"*Path to Peril* portrays terrorists and events that people fear, but do not like to think about. The story is tightly woven with some interesting twists, and speaks volumes about the government. Looking forward to the sequel."

—Michael Wang, MD, PhD (Pathology)

"The cyber technology that drives part of the story is authentic and written with inside knowledge. The story shows what kind of calamity can happen if this technology falls into the wrong hands or is developed by rogue nations and terrorist groups. The book is well researched, and is controversial and thought provoking."

—Ann Zou, PhD (Electrical Engineering)

"*Path to Peril* shows how vulnerable the country is to cyber terrorism. The digital and quantum technology in this international thriller is first rate and leaves the reader wondering if a small group of terrorists could destroy the United State's financial centers. The horrific events that happen in Portland, Oregon lend credence to the story and expose the dark side to the technology. If ever there was a book made for an action movie, this is the one!"

—D.J. Wright,
Manager (Finance and I.T. Audit Systems)

PATH TO
PERIL

To Erica,

I want to thank you and your family for all they have done for our community. Enjoy the read.

B. R. Dunn

PATH TO PERIL

H.D. DUMAN

TATE PUBLISHING
AND ENTERPRISES, LLC

Published by Tate Publishing & Enterprises, LLC
127 E. Trade Center Terrace | Mustang, Oklahoma 73064 USA
1.888.361.9473 | www.tatepublishing.com

Tate Publishing is committed to excellence in the publishing industry. The company reflects the philosophy established by the founders, based on Psalm 68:11,
"The Lord gave the word and great was the company of those who published it."

Book design copyright © 2012 by Tate Publishing, LLC. All rights reserved.
Cover design by Lauro Talibong
Interior design by Jake Muelle

Published in the United States of America
ISBN: 978-1-62147-634-4
1. Fiction, General
2. Fiction, Action & Adventure
12.10.23

DEDICATION

I would like to thank my wife, Anne, whose support and encouragement was vital for the completion of this project.

ACKNOWLEDGEMENTS

I am indebted to Tate Publishing for accepting my manuscript and publishing *Path to Peril*. What can I say about my first editor, Maryanne Wainwright, that hasn't already been said? Without her help this project wouldn't have gone anywhere. And then there is Dr. Ann Zou who helped me in the technical aspects of quantum mechanics and computing. My thanks goes to Washington State Representative, Ed Orcutt, who explained how Washington State's Congress operates and some of the differences between the State's Legislature versus the U.S. Congress. Also, special thanks to my test readers for putting up with me. I deliberately blurred the lines, in some cases, between fact and fiction in order to give the story more impact. Any omissions and/or errors are, of course, all mine. The characters in this book are entirely fictitious and any resemblance to persons living or dead is purely coincidental. And finally, my thanks to Lauren Downen, Sheridan Irick, and Nicholle Lutz, editors extraordinaire at Tate Publishing.

"Power tends to corrupt, absolute power corrupts absolutely."

—John Emerich Edward Dalberg Acton

"But a Constitution of Government once changed from Freedom can never be restored. Liberty, once lost, is lost forever."

—John Adams

ONE

INDIAN OCEAN 2008

The hot African sun beat down in fiery radiance upon the Indian Ocean off Cape Gwardafuy. The seas were glass-flat with hardly a stir from the prevailing winds, which usually came out of the east this time of year. August temperatures exceeding 105 degrees with 98 percent humidity made the ocean a veritable steam bath with tendrils of white mist twisting into the air that cut visibility less than a mile. The sun's glare was hazy but bright as Jake cuffed his right hand over his blue eyes.

"Do you see how many gun boats are out there?"

"They're thick as flies," Slade said in his gravelly voice.

"Their mother ship has to go; gunboats won't have anywhere to hide." Jake said. "Tell those sailors to hurry up, we're running low on 50s." With his usual banter, he added, "and order some croissants."

"You want coffee too?" Slade said with a grin. "Just hurry with the ammo."

Jake hated humidity, especially the kind that drapes over you like a hot, steamy blanket. The men were already dressed in full assault gear wearing Delta Force black flak jackets and full communication headgear. Sweat streamed from Jake's wavy blond hair, trickled down his handsome, tan face as he hunched his large frame over the M2HB Browning .50 caliber cannons. With tendons taut and muscles flexed to control the big guns, he peered into the mist and blazed a path of destruction toward the fleet of gunboats.

Slade, standing at his side, was manning the other gun battery off the stern of the Elizabeth Anne. Somalia pirate gunboats had been dispatched from a small, 295-foot Swedish freighter taken by pirates the year before in an attempt to overpower a larger American freighter for ransom. The Elizabeth Anne was specifically designed to handle nuclear cargo, and was consigned to the U.S. Government from Farragut Shipping, Inc. for the sole purpose of transporting nuclear materials and equipment from Iraq to the United States. Just over 500 feet she came with a stout beam and her powerful engines could propel her to thirty knots in calm seas.

Last year American troops discovered a huge stash of depleted, near-military-grade uranium, along with foreign made equipment to enrich it, in a vast underground complex in the mountains northeast of Mosul, Iraq. Because of the cargo's nature, the Department of Homeland Security (DHS) assigned its lead Intel operatives, Jake Cannon and Slade Swanson, to oversee and protect the cargo while in-transit to the United States.

They were outnumbered, but Jake knew they were in good company. Besides Slade and himself, there were a dozen black ops on board manning the other gun batteries. The ship had been especially equipped and armored for this operation because of the cargo and that they were sailing in dangerous waters off the coast of Somalia.

"Slade, toss me that RPG." Jake could smell the cordite hanging in the air. "Couple of gunboats getting too close with their 50s." He caught the tube in mid-air, unclipped a grenade from his assault belt, loaded and quickly launched the projectile into the lead boat as one of the pirates was preparing to fire his own RPG. The gunboat and its occupants lifted out of the water in an explosive pyre, flipped and disappeared under the freighter's wake. The other gunboat turned and quickly reversed course as Slade stitched the stern with a withering blast from the 50s. The boat erupted in a fireball and quickly sunk in the oil slick waters.

"Good shot," Slade yelled.

"Yeah, must have got them in the fuel tank."

Four sailors came lumbering up with two heavy boxes of .50 caliber belt feeds. As they heard the high-pitched whine of the 20 mm Gatling guns laying down a seamless wall of firepower at the Somalia gunboats, they heard an explosion seventy yards aft of the Elizabeth Anne's stern.

"Good lord, they're firing mortars at us!" Slade exclaimed.

"We're not prepared to take those kind of hits," Jake said. Immediately he got on the horn and told the captain to turn thirty degrees starboard and full ahead to get closer to the mother ship. "Doug, we're taking mortar fire. We need to get inside their range, or they will tear us apart. Over."

"Jake, I'm already at the stops," the captain said. "Over."

"I don't care, get this bucket steaming. If we take a direct hit it won't matter. Over."

"I'll do what I can, Jake. Out."

The captain rang up the chief engineer in the engine room and instructed him to spool the big diesels up to red line.

"The engines won't be able to take it for long."

"Just do it, Sly, until I tell you to throttle back."

"Your call, Cap," Sly said and broke the connection. He began to adjust the over-ride on the big diesels' output.

Just as the Elizabeth Anne turned starboard, another mortar shell hit next to her bow. One of the black ops was pitched overboard from the blast's concussion and swept under the boat. Mortar fire was now raining at a steady clip, and it wouldn't be long before they found their range.

"Holy smokes, can you believe that," Slade said. "Mother ship just took out two of their own gunboats."

"Good. I hope they take out a few more and help even the odds."

Jake was now sure that the pirates were using older, manually operated mortars and not the newer computerized GPS range finder version. The newer mobile 120 mm mortars could communicate with a ship's sonar and radar that provided range, position, and bearing of its target based on the object's latitude and longitude. Even in calm seas, the old style mortars were just a crapshoot. But he didn't want to take any chances.

"Belt feeds threaded and ready to go, pal?" Jake yelled.

"Sure are."

Jake and Slade worked well together. They had to; their lives depended on it. They both had extensive military training in the Army, Jake working as a program director for the Third Army Logistics Operation Group during the third gulf war. Slade was a marksman during the war and received his training from the Reconnaissance, Surveillance, and Target Acquisition (RSTA) School at Fort Riley, Kansas, home of the Big Red One. They both literally lived the Army's motto, "Be All You Can Be." After the war, they met when Jake completed his training with Delta Force at Fort Bragg, North Carolina, and was assigned to the counter-intelligence unit in E-Detachment. One evening Jake was invited to a stud poker game with four other members in the unit and by 0330 hours everyone was finished playing except Slade and himself. He recalled battling it out until 0600 when Slade finally beat him with a flush against his straight. Slade then walked around the table and planted his formidable 6' 2" frame toe-to-toe in front of him, looked at him eye level with hooded, dark brown eyes and said, "Welcome to the unit." He then ran a meaty hand through his short, coal black hair, saluted, and said, "You're now one of the brothers." After they both did a tour of the men of 'de oppresso liber' (to liberate the oppressed) they were tapped by Tom Ridge, DHS's first secretary, to head up the new counter intelligence unit. Jake was assigned the primary responsibility of leading the unit, while Slade worked as his lieutenant.

Jake and Slade could smell the foul stench of the cannons' smoke mixed with the ocean's humidity and sensed another kill as the 50s laid down a stream of destruction. Three hundred yards out three more gunboats exploded. Off the port side another mortar shell detonated harmlessly 400 yards out. The Elizabeth Anne steamed toward the Somalia mother ship, going for all she was worth. At flank speed she was more than world-class for a freighter.

"Buddy, can you hold the fort here?" Jake asked.

"Sure, you're going for a stroll?"

"Yeah, need to find out what happened to those croissants."

Jake collected the RPG, checked his belt for DU mag tipped grenades and headed to mid-ship to get a better shot. The Elizabeth Anne was only 2,000 yards out, closing fast on its prey. It wouldn't be long before they would be inside the range of the mortars. He was surprised that they weren't under way, especially with her flank exposed to port, and guessed that they didn't realize how fast this bucket was steaming. As they approached the Swedish freighter's port side, 1,000 yards out, the freighter finally decided to spool up her diesels and arced starboard. Too late. By then half of the black ops were laying down cover fire while the other half, including Jake, loaded their tubes and launched their deadly payloads. On the first round, three of the grenades found their mark on the freighters stern and burned through her deck plates at nearly 6,000 degrees before exploding in the engine room. On the next round, five of six grenades burned through her single hull at mid-ship, port side, and exploded in her cargo holds. The Elizabeth Anne showed no mercy and laced the Somalia mother ship's hull with two more rounds of grenades and rocket fire that burned through her like white-hot jelly. Her wheelhouse was obliterated, and the Elizabeth Anne's crew could see multiple holes punched through her cargo deck as fire and black smoke erupted into the roiling air. By now the black ops could hear sounds of exploding ammo and the freighter's klaxons wailing in the distance as she rolled forty degrees to port with heavy, black, oily soot and fire bellowing out of her funnel. Part of her keel and most of her starboard hull were now exposed as water streamed from her scuppers. The Swedish freighter was doomed, taking on water by the metric ton. Dirtied by the foul environment and nauseated by the smell of burning diesel and metal, some of the sailors aboard the Elizabeth Anne watched the destruction of the pirates' mother ship. Glimpsing through the fiery curtain of chaos, they could see the pirates trying to save themselves. Already caught in the snare of defeat, some were trying to lower the freighter's lifeboats with their davits already aflame from secondary explosions into the oily slick waters. Others simply jumped overboard, some with clothing afire, firing their AK-47s into the murky air at the Elizabeth Anne as they plunged into the black depths of the shark-infested seas. By now everyone, except the medics, was standing down, watching in awe as the Swedish freighter's bow pointed skyward and slipped slowly, stern first, into the Indian Ocean. What was left of the Somalia fleet scattered to the winds.

As the Elizabeth Anne circled, looking for survivors, Jake walked to the bow and was talking to Major Corrigan via radio about the casualty rate when a bullet caught him in the right shoulder. The impact spun him hard, and he staggered a few steps before falling to the deck.

TWO

RIYADH, SAUDI ARABIA 2009

The meeting had grown contentious; the attendees had been arguing over ways to increase Saudi Arabia's oil revenues. One group, led by the energy minister, Abdullah Al-Sakan, wanted to increase the kingdom's oil output in order to raise revenue.

The other group, which included the Oil Minister Jamal Al-Mhalifa, his assistant Al Hadi-Zafar, and his associate Dr. Seyed Mostakavi, wanted to reallocate the eighteen different refined oil classifications to reflect a better position. The action would lead to a better posture for most of their higher priced brands and push up their profits. In addition, Al-Hadi and Seyed were in the process of introducing two new refined oil types in the coming weeks that would increase revenue and give them more flexibility. The group had argued that merely increasing output production would do nothing but diminish profits in the future. The energy minister finally held up his hand and indicated that it was time to decide on the issue. After voting, consensus held for the reallocation method, although in order to keep a reasonable sense of civility the oil minister had allowed for a small increase in the daily output of oil production.

It was late Friday afternoon, and though there was still some minor business to attend, Jamal Al-Mhalifa was tired and asked the energy minister to adjourn the meeting. Abdullah Al-Sakan agreed to shelve the other business until the next time. After the meeting, the group's conversation had turned to small talk before everyone said their good-byes and went their own way.

The winter sun was setting in the west, and the sky was going dark as a cold, blustery wind began to stir. Al-Hadi once again was experiencing a migraine from the stress of the meetings. Lately these horrible headaches seemed to be increasing in duration and intensity. He smoothed his short graying hair and gave thanks to Allah that it was the middle of January in Riyadh, for in the summer the city was very hot with daytime temperatures often exceeding 110 degrees. He was trying to think through the bad news that had come out of the meeting while he and Seyed were walking to the secured parking area. But something was gnawing at the edges of his mind, and he couldn't quite put a finger to it.

Al-Hadi and Seyed met while studying in America at USC in the late seventies. Even though Al-Hadi was from Pakistan and Seyed was Iranian, they hit it off immediately because of their common bond with the Muslim Brotherhood. They kept in touch, periodically, until Al-Hadi invited him into the oil business in the late eighties. He knew Seyed was brilliant; he had attained dual doctorates in computer engineering and theoretical mathematics from MIT at a young age. He also knew that his friend had a good business background in the investment banking industry in America—perfect for their plans.

"Seyed, what were your impressions from the meeting?" Al-Hadi asked.

"Sir, I believe there wasn't much in the way of good news coming from the oil minister and Saudi's Petroleum Organization," Seyed replied. "Leave it to the Americans to foul up the global economy. Even China and the European Union bought into a substantial portion of the United Sates questionable debt, and their economies have been slowing ever since. It's amazing to see how far the market indices around the globe had fallen in the last few months. In early October of last year, the oil minister reduced Saudi's output by 100,000 barrels per day. Later that month, when the Organization of Petroleum Exporting Countries (OPEC) had met in Vienna, Austria, they curtailed total output by 1.5 million barrels per day to stabilize oil prices, although this had been over the objections of Iran and Qatar. They wanted a reduction of 2 million barrels per day. What did this get us? Not a thing. Something has to be done quickly or oil prices will continue to plummet." Seyed said, his dark brown eyes reflecting anger.

"I know. Right now it doesn't look good with oil currently trading around $40.00 per barrel, and it certainly isn't doing our cause any good." Al Hadi said, scratching his graying stubble.

"Well, at least there were some rays of hope," Seyed said. "We were able to convince the majority of attendees to reallocate the crude categories for more profit, although I don't understand why Jamal always gives in to the energy minister. Abdullah Al-Sakan has a mind of a rat, always in survival mode, always taking the easy way out, and never thinking about long-term consequences. I still can't believe how Abdullah ever attained the position of energy minister."

Al Hadi reached up and placed a hand on his friend's shoulder and in a conciliatory tone said, "You know as well as I do that King Abdallah bin Abd al-Aziz Al Saud firmly believes in nepotism and peppers his appointments with friends and relatives. But our meetings can be quite beneficial, even though it appears that some of the attendees have crawled out from the nearest rock. You really should give Jamal more credit. After all, if it wasn't for his statesmanship nothing would get done."

"I know. But you would think the sheik would vet his appointments before placing them in positions of power." Seyed said, running a slender hand through his dark brown hair.

"That's true, but who are we to question? We are only here to serve. Besides, look at all the progress we have made, especially in the last fifteen years or so."

"I suppose so," Seyed acquiesced.

"Even though at times we had to deal with some idiots, you have to admit we generally got our way." Al-Hadi said and then brightened. "Come on, Seyed, quit stewing, things are going well for us."

"Yeah, I guess you're right."

"Now how are our plans coming along?" Al-Hadi asked.

"Our people have been placed in investment banks and brokerage houses in America for three years now. Some of them have been climbing the corporate ladder as designed. However, there is more work to be done."

"What about our training programs and procedures?"

Seyed explained to his friend that he had spoken with their lead technician, Abrahim Solasti, and Solasti had told him that the training programs for each person were pretty much generic and have gone smoothly. However, as they got further along, they would need to customize the back-end procedures. This was where the real work would begin, Seyed told Al-Hadi. It would require considerable funds and testing of the plans would begin in a few months.

"You mean the U.S. brokerage houses and banks?" Al-Hadi asked.

"Yes, we will start siphoning off small amounts of funds in accounts that are inactive."

"How small?"

"In the pennies."

"Seyed, are you sure that's small enough? What if one of the their customers notices a discrepancy?"

"Highly unlikely. Values on the stock market change every millisecond. Besides, we are only testing accounts that haven't shown activity for quite some time."

"Okay, now what about the other project?"

"You mean Nano Electro technology?"

"Yes, how's it coming along?" Al-Hadi asked as he took a hanky out of his suit jacket to clean his glasses.

Seyed reflected a moment before telling his friend that the work had been very complex and progress had been slow over the last few years, but they were almost there. Even now their technology was far ahead of the United States, but funding had been very expensive.

"You know if we pull this off, the United States will probably never recover."

"That's what we're counting on. Rendering cipher keys useless on the Internet will give us the upper hand and that's why we've taken the risks and expense." Al-Hadi said. "Keep up the good work, my friend." He reached up and squeezed Seyed's shoulder to show a sign of approval.

"Thanks, sir, but we need more revenue for the project."

"Speaking of additional funds, I had a thought coming out of the meeting. You know the big American you introduced to me years ago, the one that we do arms business with?"

"You mean Felix Jamosa?" Seyed asked.

"Yes. He owns a successful textile business in Oregon, doesn't he?"

"Yes, but where is this going?"

Al-Hadi now asked his friend if Felix would be interested in bankrolling at least part of their operation. After all he had made plenty of money throughout the years profiting from arms sales they sent his way.

"I don't believe so, he's not that radical and besides he is a U.S. citizen. He would be crazy to help us."

"I suppose so. Does he have any weaknesses or grudges we could exploit?" Al-Hadi asked as he put his hanky away.

"I wouldn't know, sir. As you are aware, the only dealings we have with him are in weapons."

"That's exactly my point," Al-Hadi said as he lit a cigarette.

Al-Hadi now wondered if Felix's government knew the extent of his arms sales to rogue countries and individuals. *That's an interesting point*, he thought. They probably had enough information with their own contracts to sink Felix if the data was leaked properly.

"I wonder if his government is keeping track and knows who he is dealing with nowadays?"

"That's a great point. Do you want me to look into it?"

"Yes, please do, but do it quietly, and see if any feathers have been ruffled. If they have, let me know."

"Okay. Anything else?"

"Another angle, let's see if we can assist him in some way, such as facilitating more arms sales for him in exchange for his help." Al-Hadi took a drag off his cigarette.

"Yes, that's a good idea."

Al-Hadi hesitated for a moment and looked up at his friend before saying, "I've been thinking about this approach, and I'm sure we can find a way to manipulate Mr. Jamosa."

"You sure?" Seyed asked with a pensive look on his narrow face.

"Yes, and with his penchant toward greed, he probably has already stumbled, and we'll be there to catch him."

THREE

JAMOSA ENTERPRISES—
PORTLAND, OREGON 2008

The day started out pretty much like any other day for Felix Jamosa, except he was tired. He arrived at his building, Jamosa Enterprises, in downtown Portland, Oregon, in the 800 block of Southwest Park Avenue at 5:00 a.m. He was dressed impeccably in an Armani suit with a power red tie and a long sleeved Forzieri dress shirt, his usual attire. As typical, he was there before anyone else. He parked his custom painted, shadow blue 1995 Ferrari Testarossa F 512M in one of the two extra wide parking spots reserved for the chief executive officer in level one underground parking.

He really liked Ferraris, especially the older models with their wide slung bodies and classical looks. Sometimes on weekends when the weather was nice, he would take the "Redhead" for a spin. He liked Germantown Road not far from his loft. The road originated at Highway 30 near the St. Johns Bridge, and within three miles rose to over 1,000 feet in elevation with its horseshoe and chicane-like turns. At the top, after it crossed Skyline Blvd., the road dropped over the ridge and headed west with long straight-aways and wide-sweeping turns. He could now really get on the throttle and use all five gears and hear the deep throaty roar through the TUBI exhausts as the big V12 hurtled the car to phenomenal speeds. *Now this is really living*, he would think, with adrenaline coursing through his veins. After he parked and collected his ubiquitous brief case, he opened the steel door to the building's interior and walked to the private express elevator. The elevator, which was next to a bank of regular elevators, only went to the top two floors of the building and sublevel one through four of the underground parking garage.

He slid the smart card through the electronic card reader and then pressed his right hand to the biometric screen. The only fingerprints on file for the express elevator were the corporate officers, Felix's family, his parents Hunter and Lillian, his brother-in-law Jeffery Starr and his wife Carly, his parents Benesh and Marni, two close friends, Ed Wright and Jeremy Givans, and Molly Hill, Felix's longtime secretary.

Felix and Jeffery were the only two that had access to the top floor via a dual smart card. The 44th floor contained a penthouse suite where Felix and Jeffery sometimes entertained their contacts and suppliers. Some of them remarked that it felt like walking into a tomb since there were no windows on the floor. Felix would often joke with his clients that he was afraid of the paparazzi and would hide up here. But if truth were to be known, this was only the beginning to the floor's secrets.

From the outside, the building was configured so that the casual eye wouldn't know there was a 44th floor. The express elevator's brass wall plate only indicated sub level one through four and floor forty-three. Also, the building's blueprints and architectural drawings were replaced to show only forty-three floors and the four parking sub levels. Only Felix and Jeffery knew about the penthouse.

Felix always liked coming in early to enjoy some quiet time and reflect on recent business events to see if improvements could be made. He had a very busy day in front of him with the company party.

After exiting the express elevator on the 43rd floor, he entered his suite of offices through the outer mahogany double glass doors. He passed his secretary's desk and the hall leading off to the right, which included his brother-in-law's office and the other corporate offices, before entering a pair of solid mahogany doors that led to his inner sanctum.

His corner office, with its many windows and private bath, was large and opulent with a commanding east by northeast view of Pioneer Courthouse Square, the Willamette River, Mt. Hood and Mt. St. Helens, both attired in their impressive mantles of snow. And on really clear days, he could see Mt. Adams and Mt. Rainier. It was late December, and winter recreation was full-throttle on the mountains.

Even though he was on a tight schedule, he was in a grand mood. He and Jeffery just landed a contract with Stinson International Corporation. The company warehoused and did logistics for textile goods to the sports apparel and retail industries, domestically and internationally. The contracts, which they had been working on for the past six months, were finally signed yesterday at Stinson's headquarters in Boston. Perfect for growing the textile business and hiding their gun running activities. Because of the importance of the agreement, he was planning on celebrating with his family, Jeffery and Carly, and some of their close friends at either Morton's or Ruth's Chris steakhouse tomorrow night. He made a mental note to have Molly make the dinner reservations after she arrived this morning.

FOUR

INDIAN OCEAN 2008

In a blink of an eye, Slade was at Jake's side screaming for a medic while stemming the flow of blood with his shirt. "You all right, buddy?"

"What happened?"

"You caught the wrong end of a bullet, my man. Must have been from one of the gunboats. How are you feeling?" Slade pressed.

"A little woozy," Jake said, as he struggled to sit up.

"Lay still, buddy, the medics are on their way."

Slade stayed with his pal and applied steady pressure on the wound until the medics arrived. They had been busy at the ship's bow taking care of injuries. After they appeared and did their initial triage, found that the wound wasn't life threatening, and stopped the bleeding, the medics wheeled him to pre-op. Two hours later Jake left surgery and was wheeled into sickbay. Slade stopped by to see his friend.

"How are you doing, pal?"

"Feel like I was hit by a freight train."

"You were. The chief medic extracted a 7.62 mm slug out of your shoulder. You're lucky it wasn't a direct hit."

"How come my flak jacket didn't stop the slug?" Jake asked.

"The bullet ricocheted off something and came in at a shallow angle and went between your vest and collar bone and lodged in your shoulder. Some luck, huh?"

"Yeah, now where's my croissant?" Jake quipped.

"Jeez you just got out of surgery an hour ago, still under anesthesia, and you ask for food? Besides, you'll get sick if you eat anything now."

Jake ignored Slade's last remark. He was really concerned about the other men aboard. "How are the other guys?" Jake asked.

"Well, Hank had the same luck as you from a ricocheting bullet that got him in the right foot, but he'll survive, and Daron was really lucky."

"Meaning?"

"He was grazed in the neck, and the bullet just missed his carotid artery by millimeters. But I hate to tell you pal, we lost Sam Noland."

"What happened?"

"Remember the mortar round that barely missed the starboard bow?"

"Kind of."

"Well, Sam was at the rail loading his RPG when the shell hit, and the concussion from the blast pitched him into the water, and he was swept under the ship. I really don't think he knew what hit him," Slade said.

"Did you find anything during the search?"

"No, except for some clothing and debris from the pirates' freighter, but nothing that belonged to Sam."

"Oh man, why do we have to lose the good guys?"

"I don't know, Jake."

"Ship's okay?"

"Yeah, she's fine. Though the crew had to put out a few small fires. She's a little banged, but nothing major."

"Have you contacted David yet?" Jake asked.

"No, I was busy helping the crew put out fires, and besides I wanted to wait and see if you were okay before I called him."

"Well hop to it buddy, you don't want any withering fire from the boss, do you? And oh, bring back some croissants and a good-looking redhead too," Jake replied with his famous crooked smile.

Slade just sighed, "I'll see what I can rustle up in the kitchen, the other you'll have to do on your own."

Slade turned and left sickbay. He already knew that Jake would be fine; nothing could put that stud down for long. Before going to the galley, he thought he'd better head back to his quarters and call the chief. After walking inside, he collected his phone, sat on his bunk and punched in the code for his boss, David Peterson, deputy secretary of the Department of Homeland Security.

FIVE

RIYADH, SAUDI ARABIA 2009

Al-Hadi stubbed out his cigarette as he and Seyed walked across the street from the energy meeting and stood at the entrance to the secured parking area. Al-Hadi couldn't help but to admire the big black Mercedes Pullman limousine approaching from the rear of the lot.

The oil minister, Jamal Al-Mhalifa, had recently given it to him as a gift. Jamal, like Seyed, was extremely security conscience and wanted to make sure his trusted friend and adviser was well protected.

Even though Riyadh was relatively safe compared to other more dangerous cities in the Middle East, such as Baghdad, Karachi, and Islamabad, there were still isolated incidences of violence in the city.

At first he was against accepting such a lavish gift from his friend. But after Jamal insisted and wouldn't take no for an answer, he grudgingly accepted it only after he quipped, that he would return it if it didn't meet his standards.

When Jamal handed him the vehicle's keyless entry remote, Al-Hadi could see in the minister's dark eyes that he wasn't too happy with his last remark. He quickly added, "It was a joke, your highness."

Jamal's face, angry at first, broke out into a broad grin as he slapped his friend's back and said, "ride in it with grace; you deserve it."

As the car stopped in front of them and the chauffer exited the vehicle to secure his passengers, Seyed adjusted his lanky frame before sliding into one of the Pullman's rear seats and asked, "Is this the new limo the oil minister presented to you?"

"Sure is, and isn't she a beauty?"

"It looks like a rolling bunker." Seyed said with amazement.

"Hey, you want to know about this baby?" Al-Hadi said, as the chauffer opened the rear passenger door for him. He now grew animated as he told his friend about some of the features.

"Well the limo is built from the ground up with maximum security in mind. The Mercedes Pullman series is built in Mercedes' Sindelfingen coachworks and is different from other armored vehicles. Its protection is integrated straight into the car's frame, body, and glass when manufactured, as opposed to being retrofitted."

"You don't say."

"Yes, and the driver's cabin is separated from the totally soundproofed rear cabin by a steel framed bulkhead and five thick inches of polycarbonate laminate. And the bulkhead divider is fixed for security."

"Well, I'm duly impressed. I may want to get one myself," Seyed said, as he looked around the interior. "Jamal Al-Mhalifa must have paid a handsome price for the vehicle."

"I'm sure he did. And I must tell you that I'm grateful that he's a good friend of ours."

"I know," Seyed said.

Al Hadi took bottled waters from the micro fridge and offered one to his friend. "Thanks. This is quite the limo. So you have a full communication center back here?"

"Yes, would you like to see some of its features?" Al-Hadi asked, as he retrieved a couple of aspirin from the bar drawer and took it with his water.

"No thanks. I think I'll just look around for a while."

Al-Hadi shifted his short, bulky frame in the seat and continued. "Getting back to our plans, I heard from Abrahim that the electro magnetic pulse (EMP) portion of our quantum computing project is lagging behind. What's causing the delay?"

"A couple of things. Money of course is first and foremost, plus we are trying to determine if we should either go with the absolute zero concept in stabilizing molecular activity and string mechanics, or regulate electro magnetic voltage."

"Seyed, I'm not a scientist just a bureaucrat. What do you mean by all this?"

"In its simplest terms, before we can apply quantum computing techniques to molecular structures, we need to stabilize the ions, electrons, and photons and align them in a straight line. Otherwise our quantum computing results will be incorrect."

Al-Hadi massaged his temples, trying to ease the pain in his head, while thinking about the intricacies of his friend's statements. It was enough to give anyone a headache. "Like I said, we need to check out Felix's gunrunning activities and see if there's any way we can induce him to bankroll some of our projects. The other, I'll let you attend to. Now I'm going to relax and let the aspirin kick in. I've been fighting a headache ever since the meeting."

"That's fine, sir. I won't disturb you."

SIX

JAMOSA ENTERPRISES—
PORTLAND, OREGON 2008

Felix Jamosa was a successful but ruthless businessman and to hell with anyone that stood in his way. He ruled his far-flung empire with an iron fist. He expected perfection from each and every employee; anything less and you would receive a severe reprimand if not outright termination. His philosophy not only applied to his textile business but also to the arms trade.

Jamosa had started out nearly thirty years ago in the weapons business selling small arms such as the Beretta SC70/90 auto rifles. As his business grew, he branched out and sold other small arms that included the Beretta 9 and Glock 17 semi auto pistols. He especially liked the Glocks from Austria's Gaston Glock manufacturer. They had relatively few parts, simple to break down, clean and assemble, and were quite reliable. As his ambitions grew, it put increasing demands on his time, and he needed someone that he could trust to help build the gun business. His old high school buddy, Jeffery Starr, was just the ticket. He already worked at Jamosa Enterprises; why not help him on the side business?

Jamosa had brought Jeffery into the gun trade after he had married his sister, Carly. He had tried for weeks to get Jeffery interested in the dangerous business of running guns. After numerous failed attempts, Felix hit on an idea that he had learned from an acquaintance in the gun business that selling arms on behalf of the United States to rogue nations was nothing more than protecting U.S. interests in the name of democracy. After several tries, Jeffery finally found the ideology of advancing U.S.

policy by helping dictators backed by the United States. Jamosa also needed Jeffery because he was well educated, with an MBA/MIS from Stanford University, and a certified CPA. He was much faster and better at developing offshore shell companies and weaving them into an arcane tapestry and was quite the numbers guy.

Unlike most in his trade, Felix had been careful to create offshore companies wrapped in dummy corporations and other dubious enterprises in order to channel and hide his illicit profit. At first the sham companies were created to only launder their profits, but as time went on Felix and Jeffery offered IPO's in order to go public and trade on the world's stock exchanges. In a few year's time, their arms revenue along with their profit tied to the publicly held phantom companies now approached $300 million per year, generating almost as much profit as the textile business.

He and Jeffery got along famously, or so Felix let on. Jamosa had used the high school connection to gain his brother-in-law's confidence and trust. Once in, Jeffery excelled at the business and was promoted to president and CFO for both entities. He was the inside guy for the arms business and dealt with the finances and its involutions. Felix, on the other hand, was the outside or front guy and managed most of the contacts, sales, training, storage, logistics, and coordination.

Throughout the years they had worked hard at building their shadow and legal empires. They now had numerous shell companies scattered throughout the globe to launder their money and dozens of contacts to gain new business, while at the same time expanding their textile company, Jamosa Enterprises.

At times some of Jamosa's weapon sales stretched the envelope of ethics and legality, even by gun running standards. He didn't care, as long as it was exciting and lucrative: he was in the game. He was college educated but felt that he was from the old school, a self-made man. He could intimidate his employees, associates, and contacts, especially on a one-to-one, face-to-face up-close basis. Though he was approaching sixty, he still was a brute of a man, standing just over 6'4" with intense steely dark blue eyes, a hard athletic build, and thinning gray hair. He used his size and gruff demeanor to advantage when negotiating contracts, be it arms or textiles. He usually traveled the world alone, and personally handled all the arms negotiations. He was good and knew it.

Some of Jamosa's contacts came from military arms fairs such as the one held in Berlin, Germany, in 1983. This was where he had met Simon Duke, the king pin of gun running. Simon didn't want anything to do with him since he was new to the trade. And in this trade, no one liked competitors. In fact, sometimes people just vanished.

Simon had made his mark by supplying weapons to both sides in the Iran and Iraqi conflict in the early eighties. He had mostly managed bigger contracts such as government to government, which not only dealt in small arms but also in tanks, guided missiles, and armored troop carriers. At the time Felix was only selling small arms. He had felt rebuffed and was rudely turned away by Simon. He would remember this, and the next time they met, things would be different. Nonetheless, he had developed a couple of good contacts for small arms.

By the mid to late 1980s, Felix was one of the primary dealers shipping arms to Afghanistan during the Soviet-Afghan war. He was moving mortars, RPGs, rocket launchers, troop personnel carriers, and hand held ground-to-air (GTA) missiles such as the American FIM-92A Stinger and the 9K38 Igla missiles. In some cases the weapons he sold were Russian made, like the Iglas, and the Afghanis were especially fond of killing Russians with their own weapons.

Between the Iron curtain and the Berlin wall coming down and countries like USA, which usually didn't bring home all their weapons after a conflict, meant one thing: the arms trade was awash in guns. In one case, $3.2 billion dollars in ordnance was stolen from the Ukraine: one of the greatest heists of the twentieth century.

By the nineties and into the new millennium, the action had shifted to Africa. By now Felix and Jeffery were number one in the arms trade and were making incredible amounts of money and dope and diamonds—called blood or conflict diamonds. Blood diamonds were given their name because most of the diamond trade originated in West Africa and they were exchanged for weapons. During the nineties and beyond there were no less than thirty-two countries in conflict on the Dark Continent. Felix had a hand in almost all of them, fueling bloodshed across Africa. He was ferrying heavy weapons, automatic rifles, and ammunition to rebel groups controlling diamond mines in Sierra Leone, Liberia, Angola, and the Democratic Republic of Congo.

He had only a few gun running rules when dealing with rogue countries and dictatorships. One, never get shot with your own merchandise. Two, always have a foolproof way of getting paid, preferably in an offshore-account. Three, when being paid in dope; never sample the merchandise, just do the analysis.

After Africa, most of the action once again had swung to the Middle East, especially Iraq, Iran, Pakistan, and Afghanistan. He really didn't like dealing with those people. Most of them in the trade were idiots, and they bartered too much. Even so he made a few good friends and contacts while selling arms, especially back in the day during the Soviet-Afghan war. This is where he had met Seyed Mostakavi. They were both hard-bitten men, and Felix needed Seyed's contacts and Seyed needed Felix's weapons so they struck an unholy alliance of demon's fire.

Mostakavi was an extremely intelligent Iranian who knew his way around the Middle East. He supplied Felix with contacts to sell, transport, and provide training for his weapons. Felix felt comfortable with him, and this usually enabled him to negotiate more contracts with Mostakavi, and it enabled him a premium for technologically advanced weapons. Jamosa was known in the covert arms industry as someone who kept his word and delivered weapons as promised. However, he was not a person to be trifled with or double-crossed. On more than one occasion, some of his contacts had experienced first-hand just how vicious and calculating he could be, though he continued to profit with a good working relationship with Seyed and his Pakistani friend, Al-Hadi Zafar. In the past five years, Jamosa and Starr had procured, processed, and shipped over $300 million dollars in arms to these men, in addition to the profits they made from their sham corporations trading on the world's stock exchanges.

SEVEN

INDIAN OCEAN 2008

D avid Peterson answered on the first ring, "Hello, Slade."
Without preamble, "Sir, we have a problem. We were
attacked by Somalia pirates three hours ago."

"Is your asymmetric encryption device on?"

"Affirmative, sir."

"Now tell me what's going on," the deputy secretary said.

"Well, the ship is a little banged up, but still seaworthy. Jake
took a slug in the shoulder, and he's doing fine in sickbay, but we
lost Sam Noland, sir."

Peterson paused before answering. "Those damned pirates!
We need to go back there and kick butt and to hell with UN
sanctions." Peterson was referring to the Black Hawk Down
incident that happened in Mogadishu in 1993.

"What about search and rescue? Any indication of what
happened to Lieutenant Nolan, and were there any other
survivors?"

"No, sir. We searched the area for at least two hours and didn't
find a single soul."

"The sharks probably did the rest."

"I wouldn't doubt it. Sir, it was a well-coordinated attack. We
were badly outnumbered, and they were using an old freighter to
hide their gunboats on the starboard side. All of a sudden about
twenty of them came racing at us from about two kilometers
away, firing .50 caliber cannons. Their mother ship was also firing
at us with mortars."

"Good grief!" Peterson exclaimed with concern in his voice.

"Sir, we had a near miss off the starboard bow, and that's how
Sam was killed. In fact, the pirates were so terrible with their
mortars that they wiped out two of their gunboats."

"Good. I wish they had destroyed more of them," the deputy secretary answered.

"Funny, Jake had the exact same sentiments. We got at least a dozen of them. After we sunk their freighter, the remaining gunboats turned tail and headed to the Somalia coastline."

"How's everybody else?"

"Sergeant Hank Pendergrass and Corporal Daron Good were wounded but are doing fine."

"Well, it's a good thing we followed Jake's advice and had the ship retrofitted for battle," the deputy secretary said. "If I'm not mistaken, you're about ten days out from Norfolk Naval Yard?"

"Affirmative, sir."

"Okay, as long as Jake remains stable, we'll have you guys stay aboard to direct any other activity. Hopefully there won't be any. In the meantime, I'll open an investigation on this. Are you heading further out in the Indian Ocean?" Peterson asked.

"Yeah, the Elizabeth Anne is steaming southeast to put more distance between us and the Somalia coastline."

"Good. Now, after you arrive in Norfolk, we'll have a debriefing the next day at headquarters. By then Jake should be in better shape and well rested. I'll be transmitting your orders and instructions to you and Jake shortly. Understood?"

"Affirmative, sir."

The deputy secretary broke the sat connection. He was saddened by the loss of Sam Noland and would contact the young man's commanding officer and have him forward a hand-scribed note on the agency's official letterhead to his parents, personally expressing his condolences and gratitude for Sam's service to his country. David Peterson was a God-fearing man and never took the loss of life lightly. Thank God nothing serious had happened to his lead operatives and the cargo was safe. It was a miracle that the military stumbled upon the cache last year. He'd hate to think what would've happened if it fell into the wrong hands.

EIGHT

RIYADH, SAUDI ARABIA 2009

On their way to Seyed's house from the energy meeting, Al-Hadi leaned back in one of the luxurious black leather seats, undid his tie, stretched out his bulky frame to get comfortable, and closed his brown eyes. While the aspirin kicked in, his mind drifted back in time as he thought about the hard work that he and Seyed had done and all the plans that had been executed that enabled him to gain a key position as a trusted adviser to the oil minister in the Saudi government.

Al-Hadi knew he could never hold a government position, since he wasn't a Saudi citizen. Nevertheless, he had Jamal's ear on important issues. It was no easy task getting this far, and if it weren't for his good friend, Seyed, working together for the last twenty years, he probably wouldn't be in this position today.

It had been over thirty years since he first met Seyed. It was in their discreet mathematics class at the University of Southern California (USC) during their sophomore year in 1977. Seyed was studying for his bachelor's of science in computer science and mathematics, while he was studying for his electrical engineering degree.

By the end of summer term after their sophomore year, Seyed had completed all of his undergraduate requirements for the computer science and mathematics' programs and received his baccalaureate degrees. The night before Seyed was scheduled to leave for Boston, he confided in me about his past and how he came to be at USC.

Seyed's parents were prominent business people in Iran and owned a large Persian rug company. When young Seyed was ready for university studies, he badgered his parents to go to California and study at USC, instead of the U.K., where his parents wished him to go. His father had planned for him to attend the University of Oxford and become a Rhodes scholar.

But young Seyed had other plans, so with a winning smile and deceitful ways steadily growing, he deftly maneuvered his father to send him to the University of Southern California. He told him all wasn't lost because he was going to do his graduate work at MIT. The next day Seyed moved on to MIT while I continued to struggle in the electrical engineering program.

NINE

JAMOSA ENTERPRISES—
PORTLAND, OREGON 2008

Felix seated himself behind the large executive desk after brewing another batch of espresso when his brother-in-law entered his office.

"Hey dude, you look awful," Jeffery said, as he walked up to his desk.

"Hey, Jeff, yeah, I'm a bit tired. I didn't get back from Boston until 3:00 a.m., and I'm still feeling some jet lag."

"Are you going to be ready for the company's celebration later today?" Jeffery asked.

"Of course. I wouldn't miss congratulating the employees for helping the company reach its three billion dollar milestone. Hey, that reminds me, I need to have Molly make reservations at Ruth Chris for the families' celebratory dinner after she arrives this morning." Felix dug into his briefcase and held up a bulky envelope in his right hand.

"Ah, I see you've closed the deal with Stinson International."

"Yup, all of our hard work has finally paid off, and I want to thank you for your help." Felix didn't care for anyone's help. As far as he was concerned, he did the lion's share of the work, and without him it never would have happened.

"Jeff, you want some espresso? Cream?"

"Sure, buddy."

Felix walked back to the credenza and poured two cups of the finest Turkish black espresso available in Portland, added some half and half, and handed a cup to his brother-in-law.

"You know the Internal Revenue Service notification has been really bugging me."

"Yeah, it's bothering us all." Jeffery said.

"What really concerns me is the way the IRS is handling this. Three days after our company received the notice, they had the temerity to barge in and slap a Justice Department subpoena on my desk and tell me, in no uncertain terms, that I had two weeks to turn over the company's financial records for the last seven years." Felix straightened his tie and walked to the windows and continued. "For crying out loud, they even had the balls to serve subpoenas to Hunter and Benesh. The next thing you'll know is that they'll be serving subpoenas to our friends, Ed and Jeremy."

Felix looked out at the murky sunrise and thought about all the hard work that he had put into his textile business. It was he that had traveled the globe, buying finished textiles and selling them to the sports apparel and retail industries. Later, it was he that had set up international factories and distribution lines that had turned raw materials into finished goods, and then shipped those finished textiles to the far corners of the Earth. And it was he that had taken most of the risk during the early years of the business. At times, it was daunting to think about all the details he had to worry about and decisions he made in order for the business to succeed. Sure, Jeffery and the families and a couple of their good friends had worked hard too to ensure that the company continued to flourish. But in the end, it was he that drove the business to where it is today, and he wasn't about to let some snout-nosed government agency come in and throw their weight around. Felix turned to Jeff. "Our families have built this privately held enterprise into a powerhouse, and it's now one of the largest private corporations in the United States, and I'll never let the IRS or the DOJ stand in its way!"

"I suspect the government is investigating the company because of our side business. I thought this was never going to happen since we always had an unofficial blessing from the government to do their dirty work." Jeffery said as he sat his tall, lanky frame in the chair in front of Felix's desk.

"We have worked with five administrations and have never encountered any major difficulties. But now the Ahmad Administration is looking for diversions in the form of a scapegoat to generate shocking headlines in order to deflect attention away from the recession." Felix paused and motioned for Jeff to help himself to more espresso and went on. "You know what really irks me?" Before Jeff could answer, "the government is picking on people like us, when they should be concerned with the nation's economy. I have always thought the government should have suspended capital gains taxes for at least a year. Sure, we would have heard from the masses that it only helps the rich, and yes, it does partly. But wealth is what drives a substantial portion of the economy through spending, and this is the fastest way to create jobs and shorten the recession. The government won't even discuss this or look at overhauling the tax system."

Felix moved back to his chair, reached down to the top drawer of his desk and placed a Colt .45 on the glass top for emphasis. "If I had my way with the administration, this is how I would handle it."

Jeffery stared at the weapon with his dark brown eyes before speaking. "For Christ's sake put the gun away."

Felix ignored his brother-in-law and went on. "Congress didn't listen to their constituency about TARP. The majority of the people had wanted Congress to take a step back and thoroughly research the systemic problems of the financial industry before making their decision. But the government once again, in its infinite wisdom, had quickly passed TARP that essentially had been a piece of garbage. What did the taxpayers receive for their hard-earned dollars? I'll tell you what they received. A big fat rip off, zilch, nothing, that's what they had been given. And what about the bankers? They had received the first 350 billion dollars out of the 700 billion-dollar TARP package funded by the taxpayers. And they had received it with very few restrictions, with no oversight, accountability or transparency. Where is the money going? Need I say more?"

"I can't argue with that." Jeff said, as he walked back to his chair with another cup of espresso and ran a hand through his graying brown hair, eyeing the gun. He sat and thought for a long moment, his brown eyes and narrow hawkish face reflecting concern before he spoke. "Getting back to the IRS, this could really hurt us. We could lose everything, including the textile business, and even be sent to prison. Even though the IRS says it's investigating Jamosa Enterprises, we both know what they're after. I'm still recovering from the last two weeks, in which my team and I have spent hundreds of hours making sure the company's finances for the last seven years are in order. I suppose we could've asked for an extension, but I wanted to show the government good faith and to also show them that we were in full compliance with their demands. Even now I'm still spending time checking documents to make sure we haven't missed anything. And so far I haven't seen any surprises." Jeffery cocked a bushy eyebrow.

"Are you sure about that?"

"Yes, I'm as sure as I can be. We agreed a long time ago that we would never commingle the arms business with the textile company. Otherwise could you imagine the mess we would be in now? The government has no evidence or trail that an arms business exists. Now what's this really about?"

Jeffery knew his brother-in-law could be secretive. He was worried that Felix had too much latitude trading in arms since he mainly traveled the globe alone. He also knew that he was good at what he did, but it provided him too many opportunities to run amiss of the law. Sure selling guns at best was shady and at worst downright dirty, and he suspected Felix went too far even by gun running standards.

Felix sat in his cushy, black leather chair and thought for a moment before answering. "Well, I think the Alcohol Tobacco Firearms Agency is behind this. As you know the ATF has been shadowing us for over a dozen years, especially since our weapons company has grown so large. We've been smart and haven't provided them with a chain of evidence to prosecute us. Even though they have come close a couple of times, and in fact have caused us to lose money on more than one occasion, they haven't been able to nail us. By the time they were able to get search and seizure warrants from the Justice Department, we had always found a way to finagle ourselves out of their reach. I suspect that bastard, Jack Finley, who heads the ATF, and his lead minion, Robert Murphy, are having tantrums over us. I'm sure we have put a dent or two in their budget since they have come up empty handed every time. Enough of this, it's starting to upset me again. Now what about the legal side?"

"I just received a memo from our lead counsel, Jim Benson, that indicated a legal team has been already assembled to fight these allegations. And I'll tell you, Jim hasn't spared any expense in the matter. Felix, have you contacted any of our friends in Washington to see if this can be grounded?"

"I have, but we lost some very important contacts since Ahmad has taken office. It's getting more difficult to reach the right people to find out what exactly has happened."

Felix knew why he wasn't receiving help from his friends up on the hill. It was because of some of his underhanded deals. To hell with it! From now on he was going to do things his way and be damned with everybody and everything.

"I'll tell you one thing, though. If we go down, it will be with a loud bang. And by then, I'll be well on my way to Perdition."

Before Jeffery could speak, Molly bounded through the office's outer doors, waved at them through the open doors of Felix's office, and took her seat behind her desk.

TEN

RIYADH, SAUDI ARABIA 2009

While the limo was cruising along to Seyed's house, Al-Hadi turned his thoughts to when he had met Seyed again after graduating from USC and moving back home. It was a few years later when Seyed called Al-Hadi's parent's home in Karachi, Pakistan, on the Arabian Sea.

Two weeks later Seyed flew in from Tehran and enjoyed a traditional Pakistani dinner with Al-Hadi's family that included kebabs, rice, and Peshawari, an ice cream unique to Pakistan. After dinner, in the study, Seyed talked about his work at MIT and Wall Street. He said that he had graduated summa cum laude from MIT with doctorates in computer engineering and theoretical mathematics. He indicated that the MIT computer-engineering department was so impressed with his dissertation on Artificial Intelligence (AI) that they offered him a full ride postdoctoral fellowship. After completing his research for the Senior Simons Postdoctoral Fellowship in Computer Engineering, he said he stayed on and did further research in the AI field. From his research he submitted a couple of papers to the Association for Computing Machinery that garnered him national attention. This had led to a job with Lehman Brothers on Wall Street as a senior associate. He also indicated that he had done research for Lehman's on market predictability and that the company had copyrighted his work and was actually using some of his algorithms. Seyed confided that he had made a great deal of money working at the global financial services firm. But he had been troubled that a substantial portion of Lehman's middle management and most of the young traders were always looking for ways around the regulations and accounting rules in order to make more money for themselves and the company. They were always interested in the next quarter and didn't care about long-range strategic planning, and if it weren't for senior management, the company and shareholders would undoubtedly gone bankrupt.

Seyed said he was also troubled by the American culture, but he liked the fact that he could travel freely in the United States. And he had experienced freedom of speech, religion, and dress never thought possible a few short years ago. But he didn't like where all this was heading; there had been too much confusion, and he felt that everything was spinning out of control.

Seyd then turned his attention to his parents. His dark brown eyes reflected pain as he said his father was failing from diabetes and a chronic heart condition. He said his mother was doing fine but kept busy looking after his father. And his younger brother, Niv, had been accepted in Al-Qud, one of Iran's elite military forces. He and his brother had suspected his father, a pro-west advocate, was deeply troubled by the Islamic Revolution. Seyed added that his father was still outraged that Tehran's University students had overthrown Iran's Monarch Republic under Shah Mohammad Reza Pahlavi. He said the students had help from other factions such as guerrillas and rebel troops, which overwhelmed troops loyal to the Shah. He said after the coup, Iran was transformed to an Islamic Republic lead by Ayatollah Ruhollah Khomeini and to this day Iran was a theocratic Islamic republic governed under the constitution of 1979. Seyed said that he and his brother believed that in his father's eyes, as well as in other Iranians', Khomeini was viewed as a religious fanatic. He finally said, with tears in his eyes and rage written on his face, that his father had sold his export business, given up, and wilted away.

ELEVEN

EASTERN CARIBBEAN 2009

S everal months later, after the Somalia incident, Jake, with his
right arm in a sling from a second surgery to remove residual
bone chips in his shoulder, found himself sitting at a high stakes
poker table aboard the Oasis of the Seas. He was casually looking
at trip nines and knew he held a pretty good hand, especially
since the seven-card stud table was maxed out with eight players.
He was sitting in one of the upper card rooms off the main casino
area and had been playing for the last eight hours, ever since
the Royal Caribbean cruise ship had left the last port of call in
Roseau, Dominica. The March sun had set earlier, capping off
another gorgeous day. The winds were light, and the daytime
temperatures hovered in the high seventies with no storms in
sight. While waiting for one of the players to bet, check or fold,
he recalled how impressed he was with the ship. He was amazed
at the size of her after exploring her sixteen decks. She was truly
an elegant ship with her seven distinctive neighborhoods and
broke the molds on how cruise ships were built.

"Jake it's your call," the dealer said.

"Oh, sorry." It was the hand's showdown bet and two players
still in play. Jake looked over at the fat man sitting across from
him and said, "I raise you one thousand dollars," and slid ten
black chips to the pile at the center of the table.

The fat man paused for a moment and squinted at Jake before
he shoved ten of his own to the table's pile and countered with,
"I call."

Jake flipped his three hole cards face up and said, "Trip nines
with an ace king high."

The fat man grunted and stared at Jake for a long moment, and without saying a word, folded his hand. He stood and thanked the dealer and without tipping, or bothering to thank Jake for a night of idle conversation, left the card room.

It was 2:00 a.m. Atlantic time, and Jake wanted to cash out and call it a night. He'd won over $3,000 for eight hours of play and figured he'd better quit while the stars where still shining on him. He realized long ago that he was a conservative player and let the cards come to him before making his move. It wasn't as glamorous or tumultuous of a gambler's grit, but he found by playing this way, he really enjoyed the sport, conversation with other players, and making a good profit.

After he thanked and tipped the dealer and cashier the appropriate amount and received his updated Royal Caribbean gaming card, he headed over to the casino bar for a nightcap. He ordered a sparkling Cranapple on the rocks. While waiting for his drink, he gingerly lifted his right arm to check the pain level in his shoulder and drifted back and thought about his and Slade's last major assignment with the Department of Homeland Security.

Their boss, David Peterson, had assigned them to supervise the shipment of nuclear material aboard the Elizabeth Anne to the naval yards at Norfolk, Virginia. Their encounter with the Somalia pirates had been a close call, and they were lucky to come out of it relatively unscathed. They were prepared but caught off guard by the ferocity of the attack.

At the debriefing the deputy secretary went over every aspect of the assignment to make sure that all issues were covered and corrections were made in case there were future incidences of this nature. Peterson had served two tours in the Gulf Wars and was a retired, decorated full bird colonel. He ran the agency in a quasi-military manner. His style of management involved getting in front of problems before problems occurred, plus it would give the agency foresight for any upcoming events. The department had Knowledge Based Article (KBA) databases that not only kept track of terrorists but also threat scenarios including background, training, and associations. The agency was constantly refining, upgrading, and storing solutions in their databases. This was a critical component in the arsenal of weapons that DHS used against the war on terror.

"Hey sailor, do any good at the stud table tonight?"

Jake turned and looked up into a pair of the brightest blue eyes he had ever seen.

"Not too bad," he said. "And you, are you a fellow gambler?"

She continued to take him in, with his wavy blond hair, deep blue eyes, and tan muscular build. "Why yes I am, but I prefer playing craps to poker. I'm not good at playing games of bluff. Besides, craps has one of the best, if not the best, house odds for players."

"Ah, I see you have a bit of a head start on me," Jake mused, and took a sip of his drink. He could see a slight blush rise from her neck to her lovely face.

"Well, you wouldn't want to associate with someone that wasn't as observant as you, would you?" She teased.

"I can't argue with you there." Jake could see right off this woman was sharp and quick on her feet. "By the way, my name is Jake, Jake Cannon. And you?"

"Oh how clumsy of me for not introducing myself sooner. I'm Zoey Chamberlain, but my friends call me Zip."

"Is that a nickname?"

"Actually it's a tag that I earned a few years ago. There is an amazing story behind it. Sometime, if you like, I'll tell you the circumstances."

"That would be nice," Jake said.

"Can you excuse me for a moment? A lady needs to powder her nose."

"Oh, before you go, I would be remiss if I didn't offer a drink to someone as beautiful as you."

"Ice water would be nice," Zoey said with a smile.

"You don't drink?"

"Only rarely and only on special occasions."

"Ah, I see we have two things in common."

Jake turned and watched as Zoey headed out of the casino bar to find the nearest ladies' room. She was a striking brunette with long, sable brown hair falling around her shoulders with just a hint of silver in her locks. She looked to be about thirty with an athletic build. Her stride was long and easy, and she had that sophisticated look about her, not bookish but classical. He could tell by the way she carried herself and the brief conversation with him that she was quite intelligent and probably nobody's fool. He liked her more and more by the minute, and hoped this would blossom into something more.

TWELVE

RIYADH, SAUDI ARABIA 2009

As the limo cruised along, Al-Hadi suddenly caught a glimpse of Seyed's face. Where was he, what's going on? Is this real? They're still in his father's study, he's telling Seyed about his work on the Hub Dam located north of Karachi on the Hub River. The years are melting away as he sees himself as a young man, trumpeting his accomplishments. He tells Seyed about designing and building a reservoir that provides drinking water for Karachi and the surrounding area. He knows that he can't compete with his friend on any level, but nevertheless he is proud of his talents and skills as an electrical engineer. Even by physical standards his friend was daunting. Tall, dashingly handsome with a wiry build and wavy dark brown hair, olive complexion, flashing deep brown eyes that appeared to diminish to points of steel radiance when under heavy concentration, and that wicked smile.

Al-Hadi tells him that he saw him as a renaissance man, since whatever he touched or studied seemed almost easy to him. The results were always the same; he was simply the best. Al-Hadi knew that Seyed was one of the most gifted people he had ever met.

His friend by the age of twelve along with his native Arabic had mastered compositions and articulations in English, Russian, and Mandarin Chinese. Though he had received dual doctorates in computer engineering and theoretical mathematics from MIT at the tender age of twenty-three, he was also an accomplished author and once showed Al-Hadi a paper he wrote for a philosophy class that held brilliant arguments to the demise of democracy. After reading Seyed's thesis he realized that, in his mind, mathematics begets philosophy as easily as eloquence trumps elegance. And in some ways Al-Hadi could see this. His friend's writing was smooth, and he was able to weave philosophical arguments and counter-points throughout his composition as effortlessly as manipulating and solving extremely complex mathematical equations. Al-Hadi had also discovered, at times, he had an arcane and iniquitous side to him.

Seyed spent the night and arose early the next morning. After breakfast and some Turkish espresso, he bid farewell to the family. Al-Hadi borrowed his father's car and drove his friend to Jinnah International Airport. While in route, he was amazed after learning that Seyed was flying to the United States via Heathrow to study nuclear technology at Cal Tech. His friend turned to him and said it was time for him to give something back to his country and help bring Iran into the Nuclear age.

After dropping him off at the airport, Al-Hadi couldn't help but think about the conversations he had with him for the last couple of days. Seyed seemed so different from the days that they spent together at USC. He still had that winning smile, but somehow sarcasm had crept into his conversations, and some of his views seemed jaded and cynical.

THIRTEEN

EASTERN CARIBBEAN 2009

Jake turned back to the bar, took another sip of his Cranapple, and ordered ice water for Zoey. His sat phone rang, and he answered on the first ring, "Jake here."

"Jake, how's the cruise going, and how is your shoulder?" David Peterson asked.

"Shoulder is fine sir, and you ought to see this ship. It's the largest and most luxurious ocean liner that I have ever sailed on. We left San Juan, Puerto Rico, a couple of days ago and left our second port of call this morning, from Roseau, Dominica. Sir, is this an official call?" Jake asked, as he motioned the barkeep to put the ice water to his left.

"Yes, it is. Is your encryption service on?"

"Of course. And I must say that you really have a knack of interrupting my vacations, especially ones that lead to interesting relationships with beautiful young ladies."

"Well, Jake, sometimes that's the way it goes. Besides, you already have too many girl friends in your stable," the deputy secretary chided.

Jake thought of a comeback, but Peterson headed him off. "We have a situation that's unfolding that may require you and Slade's attention. We've been receiving Intel the last couple of weeks from Booze and Allen, Lockheed Martin and the NSA that now show a high probability of a legitimate threat to our homeland. The sources are reputable, and there is good commonality threading through the information coming from all three Intel groups that indicate a high level of credibility."

"What's this about, sir?" Jake asked.

"You'll find out at the briefing."

"Have you contacted Slade?"

"Yes, just got off the phone with him in Wasilla, Alaska. And he wasn't too happy to hear my voice either. Said something about interrupting his fishing trip on the Little Susitna in search of the world's largest spring salmon. He's as crazy about fishing and hunting as you are about muscle cars and women. He'll be on his way to Fairbanks shortly where a military transport is waiting at Ladd Army Airfield to fly him back to Washington D.C. To confirm your itinerary, you left with the department, your next port of call is Barbados. Is this correct?"

"Yes, that's correct, sir."

"And your ETA is 0700 hours Atlantic Time?"

"Affirmative, will dock at 0700 hours later this morning at Bridgetown, Carlisle Bay, Pier 6."

"Good, your orders will be forthcoming within the hour," the deputy secretary said. "Understood?"

"Affirmative, sir. This must be pretty important."

"Jake, I won't go into it now. But yes, it could have far reaching effects. I'll brief you and Slade at headquarters later tomorrow." Without any further conversation, Peterson broke the sat connection.

Jake sat at the casino bar idly stirring his drink and thinking about the conversation with the deputy secretary. Actually, he and Slade rarely were summoned while on vacation. This must be important. Otherwise, they would have at least been allowed to finish their trips.

FOURTEEN

RIYADH, SAUDI ARABIA 2009

As the big Pullman approached Seyed's house, a Wolf moon was now rising from the east. Al-Hadi now reconnects with his friend in 1989. He and his cousin on his mother's side, Mohammed Abdul Jabbar, had just seated themselves in a small café in Islamabad, Pakistan when Seyed came sauntering up to the table. After Al-Hadi introduced his cousin, Seyed said he couldn't visit long since he was discussing business with some associates, but would come and see him the next weekend. He said that he had some very interesting things to disclose, then turned and went back to his table.

After Seyed arrived Saturday morning, he inquired about the family and then was drawn to the kitchen by the wonderful aromas wafting out. Al-Hadi's mother was making halva and brewing Turkish espresso in anticipation of his arrival. Walking into the kitchen, Seyed gave Al-Hadi's mother a big hug and complimented her on her culinary skills and told her how much he loved her cooking, especially the pastries. After collecting samples and some espresso and getting comfortable in the study, Seyed proceeded to tell a story that would have seemed impossible just a few short years ago. It was hard to believe that he was the same person.

Seyed had said that after receiving his training at Cal Tech in nuclear technology and engineering, he went back to Tehran because of his father's declining health. After his father's death, he told his immediate family that he was somewhat at a loss of what he wanted to do. He explained to his mother that he blamed the Islamic Revolution and politics in general for his father's poor health and eventual death and that he needed to get away to do some thinking in order to find his way.

Seyed had said, a few weeks later, he found himself in Afghanistan fighting alongside the mujahideen (holy warriors), helping resist the Marxist People's Democratic Party of Afghanistan (PDPA) that Russia was supporting. He said, during that time, he had become quite good at negotiating differences between some of the tribal factions; they could get back to their petty arguments after the war. But for now they must unite in order to defeat their common enemy. He had gained prominence in this role, and it had eventually led to negotiations with some of the arms dealers in the region.

One day during the Soviet-Afghan war, a big American walked into one of the huts in the compound and introduced himself as Felix Jamosa. Seyed had said that he introduced the big American to Simon Duke, with whom he was currently doing business. As it turned out Felix and Simon had previously met. Seyed had said that he noticed from the big American's facial expressions and body language that he didn't like Simon. In fact, from the tension between them, there must have been some bad blood in the past.

The big American had turned his attention back to Seyed and asked what weapons he needed. That surprised Seyed, because the mujahideen bought weapons on what the dealers had, not the other way around. The American then had turned slowly to Simon and questioned, "Is this the way you've been selling arms to this gentlemen?"

The little guy shrunk in his chair and whispered, "not exactly."

The big American bristled and then had exclaimed, "Simon, speak up!"

Before Simon could say another word, the big fellow walked over and hauled his butt out of the chair by his neck and with his right hand shook Simon like a leaf, feet dancing in the air and had said, "Why, you little turd! Same old Simon, eh!" And before the little man could respond, Felix had increased the pressure on his throat until the only thing coming out of Simon's mouth was gibberish. While the big American was still clutching Simon off the dirt floor, he turned sideways and said to Seyed, "If you kill this SOB right now, the first shipment of arms is on me." Without a word Seyed had drawn his side arm and ventilated poor old Simon with two .45 rounds. Felix dropped the body back into the chair and told Seyed that Simon had been a pain in his side ever since they first met at the Berlin, Germany, Military Arms Fair in 1983.

Seyed and Felix then got down to business. He had asked the big American, "What weapons do you have?"

"It all depends. What are your weaknesses, and what areas are you not succeeding in?"

Seyed had said they were having trouble taking down Russian helicopter gun ships. "They're too heavily armored and have too much firepower."

"No they don't." Felix had said. He then told Seyed to compile a list of their weaknesses and other areas they were having trouble and to send it to him. If you do this, I'll make the Russians go away."

Felix then had indicated that the first shipment was on him, and he would be awfully appreciative if the mujahideen could provide him with other reliable contacts. The big fellow then pointed out to Seyed that shipment times for the arms would depend on the efficiency of their logistics and supply lines, and that his men would need proper arms training for the new weapons. Felix told him that his company could provide those services. It hadn't been long before everyone was using Felix, and because of that, the mujahideen was starting to slow and then eventually had stopped the Russian advance.

After hearing this, Al-Hadi just sat there in the study, dumbfounded, and said nothing for a while. Seyed rose from his chair, turned, and walked back to the kitchen for more pastries and espresso. When he returned he handed his friend a new cup of espresso. "Perhaps this will help." Al-Hadi didn't know what to say.

FIFTEEN

EASTERN CARIBBEAN 2009

From somewhere in his mind, Jake heard a soft sultry voice behind him say, "Can I join you, sailor?"

"Oh, I'm sorry Zip, must have been elsewhere."

"Well I've been standing behind you for a good half a minute, and you didn't even notice. I would have at least thought my perfume would've gotten your attention. And here I thought you were observant. It must have been interesting. Ah, I know what it was."

"What's that?"

"A girlfriend?"

"My, so interesting and yet so inquisitive. Actually, there is no girlfriend and yes, I'm not married. And what say you, my dear?"

"Oh, I'm just a free spirit trying to find my way in this world."

"It's unlikely you are trying to find your way anywhere. I have a feeling you know exactly who you are and where you are going," Jake mused.

"Well, how observant."

With a more serious stance he continued, "I just received a call from my boss and was thinking about my next assignment."

"Well I'm waiting," Zoey said as she tilted her head.

"For what?"

"Your occupation. What do you do, and does that sling have anything to do with it, or do you wear it to impress the girls?" Zoey sighed in exasperation.

"Slow down, girl!" Jake exclaimed. "As far as my shoulder, I'm doing quite well, thank you, and if you're nice to me, I'll tell you about it sometime." Jake now thought on how he would explain his occupation to her. Most of his business was classified, and he needed to be careful.

"I work for the government as a special projects manager, and sit around all day and tell other people what to do." Jake quipped. "My work sometimes takes my partner, Slade Swanson, and I to various locales around the planet."

"Come, what do you really do?"

"That's what I do."

"What branch do you work for?"

"Do you think I'm military?"

"You look it."

"Actually, I'm a civilian."

"Is that all you're going to tell me?" Zoey frowned and looked at Jake intently.

"My dear, you have seven seconds to accept these words as true. Otherwise, they will vanish into thin air, never more giving you a chance to know." Jake gave her his famous crooked smile.

"Okay, sailor, I know my boundaries."

"Good, now where were we?"

"Beats me." Zoey chuckled.

"Oh yes, let's cut to the chase and exchange phone numbers and email addresses. I have to get my weary butt off this boat at 0700 hours and fly back to Washington, D.C., complements of my boss's phone call."

"You're sure being direct," Zoey chided.

"Is there any other way?"

"Why no, I thought you'd never ask."

They exchanged information and promised to keep in touch. As Jake was leaving the casino bar, Zoey yelled to him. "Get back here, you big handsome sailor and give me a smooch."

Jake turned and took a few steps back to Zoey and gave her a passionate kiss on her luscious red lips.

"Whew, hold on sailor, you're making me dizzy!"

While still holding her tight around her waist, Jake peered down into those brilliant blue eyes and then whispered in her right ear, "Good, I want you to remember this moment because I sure will." He released his embrace, stepped back and flashed his crooked smile before turning to leave.

"Jake, before you go, I want to give you this." She stepped up to him and placed something into his right hand.

Jake looked down and saw that he was holding a silver ankle bracelet designed as a zipper. "What's this for?"

"It's my way of ensuring that you will be kept out of harm's way until we meet again. And I also want you to know that only one other man is in possession of this type of bracelet."

Uh oh, what am I getting myself into, Jake thought. "Who is he?"

"He's my brother, you big lug." Zoey feinted a hurt expression on her face and continued, "Who did you think he was?"

"I don't know. You just caught me off balance."

"Good, I like my men off balance sometimes—keeps them in line."

"Well I'm a high wire man, and your work will be cut out for you," he said as he grinned at her. "Darlin', I really have to go, need my beauty rest."

"Only if you promise to call me and soon."

"Zip, that's high on my to-do list. Bye."

Jake turned again and walked out of the casino bar and headed to his loft. He needed to get back and retrieve his orders from his boss, pack and get everything in order so he would have a quick departure at 0700 hours.

After arriving at his owner's suite, mid-ship, deck 14, he let himself in via his key card. Whenever he traveled on a large cruise ship, he chose an upper deck for the view and always at mid-ship. This usually afforded him a good night's sleep because the location eliminated some of the ship's rocking motion, especially in inclement weather.

He closed the door and walked through the kitchen, past the half bath into the living room and retrieved his laptop from the desk's bottom drawer, powering it up. He checked the battery indicator and seeing the computer was at full power, switched on the hardware encryption device. He walked back into the kitchen to get a bottle of water from the fridge and took a long pull. He logged on, entered two levels of passwords, retrieved his orders file and began to read.

March 18, 2009, 0300 hours Eastern
Department of Homeland Security
Nebraska Avenue Complex
Washington, D.C.

Jake, you are to disembark immediately after arriving at Bridgetown, Carlisle Bay, Pier 6, Barbados at 0700 hours Atlantic Time. The ship's captain has already been notified, and the first mate will expedite your departure. There will be a U.S. embassy government car waiting just outside the cruise line's checkpoint into the city. You will be dispatched to Grantley Adams International Airport in Seawell, Christ Church, Barbados where a military transport will be on standby. Your departure time from Grantley Adams is 0800 hours. You'll arrive at Fort Belvoir, Virginia, USA, at 1500 hours Eastern. Slade and you will report to DHS headquarters at the Nebraska Avenue Complex in Washington, D.C. at 0800 hours sharp the following morning.

David H. Peterson
Deputy Secretary
DHS

SIXTEEN

RIYADH, SAUDI ARABIA 2009

The killing of Simon Duke shocked Al-Hadi. When he finally regained his wits after a few sips of espresso, he turned to his friend and exclaimed, "Incredible! Just incredible."

Seyed flashed his smile and wanted to know what Al-Hadi had been doing. He ignored his remark, looked at him with anger in his brown eyes and asked if he did this for greed.

"What a question to asked," Seyed said. "Was just caught up in the moment and fired. It was in the middle of a war!"

"War or no war, it was a cruel thing to do." Seyed looked at his friend in silence.

Al-Hadi sensing a looming confrontation decided to go on and tell Seyed what he'd been up to for the last few years. He said he had received more education in the U.S., came back home and started to work for ARAMCO. He had been working with them for the last few years and had gained valuable contacts in the Saudi government, especially at the energy level. He told Seyed that he held a key position in helping the government further automate and upgrade oil production with their refineries, and more and more the oil minister valued his advice on energy matters, especially when it came to OPEC. Al-Hadi also indicated that he had good contacts in the Saudi government, especially at the energy level. He told him that his responsibilities had progressed to a point where he now attended mid and high-level government meetings, especially related to energy and oil, and now had security clearance. Al-Hadi went on and told his friend that he was now reaching the limits of his ability for solving some of the more vexing and complex energy problems for their government. And now needed his help.

At first Seyed didn't know what to say, he was caught totally off guard by the offer. He stood and took another sip of his espresso and with cup in hand turned and slowly ambled over to the fireplace. He stood there for another moment thinking, and with his back to Al-Hadi he asked in what capacity he would be involved?

Al-Hadi sat back, gathered his thoughts, and began. He told Seyed he knew that he had made good money on Wall Street while working for Lehman Brothers and that they were still using some of his algorithms on predictability and permutations, in order to do advance analysis on other companies' fundamentals before investing in them. He also knew that they were still using his Fibonacci equations in order to determine certain patterns that predict the behavior of equities over time in the commercial and investment banking world. He indicated that he needed someone like him on his team that could solve complex energy relationships involving homeland, nation-to-nation, and global energy needs. Also, he needed someone to help produce the correct ratios of the thirteen crude categories in order for OPEC to be proactive in their portfolios. This would maximize OPEC and the kingdom's profits. Al-Hadi had further told him that there might be other work that he would be involved in, but his main emphasis would be increasing profits wherever he could. Finally, he told him that he had great respect and confidence in his work and that he would excel in this position and would be well compensated. Besides, he wanted to introduce a good friend of his. He thought that Abrahim Solasti and Seyed would work well together since Abrahim was a very bright computer scientist and they could bounce ideas of each other.

Seyed took another sip of his espresso, placed the cup on the fireplace mantle, turned to his friend and said, "That's a great offer." He also said that if he had time, he could fly home occasionally and work with the minister of energy in Tehran to further advance nuclear technology for Iran. He walked over, stood in front of his friend, and asked when he could start. Al-Hadi said immediately.

SEVENTEEN

EASTERN CARIBBEAN 2009

Jake arrived at Grantley Adams International Airport in Barbados at 0745 hours, courtesy of the U.S. Embassy. He thanked the chauffer for retrieving his bags and then turned to Frank Branson, a U.S. Embassy official, shook his hand and thanked him for the fast and courteous service. He picked up his luggage and trudged off to a military transport waiting a few hundred feet away. It was an old Boeing 707 but looked to be in good shape. He hadn't seen one of these in a long time.

The weather had changed overnight to a steam bath, and Jake couldn't ever recall when the weather was so soggy this early in the spring, especially for March. He now wasn't upset that the deputy director cut his vacation short. He absolutely hated humidity.

While walking to the plane, he thought how ironic it was that he had flown to San Juan, Puerto Rico just a few days ago in first class to begin his vacation and was now leaving on an old converted military transport to fly home. He really didn't mind. *His employer isn't really the government,* he thought, *but the U.S. taxpayers, and he owes them a good return on their money.*

As he approached the plane, he could see the flight crew standing on the tarmac and a U.S. Embassy truck leaving from the backside of the aircraft. He wondered what the truck was about.

"Good morning, Mr. Cannon. I'm Major Caruthers, senior officer for this junket."

"And how are you today, sir?" Jake asked.

"Fine, sir."

"Major, you can call me Jake; I hate formality."

"Well, Jake, I see we're on the same page." Dennis said with a smile.

He was a big man, bigger than Jake, and Jake could sense a no nonsense demeanor about him.

"Good, I'm Dennis." The major smiled again and then turned to his crew and with his right hand extended, introduced them to the agent.

After the introductions were made and Jake's luggage was stowed, except for his laptop, he looked at the major and asked, "Dennis, wasn't that a U.S. Embassy truck that just left your aircraft?"

"Yes it was. Apparently, since the plane is heading back to Washington, D.C., they loaded some equipment and documents aboard to take advantage of the flight."

"Is this our government we're talking about, Dennis?"

"Yeah, it seems strange. Who would have ever thought? Perhaps the government in some small way is listening to its constituency."

"Now, if we can get the other 99 percent to think the same way, we may have something." Jake chuckled.

"I second that, sir." Dennis took a hanky out of his hip pocket and mopped his heavy brow. "How are you enjoying our Caribbean soup?"

"God, I hate humidity." Jake said. "It gets into everything and soaks you like a spring shower. How come it's so muggy this early in the year?"

"Beats me. I just fly in every so often and collect passengers and equipment and go where the Army needs me. Now let's get out of this stuff and allow me to escort you to your luxurious first class accommodations." They both laughed.

While boarding the plane, the major eyed Jake's right arm in a sling, "What happened?"

"Just a little hockey accident, nothing too serious," Jake fibbed. "You should see the other the guy."

"I don't know if I want to," Dennis replied, and they laughed again.

As they entered the main cabin, Jake could see a dozen military-style seats bolted to the floor and configured three by four. Behind the seats was a large space and a bulkhead that divided the passenger and freight sections. After taking his seat in the middle of the first row, he looked up at the major and asked what was on the menu.

"Well we have cold chicken salad sandwiches, coffee and more chicken salad sandwiches followed by more coffee."

"Ah, it's so good to be able to fly first class." Jake chuckled.

"Oh, one more thing. Believe it or not there is a power port nearby in case you need to power up your laptop."

"Thanks, but I'm just going to kick back and get some shut eye, Dennis."

The major reached up to the overhead bin and handed Jake an Army blanket and a couple of little head pillows, saluted, and then headed to the flight deck. Jake strapped himself in, using the five-point military seatbelt system. He put the pillows behind his head and would get to the blanket later if he needed. He really had nothing to do for the next eight hours except to sleep.

EIGHTEEN

RIYADH, SAUDI ARABIA 2009

The big Pullman turned off the boulevard into an exclusive neighborhood, a ways south of Riyadh, went through a pair of large sandstone pillars and headed east up a long, winding hill. The wide thoroughfare sat on a ridge and was divided by a median planted with palm trees, shade-giving acacias, and eucalyptus type trees known locally as gum trees. On both sides of the street, other trees such as tall tamarisks, similar to pine trees, were planted in rows to provide shade as well as protection from the nearly persistent wind-sand environment in the area. Varieties of cactus and phlox were planted in other areas along the boulevard. Large, well-maintained homes with expansive manicured lawns terraced up the long hill on both sides of the road. One would've thought; how could this be? This was an arid environment with annual rainfall of only four inches per year with nearly constant shifting and blowing sand. But the Saudis, like most societies, liked beautiful landscapes, and to their credit, had taken years to understand, cultivate, and expand their environment. Their landscape not only included varieties of native plants and trees but also imported species of plants and trees from around the world. Even though 80 percent of the country was desert, Riyadh was located in the Hanifa valley, and the city and most of the surrounding countryside was green and boasted many parks.

As the limo approached the top of the hill and turned right onto Seyed's drive, he nudged Al-Hadi.

"Sir, are you okay?" Seyed asked, his face showing concern.

"What? Is there something wrong?" Al-Hadi asked, as he fought for consciousness.

"Well, you seemed to be in a trance."

"No, I think I was flashing back when we met at USC, and all the things we've been through to get to this point. It seemed so real. I'm sure glad you took my offer twenty years ago. You think we've been successful so far?" Al-Hadi mused, while shifting his position in the car's seat.

Seyed looked at his comrade thoughtfully for a moment before he replied. "Yes, we've managed to accomplish most everything we set out to. And because of your kindness to allow me a flexible schedule for the last few years, I've been able to help Iran get well on its way to becoming a nuclear power."

"I know you've made remarkable progress." Al-Hadi replied.

Seyed hit the remote. The pillared xenon lit security gates opened, and the car stopped. He powered down the left rear tinted window adjacent to the pillar and slipped his security card into the slot to fetch his mail. All of his official and classified documents were delivered directly by private courier. All other unofficial correspondence was delivered to the pillar in front of the security gates by the Saudi postal system.

The limo continued up about a quarter mile on a well-lit, beautiful, wide-paved stone drive. A large two-story sandstone house came into full view with its Porte-cochere at the far northeast corner of the residence. After Seyed bade farewell to Al-Hadi, he exited the big Pullman and watched as the vehicle swung around the portico's circular drive and headed back down to the street. Seyed turned and stepped up to the portico's double security doors, slipped the security card into the slot right of the doors, and waited until the big doors opened. After he went inside, the lighting on the north and east side of the house went on. He walked through the portico's reception area and put his jacket on the clothes tree. He turned left onto a wide hall, which opened to a large well-appointed chef's kitchen on the right and taking a few more steps, he stopped and inserted his security card into the wall slot and waited for the reader to open the double glass doors to the den. After going inside, dropping his briefcase, and tossing his mail in the incoming tray on his desk, his satphone rang. He retrieved it from his suit jacket and announced, "Hello."

"Hey Seyed, it's Al-Hadi."

"Are you back at your condo?" Seyed asked.

"No of course not. I think you're expecting too much from the limo," Al-Hadi chuckled while fumbling for his lighter. "I wanted to call to impress upon you that I want you to start working on Felix's information as soon as possible, even this weekend if you're not doing much," Al-Hadi said as he lit his cigarette.

"Okay, I probably have some time Sunday. Anything else?"

"Naw. That's it. Enjoy your weekend."

"You too." Seyed disconnected.

He leaned back in his black leather chair, thinking about the energy meeting earlier today. It seemed as though almost everyone was in a panic, and some of the attendees had already forgotten that oil was at an all time high at $145.00 per barrel just last summer. Al-Hadi had reminded them that this was only a temporary setback, and oil would probably go over $200 a barrel after the recession ended. Seyed fiddled with his pen and thought just how important Felix Jamosa would play in Al-Hadi's plans. He would soon find out.

NINETEEN

FLIGHT TO WASHINGTON D.C. 2009

A s Jake drifted to the other side of the light and tried to get his mind off Zoey, he thought on how Slade's and his background were similar, at least in the last few years.

Jake's family had played a prominent role in New York's political climate for many years. His grandfather, John Cannon, was the first in his family to graduate from West Point and rise to the rank of full bird colonel in the U.S. Army during his service in the Atlantic Theater in World War II. After coming back from the war, he served as mayor of Schenectady, New York, for twelve years.

Jake's father, Michael Cannon, had attended Syracuse University in the late 1960s and graduated with a bachelor's of science in mathematics. Instead of choosing the Army and following in the footsteps of his father, young Michael enlisted in the Air Force and was sent to Castle Air Force base in Merced, California. There he received his basic B-52 training and then joined the 319th Air Refueling Wing at Grand Forks, North Dakota, where he studied and completed his advanced training on the B-52H Stratofortresses.

He served almost two tours in Vietnam, rising to a rank of captain. He flew numerous B-52 tactical carpet-bombing missions from U-Tapao RTNAF Base in Thailand during the Arc Light Operation. Under project "Big Belly," B-52 Stratofortresses were modified to carry nearly thirty tons of conventional bombs. One of the missions involved flying cells of three B-52 bombers from U-Tapao twenty-four hours per day into South Vietnam in order to support ground combat troops against the advancing Viet Cong. Flying at 30,000 feet, the aircrafts could not be seen nor heard as they unloaded their deadly ordnance one minute apart. The damage was so devastating the B-52s were instrumental in nearly wiping out enemy concentrations besieging Khe Sahn, An Loc and Kontum.

After the War ended, Michael, who had reached the rank of major, was assigned to the Chrome Dome Operation and flew B-52 maintenance missions over the North Pole until his second tour ended. After service to his country, Michael had attended New York School University of Law and received his jurist doctorate degree, going into practice specializing in government law.

On one of his cases he had met Jeff Faye, a junior senator from New York. They had hit it off so well that Jeff had asked Michael to work on an important project in one of the senator's work groups. Michael did such an outstanding job that the senator had invited him back to work on another special project. When it came time for the senator's reelection campaign, Michael was chosen to head up the reelection efforts, and the senator had won his second term in a landslide victory. That was twenty years ago, and to this day both families kept in very close contact and quite often celebrated the holidays together.

Jake remembered the day fourteen years ago he had received his nomination from the senator to be admitted to West Point. He was the second in his family to attend the academy. His family was proud of him, and to honor them and the senator's commitment to him, he made sure that he graduated at the top of his class, summa cum laude with dual bachelor of science degrees in computer science and systems engineering. After graduation, he furthered his education by taking the Material Acquisition Management program at the U.S. Army Logistics Management College (ALMC) at Fort Lee, Virginia. After ALMC he was admitted and completed the Program Management Course at the Defense Systems Management College at Fort Belvoir,

Virginia. Together, these two programs enabled him to become a top-notch systems engineer for the Army.

After completing his training, Jake was sent to the Middle East during the Third Persian Gulf War and was assigned to the Third Army Logistics Operation Group. His particular group was responsible for all combat equipment and munitions procurement, plus logistics, placement, and replacement via ground, air, and sea during the war.

Since he also had training and education in computer science, he was assigned as program director and was responsible for all project managers in the combat equipment section. His project managers were in turn responsible for teams of software and system engineers and programmers that maintained and wrote code on the servers and mainframes that were located back home and in Kuwait. The teams kept track of all ordering, including incoming and outgoing inventories of combat equipment. Other program directors in the Third Army Logistics Operation Group were responsible for supply areas such as food, clothing, and ancillary items. Jake's area was the most critical, not to imply that the other areas were any less significant in importance. But if small and medium arms ordnance, troop carriers, strikers, tanks, and artillery ground to a halt, it could put a serious dent in the war effort.

After completing his tour, Jake wanted something more daring, and he eventually applied for and was granted admission to the black ops, Army's Delta Force.

Jake was one of the few that Delta Force accepted for training outside of Special Forces such as the Green Berets, Army Rangers or Navy Seals. Even though he was in superb physical condition, or so he thought, this part of the training gave him the most difficulty. He did better in other areas of the training such as interrogation, intelligence, equipment and sharp shooting school and graduated after two grueling years of constant learning, testing, and harassment. The premise of the training: most going in were already trained to kill; all coming out were natural-born killers.

He served in the counter-intelligence group, E-Detachment (Communications, Intelligence and Administrative Support) for three years before being tapped by the former deputy secretary of the Department of Homeland Security to head up the new DHS counter-intelligence unit.

Jake knew Slade Swanson from his tour with Delta Force and as it turned out Slade and his father knew Senator Faye. Slade's father, Robert Swanson, worked for Martin Marietta, an aviation and aerospace company headquartered in Bethesda, Maryland back in the late eighties. Swanson was the director of procurement for the company's eastern division. Robert met the junior senator from New York while working with Georgia's senator, Charles Dye. Senator Dye was head of the powerful subcommittee on appropriations, which was responsible for the overall funding for the Department of Defense, including the Army, Navy, and Air Force.

The project that Slade's father worked on called for more spending on further refinements, modernization, and additions for the Air Force's aging U-2 fleet. Robert worked closely with the senators in order to get the bill through Congress.

During this process all three became good friends and would frequently go hunting together in the northern mountains of Georgia. Sometimes Slade would come along, and the senators were amazed at the teenager's hunting skills and marksmanship. On more than one occasion, the senators would remark to Robert that the Army or Marines sure could use someone like Slade in their ranks.

As if on queue, when Slade turned eighteen and graduated from high school, he enlisted in the Army. He excelled in boot camp, and because of his hunting and marksmanship skills, was sent to the Army's Sniper School for Reconnaissance, Surveillance, and Target Acquisition training at Fort Riley, Kansas, home of the

Big Red One. He graduated second in his class. After receiving his papers, he was assigned to the RSTA unit that was part of the Army's First Calvary, First Infantry Division. Slade was then deployed to the Middle East and joined up with the Army's Big Red One, the First Infantry Division in Kuwait.

In one week's time, his division's scout sniper unit, working closely with other divisions of the Third Army and Coalition Forces, was instrumental in fighting through 260 kilometers of enemy-held territory in 100 hours, destroying 550 enemy tanks, 480 armored personnel carriers and taking 11,400 prisoners. Slade's division lost only eighteen soldiers during the war. It also earned three campaign streamers for its colors: Defense of Saudi Arabia, Liberation and Defense of Kuwait and Cease Fire.

Toward the end of his tour, special ops showed interest in Slade's RSTA accomplishments, and Delta Force invited him to take their training. Slade jumped at the chance, and, like himself, did quite well in the grueling two-year training program. Afterward, Slade was assigned to one of Delta Force E-Detachment counter-intelligence units.

Jake felt and for that matter, Slade too, that both of their paths would have never crossed if it weren't for the senator from New York. They both owed him a debt of gratitude, but they were unaware of the importance that Jeff Faye would play in their lives.

TWENTY

RUTH'S CHRIS STEAKHOUSE PORTLAND, OREGON 2008

C hampagne glasses clinked and laughter rose in one of the banquet rooms at Ruth's Chris Steakhouse in Portland, Oregon. The celebratory toasts of Moet et Chandon's Dom Perignon, Vintage Rose 1996 were in congratulations of Jamosa Enterprises reaching three billion dollars in annual revenue and signing a contract with Stinson International Corporation. Stinson would internationally distribute their company's finished textile materials to Sports Apparel and retail companies throughout the world. This was a highly prized accomplishment. Stinson distributed textiles for only the big players, and their company was now one of them. Felix could now consolidate his existing distribution channels from five to two and increase his profits in the logistics area of the company.

Everyone was there, including his beautiful wife, Clarissa; Jeffery and his lovely wife, Carly; Felix's dad and mother, Hunter and Lillian; Jeffery's parents, Benesh and Marni; two very close friends, Ed Wright and Jeremy Givans; and his long-time trusted secretary, Molly Hill.

After the usual pleasantries, the conversation turned to Jamosa Enterprise's accomplishments. At the head of the table, Felix stood and, with wine glass in hand, beamed at his gathering. He recalled the company's early days from the late 1970s, working out of a storefront on Hawthorne Blvd., near 39th Avenue. Later, as the company grew through the families' hard work, he started leasing buildings around the Hawthorne and Belmont neighborhoods for additional office and warehouse space. About this time, Jeffery married Felix's sister, Carly, and was invited into the business. The textile business in retail sports apparel started to explode. The company needed more space to house their growing office staff and inventory, especially since they were now doing business internationally.

Felix's father had a long and distinguished career as a successful commercial and industrial real estate broker in the Portland metropolitan area. Through Hunter's contacts the family was able to hammer out a deal with a large property management firm to buy the old Fox Theater building in downtown Portland.

The contract called for demolishing the existing structure and building a new forty-three-story charcoal glass high-rise tower. The building was designed to include upscale retail shops on the first floor, a premier steakhouse and a large state-of-the-art multiplex cinema on the second floor—The Fox Theater. The next eight floors, including the mezzanine, were reserved for additional retail shops. The lower middle floors, ten through thirty-three, were comprised of large, elegant condominiums. The top ten floors were retained for the company. It took the financial resources of all four families, a couple of their well-heeled close friends, and some creative financing to achieve the construction of the building.

Felix went on to extol the virtues of hard work, patience, and savvy business decisions that the families and a few of their very dear friends had made throughout the years to arrive at this point. The company had recently celebrated its three billion dollar milestone—two billion in domestic and one billion in international sales. With the addition of Stinson International handling almost all the logistics that included sea-going vessels, rail, overland and air transportation, the future of Jamosa Enterprises looked very bright indeed.

Felix paused and took another sip of wine, then continued. "Even though our country and the world are currently in uncertain economic times, I believe we will pull through this and be stronger for it because of the company's strong fundamentals. In fact, I project with a little luck and hard work, the company will probably reach the four billion-dollar mark somewhat sooner than we did, going from two to three billion. And without you and all of your hard work, this wouldn't have happened."

Felix held up his wine glass to toast everyone in the room again. As he sat down, he invited Jeffery to stand and say a few words on behalf of the families, friends, and the company. Eventually, almost everyone in the room stood and praised the accomplishments, successes, and their own small contributions to getting the company to where it was today.

After dinner, everyone met in the restaurant's lobby and thanked Felix and Jeffery for a wonderful evening and bade their farewells. As everyone was leaving, Hunter motioned his son and Jeffery aside and indicated he needed to talk with both of them tonight. "Son, I've been concerned over the IRS situation for some time now, and I need clarity from both of you on what's exactly going on," he said, as he buttoned up his winter coat to protect himself against Portland's damp winter chill.

"Dad, can this wait until another time?" Felix requested.

"That's what you said last time, son, and I'm not taking no for an answer." Hunter insisted, as he was putting on his driving gloves to guard against the December cold.

"Ok, Dad, what do you want us to do?" Felix relented with a frown.

"Well, you and Jeff can drop off the wives and then come on over to the house." Hunter looked at his watch and saw that it was a quarter after nine. "Can you guys make it over by 10:30 p.m.?"

Felix looked at his friend, and Jeff nodded.

"Okay boys. I'll see you then." Hunter said, and then he took Lily by the arm and led her outside and across the street to the parking lot to retrieve their car.

Jeffery turned to Felix and asked, "What are you going to tell your dad?"

"I don't know yet! Hopefully I'll figure something out before I get there," Felix said with a slight tremor in his voice.

At that moment, Clarissa came up to her husband and asked if they were ready to go. "Yes, honey," Felix replied, and they said good-bye to Jeffery and Carly.

Felix flagged down the valet and handed him the car's ticket, and a minute later the Shadow Blue Ferrari came roaring around the corner and pulled up to the curb right in front of the steakhouse. A young good-looking man with blond hair popped out of the car, walked around to the passenger side, and opened the door for Clarissa. After she was seated and the door was closed, the young man bounded to the curb. After a short conversation about the car and a nice tip for the kid, Felix got in and drove away.

TWENTY-ONE

FLIGHT TO WASHINGTON D.C. 2009

"Hey, Mr. Cannon," the second pilot, Army Lieutenant Marge Overton, was trying to nudge him awake.

"What?" Jake mumbled as he awoke and stared into a pair of smoky gray eyes that belonged to a vivacious, petite blonde.

"Sir, I brought you some coffee and a chicken salad sandwich."

"Thanks, Lieutenant. I'm so famished that I could eat just about anything right now." Jake sat up and took the mug of hot steaming coffee from the lieutenant's hand and took a sip. "Boy, this is good," Jake said as he tried to clear the sleepiness from his eyes and then ran a hand through his hair. "What brand is it, Lieutenant?"

"I'm not sure. Before they left the plane, the embassy guys handed us a couple of thermos of coffee and some chicken salad sandwiches. I believe it's a local brand sold in Barbados."

Jake took another sip and said, "I need to get me some of this stuff, it's really good. Where are we?"

"We're just an hour from Fort Belvoir, sir."

"You're Marge, right?"

"Yes sir."

"Well, Marge, please call me Jake. I'm getting tired of being addressed as sir or Mr. Cannon."

"Okay. Is there anything else you need, Jake?"

"No, I think the coffee and the sandwich will do it. And thanks," Jake looked up at her again and flashed his crooked smile.

"Okay then, I need to head back to the cockpit. We'll be landing soon."

Jake watched as the petite lieutenant headed to the front of the plane. *She is a dish all right*, he thought. But back to business.

He needed to call Slade and see if he was available to pick him up at the Army field. If not, he'd probably take a cab to his house. He finished the rest of his coffee and sandwich, collected his satphone, and punched in Slade's number.

"Slade here," the gravelly voice floated from the other end.

"Hey, buddy, where are you?"

"Hey, Jake," Slade quipped. "We are about to land at Fort Belvoir. Where are you?"

"We're about thirty minutes out. Hey, since you'll get in before me can I bum a ride home?"

"No such luck, buddy," Slade answered. "Besides, what about all those girlfriends you keep handy, especially that pretty little redhead? I'm sure she would be more than happy to take you home."

"Not anymore, partner. Haven't seen her in a month or so, and she isn't really my type." Jake said, as he stowed the sandwich wrapper and coffee cup. "I just thought of something. There's this pretty blonde Army lieutenant flying second mate on this trip. Maybe, if she has wheels, I can talk her into a nice meal and a glass of wine before taking me home."

"Jake can't you just give it a rest and take a cab for once? What's wrong with a little solitude once in a while? Beside, your house isn't that far away."

"I could, buddy, but what's the fun in that?" Jake kidded.

"Okay, pal. Play Casanova and see if I care. But one of these days it's going to catch up with you. Mark my words." Slade warned.

"But until then, I'm going to have my fun," Jake shot back. "Did you catch any spring salmon that you were bragging about?"

"No! I was still collecting local information, fishing gear, and getting a guide. I was heading out tomorrow morning."

"Too bad, I was counting on coming over to your place in Georgetown and sampling some of that grilled salmon. I even had the wine picked out."

"Another time, pal," Slade said, as he wishfully thought about preparing and barbecuing salmon for his friends.

"Looks like there's something big brewing with the boss. He wants us both at DHS headquarters tomorrow morning at 0800 hours sharp. Slade, did he tip his hand to you?"

"No, and he rarely does."

"Okay, bubba, I'll see you tomorrow morning. Got to go and see that pretty blonde." He broke the sat connection.

He always liked to kid Slade about the opposite sex. He liked to keep his friend off balance when it came to his gamesmanship. Sometimes it drove Slade batty, and he liked that in a roundabout way. But when it came to business between Slade and him, it was serious, damn serious. Not to say there wasn't any foolishness involved when there was a break in the action. But when the cards were down, they were down. Sure, he liked the ladies as well as the next guy and perhaps even more at times. But tonight he needed his solitude. He needed to think and prepare for tomorrow's meeting. Even though there wasn't any concrete information, he needed to think about possible scenarios and to anticipate. After landing and departing the Army transport and thanking the crew, and especially Marge for a safe and uneventful trip back to the states, he picked up the prearranged cab just beyond the North entrance gate to the airfield, gave directions to the cabby, and headed home.

TWENTY-TWO

JAMOSA'S RESIDENCE—
PORTLAND, OREGON 2008

On their way home from Ruth's Chris Steakhouse, Felix told Clarissa that his father had brought up the IRS investigation again, and Hunter had insisted he and Jeffery see him tonight.

Clarissa turned and looked at her husband and asked, "Is everything all right with the IRS?"

"Sure, why wouldn't it be?"

And Clarissa with her standard reply said, "Well, I just wanted to know." She was an intelligent and thoughtful woman and always talked things through with her husband, but with his constant preoccupation as of late, it made her nervous because she wasn't sure of what was going on.

She always was a pain, he thought. He was sick and tired of her sticking her nose into his business. Sometimes he wondered why he even married her. She was getting duller by the year. In fact all his family and friends were. And then there was Jeffery, his brother-in-law, what a pain in the arse. Always checking his arms and shipment transactions. Christ! Can't a guy have a slush fund? He was the one that put the gun running business together, and he'll be damned if he answers to anyone. The only thing he was interested in was selling weapons and his gun running buddies, he mused.

Five minutes later he pulled up to their residence at the Pearl District's Waterfront building called Naito's Place. He drove around to the parking entrance on Front Avenue and stopped at the steel gate, clicking his remote. After the gate opened, he drove into the first parking level and parked his car in the Northeast corner of the parking structure next to Clarissa's triple black AMG Mercedes SL 500 Roadster and the family's Cadillac Escalade. After the elevator's doors opened to a well-appointed foyer on the twelfth floor, they walked to their penthouse in silence. Felix put his arm around Clarissa's shoulder to reassure her that everything was okay. He entered his security card next to the front door and waited for it to click open.

After closing the door, Felix turned to his wife in the foyer and said, "Honey, I'm sorry that I have to go out tonight, but Dad is really being impatient on this IRS thing."

"That's fine, dear, I understand. You need to clear up any questions he may have. If you are going to be really late please call and let me know," Clary said, as she looked at her husband.

"I will. I'm going to change into something comfortable because I think it's going to be a long night."

Clary went through the dining room and the butler's pantry into the large well-appointed kitchen. Going to the fridge she poured herself some ice water from the dispenser. *I'll need some medication for this one*, she thought. She went to the pantry and retrieved some pain relievers; stepping out of the pantry's doorway, she admired her kitchen. She loved all the high-end appliances with their gleaming stainless steel finish. This was the best kitchen she ever had; it was a breeze entertaining family and guests.

She took her ice water and medicine and walked over to the breakfast room, sitting at the table. Taking her medication, she leaned back in one of the cushy captain chairs and tried to relax for a while. She was concerned that Felix wasn't telling her the whole truth about the IRS investigation. He had always been a good husband to her and their daughter, Samantha. Lately though he seemed to be preoccupied with matters and sometimes was forgetful. She was worried about his health and hoped that he was okay. Perhaps after his meeting with his father tonight he might tell her more about the investigation.

Felix went through the foyer and great room and walked down a short, partitioned hallway into the master bedroom. Going into the walk-in closet, he changed into an old pair of jeans, sweatshirt, and tennis shoes and collected an old leather bomber-style jacket to deflect December's weather. He was dreading the meeting with his father.

He walked back into the master bedroom and dropped the jacket on the king size bed, going into the master bathroom to clean up and shave. He usually had to shave at least twice a day because of his heavy, graying stubble. Finishing, he went back into the master bedroom and stretched out on the king bed, trying to relax for a while before leaving. After fifteen minutes he arose, put his jacket on, and headed to the kitchen to get a glass of water. Clary was sitting in one of the captain's chairs in the breakfast room when he entered. He went over and took a glass from the hutch, going to the refrigerator's refreshment center and poured himself some ice water. He took a gulp and walked over to where his wife was sitting and stood behind her. Without a word, he massaged her neck and shoulders for a while knowing that she was probably experiencing one of her migraines. After a while he leaned over and gave her a kiss.

She turned, looked up at him and said, "Thanks, hon. I hope everything works out between you and your father."

"Me too," he offered. Felix kissed his wife again and left.

TWENTY-THREE

ALEXANDRIA, VIRGINIA 2009

J ake lived in an old house on an acre of land on the banks of the Potomac, a few miles south of Alexandria, Virginia. He had neighbors but not too close. He liked his privacy.

He had bought the old, run-down farmstead six years ago, right after joining DHS. The first thing he did was gut the old place and start over. The house was built in 1875 and had been remodeled twice but had been in need of major repairs. He did all the framing himself, including new raised ceilings and stairways. He had also upgraded the electrical and plumbing, plus installing a new roof and gutter system. He had hired out the painting, concrete work, and some of the finish work. Last year he had installed all new fencing, outside lighting, and a good security system. Jake enjoyed working with his hands to get his mind off of work, especially when he was vexed by a complex problem.

The house wasn't extraordinarily large by modern standards, about 3,800 square feet, but it was plenty for one bachelor. One thing it had that most houses didn't was a 3,500 square-foot garage that he had just completed. The new garage was adjacent to the south side of the house and had an epoxy-based black and white checkered floor. The large, well-lit garage showcased his five 1960s muscle cars that he had acquired over the last sixteen years.

After storing his laptop and luggage in the house, he walked outside to the garage. He flipped on the nine rows of double eight-foot fluorescents to admire his stable of cars in order to get his mind off of business for a while.

Jake and his father, Michael, had been collecting, restoring, and modifying 1960s vintage muscle cars for years. He walked up to a modified and extremely rare 1970 shadow purple 454 cubic-inch, V8 Corvette with a Can Am RPO LS7 engine rated in stock form at 465 brake horsepower. He stood there for a moment and looked over the top of the Vette at his other cars. Next to the Corvette was a metal-flaked gold 1965 Chevelle Malibu SS 327 cubic-inch V8 with 350 horsepower. His father named the car "Dax" since it reminded him so much of his old 1965 Chevelle when he was growing up. His father had told Jake that "DAX" was part of the license plate number on the old car. Across from the Malibu was an original 1970 426 Hemi Cudda "Bad Boy" pushing 425 brake horsepower in stock form. The engine was mated to a heavy-duty TorqueFlite 727 automatic transmission instead of a four-speed, since it clocked better quarter-mile times. The car was repainted in its original high gloss orange with black stripes. Next to the Cudda sat a 1965 Pontiac GTO with a 389 cubic-inch engine with tri-power rated at 360 horsepower. This was an extremely popular muscle car in its day and was often referred by its nickname, "The Goat." The last car was a modified 1967 Chevy Nova two-door post with a 396 cubic-inch engine with aluminum heads and a Muncie four-speed on the floor. *Best thing about all the cars*, he thought, *is that they all have their original manuals, MSRP, and matching numbers.*

Jake recalled how he and his father early on had decided to store all the original parts in marked bins for each modified car, in case they ever decided to restore them back to their original stock condition. Each piece of stock equipment had been pressure-washed and either chromed or painted depending on the particular component. These machines were the last of their kind, made before the dawn of computer and smog-controlled engines, and one only had to have a basic knowledge of mechanics to work on them. They exuded their own elegance of brash design and outlandish horsepower without computer intervention. The only drawback had been that they required high-octane leaded gasoline.

After fixing some dinner, he went upstairs to the master bedroom that overlooked the Potomac River, slipped into his favorite robe and slippers, and moved back downstairs to the great room. He sat down on the gray leather couch, hit the remote to the gas fireplace, and thought about tomorrow's meeting.

TWENTY-FOUR

DRIVE TO HUNTER'S HOUSE—
PORTLAND, OREGON 2008

Felix took the elevator down and walked to his Ferrari. Getting in, he looked at his music selection on the Bose system and chose Edgar Winter and Lynyrd Skynyrd, classic rock 'n' roll.

He cranked the Bose and wheeled the car out of the garage, heading south on the "Parkway" toward the Hawthorne Bridge. While listening to the music, Felix soliloquized on how he would approach his dad on the IRS investigation. He knew his dad was an astute businessman and for that matter most everything else, and he wouldn't stand for clever or pat answers.

The government inquiry came as a shock, and at first he couldn't comprehend why. He always tried to keep his weapons business at arm's length from getting directly involved with U.S. geopolitics. His goal was to help the United States push communism off the world map, and, wherever possible, help advance democratic principals. His arms company had worked well in tandem with the last four administrations, starting with Reagan's. He usually received his weapons from various stockpiled locations around the world. In other words, from past U.S. government-backed conflicts. In addition to the IRS inquiry, he couldn't understand why his arms company was now being mysteriously ostracized from receiving U.S. manufactured weapons.

It had all started with the Ahmad administration. His friends and associates on Capitol Hill, some of which he had done business with for the past twenty-five years, were no longer reachable. They wouldn't return his telephone calls or emails. If this continued it would take a sizeable bite out of his arms profit and place his sham corporations in financial jeopardy. At first he thought the pressure came from the ATF. But upon deeper reflection, he now realized he had made a huge mistake driven by his rapacious nature. George Rifkin, the fellow that helped him get started in the arms business, told him one thing you never do: never supply U.S. manufactured weapons to a country that is in conflict with a super power, unless you first get the blessings of the administration. And he hadn't with the Russian/Georgia conflict.

The President of Russia had raised all kinds of cane with the United States after he found that the Republic of Georgia, a satellite of the former Soviet Republic, was receiving U.S. manufactured weapons to help advance Georgia's cause. This could have significantly destabilized Russia's ties with the west, and even influence the actions of U.S. troops in the Middle East and elsewhere around the globe. Felix was now stuck in the middle of geopolitical mud with no easy way out. In fact, this could take its toll on the families, his friends Ed and Jeremy, and the textile business both financially and emotionally. He not only hadn't told Jeffery about this, but had also kept all the profits from the Russian/Georgia conflict for himself. *What a bonehead move,* he thought. How was he ever going to explain this to his family? He couldn't, because if he did, it would not only expose his monumental stupidity but also show his treacherous ways.

If his father pressed too far, as he knew he would, he would give him the same story he gave Jeffery about the ATF. And if needed he would even expose the arms business. Hopefully all this shocking information would throw Hunter off the trail. Felix pounded the steering wheel and swore to himself. He was now perspiring, and he needed to get his thinking elsewhere. He needed to get it together before the meeting or he wouldn't be good to anyone, especially himself.

The weather had changed to a nasty mix of snow, sleet, and rain as he moved closer to Portland's only extinct volcano that formed Mt. Tabor Park. As he approached his dad's house, he turned right on to Fifty-fifth Avenue at the top of Hawthorne Boulevard and drove one block, turning left onto a long drive. Two stone pillars lit with bright halogen lamps greeted him at the entrance and guided him in to his parent's property. The drive was bordered by an expansive emerald green lawn with a couple of large old-growth Douglas fir trees and varieties of Maple trees that had long since lost their foliage. Most of the flowerbeds planted around the property lay dormant. His parents lived in a wonderful old well-maintained French Normandy style house on a large, impeccably maintained three-quarter acre lot, right below the west side of Mt. Tabor Park—the home he had grown up in. The neighborhood was tucked away at the foot of the mountain and was sprinkled with elegant old mansions and beautifully manicured green lawns from a bygone era. Its centerpiece was reservoir number six, one of the many open-air water collection points owned and operated by the City of Portland Water Bureau.

The reservoir itself was split in half by a concrete wall, and held 37 million gallons of water per side with a beautiful water fountain in the middle. At night, the fountain was encircled by multi-colored lights that focused its beams upward into the fountain's spray, in an ever-expanding explosion of shimmering rainbow colors. Concrete sidewalks ran parallel and abutted the reservoir's three-foot stonewalls with a six-foot black wrought iron fence sitting atop that protected the waterway, and it wound nearly a mile around the water holding facility. Also, the reservoir was encircled with gas flame-style lanterns spaced every 200 feet and interlaced with the fencing. After dusk, the grounds around the reservoir were bathed in a warm romantic glow from the lanterns.

He especially remembered the summer after graduating from Benjamin Franklin High School; his dad helped him get a temporary summer position with the Water Bureau. He was assigned to take care of the beautiful lawns surrounding the old reservoir. He loved working outdoors and being around the smell of freshly cut grass, and really enjoyed mowing and maintaining nearly six acres of lawns. In the beginning he used a walk-behind, self-propelled Jacobson mower to cut the grass that took at least two full days to complete. He certainly received his exercise, not to mention a nice tan. Later that summer he received a riding mower, which pulled two thirty-inch reels behind it. This reduced his mowing time down to six or seven hours and allowed more time for him to concentrate on edging and trimming. It also gave him more time to think about his future and what he really wanted to do. At this point in his young life, he already knew that he wanted to build a business from scratch, one that he and his family would be proud of. He just didn't know what kind of business yet.

Mt. Tabor Park was a popular romantic get-away for young lovers, especially during the summer. There was many a summer night before he married Clarissa that he would bring her up here. And they would either walk around the reservoir holding hands, or he would bring a blanket for them to sit on the smooth, green rolling lawns, where they would talk for hours about their future plans. He could still vividly remember his fiancé back then, tall with a statuesque figure, porcelain white complexion, her ice blue eyes, and her shimmering, long, blonde hair cascading down around her shoulders in splashes of golden radiance.

He smiled and was moved, remembering his clumsy attempts of trying to make advances toward her with Russian fingers and Roman hands. And she, being trained in the proper etiquette of a young lady so provocative and precocious for her age, adroitly sidestepping his ungainly thrusting as if she was using a foil to deflect her opponent's parries in the art of classical fencing. He was truly amazed at her prowess and subtle musings about topics that he could barely fathom and at the same time doubted his doubts that she was intellectually superior to him.

⸻◆⸻

Felix's mind drifted back to the present while he drove up the long drive. He peered through the car's windshield and could see the reflection of ice crystals glistening like diamonds fading in the night to a crystalline curtain's gossamer edges of his car's headlamps and feel the crunch of snow beneath his tires. He again looked up at the car's thermometer/compass and saw the temperature had fallen to twenty-eight degrees because of the change in elevation. The car's wipers were now crusted with ice as it snowed in earnest, and the icy east wind brought December's vengeance as it danced its swirl and sighed among the fir and maple trees.

Arriving at the house, he could see Jeffery's black 740 Beamer along with Jeffery's father's old white Caddy parked in the driveway. Alarms went off in his head; he wondered why Benesh was here? Even though the IRS was investigating him, he didn't recall at the restaurant that Benesh was invited. It finally dawned on him that his dad really meant business this time.

TWENTY-FIVE

DHS NEBRASKA COMPLEX—
WASHINGTON D.C. 2009

As Jake drove the government-issued Ford into the gated underground parking structure at the Department of Homeland Security headquarters on Nebraska Avenue, he noticed Slade's black Range Rover two cars in front of him. He parked his Ford next to Slade's car. They both got out at the same time, and Slade stood there for a moment thinking about Jake's 1967 Chevy Nova muscle car squirreled away in his garage before he asked Jake for the umpteenth time if he was in the mood to sell it. And Jake, for the umpteenth time, declined the offer. Ever since Slade had laid eyes on the fire orange Nova, he was continually after Jake to sell him the car.

"Come on Jake, why not? You would still have four gorgeous muscle cars left in your garage."

"Yeah, buddy. But that would upset the ratio of muscle cars to girlfriends. I always like to keep it one-to-one you know. If I ever have less than five girlfriends, I'll consider it." Jake said and flashed his crooked smile at Slade.

Slade slapped his friend's shoulder as they walked toward the elevator, "Here it is 0730 hours, and you're already talking about your girlfriends. Don't you ever give up, pal?"

"Why should I do a thing like that when I'm having so much fun?"

Slade half frowned, ran a hand through his coal black hair, and changed the subject. "I wonder just how important this meeting is and what plans or scenarios David will address us with?"

"We won't have to wait long," Jake quipped.

"Indeed."

They exited the elevator on the fifth floor and headed to a small break room to fetch some coffee, continuing on to their respective offices to do last-minute preparations. Like there was any planning to do.

Jake arrived at the deputy secretary's corner office on the seventh floor at 0800 hours sharp and went in. Slade was already seated alongside the team's computer guru, Dr. Tonia Franks. Seated next to her right was Dr. Clyde Ferris, Homeland's neural net expert, and sitting across from Slade was Tom Morrison, Homeland's database director and profiler. Rounding out the group was David Peterson, and, to Jake's surprise, the secretary of DHS, Mary Knappa, seated at the far end of the table. He knew now that this was extremely important as he walked around the other end of the large oak table and sat next to Tom, nodding to the team. After some of the team poured coffee from two carafes and the usual pleasantries were exchanged, the secretary stood and started the briefing.

"I'm sorry I had to call some of you in while on vacation," looking at Jake and Slade. "But we have been receiving troubling information from the intelligence community in the last few weeks that could put our country into a dire situation if left unchecked. The data we have received from Booze and Allen, Lockheed Martin, National Security Administration (NSA) and other reputable sources indicate a possible take-down of our nation's economy through computer espionage."

With those words red flags where going up in everyone's mind. Jake asked, "Ms. Secretary, what kind of computer espionage are we talking about?"

"Jake, hold on," the secretary said. "I'm going to let David brief everyone. I'm here today to impress upon each and every one of you just how paramount this investigation is."

The secretary nodded to David, who was sitting at the opposite end of the table to begin the briefing. Peterson stood, placed both hands on the oak table, and leaned his short, wiry frame toward his audience before he began. His brown eyes commanded their attention. The deputy secretary had worked in the government since his last tour in the Gulf Wars, either as an elected official or as a government bureaucrat. He had always taken his career seriously and worked tirelessly promoting good sound fiscal judgment, clear logical thinking, and extreme work ethics. He was a hard taskmaster, but he treated his people with respect and dignity. And when the chips were down, he always stood behind his team. With Dave you always knew where you stood, and he expected the same from his friends, colleagues, and employees.

"As you all are aware, we gather intelligence on thousands of individuals and groups that involve homeland security from a variety of sources. Most times the information runs the gamut from insignificant to bombings, and in rare cases can include nuclear threats. This time it's different. The events that I'm going to discuss with you are indeed chilling, and can be more horrific in some ways than taking down one of our cities through thermonuclear detonation." The deputy secretary paused to let his remarks set in, took another sip of coffee, and seeing that he had everyone's undivided attention, continued.

"The intelligence we are receiving indicates that there are certain sources in the Middle East that are working to bring down our financial institutions through cyber terrorism. And you know full well if they succeed it will not only take out the United States economically but also the other G20 nations of the world, in a domino effect. This insidious threat is possible because the majority of brokerage and banking transactions are now interconnected throughout the globe. Overnight, governments, corporations, and individuals will lose all of their investments and savings. Two words come to mind: Financial Armageddon!"

TWENTY-SIX

HUNTER'S HOUSE—
PORTLAND, OREGON 2008

Felix parked the Ferrari on the RV pad along the west side of the double garage, walked to the front entryway, stepped up onto the slate porch, and rang the door bell. His father answered the door after the second ring, inviting his son inside. Hunter took his son's bomber coat and hung it on the coat tree in the entry hall, and without a word led him to the large office.

Walking to his dad's study, he remembered how comforting the old house seemed to him as a child, with its many nooks and crannies and its warm and inviting dark interior. At times, and especially on nights like tonight, it felt as though he were living in a cave in the woods. The house had been built by old-world craftsmen in the 1930s and still held together as if it were almost new. It simply was a marvelous old home with lots of character displaying its many built-ins, leaded glass windows, and heavy dark mahogany and walnut throughout. Even though the house and the neighborhood were relegated to the realm of the superannuated long ago, it reluctantly deferred its prominence to newer neighborhoods, such as Forest Heights on the west side with its glitz and glamour. This house and its neighborhood would stand the test of time.

He remembered the one room he couldn't go in as a child while his father was away. Hunter told him the study was his place of business with sensitive documents and contracts lying about and didn't want them disturbed. The entire room was done in wall-to-wall gleaming dark mahogany, including the ceiling with its solid mahogany beams arching across the room.

Cabinets and bookshelves flanked the back wall with its large gas fireplace and impressive mantle in the center. Bookshelves were lined with philosophical readings from Bacon to Mill, Descartes to Nietzsche, Shakespeare, works from William F. Buckley Jr., and some of the twentieth century's great novelists including Hemingway, Steinbeck, Faulkner, Fitzgerald and Frost.

In his earlier years as a commercial real estate broker, his father would occasionally invite unsuspecting clients up to his house, usually during the evening, to discuss business. In his study he would always have the fireplace going, even in the summer, with heavy drapes drawn, and he would ply them with high quality Cognac in heated snifters and fine Havana cigars. Hunter was a master negotiator, dressed in mediator clothing, and shrouded in the cloak of a conciliator. He could step into an argument with a client or, for that matter, arguments between clients, and defuse the situation with sound logical advice. He could win over his opponents in a non-threatening manner.

He sometimes appeared to others as an enigma, and he used this to know when to weave and where to jab. He especially enjoyed applying his adaptation of Machiavellian principles on the poor souls. Hunter always waited with his closing until they began to squirm, wilt, and slump in their chairs, sweating profusely in their soiled dress shirts with their undone ties and rolled-up sleeves. By now his clients were trying to peer at his father across his desk through a thick haze of cigar smoke, excogitating their next move. He knew the walls were closing in on his prey, as the coral green flames from the large gas fireplace danced its rhythm of trance off the shimmering polished mahogany walls. In retrospect, it seemed as though the poor fools were queuing up to walk through the doors of one of Old Portland's smoky opium dens, sitting down and stoking their pipes with the flames of ignorance and stupidity before doing their bidding with the devil. He rarely went to these extremes, but when he did they were usually on important clients with large projects.

At the study Hunter opened the double solid mahogany doors and ushered his son in. Jeffery and his dad, wearing their yarmulkes, were already sitting on comfortable old leather wing chairs on the right side of the study. They were next to the large gas fireplace, going full bore, both sipping Hennessy XO Cognac Extra out of their heated snifters.

Whenever Jeffery was around his white haired bespectacled father he always wore his *kippa* to honor him and *God*. Even though Benesh and his wife Marni were diminutive in stature and their only son towered over them, Jeffery always treated them with the utmost respect. Benesh's mind worked slowly and methodically, and he usually took his time to chew over his thoughts before making decisions or speaking. On occasion, when he got excited or agitated, his speech would sometimes come out jumbled or he would stammer. However if people took him too lightly it could prove to be a fatal mistake. He was nearing eighty, but still had a razor-sharp mind and a dry sense of wit.

When Hunter closed the study doors, Felix turned to his friend and said, "Jeffery, I see you are enjoying one of Dad's fine Havana Cohiba cigars. How is it?"

"Absolutely delightful, especially in combo with the Cognac."

"Well, enjoy it while you can. It appears we will be in for a long, arduous night." Felix said solemnly.

TWENTY-SEVEN

DHS NEBRASKA COMPLEX— WASHINGTON D.C. 2009

B ehind him, the deputy secretary peered through the bank of windows facing the March sun before looking at Mary Knappa, the DHS secretary. After turning she nodded for him to continue. Peterson gathered his thoughts and began. "We can't imagine the calamity, confusion, and outright terror that this will create. It could throw the world into a depression the likes we've never seen, not to mention all the finger pointing and accusations that could eventually lead to another world war. If this happens global hyperinflation would soon follow, and all the wealthy nations will have no choice but to crank up their printing presses in order to fund their war machines. Even without global confrontation, countries would still have no choice other than printing more currency. Though we believe the target is the United States, it doesn't preclude the fact that the terrorists can probably pick and choose which G20 country or countries to cyber-attack. The main thing to understand is it probably doesn't matter which country. If any one of the G20 nations are cyber-attacked, the world will probably step into an abyss, and it will take decades to recover, if we ever recover." The room was so quiet one could hear a pin drop. The deputy secretary looked at everyone again, and he could see the stunned looks on every face.

Dr. Tonia Franks, the head of homeland's information technology, was the first to recover. "Mr. Deputy Secretary, how can this be? I've devoted my entire career and most my of life to the IT field, and I know that all of the major financial institutions in this country have extremely powerful, sophisticated, and complex hardware and software firewalls to stop this sort of thing. Our country has always been at the forefront."

"Well Dr. Franks, if this is an idle threat, which I don't think it is, other parts of the world have apparently caught up or even exceeded us in this area," the deputy secretary said as he put down his coffee cup.

"Sir, regardless if they can pull this off, do we have working computer models in place to see if the threat is creditable? And if so, can we advance these models to quickly come up with a plan of action?" Jake asked.

"Only minimally. This caught us off guard," the deputy secretary said, looking at Jake. Now David paused, looked out at the March weather before turning and measuring everyone's expression in the room. "First, I want to say that we're not sitting on this. Homeland Security, in conjunction with the FBI, are in the process of setting up a national task force comprised of forensic computer scientists, profilers, database specialists, Artificial Intelligence (AI), network, security and firewall experts, and other essential personnel, including a couple of notorious black hat hackers to investigate this. And if needed, we will commandeer additional computer experts and others from the private sector." Peterson looked at Dr. Franks. "Tonia, I want you and a few of your hand-picked computer experts to aid the FBI on their end of the investigation. Think of this as another Y2K scenario but with much more serious consequences. Your team will be given security clearance and access to the government's IBM and Cray supercomputers to conduct tests you deem feasible. Understood?"

"Yes, sir. Dr. Ferris, Tom Morrison and I will organize our team right after this meeting. Sir, who are my contacts with the FBI?" Tonia asked.

"I spoke with the FBI assistant director, Dan Johnson, yesterday, and he indicated that your counterparts for you and Tom are Ben Jenkins, head of computer security, and Sam White, lead member of the FBI's profiling team. Also, the DOD, ATF,

CIA, NSA and all of our private Intelligence Agencies, and even sections of the Armed Forces are now a part of this investigation and have given this priority one. DHS has now elevated the threat advisory system to yellow (significant risk to terrorists attacks). Your team's primary focus is to work with the other agencies to uncover how they plan to do this and determine if any part of their plans are already in place, and if so, how to disable them. Understood, Dr. Franks."

"Affirmative, sir."

"Sir, I've been thinking about what you said in regards to the United States being placed in dire consequences if the terrorists succeed. Have we run any studies off of our KBA?" Jake inquired.

"Yes we have, but as I indicated the models are not fully functional to work with these types of scenarios and threats, and certainly not of this magnitude. We have already formed a pre-team to gather as much pertinent information that we can from our existing databases. Mr. Morrison, can you step in and briefly describe what your team is doing?"

TWENTY-EIGHT

HUNTER'S HOUSE— PORTLAND, OREGON 2008

"Son, would you like some Cognac?" Hunter asked, as he motioned Felix to sit down on a wing chair next to the fireplace.

"Might as well, Dad, perhaps it will ease the pain," Felix muttered.

"What do you mean by that remark?" Hunter snapped.

"Dad, I know how you operate and where this little soiree is going." Before Hunter could speak, Felix turned to Benesh and asked, "When were you invited to this little gathering?"

Benesh cleared his throat and motioned to Hunter. "Son, I invited him before we left the steakhouse tonight," Hunter said as he handed Felix his Cognac.

"Why didn't you tell me in the lobby?" Felix asked, while taking his first sip.

"I didn't think it was that important, and besides he has every right to be here. After all, he's being investigated too," Hunter, said in a loud tone.

"Yeah I know dad, but—"

Hunter, still standing, cut him off and looked directly at his son with those piercing blue eyes and exclaimed, "There's no buts about it! Benesh and I want to know what's going on, and we want to know tonight!"

Now Felix stood, faced his dad and said, "I just can't tell you much right now. Besides the less you and Benesh know the better off you two are."

Hunter stepped in closer to his son, and even though he was close to eighty and was a couple of inches shorter, he still didn't take spin from anyone, especially his family. "Son, have you lost your upbringing? Haven't I always taught you to respect and always be honest with people?"

"Yes, you have. But in this case, I think it is absolutely imperative that you know as little as possible." Felix shrugged his shoulders and waited.

Hunter stepped back from his son and took another sip of his cognac and said, "Now you really have my interest."

Benesh stood and said, "Felix, please let us know, and if I think this is as important as I think it is, it certainly is crucial that we know every little detail."

Felix put his drink down, threw up his hands and looked in Jeffery's direction, and bellowed, "Well are you just going to sit there and say nothing?"

Jeffery, taking a puff on his cigar and letting out the smoke slowly while he composed himself, said, "Dude, you know we have talked often about this day, and if it ever came up we would think of something. Well, guess what? That day, or rather that night, is here, and we're still unprepared." Taking another pull of his cigar, he continued, "Even though we always thought it would be best to shield our fathers from this, I think we better come clean."

"But, Jeffery," Felix dived in.

"Let me continue and don't interrupt me again." Jeffery glowered and went on. "I was speaking to our lead counsel, Jim Benson, the other day about the investigation. And you know what he said. Jim looked me directly in the eye and asked me twice whether there where any details on the accounting and finance procedures, however small or insignificant, that he and his team should be aware of. I asked him why he was so adamant. And you know what his reply was?" Jeffery now stood and looked directly at his friend and brother-in-law and continued. "He said, 'Even though you might think you have a bulletproof case, you would either be stupid or a fool to let our legal team go up against the government without knowing everything. Because if we do, our team will get caught with their collective pants down, and as a consequence, you might as well kiss the company good-bye. And can you imagine what kind of pratfall it would create for the families?'"

Felix looked at his friend for a long moment and then turned to Hunter and said, "Dad, I have two conditions."

"What are they, son?"

"First, can you refresh my drink and get me a cigar? And second, I don't want any interruptions until I'm finished—you can fire away then. Agreed?"

"Agreed, son."

Felix excused himself to go to the bathroom, while Hunter walked over to the other side of the large study to make another round of drinks at his private bar. After the drinks were made, he stepped around the side to open his Executive Puro Humidor. He remembered how thrilled he was when he received the Humidor from his son and Clarissa on Hunter and Lillian's fiftieth wedding anniversary. Lily didn't think much of it, but he sure appreciated it. Besides, Lily couldn't complain, she received her own gift, more Waterford crystal. He recalled he had given his son a fine Cuban Montecristo after loading the humidor that evening. Ordinarily Felix didn't smoke, but he did like the Montecristo, so he chose another one for him.

Felix closed the hall bathroom door, walked up to one of the double sinks and peered into the mirror and saw he didn't look so good. He began splashing cold water on his face; *this was going to be a long night*, he thought. Before leaving he glanced at the bathroom window and could see from the adjacent garage lights that snow was continuing to fall. He would call Clary soon and let her know that he was either going to bum a ride with Jeffery or spend the night here. He certainly wasn't going to drive the Ferrari home in the snow.

Just then Felix's smartphone rang, and he punched in. Byron's mug appeared on the screen.

"Felix, Byron Sokowski here—how goes the battle?" Sokowski sat back in his leather chair and waited for a response. He knew this wasn't going to be easy. He worked for one of the deputy assistant secretaries in the Bureau of Arms Control, Verification and Compliance back in D.C. and had a loose-working relationship with arms appropriation.

"Not good. Where have you been? I've been trying to reach you for days. Wait a minute; why are you calling at this hour?" Felix asked.

"We're in an emergency committee meeting, and I had some time and decided to call. Felix, what were you thinking supplying arms to the Republic of Georgia?" Byron asked.

"I don't know? Is there any way to work around this, any way to patch it up?" Felix pressed as he took another look at himself in the mirror.

"I don't think so. You really screwed up this time. I've told you before, the arms business is a dangerous occupation and there are too many ways to foul up. Why didn't you just stick to your textile business? The way I understand it you are doing quite well," Byron surmised.

Felix pause for a long moment before answering; he didn't know what to say. "Byron, is there anything you can do?"

"I'll snoop around; that's all I can say. Felix, I need to go; the committee will reconvene in a few minutes. Good luck."

"Thanks." The line went dead.

Felix put the smartphone back in his pocket, sat on the commode, and leaned over with his face in his hands, thinking. *What in tarnation is going on? So I made a mistake, so what. It's not the end of the world. Well screw them*, he thought. *I'll find a way to fix this.*

TWENTY-NINE

DHS NEBRASKA COMPLEX— WASHINGTON D.C. 2009

Tom Morrison stood and faced the deputy secretary. "As you know, we don't have a formal behavioral science division like the FBI, but we do okay. We are gathering our mathematicians, computer scientists, medical staff, behavioral scientists and sociologists to build profiles to address this particular threat. Based on our intelligence harvesting, the first thing we'll do is to identify and categorize terrorists with advance computer technology skills. Second, we'll be in the process of contacting schools where they received their education and at what universities they were employed, either as a teacher or some other academia post, such as a researcher. We'll also be looking at their employment backgrounds in government and in the private sector. Third, we'll be examining their medical histories for any psychosis or other psychological or physiological problems. Fourth, we'll be checking with their relatives, neighbors, friends, colleagues, and any related activities in order to cobble together possible patterns in their relationships. This work will allow us to build all-inclusive profiles on these people. Once the profiles are completed and loaded into our databases, we will apply powerful commonality search engines to determine if there are certain traits and patterns shared between the terrorists and any associations they may have, and if so, is there linkage between them. Further, we're also in the process of building a criteria matrix based on I.Q., type of skill, skill levels, culture, personality traits and unusual events such as life-changing situations. Finally, we'll add other factors such as traveling habits that would make them prime candidates for the investigation. Taken together this will give us a window into their activities and how they think. We will know them better than they know themselves, and since we will be working with the FBI, I will be sharing this information with Sam White and will forward any profile data we have built to date. They're legendary in this area."

Jake turned to Tom, "Have you found any individuals or groups that stand out, other than Felix Jamosa, Jeffery Starr, and their relatives and associates?"

"Not yet. We're still early in the process."

"How about linkage from Felix or Jeffery to other people?"

"Nothing so far."

"What about groups such as al-Qaeda and the Taliban?"

"Same answer," Tom said.

Jake looked at the deputy secretary and said, "Wouldn't you think before any multi-nation war broke out there would be massive civil unrest in the affected nations? And if so, wouldn't the countries be too busy protecting their infrastructures from civil disobedience and criminal activities before launching into war?"

"Good point, and yes, we have taken that into consideration. But that doesn't preclude opportunistic rogue nations such as North Korea or Iran initiating a preemptive nuclear strike while this is going on. Jake, any way you look at this, it's just a nightmare."

"I totally agree, sir."

Dr. Clyde Ferris spoke next. "As you know, my specialty is neural networks and botnets, and I'm not sure how much help I can be of service here. You mentioned that DHS and the FBI are forming a national task force to address the threat. Mr. Deputy Secretary, can you further clarify who will be leading this investigation? I mean, what agency will assume the responsibilities of creating a central clearing house to filter the intelligence and coordinate all the activities between the agencies involved in the probe?"

The deputy secretary brought his full attention to Dr. Ferris. "That's an excellent question, Clyde. President Ahmad and his cabinet are already working on this. Though I suspect since this involves national security, it will fall under our umbrella." David Peterson leaned forward in his chair and looked at Clyde. "Don't you ever sell yourself short, Dr. Ferris. You're one heckuva computer forensic scientist and neural network expert. I'm sure you will be a key person in this investigation on the computer technology side."

Clyde bowed his head and peered through his thick horned-rimmed glasses as if looking at a spot on the table and whispered, "Thank you, sir."

Now the deputy secretary looked around the table and asked for any further questions. Everyone was quiet. He nodded at the secretary, and Mary stood to give her final remarks before the meeting was adjourned.

"As most of you know, since I was appointed to this office, it has been only the second time that I have attended a high-level briefing with you. I can't impress upon all of you enough how vitally important it is for these scoundrels not to succeed. I fear if they do, it could send the world back to the seventh century, and Allah will reward them for their efforts, or so they will think. Now let's get crackin'." Everyone left the deputy secretary's corner office in a somber mood. Jake motioned to Slade to meet him in his office.

After Jake closed the door, his buddy wheeled around to face him directly and said, "Jesus, can you believe what we just heard?"

"Hardly," Jake said in a solemn voice. "Pal, this is for all the marbles this time. We better be on our 'A' game."

"I agree. But we've always approached our jobs that way," Slade said.

"Well, I got news for you, partner. We're stepping it up to 'A++', if there is such a thing." Jake replied.

"I hear you," Slade acknowledged.

"And to think that they may be able to pull this off without discharging a firearm or detonating a bomb!"

"Or flying commercial airliners into buildings," Slade added softly.

"Okay, let's get down to business. I just hope they don't have their plans in place and ready to execute. The computer, forensic, and database teams are really under the gun on this one," Jake mused.

"Yeah," Slade countered, "we all are!"

"I wonder about this Jamosa character. He didn't show up on DHS's radar for any known linkage to other groups, but he will," Jake ventured.

"Yeah, I'm sure he will. Got to go, buddy. Need to get some work done before noon. Then I'll be checking out some fishing gear at a new sporting goods store not too far from here. See ya."

"Later, man." After Slade left, Jake sat back in his chair wondering about all the events that have taken place recently. He had been so busy that he had hardly any time for Zoey. He had only had time for a quick telephone call and a couple of emails to her. *What a fine gentleman he's turning out to be*, he thought. Sure, he liked the ladies, but Zoey caught his attention. She was not only smart but he also could see that she had a firm resolve, a resilience about her uncommon with most people these days. Somehow he would have to find time to get to know her better.

THIRTY

HUNTER'S HOUSE
PORTLAND, OREGON 2008

What have we gotten ourselves into? Hunter thought, while serving drinks from the tray to Benesh and Jeffery. He turned just as his son entered back into the study, handing him his drink along with the Montecristo. Felix pulled his wing chair out to the center of the room so he could face everyone. It was getting too warm sitting next to the fireplace, and he needed to pace; this wasn't going to be easy. He stood by his chair and took a few seconds to gather his thoughts before he began.

"Dad, do you remember when I was about eight or nine years old, and we went to the basement one summer day, and you opened up your gun cabinet? As I recall, you showed me an old Winchester Model 52B Sporter LR, twenty-two-caliber rifle that belonged to Grandfather. You know the one, with its ten shot magazine, checkered pistol grip and Lyman 'F' peep sights."

"Yes, that was a doozy of a rifle for its day." Hunter opinioned.

"Do you remember how my eyes lit up when I first saw that old rifle, with it being in such excellent shape, polished blue? And then you carefully handed it to me and told me that we would do some target practice. In the meantime you taught me how to break it down and clean the old rifle. A week later after we got back from the gun club you told me that I was a natural."

"Yes, I did, son," Hunter said with pride in his voice. "You not only learned how to shoot accurately, and very quickly I must say, but what surprised me is that you were very good at breaking down the old rifle and cleaning it thoroughly."

"From that day on I fell in love with weapons. It was as if I was transformed into some powerful being when holding those instruments in my hand. I now could feed, protect, and apply justice. Although it did take me a couple of years to fully comprehend what you said to me that summer: 'whenever someone picks up a gun they must realize that they are now held accountable for the terrible responsibility and consequences for the use of that weapon.'" Felix took another sip of his cognac and continued. "That fall, after you trained me on a Winchester 270, you took me to the coast range east of Tillamook, Oregon. And I'll be darned if I didn't get a white-tailed buck! He was a five-pointer and a beauty. From then on, I always went deer and elk hunting with you and your friends or with some of my friends until I was about sixteen."

"Why did you stop, son?" Hunter puzzled.

"You should know Dad; two words—girls and cars." Everyone chuckled while Felix paused, smiled and went on. "As you know, I really didn't stop. I just took a short hiatus until I married Clary. I'm sure you remember your sixty-fifth birthday when Clary and I invited you and Mom over for dinner and afterward, in the den, I handed you a Freedom Arms Bear Track case and told you to open it. And when you did you saw those two revolvers, two spare 5-round cylinders with two top-mounting Leopold scopes inside. You looked at me, and I said they're for our first African Safari. I remember you taking one of the revolvers out of the case, a model 83-field grade with a matte finish. You examined it and said that it was the finest handgun that you had ever seen. You picked up the other revolver, a model 97 premier grade with a bright brush finish and held it up to the light to see its fine craftsmanship and said you didn't think we could use revolvers to hunt big game in Africa. And then I explained that a company in Freedom, Wyoming, in my opinion, makes the best handguns in the world, and these weapons are more than capable of bringing down any of the dangerous seven in Africa."

"Where is this all going, son?" Hunter said impatiently.

"Dad, I guess I'll just cut to the chase. In any event, I wanted you to know how much I like weapons."

THIRTY-ONE

OGDEN, UTAH 2009

The morning sun was just rising above the far northeast section of the Wasatch mountain range. The leaves had given way to another November sunrise. It was crystal clear but a chilly morning when Jim Coffey arrived at his office on the sixth floor at the IRS regional center in Ogden, Utah. He was the assistant regional director for the Western region of the U.S.

The FBI recruited him twenty-two years ago after graduating from LSU. He was assigned to the Phoenix, Arizona office as an assistant agent after he completed his studies at Quantico. But after receiving his commission as special agent in charge, he wondered if he wanted to stay with the bureau. He eventually moved to the IRS as an audit supervisor. He was now part of a great team that prided itself on out-of-the-box thinking. He really enjoyed his work; and this helped him to move quickly up the management chain, first as a department head, then director of operations, and finally to his present position.

He thought about the assignment that the regional director, Bill Sorenson, had handed him some time ago. Normally he didn't get directly involved with tax investigations unless they were high profile cases. In this particular instance it seemed a bit unusual since he didn't even recognize the person's name or company that was targeted for the probe. In fact, he didn't know anything about Felix Jamosa or his company, Jamosa Enterprises. Bill only had told him that the order came from high up in the Ahmad Administration. Bill indicated to not only check into the company's finances but also uncover any offshore operations if they existed since this was the area they were interested in.

Finally, he was specifically instructed by the regional director to really go after this one and use whatever resources necessary.

Bill had said that the request came directly from the Treasury Department involving the ATF. Apparently, the ATF had suspected that Felix Jamosa and his brother-in-law, Jeffery Starr, had been dealing arms to dictatorships and rogue nations for quite some time. In fact, the ATF Director, Jack Finley, at the Denver, Colorado, division office had told Bill of one particular incident that really aggravated him. A couple of years ago one of his best field agents, Robert Murphy, and his team had shadowed an Iranian freighter off the Libyan Coast of Africa in the Mediterranean Sea. The team had stopped the vessel in international waters and boarded it on the pretense that they suspected the freighter was leaking fuel. Before the team went down to the engine room, Robert had checked the boat's registration log and asked the captain for the cargo's manifest. Before the captain handed him the manifest, a big American appeared at the captain's side and told the field agent in no uncertain terms that he had no right to inspect the ship, including its manifest. He indicated that if the vessel's registration checked out, the ATF team must depart the ship immediately since they were on a tight schedule. Murphy had told the American that they believed the vessel was leaking fuel and had to check below before leaving the ship. Murphy then told Jack that the big American was indeed Felix Jamosa, the same person that the ATF had been tracking on suspicion of gun running, and had had run-ins with him before.

After his team checked the engine room, Robert had pointed out that there were some minor fuel leaks that needed to be repaired. He indicated the registration seemed to be okay, and the team departed the ship. On the way back in their vessels tender, he thought he noticed something peculiar about the registration numbers on the ship's starboard side of the bow and decided to take digital photos of the numbers. He also took pictures of the vessel's water line in relation to its plimsoll line. He wanted clear evidence in case the vessel had a change of cargo before it reached its destination.

Jack Finely said that Murphy called him on his satellite phone and apprised him of the situation. Jack had then called the Department of Defense (DOD), and had given them the coordinates of where the ship was located, and requested satellite surveillance of that particular patch of the Mediterranean. DOD indicated that it would be four hours before one of their keyhole image satellites, in geosynchronous orbit, would be in position. Once the satellite digital pictures of the ship were taken, the encrypted images were downloaded to the agency's sat-com computers, reviewed and then sent to ATF via coded top-secret encrypted email on the agency's Virtual Private Network (VPN).

In the meantime the freighter had altered course and headed southwest toward the Libyan seaport of Tripoli. When ATF received the satellite surveillance photos seven hours later, there seemed to be enough evidence in the pictures to indicate an anomaly on the registration, and search and seizure warrants had been issued for the ship. Murphy and his team waited for the freighter to steam back into international waters. Forty-eight hours later they stopped and boarded the Iranian vessel, and Murphy issued the warrants to the captain. They checked the ship's log, and it hadn't been changed, except for the emergency stop in Tripoli. Their destination was still the seaport of Karachi, Pakistan, via the Suez Canal, Indian Ocean and the Arabian Sea, and their manifest indicated that the vessel was carrying fertilizer and grain. Sure enough, that's what they found.

Robert asked why they had steamed into Tripoli; it wasn't a port originally listed on their log. Felix told Robert that since his team had been so gracious and alerted them about the suspected fuel leak, the captain decided to make an emergency stop to check the ship's engines. When Robert asked about the registration, the captain said there had been some rust on one of the numbers, but it had been repaired while in port.

In addition to the freighters log appearing to be in order and the manifest matching their physical inventory and the vessel's water/plimsoll line relationship not having changed, Robert had a very weak argument on the allegations of a registration change. Besides, the damage had been done. The switch had been made, and no evidence had been found.

Robert had wanted blanket authorization to stop and check registrations on any ships leaving Tripoli within the next seventy-two hours, since he now suspected there was a good possibility one of the freighters might be carrying the transferred weapons. Jack had asked how he proposed to do this, with a crystal ball? The only solace ATF could see was that Felix must have paid a steep price for getting permission from Libyan's military dictator, Colonel Muammar al-Qaddafi, to swap out weapons for grain and fertilizer. Either the colonel had kept the weapons or the guns eventually found their way via a circuitous route to their final destination.

Coffey, after hearing all of this from his boss, could only shake his head and wonder what the heck was going on. He was an IRS agent directing teams to uncover corporate tax evasion and malfeasance, not a modern day pirate on the high seas. *Besides*, he wondered, *what is a plimsoll line?* He later found that it was the load line of a ship. The purpose of a load line is to ensure that a vessel has sufficient freeboard and thus adequate reserve buoyancy and is certified by a load line certificate. In other words, the ship's cargo weight cannot decrease the reserve buoyancy of the vessel to a point where the water line is higher than the load line or plimsoll line markings. Otherwise, the ship's load line certificate would be out of compliance, not to mention putting the ship in harm's way of sinking.

Jim Coffey cleared his mind and thought about the weekend ahead. It was Friday morning, and he was looking forward to spending the long weekend with his family on a skiing trip to Park City in Southern Utah. That's where he had taken his wife,

Jill, on their honeymoon fifteen years ago, and they had been going back every two or three years. Besides, his two boys, Mark and Sam, liked the slopes, and it wasn't too far away. Visiting Park City was like slipping through a rabbit hole—it was quick, convenient, and a complete getaway. But first he had to get through the morning.

THIRTY-TWO

HUNTER'S HOUSE—
PORTLAND, OREGON 2008

Still standing, Felix took another sip of his cognac. "During one of my textile trips to Asia, shortly after we went international with Jamosa Enterprises, I ran into a very interesting gentleman who knew some of my business associates. He was from the United States and shared the same interest in guns and hunting as I did. We both had some spare time to burn in Shanghai, so we agreed to have dinner the next evening. During dinner our conversation turned to weapons, and whom we thought made the best American rifles and handguns. Then he launched into military weapons, which I didn't have much knowledge of. He seemed to know his stuff. After dinner it was still early, so he invited me back to his hotel bar, not far from the concert hall, and we continued where we left off. He was telling me how lucrative the arms business was. I really didn't believe some of his boastings, but one thing he imparted stayed with me: if you are really good at arms sales and you provide a covert service to the government, they generally will leave you alone."

"My word! Why was he telling you this?" Hunter exclaimed, as he was coming back from the bar with more drinks.

"He said that maybe he was in need of a backup, and if I was interested to give him a call. He left his contact information with me. We finished our drinks, squared the tab, and as we left the hotel bar, he asked me to give it some consideration. I told him that I wasn't interested. Besides, I was too busy with the textile company."

As Hunter handed his son another drink, Felix continued. "Three months later, I happened to run into him again in Mexico

City. We started talking, and he told me that the Salvadoran Civil War was heating up. The conflict was between the U.S. backed right-wing military government of El Salvador and the Farabundo Marti National Liberation Front (FMLN), a coalition or umbrella organization of five Marxist guerrilla groups. He said he needed someone that he could trust to oversee the transfer of weapons to the Salvadoran government. It would be an easy assignment since the weapons had already been arranged to arrive there in the next couple of days. He said I would be supplied with the necessary documents, hop a jet from Mexico City to San Salvador, meet with the government officials, inventory the weapons, have the documents signed, collect the money and fly back. Wouldn't take more than forty-eight hours. I asked him why he was involved. He stated he was helping the U.S. government stem the tide of communism in the Western Hemisphere."

"Why did you even listen to him, son?" Hunter asked.

"Let me finish, Dad. I then asked him why he wasn't taking care of this himself. He answered that he had some very pressing business elsewhere on the globe and couldn't be in two places at the same time and didn't trust a wire transfer by the government. He then impressed upon me that the Salvadoran government absolutely needed this business taken care of in the next forty-eight hours. I asked why he thought he could trust me with the cash. He said he knew where to find me and why would a successful businessman with a legit company blow the transaction. He had a point. He said to wire the money to him and take 10 percent off the top for my trouble. He jotted down the instructions for the wire transfer and said he knew where to locate me and would catch up with me later to collect the documentation. After some thought I told him that I would do it."

"Son, you didn't!" Hunter exclaimed. "Who is this guy, what's his name?"

"Dad, that's unimportant, and you really don't want to know if you get my drift."

Felix said, "Dad, I can't explain why I agreed. I only know after I said yes I got this strange feeling, as if being on some kind of high. I felt so exhilarated. Besides, I was doing a patriotic service for our country."

"Felix, serving your country in the military is patriotic, not running guns," Hunter intoned with a stern look toward his son. "Besides, patriotism involves fighting for your country's values and honor and not some selfish need to profit!"

"Dad, let's not get hung up on semantics right now. Do you not want to hear me through?" Felix pleaded.

"That's not semantics, that's a fact. But please continue," Hunter relented.

"The Salvadorian transfer went smoothly, and the money was good so I started running guns for him over the next twelve to fifteen months until I developed enough contacts on my own. At that point I started my own arms business."

Benesh jumped up and asked, "Is my Jeffery involved in this?"

"I'm afraid so, Mr. Starr."

Benesh turned to his son and stammered, "Jeff…Jeffery, how could you do this?"

"Father, please let Felix continue, and we'll address this later." Jeff motioned for his friend to go on.

Felix took another puff of his Montecristo and continued. "At first, I was doing all the arms business, that included creating the offshore sham companies in order to hide the arm's profits. However, not too long after Jeffery came into the family textile business we talked about the possibility of him structuring the offshore accounts for the arms business. With his education and experience in business accounting and computers, I knew he would prove to be much better than I. After some convincing Jeffery finally relented, and I must tell you Benesh, your son is an ace at running the numbers and building offshore companies." Felix looked at Hunter and motioned for him to wait.

"First, I want to impress upon everyone that in no way are the arms' profits being funneled through our textile business. The business and its finance and accounting are 100 percent legit and always have been. Next, and I might as well get this out of the way, all the offshore corporations and companies that Jeffery and I have created are owned and operated by dead people."

"Dead people!" Hunter and Benesh exclaimed in unison.

"How can this be?" Hunter said incredulously.

Felix ignored their statement and looked at his watch and saw that it was already 1:00 a.m. Before going much further, everyone needed a break. "This is going to take awhile, and we need to call our wives and let them know we are going to be very late." Jeffery and Felix excused themselves to make their calls and left Hunter and Benesh to their own thoughts.

Benesh stayed behind, talking with his friend. "Hunter, can you believe this? Dead people!"

"Quite frankly, at this point, I don't know what to think." Hunter said, as he was shaking his head. "I only know this is a much larger problem then I initially thought."

"What about our textile business? What's going to happen to it?" Benesh asked.

"I don't know for sure, Ben, but I do know that by their actions they have placed our families and Jamosa Enterprises in jeopardy."

Hunter and Benesh stood, stretching their legs. "Do you need another drink, Ben?" Hunter asked, standing with his hands in his pockets.

"Well, I'm already past my limit, but seeing as we are going to hear about the deceased running corporations, you might as well keep pouring for me. This is going to be a long and interesting night," Benesh sighed. He walked over to the bar and used the phone to call Marni. In the meantime, Hunter collected all the glasses and headed back to the bar to make another round of drinks.

THIRTY-THREE

OGDEN, UTAH 2009

Jim Coffey picked up the phone and punched Steve Kronoski's extension, his department head. On the third ring, Steve answered with a cheery hello.

"Steve, it's Jim. How are you this fine morning?"

"I'm good, just came in a few minutes ago," Steve said, as he was getting his first cup of black coffee.

"We're still good for 9:00 a.m., right?" Jim asked.

"Yeah, my crew and I will be meeting you in conference room 514A," Steve said, taking his first sip of coffee. He continued as he put his cup down on the desk. "I hate to bring this up, but you have been really pushing my staff and I on the Jamosa file."

"Well Steve, you only have to look as far as the regional director to get that answer. As I said before, it's a high-profile case, and Bill indicated that it's an important investigation for the Ahmad Administration," Jim replied, standing to get a better view of the November sunrise.

"Okay, boss, I'll see you at nine." Steve punched the disconnect on his desk phone. Sipping his coffee he rang Gene's office and put him on speakerphone.

"Gene, are you and Ted prepared for this morning's meeting with the assistant director?" Steve said, as he pushed his chair away from the desk and walked to the credenza for a coffee refill.

"What, no good morning or how are you before you launch into the morning's business?" Gene chided.

Gene McIntyre was the chief investigator of corporate financials for the Western Region. He was a dedicated and bright CPA and one of the agency's young rising stars. His specialty was proprietorships, corporations, holding companies and offshore trusts. He would often lay awake at night and dream about ways that these entities could maneuver and manipulate their statements. They usually did this by timing, substitutions, deletions, additions and other dubious and arcane methods in order to show a more profitable bottom line and a better return for their shareholders and owners, not to mention better compensation for their officers. In this particular case, Gene was not only interested in Jamosa Enterprises' accounting and finance procedures to hide money, but also, more importantly, where the source was coming from and where the funds were going.

"Sorry, buddy," Steve mumbled, and went on. "The regional director is really turning the heat up on this one, and I want to make sure that everything is in order before the meeting."

"So far Jamosa's accounting procedures look pretty straightforward for the textile business, and I haven't been able to uncover any funny stuff. As far as the possibility of offshore accounts, I'm drawing a blank. Perhaps Ted will have better news," Gene replied, looking at his watch.

"Is Ted here and ready?" Steve asked.

"I believe so, though the last time I saw him was yesterday afternoon wandering the halls, peering down at a document through his geeky glasses, and scratching his disheveled head of hair and muttering to himself."

"Gene, he better be here and be prepared." Steve huffed. "This investigation is taking more time than expected and the administration wants answers."

"I'll round him up and make sure he's at the meeting."

"Okay, I'll see you guys at nine a.m."

"We'll be there," Gene replied and hung up.

Gene thought back and remembered the first time he had met Ted Hamilton. Three years ago, Steve had brought the kid into his office and introduced him. The kid was a nerd all right, long and lanky, wearing heavy plastic, black, horned-rimmed frames with thick coke bottle lenses. But what really caught Gene's eye was his mousey brown hair that wanted to run away, a grey tweed jacket with a purple paisley tie, and a yellow shirt with brown horizontal stripes and khaki colored corduroy pants that were too short for him, not to mention his white athletic socks and ragged dirty white sneakers. His attire was so loud a person needed sunglasses. After the formal introduction the kid had been quiet, standing there shifting from one foot to the other and listening to the conversation. Steve said that Ted would join the team and to make him feel at home. Gene remembered saying to Steve with a raised eyebrow, "He is, is he?"

Steve snorted back, "You're also his mentor," and wheeled on his heels and left the office with Gene sitting behind his desk, wondering how this was going to work out.

Ted was still standing, still shifting his feet. Gene and Ted then went through the usual pleasantries of where he had received his degrees and how he came to be with the IRS. It didn't take long to realize that he was a bloody genius when it came to unraveling very complex corporate structures such as companies wrapped in corporations, especially the offshore variety. Despite his idiosyncrasies Ted was a genius at unraveling companies and boundaries that separated them.

Gene called Ted, to see if he was in and thank God he answered the phone. "Ted here," he offered.

"Hey dude, you ready for the 9:00 a.m. meeting with the head honcho?" Gene quipped.

"Yeah man, I'll bring what I have, but I haven't been able to make a connection to any offshore accounts that could be associated with Felix Jamosa or Jamosa Enterprises. In fact, I haven't found anything at all that would provide a link."

"You're saying everything looks clean?"

"I'm afraid so, boss."

"Okay, come on over to my office with your information and let's discuss this further before the meeting."

"I'll see you in a few," Ted replied.

Gene hung up the receiver and kicked back in his chair. This was going to be a strange meeting, especially without much supporting evidence. "I guess we'll find out," he mused.

THIRTY-FOUR

NEW YORK CITY, NEW YORK 2010

A group of older, silver haired, and highly polished gentlemen walked down the halls of greed to their chamber of wisdom on the top floor of Steel National Bank of New York. Not your average ordinary people, they all hailed from prominent east coast families, save one. Cloned from Ivy League schools with advanced degrees in money and finance, wearing Giorgio Armani and Brioni suits, the corporate officials entered the boardroom to vote on the government's Troubled Asset Relief Program (TARP), created from $700 billion of taxpayer money.

Congress had enacted TARP to alleviate the banking and credit crisis brought on by years of deregulation, aggressive lending practices, un-enforcement of existing regulations, Congress' lack of knowledge, and inaction to correct the problems that they and past administrations had caused in the first place. After the bank's executive officers had discussed the benefits and drawbacks of the government's program, a vote would be taken to either accept or reject money from TARP. Time was running out on the program, and the officers needed to act.

Everyone took their seats, and the secretary called the meeting to order. The bank's CFO, Frank Mulligan, watched as his boss, Jack Scanner, CEO of the bank, stood at the other end of the highly polished Brazilian cherry board table and discussed the merits and pitfalls of receiving funds from TARP.

Frank didn't care for Jack. He hadn't paid his dues like Frank, and he really didn't care that he knew very little about him. Four years ago, Jack Scanner had suddenly appeared on the scene, compliments of the board of directors.

Apparently malfeasance had caught up to Jack on his last job as director of finance for a holding company that did nothing more than acquisitions and mergers. The holding company would swoop down on other vulnerable companies through hostile takeovers and spin them off in order to sell the pieces to the highest bidder. Loyalty didn't play a part in the companies they sold or the employees that worked for them. They were only interested in how much gold they could accumulate. After a little digging, Frank found out that Jack's father, a member of the board of directors, had apparently blackmailed other members, including the chairman, to get his son in as the new CEO. Jack's father had damaging personal information that if let out would put a serious dent in some of the board members' reputations, and possibly lead to terminations and civil and criminal penalties.

To make matters worse, Frank had a long-running battle with Jack on how to run the bank's finances. Jack continually tried to take some of the bank's liabilities off the books in order to impress Wall Street and get favorable quarterly reviews from analysts. Profit drove Jack: the more the bank made each quarter, the higher the company's stock. Plus more funds could be used to purchase additional stock options and increase his annual salary, not to mention more lavish vacations. And, there was always the bonus. Frank was amazed that Jack didn't care that the bank's true debt-to-asset ratio was out of control, approaching twenty-five to one—pure craziness. Jack just wanted more money. Frank tried numerous times to alert the board, but each time the information fell on deaf ears. Greed drove the board of directors and other officers in the company. Something had to be done and quickly.

With effort Frank settled his short arthritic frame, racked with pain, back in the cushy leather chair and listened to his boss's nonsense. He didn't know how he had been inflicted with rheumatoid arthritis, only that some of his family members were also burdened with the scourge. Frank was a likeable guy but very serious and professional when it came to business. Raised in a poor family with seven siblings he knew the hard scrabble life too well and took pride in how far he had come. Even though he was a little guy with deteriorating health, he didn't take flack from anyone, especially people like Jack. He had a hard time coming to terms with the corporate world of today with their weak ethics, short-term strategies and their penchant for greed.

Jack was saying that when he had discussed TARP with other banking officials around the nation, he had found there weren't any unexpected problems of receiving the money. His good friend, Charley Tolland of South Carolina National bank, had told him it was all blue sky ahead. Charley had indicated that most banks in his region, if in relatively good shape, had received money from TARP, even though they didn't ask for it and furthermore didn't need it.

"What do you mean by blue sky?" Frank asked.

"Well, I asked Charley if he had applied for TARP, and he said he'd be a fool if he hadn't," Jack said, while pouring coffee from one of the two gold-plated coffee carafes on the table.

Frank peered at Jack over the top of his glasses and pressed on. "What's Charley doing with the funds?"

"Charley said he might sit on the money and do nothing because he didn't know the true losses of bad assets on the bank's balance sheets, or he might use the money to acquire other, smaller banks or even invest in other companies' stocks. He told me it's free money."

"Jack, what's wrong with you?" Frank questioned and went on before his boss could speak. "There's no free lunch, especially with the government and taxpayers' money."

"What do you mean?" Jack said, and took another sip of Hacienda La Esmeralda's Geisha coffee grown in Panama that retailed more than $104.00 per pound.

"Do you honestly believe the government is going to hand over millions or possibly billions of taxpayer dollars to our bank without anything in return?"

"Frank, don't you interrupt me again!" Jack rebuked. "I was getting to that."

"We'll see," Frank said under his breath.

"What?" Jack's face flushed.

"Nothing, just clearing my throat." Frank shifted in his chair, feeling the pain in his right hip.

"Now, where was I," Jack mumbled to no one in particular.

"Oh, yes. Charley said the restrictions and oversight didn't exist on how to use the money, outside of limiting dividends and CEO annual pay. Charley had said that months later the board of director's had issued a proclamation for added incentives. The incentives had been used for the officers' bonuses and for more stock options. He said he had also spruced up the central bank's offices and branches with elegant new office furniture, oil paintings, and Persian rugs."

"What?" Frank, indignant, slowly stood and squinted as the March sun shined through the boardroom's glass windows. He shook his right index finger at his boss and said, "You're telling us that Charley spent some of the TARP money on sprucing up his bank and branch offices with expensive furniture, oil paintings, and fancy rugs. Apparently, Charley has gone off his nut!" Frank now used his right index finger and gave the universal circular sign for lunacy. Everyone in the room laughed except Jack.

"Christ, Frank, you can't refer to my friend like that!" Jack bellowed.

A smile crept across Frank's face as he and the other executives watched, while coffee-stained spittle flew out of Jack's mouth and dribbled down the front of his starched Raja white dress shirt and decorated his red Pancaldi silk tie.

"Well, Jack, I got news for you. I just did." Frank fired back, his brown eyes blazing.

"That's not…not re…respectful." Jack stammered.

"Oh, go on with your spiel, Jack. I'm sure it's enlightening." Frank knew he had Jack on the run now and knew Jack hated it when he got the better of him, especially in front of the other officers.

Jack hesitated a moment. He knew if he continued down this path, arguing with Frank, that Frank would chew him a new one, so he stayed on course. "Charley said he couldn't believe that congress had not only passed TARP quickly, but also without any foresight that clearly specified a detailed plan for restrictions and rules for the taxpayers' money."

Frank slowly eased himself back into his chair, gingerly clasped his hands behind his head, leaned back and listened to his boss drone on, and thought how this was all brought about.

THIRTY-FIVE

HUNTER'S HOUSE
PORTLAND, OREGON 2008

W hen Felix and Jeffery came back to the study and everyone was comfortable, Felix took his post next to the leather wingback chair in the middle of the room. After Hunter had distributed the drinks, Felix took a long pull from his snifter, turned to his audience and waited.

Hunter was the first to speak. "Son, what are you saying about the dead?"

"Just a minute, Dad, let me back up and explain the whole story," Felix replied, and then went on. "Usually when selling arms to rogue nations and military dictatorships, there is very little if any documentation involved in the transactions, for obvious reasons. No one on either side wants any transparency or traceability to come back to haunt them. Unlike most arms dealers that provide no buffers between themselves and their profits, Jeffery and I took the unusual steps to set up some very sophisticated defenses to distance ourselves from the arms profits."

"But what about the dead people?" Benesh insisted.

"I'm getting to that," Felix replied. "We are not only responsible for the sales and weapon's logistics, but we often train the lead people; if you will, the lieutenants, sergeants, and other designated personnel. This allows them to instruct their troops in the proper use and cleaning of the weapons. Even though there is very little documentation, we do require sign-off signatures of people that we personally instruct so their commanders can't come back and complain their people weren't properly trained. This not only takes the responsibility off us, but at the same time it ensures to the commanders and dictators that we know what we are doing. This enables us to gain their respect and garner more contracts and possibly more contacts. Though unbeknownst to them there is another equally important reason for doing this: after we receive the field leaders' signatures, there is roughly a 65 to 80 percent chance that they will be dead within the year."

Hunter interrupted, "Are you saying that you have a hand, either directly or indirectly, on the soldiers misfortunes after you collect their signatures?"

"No, of course not. I only meant that the junior officers and noncoms have a very high mortality rate, and because of this they are excellent candidates to become our future corporate officers posthumously. So in the meantime, and hopefully before their demise, we duplicate their legitimate signatures on corporate documents that we create, and then we record them with the proper authorities in the countries we are doing business."

"What if there's a chance that some of them survived and somehow found out about your plan, and decided to blackmail you or simply take the companies away from you?" Hunter queried.

"First of all, how will they know? Second, we really don't care; we never own the companies. And third, even if they found out they own one or more of the companies, there's never any money to take, it's all on paper. You must realize that almost all these people have no more than a rudimentary education, if any education at all. And even if they somehow passed this information to the right sources and they investigate, they quickly will arrive at a dead end."

Felix moved to prove his point. "For the sake of argument, let's say that they are very lucky and are able to trace the companies all the way back to its parent corporation. Now what? Like I said, it's literally a dead end. More importantly, how would they ever know? That's really the key."

"Do you issue initial public offerings (IPO's) and are these companies trading on their respective country's stock exchanges?" Hunter asked.

"Yes, they are. To give you a clearer picture: we do business in countries with shell companies that are wrapped within corporations that trade on their respective countries' stock exchanges. Also companies can trade on the world stock exchanges in countries without markets, such as Afghanistan."

"How can you do that?" Hunter pressed.

"We create sham companies in those countries and wrap them into corporations that trade on another country's stock market."

Benesh stormed out of his chair and was shouting and stammering, "You…you just mentioned the Middle East. Are you and Jeffery helping the Arabs?"

"Well, yes and no. When the opportunity presents itself, we do help the United States advance pro democratic values to hostile regimes throughout the world."

Benesh took a long moment to settle his nerves before he spoke. "Felix, do you know who you are dealing with?"

"Yes."

"You better read your history, son. I'm sure you know that Christians had conflicts and wars with the Muslims for centuries, including the Holy Crusades."

"I know, Benesh, but we are only doing business with them, not fighting them." Felix explained.

"Do you also know that the Arab world wants to wipe my homeland off the face of the earth?" Benesh pressed.

"Yes, I do, but with the United States being friends and allies with Israel, it will never happen." Felix replied.

"How can you be so sure, especially in light of what happened in Germany during World War II?" Benesh solemnly asked.

Felix was getting tired of the badgering and glowered, "I'm not."

Hunter stood and bellowed, "We can carry this conversation on at a later time. I want my son to finish his story!"

Meanwhile, Benesh had turned to his son and was berating him with unkind remarks, to put it lightly.

Hunter looked at his son who shrugged, and then Hunter directed his attention to Benesh and Jeffery and shouted, "Could we please have your attention now?"

"Okay...okay," Benesh replied.

Hunter ran his hands through his thinning white hair and asked out loud, "Now where were we? Oh yes, phantom corporations that trade on the world's stock exchanges. My God! Did you ever think about all those countries and shareholders?" Hunter asked.

"Yes I did. You have to remember we control the number of shares outstanding that are issued through IPO's. We also control the movement of shares on the exchanges through injections of cash. These fictitious revenue streams are used for the company's monthly P and Ls and other company reports such as quarterly, semi and annual financial statements, and tax documents. As a result, we can generally control the upward as well as the downward direction of the company's stocks. In essence, we control short selling as well as going long and also margins. You have to remember that markets are basically controlled by greed and fear, and as long as the company's stock is moving up, greed takes over and usually no one will sell. And if they do take profits, we can cover it. In down markets, which for our companies are usually quite rare because we control and manipulate our earnings, there are not too many cases where we need to cover sells. As a result we generally keep all the shareholders happy because we are usually making profits about 70 percent of the time. We certainly don't want to show a rate of return more than that because we could conceivably tip off the authorities. Besides, we have sophisticated programs that generally reflect the direction of our company's stock within its industry based on that country's economy."

"Well, you've partially answered my next question. How are you controlling all of this? You certainly can't do it all by yourself?" Hunter asked skeptically.

THIRTY-SIX

OGDEN, UTAH 2009

A few minutes later, Gene heard a knock on his door and said, "Come in." Ted sauntered in and took a seat in front of Gene's desk. "Ted, where are your manners?"

"Huh?"

Gene motioned to the door behind Ted and said, "Close the door please."

"Oh, sorry, boss." Ted stood and closed the door and took his chair again.

"What's with this Grateful Dead T-shirt you're wearing?" Gene asked. "Didn't you remember there is an important meeting scheduled today?"

"Yes I did, but I forgot to change into a dress shirt this morning. I've been feeling a little frazzled with this Jamosa investigation."

"I hear you," Gene quipped. He walked over to the credenza and pulled out a white dress shirt and tie and gave them to Ted. While Ted was changing, Gene thought how he had to occasionally bail out his friend on certain things. He suspected that Ted was autistic in some ways. *I guess that's the price you pay sometimes for being as brilliant as Ted.* Even though he lacked social skills and dress etiquette, there wasn't any denying when it came to his friend's ability to do his job. "Anyway, are you prepared as best you can?"

"I just don't understand," Ted said. "I can't find anything."

"Even after the Justice Department issued special warrants that allowed us to subpoena their personal financial records for the entire family and their two close friends?" Gene asked in amazement.

"Boss, like I said, I don't know what to say other than we need to find the missing key."

"Well I support that, Ted. I think our emphasis will be on fact finding. We'll give them what we have, but at the same time we're going to be digging for more information. I think that's our strategy, don't you agree?"

"I think that's the only avenue we have."

"Where's your notes and information?" Gene asked.

"They're still in my office. I'll retrieve them on the way to the meeting."

"Didn't I say to come to my office so we could compare notes?"
"So?"

"Why didn't you bring them?" Gene asked.

"Didn't need to," Ted, pointed to his head.

"Oh, I keep forgetting about your photographic memory."

"That's okay, most people do."

"So, do you have anything at all?" Gene asked as he looked at his watch. "Oh, it's almost nine. We can go over your findings at the meeting." Gene grabbed his folder for the conference, stuffed it in his briefcase as he and Ted headed out of the office, swinging by Ted's office to collect his reports and then went on to the assistant director's conference room.

THIRTY-SEVEN

DHS NEBRASKA COMPLEX WASHINGTON D.C. 2009

David Peterson looked out the windows of the seventh floor conference room at DHS headquarters, ran a hand through his coarse, gray hair, turned and asked if everyone was ready. His mood was as foul as the D.C. weather. It had been spitting snow on and off for the last two weeks in November and was now getting ready to brew up an early Nor'easter. He could tell by the solemn looks on his team's faces that they were fully aware of the enormity of the situation. "Okay, what do we have so far?"

Tonia Franks was the first to respond. "Sir, our team has been in close contact with our counterparts at Quantico, and we are still drawing a blank. Tom Morrison and I have been working with the FBI behavioral and profiling departments, and Sam White and Ben Jenkins are encountering the same difficulty as we are. We also have been working with Steve Kronoski, Gene McIntyre, and Dr. James at the IRS in Ogden. They profile businesses like we profile individuals, and they haven't identified any candidates. It's as if we're chasing ghosts. The problem is we haven't received enough information, so we are confined to profiling Middle Eastern terrorists that may or may not have a connection with Felix Jamosa and Jeffery Starr. Tom and our team have looked at hundreds of suspects so far. As Tom indicated in our last meeting in which he explained profiling criteria, we have done nothing but adhere to the strictest standards and the newest techniques, including Perpetrator-Motive Research Design (PMRD). One bright spot though, when and if we find a smoking gun, we'll be on it quickly because of all the extensive preliminary work."

"Tonia, there's no if, only when," the deputy secretary snorted. "I understand, sir, but we don't like being in this position."

"Well, who does?" Peterson huffed. "Dr. Franks, we must have patience."

"Sir, you of all people should know how important it is to move on this quickly. After all, the United States and possibly the world's economic infrastructures are at stake here."

"You don't have to remind me, Dr. Franks. Our secretary, Mary Knappa, is planning a high-level meeting with all the affected agency heads as soon as we receive enough information. She intends to make sure that all the agencies are well coordinated and ready to act on this when the time comes. Now, in addition to individuals, what groups has your team been profiling?"

"For starters we've looked at al-Qaeda, Taliban, Lashkar-e-Taiba and others, sir."

"Anything?"

"No, sir. But we'll keep looking."

Without waiting for any further response, the deputy secretary looked at Tom Morrison and asked, "Tom do you have anything to add?"

Tom cleared his throat, fidgeted with his hands and said, "Not really, sir. I'm as baffled as Dr. Franks. Like Tonia said, when this breaks we'll be ready to go."

"Okay, Mr. Morrison. What about you, Dr. Ferris? Have you come up with any ideas or uncovered anything?"

Clyde adjusted his thick, horned-rimmed glasses and nervously peered at his notes and proceeded cautiously. He could tell his boss was in a nasty mood. "No, sir. It's too early in the investigation for me to be of much help. As you know, my specialty is neural networks and botnets. I do however have an idea or two."

"We'll, shoot, Dr. Ferris," the deputy secretary said.

"I think we already know a couple of things about these guys. From all the difficulty we're having, I'm sure they're clever and careful. And unlike some gunrunners they are well established. They undoubtedly have plenty of resources and know their way around the globe."

"We know that. Otherwise, we would be on to them by now," Peterson replied.

"I know, sir. Dr. Franks said something earlier that piqued my interest. She said, 'It's as if we're chasing ghosts.' Perhaps they are."

"What do you mean, Dr. Ferris?" Peterson leaned his short, wiry frame toward Clyde, listening intently.

"I mean if we are *chasing ghosts*, then they must have disguised their resources."

"Could you enlighten us, Dr. Ferris?" the deputy secretary pressed.

"I'm not sure how this all works, at least not yet. I do know we are up against some very savvy people, and yes, they're probably using dummy companies. Most dubious organizations use this method. But I believe they have taken it a step further and are using some type of mechanism within their companies to hide their illicit profits. Perhaps they are hiding their companies."

"Interesting, and how would they do that?" the deputy secretary queried.

Dr. Ferris looked down at his notes and mused, "I'm not sure."

"If you figure this out, you beat feet to my office. You understand, Dr. Ferris?"

"Yes, sir."

The deputy secretary knew that Clyde could think outside the box and at times came up with some crazy schemes. But sometimes his ideas hit the mark.

David Peterson paused, measured his audience, and then said, "Jake and Slade will be dispatched to Islamabad, Pakistan. There, they'll meet with a Pakistani Muslim pro west sympathizer, Mohammed Abdul Jabbar, whom we believe has critical information in regards to the investigation."

"What's the connection with him, and more important can his information be trusted?" Dr. Franks asked.

"Tonia, it appears that we got a lucky break awhile back. As you know we've been keeping track of Jeffery Starr and Felix Jamosa ever since they got into geo-political mud over the Russian/Georgia conflict. We've been taking names, and as it turns out, we have found that Mohammed knows Maria Gonzalez, a Pakistani interpreter that works for the American Embassy in Islamabad. More importantly, Maria is a friend to Mohammed's mother, Fara Jabbar. We've been in contact with Maria for some time, and she has assured us that Mohammed is a forthright gentleman that can be trusted, and he is genuinely concerned about the possible impending firestorm between Jihadist Muslim radicals and pro western nations."

He paused again and looked at everyone before going on, "This information has been corroborated by an old friend of Jake's, Paul Paulson, who is one of the Embassy's attachés. Paul has established a definite connection between Felix Jamosa and two Middle Eastern suspected gunrunners and terrorists, Al-Hadi Zafar and Dr. Seyed Mostakavi, through another source. Jake indicated there is more on the table and that he needs to meet with Al-Hadi's cousin, Mohammed, to uncover the rest of the information. Perhaps this is the break we've been looking for."

"Sir, you are saying that Mohammed Abdul Jabbar is related to Al-Hadi Zafar?" Tom Morrison asked.

"It appears so, Tom," the deputy secretary said.

"Interesting, sir."

"Well, regardless of the connection we need to get down to the bottom of it."

The deputy secretary stood and looked at everyone for additional input but could see from their faces they were deep in thought from Dr. Ferris's remarks and the new information just given to them. David Peterson cleared his throat loudly to get everyone's attention and asked, "Is there anything else, team?" Everyone shook their heads no, stood, and walked out quietly.

He knew their minds were working furiously on the new information. So was his. Before going on to other business, he sat back in his chair and thought about what Clyde had just said. It was tantamount to invisible companies. *What are they and how would they operate?* he wondered. *And is there a connection between Felix Jamosa and other terrorists? Just more items on my plate*, he thought.

THIRTY-EIGHT

HUNTER'S HOUSE
PORTLAND, OREGON 2008

Felix paused on Hunter's last question and thought on how to answer it. "That's true, Dad, we can't operate the corporations by ourselves. We use sophisticated software and artificial intelligence programs developed by Jeffery, Abrahim, and a team of highly skilled programmers. These programs control all the day-to-day operations that include issuing the proper accounting and financial reports to the various government authorities and agencies. In addition to covering shareholders' positions with cash, we also need to issue the companies' cash disbursements during the course of a business year. These can include business licenses, regulatory fees and other items such as an occasional bribe. When appropriate the systems alert us, and then we prepare and disburse checks as required."

"What about communications?" Hunter asked as he was adjusting his seating position."

"What do you mean?" Felix quizzed.

"You surely can't have the deceased communicate."

"Oh yes we can, and we do so on a regular basis."

Benesh and Hunter looked at each other again with strange expressions on their faces, and Hunter finally said, "I have to hear this, son."

"As far as telephone inquiries, we use a complex computer voice/prompt system to discourage most inquires, except from a list of pre-identified officials that we need to communicate with. These specific telephone calls from the list are automatically forwarded to our landlines and smartphones. And from our end, the conversations are handled through language translation devices, voice synthesizers and telephone spoof cards/programs."

Hunter looked at his son again and said, "I know what language translation devices are, but how do voice synthesizers and spoof cards work?"

"Voice synthesizers mimic the person's tone, inflection, and pitch of his or her voice. Dad, I know what you're next question is, so let me continue. We can record a person's voice from different media sources, such as television, radio, and computer, or directly from the person when he or she was alive. If there's any white noise or other distractions in the background, we can fade them out with software. We can pull all this together when speaking to a live person through a deceased voice. While the deceased is speaking through our voice, our voice is translated into their language or dialect and then the voice synthesizer matches the modulation of the deceased person's voice we want to mimic. Technically, we superimpose the sound signal of the deceased person on a continuously transmitted carrier sine wave to the sound signal of our voice. As a result, we can now speak in the tone, inflection, and pitch of the deceased person.

"Additionally, telephone spoof cards are used when caller-ID is in session. This means when you place a call, if the person on the other end has caller-ID, he or she receives the identification of the person placing the call. So when we place a call, we merely program the spoof card for the person we want to be. We can also spoof the location of the call. This adds another level of authenticity. It guarantees to the person on the other end that he or she is indeed speaking to the right party and the location where they're suppose be if that should be the case."

"What about incoming calls when you're not there?" Benesh asked.

"We have a miniature switchboard operator in our phone system to direct the intended messages to the right people."

Benesh looked at Hunter again as if he wanted to say, "is your son for real?"

Felix caught the sideways glance and prefaced it with, "let me explain. What I just said is exactly the way the technology works. When a call comes in, a pre-recorded message asks the caller to identify himself and either say the person's full name they wish to speak to or enter their name via the telephone's keypad. Now the information packet is sent to the telephone's internal send/receive program, called "exchange" to determine if it's on the real time list of names. If it is, it captures the phone number next to the name and places the call through to the intended recipient. If we don't pick up the forwarded call, a greeting message comes on matching the voice the caller wanted to reach and instructs the caller to leave a message. Of course, we will return the call later using the language translator and voice synthesizer, or in some cases we indicate the person's voice mail hasn't been set up yet. Otherwise, if the name isn't found on the list, the caller receives a message indicating that they have reached a wrong number."

Hunter jumped in and now asked about emails.

"Dad, when emails arrive they are sent to a program called mailit. The program checks the incoming mail address against a real time mail address list to see if it's valid. If it is, it sends it to that particular person's email address and places the message in that person's queue. If it isn't on the list, it sends back a mailer-daemon style message from a mirrored IP server indicating an incorrect email address, usually in the form unknown user account."

Benesh now asked, "Felix, what'd you mean by a mirror IP server?"

"The mirrored IP server's address is untraceable."

"Why is it untraceable and what does that really mean?" Benesh persisted.

Felix looked at Jeff and said, "Why don't you handle the discussion about the Internet and server networks, you're more knowledgeable on this subject."

THIRTY-NINE

OGDEN, UTAH 2009

As Gene punched the button in the elevator for the fifth floor, he had an uneasy feeling that the assistant director would be laying a bombshell on them. Otherwise, why was this so important? The first tip was when the Justice Department had issued executive order/warrants. This enabled the IRS wide-ranging authority to go after its subject. He knew there would be more surprises. He and Ted exited the elevator, turning right and going down a long carpeted hallway opening the double glass doors to the conference room. As they entered the room, Gene saw that everyone was already seated around the large conference table. The assistant director, Jim Coffey, standing at one end of the table, looked up and motioned them to a couple of vacant chairs. The assistant director then half turned and looked out the large glass windows at a clear, crisp, fall day to collect his thoughts before speaking.

"Gentlemen, I have called all of you here today to discuss an important investigation that the Ahmad Administration is undertaking with the Justice Department, DOD, FBI, CIA, NSA, ATF and Homeland Security in regards to Felix Jamosa and Jamosa Enterprises. Also, Booze and Allen and Lockheed Martin are in the mix for intelligence gathering and corroboration. Further, Homeland Security has recently raised the threat advisory system to orange (high risk of terrorist attacks)." Jim paused to pour more coffee from one of the two carafes on the table and to let his remarks sink in before continuing. He looked at his department head, Steve Kronoski, and saw concern written on his face.

"Jim, how come there are so many agencies involved and the threat advisory system has been raised to orange?" Steve asked.

The assistant director looked at everyone in the room. "I know you all have a lot of questions, but please hold your remarks until I'm finished. Okay?" everyone nodded, and Jim continued. "I know most if not all of you are wondering why so much heat is coming down with this investigation and why there hasn't been much information forthcoming. Well, it's because the regional director has been receiving so many updates from these agencies from day one of the investigation he decided to withhold some of the facts until all of you have at least done your assigned preliminary work. And I'm here to tell you this is big. Now let me address why so many agencies are involved and why so many extraordinary steps are being taken for this probe. At first the inquiry only involved an arms dealer being snared with his pants down. As you may recall, over a year ago there was a conflict between Russia and the Republic of Georgia that involved a dispute over territorial sovereignty. It appears that Mr. Jamosa was supplying weapons to the Republic of Georgia to help further their cause. It's a well-known fact that arms' dealing by individuals has been going on for decades and sometimes with government approval. But when it involves interfering with a super power, well, you can guess the ramifications. Our government had no knowledge of this until Russia's prime minister, Vladimir Putin, informed our president that they have evidence showing U.S. manufactured weapons in the hands of Georgian rebels and that they have identified the gun runner as being Felix Jamosa, a U.S. citizen. You can imagine the uproar that it created and that's why part of this inquiry involves the IRS looking into the family's personal and business finances. But more importantly, it now appears from recent intelligence that Middle Eastern terrorists are preparing an attack against the United States and that Mr.

Jamosa may have ties to it. At least that's what we have recently heard from Homeland Security. We don't know the targets yet. However, we think the delivery mechanism being used for the cyber-attacks involves some form of computer espionage." Jim paused to get his breath and motioned to Steve that he would have his turn soon. "Because of this new information, a joint task force has been created and a cabinet level decision has been made to establish Mary Knappa, secretary of the Department of Homeland Security, to lead and coordinate the investigation with all the aforementioned agencies. Central command and a clearinghouse have been established with her deputy secretary, David Peterson, and he will act as a liaison between their agency and all of the other affected agencies. He will also manage the day-to-day operation of this endeavor and all intelligence will be filtered through his group, since they're responsible for homeland protection. Further, the Justice Department has issued National Security Letters on warrants that gives the DHS and some of the other agencies the authority to eavesdrop on all suspected terrorist activities that are even remotely connected to this investigation. The warrants address all forms of communication including cell and landline telephones and emails. Finally, its imperative that all lines of internal communications between the agencies remain open and that we all share information without any concealment. In other words, even if you receive communications that may appear innocuous to you, nonetheless the information must be forwarded to David Peterson's group. There will be no petty rivalries between the agencies, and any grandstanding, exclusivity or one-upmanship will not be tolerated. Is this understood?" Jim paused again and looked at his team, and he could tell by their silence and rapt attention that everyone agreed. "Just to bring you up-to-date, I spoke with David Peterson a few days ago, and he indicated that he is sending a counter intelligence team to the Middle East to gather information from a pro-western advocate that could furnish key and reliable facts to the investigation. That's all I have for now, except to say that I want everyone to redouble their efforts for the task at hand. Understood?" Everyone nodded. "Steve, can you address the information our teams have uncovered so far?"

FORTY

NEW YORK CITY, NEW YORK 2010

Frank Mulligan had started out at Franklin Beneficial Savings and Home Loans in Portland, Oregon in 1974, as a young loan officer. Back than, requirements for receiving a home mortgage had been narrow and restrictive. Outside of private parties who used their own money and assets to provide funding to other people such as holding a mortgage via a land sale contract, there had been three basic ways for consumers to acquire home mortgages.

Vets could acquire loans through the VA with nothing down. FHA, established in 1934, required three percent down for first time homebuyers. Conventional mortgages were the last choice and required 20 percent down. Banks and savings and loans held their own paper back then. The mortgage guidelines had to be strict. Otherwise the balance sheets of the institutions issuing the notes would be directly affected. Further, bank industry regulators expected banks and saving and loans to follow the rules. The regulations stated that banks had no more than a one-to-one relationship for outstanding loans against the banks' asset base.

The first cracks in the finance and investment industry dam appeared when Congress passed the Community Reinvestment Act (CRA) of 1977, during the Carter Administration. The CRA required banks and saving and loans to open branches in minority neighborhoods, and the regulations pressured them to lend to uncreditworthy borrowers based on race. To further compound the problem, President Carter deregulated portions of the banking industry on March 30, 1980. Years of standard and prudent banking practices were disappearing.

While Frank was moving up in the company during the 1980s, things had changed even more. Now, banks and saving and loans sold their mortgages to other lenders, and they in turn serviced the loans. Pressure continually mounted from the government for banks and S and Ls to provide more loans to lower income people, including more minorities.

Frank shook his head as he thought how quickly the banking industry guidelines had been unraveling, especially during the S and L crises in the late eighties. A substantial portion of the banking industry had taken on debt-to-asset ratios that had violated government requirements. In some cases the banks' debt load had been four times greater than their asset base. More cracks in the finance and investment industry dam appeared.

In the early nineties the Clinton Administration had expanded the Community Reinvestment Act regulations. Now the CRA was pressuring lenders to make even more questionable loans. Refusal meant being publicly branded as racists. No fewer than four federal bank regulators required a financial firm's portfolio to be in compliance with the new CRA regulations. Failure would mean dire consequences. Non-compliance meant banks might not be allowed to expand liquidity via loans from the Federal Reserve, add new branches, or acquire or merge with other banks. The CRA was rating each bank's lending portfolio on the diversity of their lending practices. Now the government was really playing economic hardball.

Banks were now selling unstable mortgages to Fannie Mae and Freddie Mac after Congress gave them authority to purchase the instruments from commercial and investment banks, then repackage and securitize them for resale on the open market. Banks were also able to allay exposure to their sub prime portfolios and pass on all the risk. During the late nineties and in to the next decade, Congress passed a series of bills that essentially allowed banks to have free reign over the financial markets. New products were coming out daily in the form of engineered financial hybrids called credit default options (CDO) and credit default swaps (CDS). Regulatory agencies didn't have the manpower or expertise to manage these newly engineered financial hybrids. Now the finance and investment industry dam was crumbling. *God, where is this all heading*, Frank thought.

FORTY-ONE

HUNTER'S HOUSE—
PORTLAND, OREGON 2008

Jeffery Starr turned to his father and began. "I'm going to keep the discussion about mirrored servers and the Internet simple, direct, and much of which is to follow will only apply to our case. Father, the Internet evolved from the Pentagon's Advanced Research Project Agency (ARPA). The forerunner to the Internet was launched in 1969 between UCLA and Scientific Data Systems in Menlo Park and was known as the ARPANET. The Internet was turned over to various public entities and went live in 1995. In the intervening years, protocols were developed and tested by various organizations and people, including academia in order to systematically identify and direct traffic on the Internet. In its simplest form, you can think of the Internet as an old-fashioned mail system. A township is planned with its business core being the center and surrounded by its suburbs. The township itself would be considered a network on the Internet, and the houses and business locations would be considered computers. Like addresses for houses, computers also need unique addresses."

"How do the addresses work?" Benesh asked.

"Just like the US mail. Headers on information packets contain Internet Protocol (IP) addresses of return and receiving locations of computers. In other words an Internet Service Provider sends the information packet to a router that governs traffic on the network and sends it to the receiving IP address."

"What are protocols?" Benesh asked.

"Father, they're established rules to identify, prioritize, and guide traffic on the net."

"Oh, I see, just like mail prioritization and classifications."

"You could say that."

"But how many protocols are there?"

"Father, I'm not going to describe protocol hierarchical architecture or root servers that are vital in every TCIP connection, it's beyond our discussion. Now where was I?" Jeffery asked to no one in particular. "Oh, yes, regional and local Internet Service Providers (ISPs) were established to provide hubs for traffic on the net. Whenever computers for a household or a group of computers for a business were installed, the ISP would provide static or dynamic Internet Protocol (IP) addresses to its customers. Larger companies required static or dedicated IP addresses because of their high traffic volume and many business functions, whereas homes usually were issued dynamic IP addresses." Jeffery looked at his father and motioned for him to wait. "Dynamic IP addresses are rotated from an address pool and assigned to individual users on a first-come first-served basis. As soon as these users are through using the net, the addresses are reallocated to the pool for others to use. This method allows for a smaller number of IP addresses being live on the net at any given time. However, the limits are fast approaching the current IPv4 scheme. Because of the rapid growth of the net, a new IPv6 scheme will need to be assigned in the near future to allow for expansion. Also, all IP addresses and domains are registered for use on the Internet."

"What…what are domains?" Benesh interrupted as confusion, once again, crept into his voice.

"They're tags or names that act as substitutes for a series of numbers and dots that represent IP addresses. It is far easier to remember names rather than numbers."

"Why do they have to be registered?" Benesh pressed.

"Because it aids law enforcement agencies to track down unscrupulous users on the net."

"Couldn't an Internet Service Provider register a fictitious company name and address for the purpose of doing illegal activities on the Internet and thus keep the authorities from finding them?" Benesh asked.

"Yes, they could. But authorities can ping any IP address with a sniffer to see if it's live, and if it is, they can use trace route software that will uncover the IP address. They can then shut it down and use good old fashioned detective work to locate the ISP and thus the IP address."

"But what about mirror IP servers?" Benesh persisted.

"Father, I'm getting to that. I was giving you the basics on how the Internet was set up and operates so you could understand what I'm about to say," Jeff said. "What we have done is create our own botnet that mimics the Internet in cyberspace. Meaning we have developed our own network of computers and servers using distributed computing hardware and software. A botnet can have many uses such as running malicious software that attacks other networks and computers. Our botnet has physical and virtual servers running twenty-four hours a day, and our virtual server scripts constantly query other physical server sites outside of our botnet on the Internet, in order to mimic other physical servers' IP addresses. Simply stated, this is the mirror process, and if authorities are looking, they can't get a fix on us because our virtual servers have already moved on to someone else's physical server. Please understand the entire process happens in milliseconds. This was the process that Felix mentioned earlier in relation to email scripting. You still with me, Father?" Jeff asked.

"Yes, son, I am. But what do you mean by moving on to the next physical server?"

"It only takes a millisecond or two for our virtual servers to mimic the physical server's IP address before they move on to the next one. The authorities have less than one chance in a million to have their sniffer and trace route software at the right place and time when our virtual servers are mimicking other physical servers' IP addresses."

"Couldn't the authorities lay in wait for one of your virtual servers to show up and then nail you?" Benesh quizzed.

"That's virtually impossible. Our servers rove the Internet on a random basis. And there are billions of physical IP addresses out there in cyberspace, and they are growing daily. It would be a virtual needle in the haystack. Because of this there is no way for the authorities to trap us, just like there is no way for them to uncover the true identity of our sham companies." Jeff now placed a hand on Benesh's shoulder and asked, "Now do you understand, Father?"

Benesh looked at his son and said, "How ingenious. No one can find where you are at any given time."

"That's right, Father." Jeff said and then motioned to Felix to continue.

FORTY-TWO

OGDEN, UTAH 2009

S teve Kronoski looked at the IRS assistant director and said, "unbelievable."

"Yes it is," Jim Coffey replied as he took his chair.

Steve directed his attention at everyone and said, "I think I can speak for all of us here and say how vitally important our duties will be from now on out." The team nodded their understanding. "Okay. First, I'll have Dr. James provide his team's progress working with Dr. Tonia Frank's team over at DHS. Next, Gene and Ted will report their findings on Jamosa Enterprises and any offshore operations they might have. And then the assistant director and I will wrap the meeting." Steve looked across the table to Dr. Dean James and motioned for him to begin.

Dr. James cleared his throat, stood and looked at the assistant regional director. Dean was a tall, lanky, distinguished looking African-American that was respected and sometimes feared throughout the agency. He was a no-nonsense guy that drove his team to the breaking point at times, but always respected his team members and gave credit where credit was due. "Sir, we have been in close communication and sharing information with Dr. Tonia Frank's team at DHS." Dr. James nodded at Gene then continued. "We have also been working with Gene McIntyre's team, providing them with Jamosa's family and business income tax history. Further, we have forwarded tax and other information crucial for tax evasion methods to Dr. Frank's team in order for their behavioral science group to generate profiling data to us for Mr. Jamosa and Mr. Starr. In other words, we are looking for specific traits and conditions that would compel someone to cheat on their taxes. Even though on the surface it may seem that this isn't central to the Jamosa Enterprises tax investigation, we are not taking any chances."

"Is there any evidence or peculiarities that you have uncovered, Dr. James?" the assistant director asked.

"Well yes and no. Both of their personal and corporate tax histories look clean. However, I believe Mr. Jamosa is far more of a risk taker than Mr. Starr. It seems that Mr. Jamosa is inclined to take chances, especially because of his avarice nature. He enjoys operating in clandestine ways."

"So there's evidence of tax evasion?"

"I didn't say that. However, that is not to say that they're not evading taxes," Dr. James added.

"We need to find evidence, Dr. James," the assistant director retorted. Jim nodded at Dean and then said, "Okay, let's move on. Gene, what have you found?"

Gene McIntyre peered down at his notes for a moment, looked up at Dr. James and said, "Thank you, Dean. You and your team have provided excellent information by crosschecking our work on Jamosa's tax histories and your profiling data has been most helpful. Even though their histories look clean at this point, you have given us a revealing picture on how they think and act." Gene nodded at Dr. James and went on. "I'm sorry to say that we haven't uncovered any concrete evidence so far with respect to their company's accounting methods. Ted and I have taken the outside view first and have poured over their income statements, balance sheets, cash flows, transactional analysis statements, P and L and annual reports, and all of them looked good. We've also inspected their company's stock options and profit sharing plans and still nothing. There also appears to be no evidence or anomalies that would indicate any concealment of outside funds nor any existence of offshore companies."

"What have you done internally?" Steve asked.

"I'll let Ted go over those details with you, sir."

Ted Hamilton stood awkwardly, pulled at his tie and said, "Mr. Coffey, Mr. Kronoski, I find this puzzling."

"What do you mean, Ted?" Steve questioned.

"I mean I have thoroughly investigated their family and business transactions that could even be remotely connected to this inquiry. I have examined connections with Felix's father and mother, Hunter and Lillian, and have found nothing unusual. I've analyzed their checking, savings, and other accounts through their credit union and banks, and I have found nothing suspicious that would suggest a money-laundering scheme. I have also checked their incoming and outgoing funds on their portfolios and life insurance policies and received the same answer. Further, I have inspected all of their real estate transactions listed through public records, and all other assets and liabilities, gifts and trusts, and still nothing. And, that's going back forty years. In other words, I have verified and studied all financial contracts that they have had with other parties throughout the years and uncovered nothing of a dubious nature."

"What about Felix and Clarissa's holdings? Are there any suspicious financial activities that you have been able to uncover?" Steve pressed.

"I took the same steps as I did with their parents, although there was much more to wade through. I did find that there were two other people involved in a real estate and property management transaction on purchasing the land and building for Jamosa Enterprises. Again, these transactions are public record and occurred over twenty years ago."

"Who are they?" Steve asked.

"Ed Wright and Jeremy Givans."

"Have you thoroughly checked their backgrounds?" Steve asked.

"Yes, and they're also clean."

"What about Jeffery and Carly Starr?"

"Same thing, nothing."

"How about Jeffery's parents, Benesh and Marni?" Steve persisted.

"Same thing." Ted looked at Gene and asked, "Should we check Benesh and Marni's parents' backgrounds?"

"No, I don't believe so. Benesh and Marni's parents are both deceased. And that is also true for Hunter and Lillian's parents."

Steve interrupted. "We may look into their financial histories because you never know what we'll find. Even deceased people have business records, and sometimes they can still have substantial holdings, especially in trust accounts."

"Point taken," Gene agreed. "We'll check their histories."

"Gene, who else is left?" Steve asked.

"Felix's personal secretary, Molly Hill.

Gene nodded for Ted to continue.

"Outside of a couple of ordinary real estate transactions for the last twenty years, Molly Hill's financial records show no other major activity or any evidence of collusion. The real estate transactions involved homes that Ms. Hill had lived in during this time, and they are modest properties. Sir, I've looked high and low, and everything and everyone appears to be normal. It's almost like they have been preparing for this event for a long time," Ted said before taking his chair.

The assistant director checked again, "What about offshore companies? Have we found any? And if so, what are their relationships with Jamosa Enterprises?"

Ted looked at the assistant director, shook his head and exclaimed, "There is absolutely nothing, sir! I know there is money somewhere out there; I can smell it. Otherwise, it's either they never existed or they really know how to cover their tracks."

Coffey leaned forward in his chair, looked at Ted and said, "Don't beat yourself up, son, you're doing a fine job. We just need a break, a starting point to unravel this mystery. One thing we can do right away is have the Justice Department lean on banks that have offshore accounts in Switzerland, the Caymans, and the Eastern Caribbean government to name a few. We've been making good progress in this area, on similar matters, for the last year or so."

"Yes, we have. But we need numbers," Steve said.

"If that's where they're hiding their money, we'll find it, Steve," the assistant director said. "One final matter before I adjourn the meeting. I think its time that we fully brief our lead counsel, Timothy Deering, about this investigation so his team can start the deposition process. It'll be interesting to see what we find out. Is there anything else?" he asked as he looked around the room. Everyone remained quiet. "Well then, let's get to it. We have a lot of work in front of us, and don't forget no matter how innocent the information may seem, please forward a copy to DHS."

As Gene and Ted left the conference room, Gene turned to Ted and said, "I knew there was a bombshell somewhere, and it just landed."

"Yeah, and it's a big one!" Ted exclaimed and went on. "Computer espionage? What are they trying to do, bring down our financial infrastructure?" Ted asked.

"Well, buddy, it looks like we're going to find out," Gene said solemnly.

FORTY-THREE

ISLAMABAD, PAKISTAN 2010

The military transport, a Boeing 767, descended through the crisp, clear blue skies into the smog of Chaklala Rawalpindi before touching down at Benazir Bhutto International Airport. The winter sun was just setting off in the distance over the Margalla Hills. Rawalpindi was a working city known for its heavy industry. Its sister city Islamabad, capital of Pakistan, was a few miles to the northwest and was the country's cultural and educational center. The Himalayan foothills, north of the capital, afforded its citizenry with many hiking trails and great views as well as wildlife and had been established as a national park in 1980. The country's seat of government was moved from Karachi to Islamabad in 1960, and the new capital was developed as a progressive city with its burgeoning transportation system providing easy access to most areas of the country. Plus, the old capital adjacent to the Arabian Sea made it far more vulnerable to attacks. After Jake and Slade departed from the plane, collected their luggage, and thanked their air transport's crew, they headed for the American Embassy car parked a few hundred feet away. As they neared the black limo, the chauffer got out and opened the left rear passenger door. A tall, blond American stepped out and held out his hand. "It's been awhile, my friend. How are you, Jake?"

"Fine, Paul. And how is Islamabad treating you these days?" Jake asked.

"Good, except for those pesky Taliban hombres." Paul Paulson was one of a half a dozen attachés assigned to the American Embassy in Islamabad, Pakistan, and knew Jake from the days when they served in the Army.

"Paul, this is my partner, Slade Swanson."

"Well, how are you, Slade? I've heard a lot of things about you."

"Hope they're all good." Slade chuckled. He already knew he was going to like this guy.

"Well, mostly," Paul replied with a grin.

"Okay, let's break up this mutual admiration society and get down to work," Jake said, as he was helping the chauffer stow their gear in the limo's trunk.

All three got in the back of the town car and made themselves comfortable for the trip to Islamabad. As the limo left the apron to the tarmac, Paul hit the remote to seal the rear passenger compartment. Jake asked, "Paul, have all the arrangements been made?"

"Yes, my friend. Mohammed Abdul Jabbar will be meeting with you and Slade tomorrow afternoon at the safe house. I must forewarn you, though, he is very skittish and nervous about this."

"Yeah, you mentioned that on the phone. Is he going to show?" Jake asked.

"Yes. We have his mother's friend, Maria Gonzalez, staying with the Jabbars at their house this evening. Maria went to the central produce market today and picked up some fresh veggies and commandeered some filet mignon steaks from the embassy kitchen with her dazzling personality. She called Mohammed's mother, Fara Jabbar, yesterday to make arrangements and told her since she hasn't seen her for a while; it would be nice to get together and catch up over a nice homemade dinner of beef Sis-Kabobs and Pakistani wild rice. The treat was on her. She also inquired about Mohammed, and Fara told her that he was home and that they would both be looking forward to seeing her and enjoying some of that wonderful American beef with her. Maria will bring him over tomorrow at 1400 hours our time. You've been briefed about Maria?" Paul asked.

"Yes, we received the information on her a few days ago. Like you said, she's a good friend of Fara and also knows Mohammed quite well. And, I might add, it was a series of fortuitous events that led us to this information."

"Indeed it was."

"So is Fara aware of what's going on?" Jake asked.

"Heavens no, there's no need to involve her, and Maria has assured us that Fara knows nothing of this. Anything from the bar?" Paul asked.

"No, I'm fine."

"How about you, Slade?"

"Paul, if you don't mind I'll take a bottled water. I'm a little thirsty from the trip."

After handing Slade an ice-cold Cascadian bottled water, Paul slapped Jake on the shoulder and said, "Okay, gentlemen, I'm taking you out for some authentic Pakistani food this evening."

"Sounds good to me. We're both starved. Military rations aren't exactly to our liking," Jake quipped.

"Don't remind me, buddy."

As the limo headed North toward the twinkling lights of Islamabad, Jake pulled out the dossier on Mohammed. All three then discussed Mohammed's background and strategies on how to engage him.

FORTY-FOUR

HUNTER'S HOUSE
PORTLAND, OREGON 2008

"Now, lets see. Where was I? Oh yes, e-mail and voicemail," Felix said. "If the caller or sender cannot reach the recipient they either think the person has left the company, has changed their e-mail address, telephone number, or their e-mail and voicemail haven't been set up yet. Oh, I almost forgot one thing. We can also receive live telephone calls via computer, and we can decide if we want to accept the call or let it switch over to the recipient's voicemail. If we take the call, we activate the interpreter and voice synthesizer software for the deceased person. And if the caller has caller-id in session, the telephone spoof program is mobilized. Otherwise, the message is sent to the recipient's voicemail, and we can call later using the same technology."

"What if family, friends, or associates call?" Benesh inquired.

"We don't give out these numbers except to government and business officials we need to deal with. We don't want anyone else to know about these numbers. Besides, why would family and friends be calling their dearly departed? Does that make sense?" Felix asked.

Benesh thought for a moment and answered, "I guess it makes sense in a clandestine world."

"What about video conferencing?" Hunter asked.

"We don't use that method, at least at the present time," Felix replied and went on. "This is still relatively new, especially in third world countries. However, we are currently working on AI programs that generate three-dimensional holographic human-like avatars. The most difficult part of the process still lies ahead. This involves gait dynamics, fractals and falls, and other areas of movement science that simulate human movement and actions. When completed, this will add another layer of authenticity to our deceased corporate officials or, for that matter, anyone else. At first, these deceased officials will only be seen and heard within their office confines. Eventually though, these holographic representations will be seen in all kinds of settings under a controlled environment."

Hunter cocked his eyebrow. "Wait a minute. You are telling me that you will be parading the deceased out in the open when you develop this technology? That's preposterous. How can you expect that family and friends will not recognize some of these dead people?

"We'll be editing and altering some of the deceased (avatars) and creating new ones for others once the new technology comes online."

"Oh, I see," Hunter uttered softly, thinking with a far away look on his face.

"But doesn't anyone ever get suspicious because no one ever interacts with a real person?" Benesh puzzled.

"Yes, that can create problems. But you have to realize that there are some affluent and very powerful people out there that like to remain anonymous for one reason or another. The late Howard Higgins and K. Paul Netty were prime examples of this. Actually, there are more people than you would think. As some people get older and amass more wealth and power, have seen and done most everything, they want to be left alone."

Hunter and Benesh nodded to Felix, and Hunter said, "I can see your point, son. Though it doesn't hold true for everyone, since many people aren't reclusive by nature."

"That's true, Dad. But I believe the percentage of wealthy and powerful people that are or tend to become reclusive over time is significant enough not to pose a problem for us. Besides, most of these individuals do not want easy access because of the criminal element in our societies. In addition, the way things are moving, I'm sure technology will overcome these barriers in the not too distant future."

"Son, we're not talking about the wealthy here. We're talking about soldiers. Why wouldn't some of their loved ones get suspicious," Hunter argued.

"We're talking third world countries here. No education, confusion everywhere and superstition running rampant. Who cares anyway? Besides, like I said, we'll address the issue when the time comes."

Hunter stood, put his hands in his pockets, and looked at his son and said, "To sum this up, you have virtual phantom companies that trade on stock exchanges throughout the world. And because of these sophisticated systems, these companies can handle all corporate earnings and reports and in most cases automatically send them to their respective government agencies. Also, these programs generate all paper flow and documents for all these companies' internal systems, such as inventory control, payroll, accounting and financial reports. Other advanced systems control communications. Further, there is very little intervention on your part except when you need to respond to government, business and shareholders via e-mail, telephone and an occasional fax, in order to periodically disburse checks, information, and statements. And you can respond anytime, anywhere in the world. Finally, anytime you wish, you can pull the plug and take all the shareholders', businesses' and governments' money and vanish without a trace. Is this correct?"

"That's correct, Dad."

"One more thing. Are there other people doing this? I mean, we could have dozens, perhaps hundreds or more of these virtual or phantom companies trading on the world's exchanges, and no one would ever know including the governments?" Hunter asked, as he stared at his son in disbelief.

"To answer your first question, I do know of one, and his name is Bernie Maddoff."

"Yes, and he's a scoundrel," Hunter opinioned.

Felix took another pull of his drink and then continued, "You take a very smart individual like Bernie and apply his business savvy, and you wouldn't believe how much wealth a person like that can amass. Although I really think Bernie had some help in his scheme. Of course he's operating on a much smaller scale then Jeff and I, creating and using hedge funds instead of phantom corporations. But he still did plenty of damage to the tune of at least $100 billion dollars. And he probably did it without any sophisticated software, except for trading. And as far as your second question, are there more Bernie's or phantom corporations out there? I'm sure we wouldn't know until it's too late. Dad, you have to understand, it doesn't matter how the wolves are dressed: they all use the same scheme. It's called Ponzi. Charles Ponzi first utilized the scheme in the roaring twenties. And since there's little or no regulation and oversight from the SEC and other regulatory bodies probably throughout the world—well, you get the point. We could be looking at a disaster the likes the world has never seen!"

"And what about you, son, when you decide to quit? Will the shareholders, governments, and businesses be left holding the bag?" Hunter asked, shaking his head again.

"Dad, we're not dissolving the phantom corporations for some time. When we do I think the shareholders will have made enough profit to offset any losses they might have incurred, since we help drive up the shares in value," Felix replied.

"You're telling me that you own the majority interest of your companies' common and preferred stocks, and you have for the whole duration?" Hunter countered.

"No, Dad, but we have been buying back stock for some time now and are now approaching forty-five percent ownership in most of our companies."

"Damn it! Listen to me! Who do you think you're kidding, son?" Hunter slammed his fist down on the bar, and Felix had flashbacks, seeing others sweating across from his father's desk. He wondered if he now had that same terrified expression on his face. "You'll never do it. It's called greed," Hunter bellowed.

Felix slowly replied, "No, we will, and besides, the intent of the operation was never to default on the shareholders but to hide money and documents from the IRS or anyone else in case they came looking. Just to show you our plans, we have already purchased land in Afghanistan with some of our phantom companies' profit. Also, we're making arrangements to purchase some old pieces of rock-crushing equipment including a loader, cat, and a couple of dump trucks. We can quickly develop a rock quarry and put up a couple of warehouses stored with stone and rock products in case local authorities or the country's government get too close. In fact, the paper flow and documentation already show that we ship stone and rock products to some of our shell companies. They in turn can ship to legal entities that can use our stone and rock products for the industrial, commercial, and residential markets."

"Have you been doing this?" Benesh asked as he looked up.

"No, but we can. Actually, we can package this and have a legitimate operation up and running within a couple of weeks or so. We're betting we can have the operation going before any authorities arrive, especially in third world countries. And then there's always the bribe factor."

Felix directed his attention to Hunter and said in a conciliatory tone, "Dad, to put you at ease, when we wind down the arms business someday, we will probably convert most of these companies to legitimate businesses. And if the IRS pokes their nose into our businesses on foreign soil, don't you think the U.S. government would be risking an international incident? Jeffery and I think so. *He is never going to convert these companies unless it's under a threat of a major investigation,* he thought.

Hope it's enough to convince Hunter, though. Now, have I left out anything?" Felix asked as he sat his weary bones down in the leather wing chair.

Hunter and Benesh thought for a long moment and then Hunter said, "Son, I don't care if you can fool the best governments on the globe, this isn't morally right and you know it."

"Dad, it's in my blood, and I enjoy it."

"Son, you need help. We can help you, Felix." Hunter said quietly.

Benesh turned to his son and asked, "How could you be part of this?"

"Father, I don't know what to say right now. I need some time to think about this," Jeffery replied as he rubbed his tired brown eyes.

Hunter looked at his watch and saw that it was after 4:00 a.m. "It's extremely late, and I'm sure that it is still snowing out. I would like all of you to stay over, and perhaps we can continue this at breakfast. I still have some additional questions."

They agreed to stay, and Hunter took them upstairs to the guest bedrooms. When Hunter arrived at the door to his son's childhood bedroom, he told Felix that they would talk further and then wished him goodnight, turned, and headed back to the study. Before he got too far down the hallway, his son whispered, "I thought you weren't going to interrupt me tonight." Hunter softly chuckled to himself and continued down the hall.

In the study he opened two opposing windows and peered through the screen on one of them. Sure enough, it was still snowing. He turned on the ceiling fan to ventilate out the cigar smoke and moved the wing chairs back to their proper places. He collected the barware and put them in the bar's dishwasher, turned it on, and sat down to think over the night's proceedings. Hunter was stunned at what he had heard from Jeffery and his son tonight. He could hardly wrap his mind around the depth and level of their deceit. He thought, *who gave my son and Jeffery the right to play God with others' money?* After the cigar smoke cleared, he stood, closed the windows, turned off the lights, and went upstairs to the master bedroom to get some rest. He wasn't sure if he was going to get much sleep.

FORTY-FIVE

NEW YORK CITY, NEW YORK 2010

Frank heard a voice tunneling into his thoughts. "Mulligan, are you there?"

"What is it, Jack?" Frank puzzled, as his mind fought back to the present.

"I asked if there is a quick and easy way to roll some of the liabilities back onto the bank's balance sheets?"

"Why? Is your conscience getting the best of you?"

"Yes, it is." Jack lied. "I think it's about time we turn over a new leaf and act responsibly to the company and it's shareholders," he said, in his most earnest tone.

"Jack, why would you ever do that? Even though it's the right thing to do, you do realize the bank shares will plummet, and the officers, employees, and stockholders will lose value. Plus, you will fall out of favor with Wall Street."

"That's okay." Jack lied again. "I know it'll be a struggle until the bank's stock recovers, but we owe it to ourselves, the economy, and the taxpayers. Hopefully, the banking industry as a whole is also thinking the same way."

As Frank reached for his coffee, he saw his friend, Clarence Gleason, the company's CIO, rise from his chair to address Jack. With concern written across his friend's face, Clarence interjected by saying, "Jack, I can't believe what you just said. Let's call a spade for what it is. How gullible do you think Frank and I are?" Clarence then looked over at his friend before taking his seat again.

Frank now stood from his chair, squared his shoulders as best he could and faced his boss and bellowed, "You SOB, I know why you're asking this." Frank went on without giving his boss a chance to respond and looked at Clarence, and the CIO nodded as if to say, "you go get him Frank."

"You want to roll more liabilities back into the bank's balance sheet in hopes of showing the government how poorly the bank is doing, in order to get a larger share of the TARP funds. This is nothing more than REPO 105, popularized by Lehman Bothers, where commercial and investment banks off load some of their more toxic securities to holding companies prior to scheduled audits then move them back afterward. Let me explain something to you Jack. First of all, it won't work unless the government really drags its feet because it will take at least two or three quarters to work in the debts, in a meaningful and logical manner, back onto the bank's balance sheet. Second, we are running out of time. Third, and most important, you just showed us all what a scoundrel you really are."

Now some of the other officers and the secretary were looking at Jack with shocked expressions on their faces and shaking their heads.

"If you think Clarence and I will play your little shell game with the government, you're sorely mistaken."

"Frank, it was only a rhetorical question. A little brainstorming doesn't hurt, does it?" Jack asked, trying to defend himself.

"I know what you're up to, and it's hogwash. You hear me? Hogwash." Frank bellowed again. "Even if you get approval from the board, it's just not going to work." Frank was on a roll now and continued speaking while looking at some of the other corporate officials in the room he suspected to be as rotten as Jack. "I know if you and your cronies approve this, the first thing you'll do is cash out your stock options before the company's stock plummets."

"Now, look here Frank," Jack tried to interrupt.

"Let me finish, and then you'll get your say!" Frank glowered in a low voice filled with rage.

Jack stared at Frank and said nothing.

"I know why you were let go from KKR. It's called malfeasance. You know, dereliction of duty."

Clarence and the other executive officers in the room were now shocked and could feel the heat and intensity build between the CEO and CFO. It was almost palpable.

"And now you're trying the same crap here. Just like KKR, Enron, and other Wall Street firms, it's the same old replay: Cash out and screw everybody."

Jack's face was bright red now, and you could see the veins stand out on his neck and forehead as he stood and shouted, "That's quite enough, Frank. Sit your butt down!"

As the two executives stared at each other across the table, Frank finally said, "I'm finished," and sat down.

Jack stood a moment longer trying to regain his composure and then sat. "You're finished all right."

Frank knew he had overstepped the boardroom's boundary of etiquette and civility. He didn't care anymore. He'd been preparing for this day for the last two years. He knew he needed to calm down and think about more pleasant things or his blood pressure would get out of control.

FORTY-SIX

ISLAMABAD, PAKISTAN 2010

A t 1345 hours local time the next day, Jake and Slade descended the stairs to the gathering room at the safe house and took their seats on a braided leather couch to await their visitor. They poured themselves some black Turkish espresso from a decanter on the coffee table, helped themselves to some Pakistani pastries, and then discussed how they were going to question Mohammed. Jake looked again at the dossier on Mohammed to check out more facts and then turned to Slade and said, "Since he is so twitchy, I think we need to put him at ease before we start questioning him. What do you think?"

"That's a good idea. Let's get him to talk about sports, especially soccer. Then we can move on to his education and what he does for a living and does he have any hobbies. Then we can address his friendships and hopefully this will lead him to our questions."

"I think that's a good plan, and it will also allow us to see how close his answers match the information in the dossier," Jake said, picking up his espresso cup for a sip. Just then the front doorbell chimed, and Paul came out of the kitchen to let his guests in.

As Paul let Maria and Mohammed in, Jake and Slade stood and turned to their guests. Paul led Maria and Mohammed over to the pair of Homeland Security agents and introductions were made. For the next half hour, they bantered about the progressive nature of Islamabad and Mohammed's relationship with Maria. Finally, Paul stood and motioned for Maria to follow him and said, "Well, Maria, we're having too much fun! I suppose it's time to leave so they can get down to business." Maria nodded, said her good-byes, and followed Paul out of the room. Jake could sense that Mohammed was now relaxed and was actually quite an affable person. He had even indicated for them to call him Mo.

"Mo, do you need anything before we begin, any more espresso or pastries?" Jake asked politely.

"No, I'm fine. Though I am a little warm from the fireplace, but it feels good."

Jake then took the lead. "Okay Mo, what do we have here?"

"Well, where should I start?"

"You can begin wherever you like," Jake said, as he stood and walked over and dialed down the fireplace.

"I guess I should mention my cousin, Al-Hadi Zafar on my mother's side. Do you know of him?"

Slade looked at Mo for a moment to gauge him before speaking, "Yes, we know of him through his long-time friend, Seyed Mostakavi. In fact, if I recall correctly, they first met and studied together at USC over thirty years ago and have remained close friends ever since."

"So you also know Seyed?"

"Yes, we know that he and the mujahideen had been receiving arms through Felix Jamosa during the Soviet-Afghan war in the late 1980s," Slade said and poured himself another espresso.

"Ah, you know Felix too, and do you know how brilliant Seyed is? It seems to me the smarter the individual the more dangerous they can become."

"That's a good observation, Mo, especially in Seyed's case. His I.Q. is off the charts, and he is probably one if not the most gifted person living today. However he is ruthless and treacherous and cares nothing about anything or anyone, except his family and Iran." Slade said as he took a sip of espresso.

Jake looked at Slade and then said, "Mo, we know that you're well educated and a really bright fellow yourself, and closely follow your Muslim beliefs. But really, why would you want to help us? You surely know that our western ways are flawed, and sometimes it appears our culture is self-centered. There really must be a deep-seated reason or even fear why you want to do this?" Jake knew that there were other ways to get answers from potential adversaries, especially if they were hostile. But Jake's instincts told him after studying Mohammed's dossier and conferencing a call with Paul and Maria earlier that morning that Mohammed was a sincere and undoubtedly an honest individual and saw no need to use strong-arm tactics.

Mohammed sat there for a long moment to think through his thoughts before answering. "I know every society has its problems and that there isn't any country on earth that can cast the first stone. And being pragmatic, there's no such thing. In almost all cases, its not the people that are at the root of evil but their country's governments."

"Well spoken, Mo," Slade interrupted.

"Let me finish," Mo said with anger flashing in his dark brown eyes. "Somehow the people of our planet have to find a way to control and turn the tide of evil, or all will be lost. I have no ill intentions for societies that recognize their mistakes and try to overcome them. In fact, I believe the people of the United States are basically good and a very giving society. You see it every day by their wealth of generosity, stepping in and helping their less fortunate brethren, especially when natural disasters strike. But their government needs to be reined in. And that's the problem."

"Mo you're not getting into the geo-political arena, are you?" Jake questioned.

"No, I just wanted both of you too know in simplistic terms that it's not the Muslims or your people causing strife, it's the governments and radical factions around the globe. There are fanatical groups in every religion and society that can cause trouble but in the end it comes from the governments."

"Mo, Slade and I really share your concerns and agree with much of what you just said. But we need to get to the problem," Jake prodded.

"Okay, I'll strike the heart of the matter. On occasion I've had the good fortune of being with my cousin, Al-Hadi and his friend, Seyed, while they were discussing business and expressing their opinions on various topics. I remember one time sitting with my cousin at a café here in town in 1989, and Seyed came over to our table to see Al-Hadi. My cousin introduced me to him, and after some small talk Seyed went back to his table next to ours. I've always been good at observing people and quite frankly I'm the curious sort, and so I eavesdropped on Seyed's conversation with three other people sitting at his table while my cousin and I were having lunch. From their discussion, I could tell that Seyed was heavily involved in the Soviet-Afghan war and solely relied on Felix Jamosa for all of their arms. He was making arrangements for the other three people to receive weapons, and it appeared he was recommending Felix, since he and Felix were such good friends. He also told his comrades that he had killed another arms dealer in front of Felix because Felix didn't like him."

"From what you just said, it appears your cousin and Seyed aren't too careful about who overhears their conversations. I can't believe they're this careless." Jake said.

"Actually they're not. Let me rephrase what I just said."

"By all means," Slade quipped.

"Al-Hadi likes me around a lot of the time. I guess he thinks I am his lackey, always getting things for him and his friends, making reservations, getting beverages and generally picking up after him. You could say that when I'm around, I'm not around. After hearing some of his conversations early on, I made it an art to be seen but not seen." Mohammed volunteered.

"But doesn't that offend you?" Slade asked.

"Yes it does, but he is my cousin, and he can be very kind and giving at times."

"Okay, where's this leading to?" Jake asked.

"I'm getting there. From that point on, I was usually all-ears whenever I was around Seyed. Did you know he is practically and single-handedly pulling Iran into the Nuclear age?" Mohammed offered.

"Yes, we suspected as much. Otherwise it would have taken Iran much longer," Jake said.

"So you know that Seyed can be a very dangerous person?"

"Well, what does treacherous and ruthless mean?" Jake countered.

"I see your point." Mohammed replied.

"Now can we continue?" Jake pressed.

"Okay. Do you guys know Abrahim Solasti?" Jake and Slade looked at each other and shook their heads. "He's a Sudan national that Al-Hadi recruited in the late 1980s to help work on distilling and allocating Saudi's crude oil categories using complex mathematical models. After Seyed joined Al-Hadi's team around 1990, he and Abrahim became good friends, since they both were brilliant and could play off of one another. For many years Al-Hadi, Seyed and Abrahim worked with ARAMCO and the Saudi government with the blessings of their friend and confidant, Oil Minister Jamal Al-Mhalifa. Even though none of them, including Al-Hadi, were Saudi citizens they managed to gain the respect and trust of the oil minister. Throughout the intervening years, they had eventually leveraged Saudi's oil consortium to lead OPEC in most of their decisions. But by now they had bigger ambitions. I once overheard my cousin speaking on the phone with Seyed, about four years ago, discussing the economic infrastructures of all the advance nations. Al-Hadi told Seyed that it was about time to put their plans into motion because T1 communication lines throughout the world now tie together all of the leading powers' financial transactions."

Slade let out a low whistle and then said, "So that's what they're doing."

"I believe so."

"Do you know what country or countries and the financial institutions they've targeted?" Jake asked.

"Well I know the United States is on the top of their list, but I don't know what financial institutions they plan to cyber-attack."

Jake rubbed his face and asked, "Mo, you said you first heard about this four years ago?"

"That's correct."

"Why didn't you come to us sooner with this information?" Jake asked and went on. "I know you must have realized what kind of chaos this could unleash on the world's financial systems. After all, you are bright guy and well educated in computers and chemistry."

"That's part the problem, Jake. With my background I knew how difficult it would be for them to pull this off. Plus, I was scared. I kept it to myself until now, and the only reason why I came forward is because of something I overheard recently."

"What's that?" Slade asked as he looked at Jake.

"I don't know exactly how to put this. It seems so unbelievable I can barely comprehend what I heard. Two words come to my mind: phantom corporations."

"What...what is that supposed to mean?" Jake asked as he was shaking his head. "I feel like we just entered the realm of paranormal discussions."

"Unbelievable!" Slade exclaimed.

Mohammed paused and took a moment to study the two agents' reactions before going on. "I know, it sounds almost unimaginable."

"In what context did you hear this?" Slade asked solemnly.

"One night not too long ago I asked Al-Hadi if I could be invited to an official state reception being held at Seyed's house in Riyadh."

"Why did you ask your cousin for an invite?" Slade mused.

"There was a young graduate student from the university that I wanted to meet and—"

Jake interrupted and asked, "Was the student of the opposite sex?"

"Why yes. Why do you ask?"

"You sure that you didn't have any other intentions besides business for this young lady?" Jake kidded.

"No...no, she's studying at King Saud University and just published an exceptional paper on petrol-chemical reactions and extraction techniques, and I wanted to discuss it with her. Also, Al-Hadi wanted me there in case I needed to drive him home."

"Doesn't Al-Hadi have a chauffer?" Slade asked.

"Usually he does. I guess he figured if he invited me to the reception, he would see that I would be useful in some way. I remembered getting quite warm and stuffy at one point during the evening so I stepped out on Seyed's back patio to get a breath of fresh air and sat on a lounge chair at the far end."

"Were any of the patio lights on, Mo?" Slade questioned.

"No, it was quite dark. And like I was saying, I was sitting there, and five minutes later Seyed comes out, and I find that he is on his satphone and having a heated discussion with Felix Jamosa. He was telling Felix that it wasn't his fault that the three dimensional holographic software wasn't accurately representing the deceased avatars for his phantom corporations. Well that certainly got my attention after hearing that! They continued talking until Seyed finally said he would look into it as soon as he could, but in the mean time he would remotely shut down that portion of the system. He told Felix that he would have to rely on the other sections of the system for the corporations' incoming and outgoing communications. He disconnected the satphone and went back inside."

"So you're saying that they use dead people to run the companies through their holographic representations?" Slade queried.

"Yes."

"Did Seyed elaborate on the other forms of communication?" Jake asked.

"No, but it's logical to assume that would be e-mail and telecommunications."

"I would think so," Jake agreed.

"Mo, do you know why they set up these so-called phantom companies?" Jake pressed.

"Well, it's probably to channel their illicit gains from their arms' sales."

"Interesting," Slade said.

"Are you sure that Seyed didn't see or hear you?" Jake asked.

"Yes, I'm positive."

"Well, I hope so for your sake, Mo. Otherwise, I don't think your life would be worth a tinkers damn. Did he indicate any of the deceased names, where they were from or in what period of time they were deceased?"

"No, Jake. That's all I heard, and after hearing that I was so scared that I could scarcely breath."

"I would imagine, Mo. Now, is there any other information that you would like to share with us?"

"That's about it. Isn't it enough?"

"I believe so. Now we would like to discuss something with you," Jake said. "First of all, we want to thank you for being so candid with us. Second, I'm sure you realize that you could possibly be in great danger."

"Yes, the thought has occurred to me, and that's another reason why I decided to come to you."

"Mo, do you have Paul Paulson's private number?" Slade asked.

"No, but I have Maria's number."

"Okay, this is what we'll do." As Jake was giving Mo instructions, Slade jotted down Paul's number and gave it to Mohammed and then went to fetch Paul. Maria and Paul came back into the gathering room, and Paul took Mohammed aside for further instructions while Maria spoke to the Homeland Security agents. Just then the gathering room's front window exploded with glass shards flying everywhere.

FORTY-SEVEN

HUNTER'S HOUSE—
PORTLAND, OREGON 2008

At breakfast, Lily served her husband, Hunter, his favorite. He always liked scrambled eggs with goat's cheese, Prosciutto ham, dark Russian Rye toast and plenty of Seattle's Best hazelnut coffee. After Lily cleared the dishes away and left two full carafes of coffee on the table, she left the breakfast room. The conversation turned to last night's topic. Hunter looked at his son, Felix, and then Jeffery Starr and his father Benesh before speaking. "Son, I don't know about you, Ben or Jeffery, but I couldn't sleep well. I kept coming back to why is the IRS after us? What is the problem?" Before Felix could speak, Hunter continued. "The way I see it is that you either stepped on somebody's toes in Washington or crossed one of your gun running buddies, and they leaked some harmful information to the boys up on the hill. Either way, Ben and I need to know what's going on." Benesh nodded at Hunter with approval.

Felix didn't know if Hunter was laying a trap, so he stayed with his original plan. "Dad, it's neither. What Jeffery and I think is that the ATF is so frustrated with us that they went to the administration and applied pressure through the Treasury Department. You have to understand this agency has been shadowing us for years and has always come up empty handed. And I know this has put a sizeable dent in their budget, not to mention their pride, and they're probably getting real tired of it."

"Son, you mean the Alcohol, Tobacco and Firearms agency?" Hunter queried.

"Yes, Dad, the arms trade falls under their jurisdiction."

"But what made them so mad?" Hunter pressed.

"They've been trying to look into our business since the mid nineties."

"Yes, go on, son," Hunter encouraged.

"Since then they have dedicated a substantial portion of the agency's budget on resources, which includes satellite surveillance, computer time on the Department of Defense mainframes, equipment such as boats and planes, and legal document preparations, not to mention the amount of hours spent tracking us throughout all these years, I suspect they are really steamed."

Benesh stepped in. "What is it with you, some kind of cat and mouse game?" Benesh looked at his son and went on. "Don't you know who you're up against and how serious this is?"

"Yes, we know its serious and what the consequences are." Felix answered, while pouring himself another cup of java.

"Then why do you and Jeffery do it?" Benesh puzzled, still looking at his son.

"In a word, its money, and besides, it's living on the edge for me, and I like the rush."

While Benesh was shaking his head, Hunter stepped in and exclaimed, "Enough of this! I want to know exactly why the ATF is coming down so hard on you."

"Like I said, Dad we are causing too much pain and money for the agency."

Before Hunter could ask anything else, Felix continued, "Let me give a couple of illustrations. In the mid to late nineties, we were supplying arms to the Revolutionary United Front (RUF) in order to help their cause in a civil war against Sierra Leone's corrupt government. At the time we were using an old twin-engine DC-4 prop to transport arms to the RUF. On one occasion, our plane was illegally forced down to an abandoned airstrip in the middle of nowhere by an ATF plane. After we landed, Robert Murphy and a team of ATF agents rushed us with guns drawn, and Murphy showed his badge and said we were under arrest.

I told him I wanted to see the warrant, and the only response I got from him was a crack on the side of the head with the barrel of his gun. While my pilot, Duke Morrison, and I were being read our Miranda Rights, other field agents disabled the plane's engines. The team snapped pictures of the plane's cargo, took my satphone, and threw us a couple bottles of water. Murphy told us they would be back the next day to seize the cargo for evidence and transport us to the states. After they left Duke and I got a couple of wooden crates and a couple of revolvers and ammo off the plane for our protection. We sat down on the empty ammo boxes and pondered our dilemma. Here we were, Dad, out in the middle of nowhere with just a couple of bottles of water for nourishment. Thank God we had weapons for protection. Pretty soon some of the local natives came out of the bush to stare at the plane, and then the idea hit me: Open up the plane and let the local population cart away the merchandise. It's only money, and I can always make more."

"You didn't!" Hunter and Benesh exclaimed together.

"Holy smokes, that's incredible," Hunter exclaimed again.

"The local establishment took more than just weapons. They removed everything they possibly could that wasn't securely fastened down. When they were finished, the plane, or rather what was left looked like a big-gutted silver tube. Anyhow, the aircraft was reduced down to scrap value. Like I said, its only money, and I sure didn't want to rot away in some federal prison cell," Felix said quietly. "Dad, you should have seen the looks on the ATF agents' faces when they arrived the next day and found the weapons gone and the plane dismantled."

Jeffery laughed at the vision of a silver tube he had conjured up in his mind, and Benesh gave his son a stern look across the table. Felix continued, "The cost of the weapons and the plane was well worth the looks on all of their faces. Murphy let out a howl of expletives that a drunken sailor would be proud of as he approached me. The next thing I knew I was lying on the ground again with the other side of my head bleeding and throbbing. Murphy looked down at me and started to swear again, and then he smiled.

"He said, 'You think you're smarter than me? You think you can jerk me and the agency around, huh Felix? Well I've got news for you, buster. From now on, I'm going to be your worst nightmare. I will be hounding you day and night wherever you're at and wherever you go, and eventually justice will be served!'"

"After Murphy and his team left, we rounded up a few of the tribesmen to guide us, and three days later we were in the provincial capitol of Kenema. I received some medical attention for my head wounds, and a couple of hours later Duke and I were on a plane headed for Sierra Leone's national capitol, Freetown. The next day Duke and I boarded a flight back to the states. As you can guess we never were taken into custody, and we didn't hear from Murphy again for quite a while. Dad, do you want me to go on? I can tell you about the Iranian freighter incident." Felix offered.

"No, son, that's quite enough. I think I see the picture, especially with the ATF. It appears that they not only bungled your situation, and, if I recall correctly, they also showed incompetence at Ruby Ridge and Waco, Texas. And I hate to think of other incidences that we are not aware of." Hunter continued, "So together with the IRS they are out to get us because you have embarrassed them and given them a black eye. Is that about right, son?"

"I believe so," Felix answered.

Hunter stood and hooked his thumbs in his pant's pockets and looking directly at his son, "I have one final question, and this one has been keeping me up nights. Why did we get the subpoenas from the Justice Department? If I recall correctly the Justice Department handles criminal, not civil cases. If it was a civil case I imagine the subpoenas would have come from the Treasury Department."

"Dad, that's been bothering me too, and for the life of me, I just don't know," Felix lied with a solemn face.

"We'll find out, won't we, son," Hunter said with a concerned look, and went on. "Do you and Jeffery have your legal team in place, and have you addressed your strategy yet?" Hunter queried.

"Yes, we are currently working on this, and our lead counsel, Jim Benson, said we have nothing to worry about as long as Jamosa Enterprises is following the letter of the law."

"And is it?" Hunter asked.

"Yes, it is Dad."

"What about us?" Benesh asked.

"Jeffery and I will be calling you and Dad in a few days to arrange a meeting with our legal team to go over your involvement, or rather the lack of. To be honest, I don't know why you and Dad are in the middle of this. I think the government knows that they have nothing and are just throwing darts at the wall to see what sticks." Felix argued.

"Before we leave this conversation, son, I want you to know that I would never condone yours and Jeffery's actions in this endeavor. And I'm sure that Ben would also agree with me." Hunter said solemnly, as Benesh nodded toward him.

"But Dad—"

"Let me finish," Hunter glowered.

"If you weren't my son, I would be throwing you out on your ear. And, if we get out of this mess, you will take Benesh's and my advice and get out of the arm's business. Do you understand?" Hunter intoned.

"Yes, Father, Felix lied." He stood and looked as his dad and said, "If you would have let me finish, that's what I was going to say. Jeffery and I will wind down the weapons business."

"Good, now let's concentrate on winning our case and let Benesh and I know when we need to meet with your legal team," Hunter said.

After breakfast Felix bummed a ride with Jeff and left the Ferrari parked since there was snow on the streets. They thanked Lily for the fine breakfast and said their good-byes to everyone. As Jeff was taking his brother-in-law home, he wanted to talk more about the morning's events. But before he could speak, Felix indicated that he wasn't feeling well, probably from the goat's cheese, and wanted to rest. His insides were in turmoil, but not from the breakfast. His guts were being gnawed from fear of the upcoming investigation. He hated himself for lying to everyone, especially his father. Even though, technically, it was an omission. He thought, *when everyone finds out, which they probably would, there would be severe consequences. He would have to trust his instincts and play it close to the vest. And more importantly, he didn't want to quit running guns—he still received a rush from it.*

FORTY-EIGHT

ISLAMABAD, PAKISTAN 2010

Jake and Slade could hear the staccato sounds of a pair of AK 47s firing on full automatic at 600 round per minute. The two glass swan lamps on the end tables shattered as the gathering room's back wall was raked with 7.62 mm slugs. In an instant, Jake slammed Maria to the floor while Slade was flipping the nearest leather couch on its side for some protection. The front door's beveled glass and the dining room's chandelier disintegrated in a collision of glass and bullets. Suddenly the Kalashnikovs went silent as the assassins slammed fresh thirty round banana clips into their hardware. Jake yelled, "Get Mo and Maria into the kitchen now!" As Paul was pushing them toward the kitchen, Jake yelled at Paul again, "Are you armed?"

"Collecting a weapon in the kitchen," Paul yelled back as he hustled Mohammed and Maria through the kitchen door.

"Watch the rear," Jake shouted as he saw them disappear into the kitchen. Jake then slid across the floor to the rolled over couch. "Slade, cover me while I get to the front window. Need to see what we're up against."

Slade pulled out his Freedom Arms Model 83, .454 Casull revolver and flipped the safety. The big gun roared as he laid down cover fire through the blown-out front window as the AKs chattered again. Jake bellied to the window to assess the situation.

Jake and Slade didn't use the DHS issued side arms, except for backup. In fact, whenever they were on field assignment, they always brought their Bear Track cases—toting revolvers, scopes and spare cylinders. They both agreed that Freedom Arms made the best side arms in the world for reliability, accuracy, and stopping power.

At the window, Jake motioned with two fingers of his left hand and said, "One's using an old pickup for cover, and the other one is circling around to the right to come up the side stairs of the front porch." Just then they heard the blast of a 12-gauge shotgun coming from the rear of the house. Moments later they saw Paul crouching at the kitchen door covered in blood.

"You okay, Paul?" Jake yelled.

"Yeah, but you should see the other guy," Paul said as he was using a hanky to wipe blood and brain matter from his face and neck.

"I see you decided to come to the party in red." Slade chuckled.

"Is there any other way?"

As Slade chuckled again, he asked, "Anymore back there?"

"No, I checked, and it doesn't appear so," Paul offered.

"Well, keep a sharp eye out, I think we have the front covered," Slade instructed.

"Where are Mohamed and Maria?" Jake queried.

"They're still in the kitchen behind an upturned table. They're fine."

"Paul, how's the basement for protection?" Jake asked.

"Good. It has a steel reinforced door for the walk up, and there's a couple of side arms stashed down there."

"Get ready to get Mo and Maria down there. Still not sure what we're up against," Jake said.

As another volley came from the AK-47s, Paul ducked back into the kitchen to get Mohammed and Maria. Jake and Slade returned fire with their revolvers. Jake, now on the floor, reached up and ever so gently opened the front door a bit so he could get an angle of the side stairs leading to the porch. One of the gunmen was coming up the side steps. Jake pushed the door just a smidge more and laced the assassin across his chest with a couple of .454 rounds. The man leaped backwards off the stairs as if pulled by a set of invisible puppeteer's strings. Just as Jake was about to tell Slade that another one of their guests had decided to leave the party, the other gunmen jumped in his truck and rocketed down the street before Jake could get off a shot. He knew the gunman lying off the side stairs of the porch was stone cold dead and that the big .454 rounds did their work by leaving saucer-sized holes exiting his back.

"Wow, that's one mean hotrod!" Jake exclaimed. "Okay, let's hustle Mo and Maria to the basement, and then we can check things out."

After Maria and Mo were safely ensconced, the two agents and Paul checked the rest of the house and property and found nothing but the two dead would-be assassins.

Jake then looked at Paul and said, "Call the Pakistani authorities. While you're at it get a couple of high ranking American Embassy officials over here. I think we need to put Maria and Mo under protective custody at the embassy until we at least know what's going on."

"Good idea," Paul said. "It's better to have them under lock and key at the embassy where they are easily accessible and undoubtedly better protected."

Paul grabbed the house phone while Jake and Slade set about the business of thoroughly checking the suspects for identification and any other evidence that would give them a clue as to who they were. After Paul made the calls and the two DHS agents were done with their search, they led Mo and Maria out of the basement. Paul then cleaned up while Jake and Slade talked to the pair. Jake asked them if they were okay. Still too stunned to speak, they both nodded yes. Jake continued, "After the Pakistani authorities are done questioning you, we are moving both of you to the American Embassy and putting you under protective custody. We need to find out what exactly is going on, and we may need to question both of you further. I hope you both understand?"

Mohammed was the first to speak. "I can't believe what just happened here. I mean I knew this was important information, but to send assassins after us? We're talking about my cousin,

Al-Hadi Zafar. We grew up together, played soccer together and attended family functions together—we were so close. And now this!"

"People change, Mo," Jake said. "Besides, we don't know yet what exactly happened here today, except gunmen were sent to take your lives. Perhaps it wasn't your cousin but one of his friends without his knowledge."

"That's true. Maybe it was Seyed?" Mohammed mused.

"What about me?" Maria asked, as she was trying to calm her nerves.

Jake studied her for a moment before he said, "Both of you will be placed under security, and your movements will be restricted until we find out what's going on." Jake gave her his famous crooked smile and added, "Besides, you're already an embassy employee; plus this will give you and Mo a chance to recall events leading up to this and possibly uncover some information that might be helpful."

After the Pakistani police left and Mo and Maria were whisked away in a bulletproof American Embassy limo followed by another car of Embassy security personnel, Paul and the two DHS agents sat and discussed what had happened.

"Good call, Jake." Paul said. "If it wasn't for the embassy officials, our friends would have been in Pakistani custody, and control would have been taken out of our hands."

"That's exactly what I was afraid of. Though their lives could still be in jeopardy," Jake said.

The three continued their discussion until Jake turned to Slade and said, "I think it's time to call the deputy and apprise him of the situation."

FORTY-NINE

NEW YORK CITY, NEW YORK 2010

"Frank, Frank Mulligan, how do you say?" Jack asked.

"What?" Frank puzzled as he looked at Jack. Frank was so wrapped in his reflections that he had almost lost sight to the reason why he was here.

"How do you vote on the TARP proposal?" Jack said impatiently.

"Nay."

"Fred, what say you?"

"Yea," Fred responded and slapped the massive cherry table for emphasis.

"Okay, the vote is four to two in favor of the yeas," Jack happily said.

With that, Frank tossed an envelope in Jack's direction. Jack peered down at it and asked, "What's this?"

"What do you think it is? It's my resignation, you idiot!" Frank glowered as he stared at his boss. "I'm through with this company. I can't believe the officers of this bank, except for Clarence and I, just voted to accept TARP funding from the government."

Jack smiled and looked on in triumph as Frank continued.

"You know as well as I the bank doesn't need it. You're no better than the people that engineered the hybrid products in the boiler rooms on Wall Street and in Europe. Screw Main Street and the taxpayers, right?" Frank asked, getting more agitated by the second. Without allowing his boss to answer, Frank stood and gave him an icy stare that could freeze hell over and finally exclaimed, "Heaven help us all!" He then abruptly spun on his heels and walked out of the boardroom with Clarence following close behind.

"What are you going to do now?" Clarence asked.

"Well Clare, I'm going to do what I've been wanting to do for a long time."

"What's that?"

"Write."

"What are you going to write about?"

"Lot's of things. But to begin with, I'll write on how business and the economy used to operate in this country years ago and why and how it's spiraled to its present state. I'll write compelling stories about terrorists and weave sound and logical solutions in my novels to my reading audience through twenty-first century technology and other measures to right our country. You know as well as I, Clare, that we're a republic, and the people of this great nation have the ultimate power to set things right with their vote. And they will need help with technology on how to vote from now on in order to accomplish this. If this doesn't happen then I believe this country, as we know it, will fail in a few years. I just hope there are enough of us out there to stop this."

Frank didn't want to alarm his friend any further. But he couldn't help to think that somehow the decline of the U.S. economic fiscal policies and how the government operated in the past thirty-five years was on a collision course with future terrorists' activities both foreign and domestic, and in some way he had to help.

The two friends exited the elevator and walked through the massive bronze front doors of Steel National Bank of New York, one hopefully for the last time. They stood there on the wide marble steps, facing each other in the chill winds of March. They turned and both looked up at the massive glass and steel tower in the Manhattan district and said their farewells and promises to keep in touch. They took their own paths into the future: one thinking on how to right Steel National Bank of New York, the other pondering the destiny of the United States.

FIFTY

ISLAMABAD, PAKISTAN 2010

Jake placed the call on his satphone, and the deputy secretary picked up on the second ring. "Peterson here." Even though it was 0100 hours Eastern Time, the deputy secretary sounded wide-awake.

"Sir, it's Jake, and I'm afraid that I have some bad news for you. There's been an attempt made on Maria and Mohammed's lives," Jake said solemnly.

"Are they okay?"

"Yes, sir, everybody's fine. At my behest I have placed them in protective custody at the American Embassy in Islamabad."

"Good thinking. Now, is your encryption on?"

"Yes, it is, sir."

"I'll make a follow-up phone call to make sure they stay put," the deputy secretary said. "Now tell me what's going on, Jake."

"Well, sir, three armed assassins dressed like Taliban fighters showed up at the safe house where we where staying earlier today and opened fire on us. We managed to take two of them out, but the other one got away."

"Did you get a good description on the fellow that escaped?"

"No, but I made his truck, and I have to tell you it was a rocket. One second it was parked in front of the safe house, and the next second it was down the block—couldn't even get a shot off." Jake said.

"How about the other two, is either one of them still alive?" Peterson asked.

"I'm afraid not."

"Did you make them?"

"No, sir, but Slade and I are downloading the six security cameras' disks to my laptop, and when it's completed I will send the video streams to Dr. Franks. Perhaps her team can identify them and the truck."

"Now, what did you find from Mohammed?" Peterson queried.

"We received some disturbing news from him, and at times it bordered on the bizarre," Jake said. He told the deputy secretary everything he had heard from Mohammed.

"You're right, Jake, some of this is approaching the twilight zone. Are you sure this information can be trusted?"

"I know it seems pretty strange, but he appears to be quite earnest and forthcoming in his statements. Slade and I have discussed this with Maria, an embassy employee that knows Mohammed and his family quite well, and she indicated that he is an honest and sincere person. Plus he's confirmed what we already know about the terrorists targeting our banking industry, and as you know his background is clean."

The deputy secretary paused on the other end before saying, "Jake, as you already know we have suspected a possible plot against our government to take down one or more of our financial institutions, and that in itself is bad enough. In fact if they pull this off it could lead to financial Armageddon. And now the possibility of phantom corporations, incredible!" The deputy secretary exclaimed. "Look, I want you and Slade to stay in Islamabad for the time being and make sure that security is tight for our friends and to lock down the safe house and its surrounding area. Are the deceased still on site?"

"Yes, I made sure of that. Shortly after we secured the property, Paul called the embassy and after explaining the circumstances requested that they send over a senior official. Two high-level embassy officials arrived and assured us that proper notice had been given to the Pakistani government that gave us the authority to impound the property because of its international repercussions. However, before the Pakistani police left today, we had a minor disagreement whether they had the authority to remove the evidence from the site. We were surprised that they wanted to remove all the evidence first and do forensics later. They probably would have destroyed most of the evidence if they had gotten their wish. In fact, they were so adamant of controlling the situation that district and regional police authority showed up to take command of the scene. If it wasn't for our embassy officials being on site they may have gotten their way."

"Jake, we are now working under extraordinary circumstances that may well cause our nation and the world irreparable harm. As far as the financial take down, I need to know if they're going to do this remotely or on site?" the deputy secretary asked.

"Yeah, that was one of my questions for Mohammed, and he said he didn't know."

"Jake, we need to find this out and soon. This will determine what kind of action we'll take. We also need to identify what institutions they plan to cyber-attack. This is major, Jake. We need to know."

"We'll find out," Jake said and then asked, "What about forensics, sir?"

"We will have a forensic team on site within twelve hours so keep it locked down. Now, is there anything else?"

"That's it for now, sir."

"Good, now get me more information," the deputy secretary said and broke the sat connection.

David Peterson sat back in his leather chair, folded his hands in a tent, and mentally jotted down what needed to be done. First, he would check with Dr. Franks to see if her team had identified the suspects or the truck after she received the information from Jake. He knew the chances were slim. He also knew that the secretary would personally handle the request and put the nation's best forensic team on site as soon as possible. Perhaps with the assassins' DNA evidence from forensics it would give them a better shot. They had been fortunate to confirm that the terrorists were targeting U.S. financial institutions and that they were using sham companies to funnel their illicit gains from their gun running activities. If there were enough of them it could cause a worldwide economic meltdown. Once the secretary was privy to all the troubling news, she would escalate it to cabinet level decisions and the threat advisory, no doubt, would be put on red. David shook his head and thought, *Our government needs to move on this fast or God help us! The country has the technology to do it, but do we have enough time?*

FIFTY-ONE

OGDEN, UTAH 2010

The day after Bill Sorenson flew back from Washington D.C., after meeting with the other agency directors arranged by the secretary of Homeland Security, Mary Knappa, he called his assistant director, Jim Coffey, into his office.

"Jim, how's it going this morning?" the regional director asked.

"Bill, the bigger question is what did you find out at the meeting yesterday?" Jim asked. "I'm sure we are looking at a very serious situation, otherwise there wouldn't have been an agency summit."

"Before we start, would you like some Costa Rican coffee that Jill and I brought back from our last vacation?"

"Yeah, that would be great."

Bill poured a cup for his friend and began. "Speaking of vacations, there won't be any until we finish this investigation."

"I knew that was coming. Now what's going on, Bill?" Jim asked as he took a sip of the dark roasted coffee.

"Before I brief you on the Jamosa investigation, I want to inform you on the summit meeting. DHS Secretary, Mary Knappa, chaired the meeting and indicated that there is now a worldwide effort underway to stop this insidious threat and that DHS has now elevated the threat advisory system to its maximum level, red. Jim, we have never been on this alert level before. In fact, the secretary, after conferring with the other cabinet members, will advise the president to request that the other G20 nations follow our lead. All of the world's developed nations' governments, law enforcement, and intelligence agencies will be put on high alert. The countries' agencies range from Interpol to the legendary Israeli Massod."

"Wow, world-wide effort. This is more serious than I expected." Jim intoned.

"Like Mary Knappa said, if the terrorists get their way, it'll create a domino effect in taking out most if not all of the world's economic infrastructures. It doesn't matter which advanced country the terrorists target, the end result will be the same. And this isn't all of it."

"What are you saying?" Jim asked.

"Now brace yourself because what I'm about to tell you will seem a bit strange. We finally got a break on Felix Jamosa. The reason why Gene and Ted were having so much trouble finding any evidence on off-shore accounts connected to Jamosa Enterprises was because Jamosa's international shell companies are buried within phantom corporations that have deceased corporate officers running them."

"What did you just say?" Jim exclaimed.

"You heard me. It appears that some of the deceased corporate officials where at one time part of the mujahideen resisting the Marxist People's Democratic Party of Afghanistan (PDPA) during the Soviet-Afghan war in the late 1980s."

"Bill, this is getting stranger by the minute."

"I know. Apparently Felix Jamosa and Jeffery Starr think by installing deceased people to do their business it will shield them from prying eyes. And as crazy as it sounds, it does have a sort of peculiar logic to it. The reasoning goes that if their phantom corporations come under governmental scrutiny they can hide behind these corporate officials and still maintain control. After all, it's pretty difficult to subpoena dead people."

"That's crazy," Jim said. "Besides, I'm sure they're breaking numerous laws by doing this."

"That's probably true," Sorenson stated. "But don't forget their primary reason is to hide their illicit gains from their arms business, and if anyone gets too close they can pull the plug and vanish without a trace. And to make matters worse, even if we find them I'm not sure how the government would prosecute since I don't believe we have regulations and laws that cover this; our legal system hasn't caught up to the technology yet."

"I see your point, Bill. But how on earth does he do it?" Jim asked.

"We're not sure yet, but I'm sure it's not through the heavens."

They both chuckled and Bill continued, "Apparently the boys over at DHS got a break when a disenchanted Muslim stepped forward and blew the whistle on Mr. Jamosa and friends. What we've been able to cobble together is that they use extremely sophisticated AI and communications software and hardware in order to pull this off."

"Incredible!" Jim exclaimed.

Sorenson took another sip of his coffee and continued. "Wait! You haven't heard the rest of it, and it is downright frightening. If this is the medium Mr. Jamosa uses to launder his arms revenue we see no reason why these phantom corporations cannot run on the world's stock exchanges."

"You have to be kidding!" Jim exclaimed again.

"No, and this allows them to basically control the movement of shares on the exchanges through their illicit revenues and provides them with a steady stream of profit through their investments. And if they disappear—well you can imagine the losses that will occur for the shareholders, governments, and businesses. Now this begs the question: if they're doing it, who else is?"

"My God, Bill, this sounds like an episode from the *X-files* or *Fringe*," Jim said.

"I agree. Now this is what we need to do. Dr. James and your team will continue to work together to help solve Jamosa's tax evasion case. Dr. James's team will provide the IT expertise to help your team to identify the deceased mujahideen that are involved in this scheme. Also, the agency has budgeted extra funds to hire outside experts from the private sector to help us in this investigation. Frank Mulligan will be introduced at tomorrow morning's meeting and will be assigned to your team, Jim."

"What does he do and who is he?"

"He thinks outside the box, and for this case that's exactly what we need." Bill fiddled with a pen on his desk and thought what he would say next. He knew that he needed to broach this topic delicately since Jim's brother's position was recently outsourced at Siemens. "Look, no offense to you or your team or even the agency, but you know as well as I we're basically auditors. Granted we're experts at tax evasion and do our work extremely well, but at the end of the day we're still bean counters. Frank has a vast amount of business and finance experience going back nearly four decades, and he knows all the nuances on how corporations work to deceive governments and their shareholders."

"We also pride ourselves for going beyond the borders," Jim said.

"Yes we do, and don't get me wrong, but we don't have the experience this guy has. He not only thinks beyond the box, but beyond the beyond. Frank is well educated and came up through the ranks with his shirt sleeves rolled up. There wasn't any free lunches or influential relatives or friends that helped grease the skids for him. Just to show you how tough and ethical this man is he resigned his last position as CFO of Steel National Bank of New York after uncovering numerous violations that the bank had made against the regulatory agencies. In my book that takes guts. Jim, he's not here to take anyone's job. He's only here as an outside consultant to help us unravel this mystery. Understood?"

"Understood, boss."

"Now get together with Dr. James and let's see if we can crack this walnut."

"Bill, you can count on that, and I'll see you at tomorrow's meeting."

"Ciao, my friend."

After Jim left his office, the regional director pushed his coffee aside, stood and walked over to the bank of windows and peered out. Off in the distance he could see the Wasatch Mountains looming large with their mantle of glistening white snow shadowed by the sun reaching for the sky. Spring was at nature's doorstep, and the mountain range looked particularly beautiful this time of year, especially with the sun peeking behind. He didn't want to alarm Jim with too much information on the bigger problem. He knew he already had his plate full on Jamosa's tax evasion inquiry. Bill thought that Jim, even for a person in his position and background, was still struggling to get his mind around the concept of phantom corporations, let alone fathom the intricacies of toppling our financial institutions. One thing Bill questioned: Was technology moving too quickly?

FIFTY-TWO

PORTLAND, OREGON 2010

"I gather the papers that I sent you were in order," Felix said. "We had no problem getting through customs in Seattle. The documentation was very authentic," Al-Hadi offered. "The connecting flight to Portland was short. I didn't realize how close the two cities were to one another."

"Yeah, only about 180 miles apart," Jeffery added.

"How was flight from Riyadh?" Felix asked.

"It was too long and tiresome, even in first class, and I'm getting too old to hop around the world anymore. Besides, the food isn't as good as it once was, and they're too many rude passengers," Al-Hadi complained.

Seyed chuckled and said, "Come on it can't be that bad. Besides, we're here now so let's relax and enjoy our stay and take in the beauty of the Pacific Northwest."

As the conversation continued between the four terrorists, Felix decided while driving back from Portland International Airport he would take a side trip before discussing business. It was such a beautiful spring day he couldn't resist showing his guests how truly impressive the Northwest was. Perhaps by showing Al-Hadi the Washington Park Botanical Gardens on a beautiful day it would put him in a better mood.

As they drove past the tennis courts and wound through the gardens, Jeffery pointed to the rows of beautifully manicured roses and said, "Now this is paradise."

After parking the Escalade and all four exiting the car for the view, Felix pointed toward the City of Roses with Mt. Hood and its mantle of snow framed in the background and said, "Well, what do you think of this picture?"

"Praise be to Allah!" Al-Hadi exclaimed. "What a view. I've heard so much about Portland with its progressive nature and MAX, its transportation system, but I didn't realize how beautiful the city was. You are fortunate to live in such a place."

"Yes, we are," Felix said and pointed again. "Do you see that silver and charcoal colored building down there gleaming in the afternoon sun?"

As Al-Hadi and Seyed peered into the distance at downtown Portland, Seyed motioned and asked, "Is that Jamosa Enterprises?"

"Yes, it is. Forty-three stories of office space, retail shops, and condominiums," Felix proudly offered.

"Very nice," Al-Hadi said. "Now where are we staying, Felix? I've heard that Portland has some rather nice hotels."

"I've reserved a couple of nice suites at the Benson Hotel, and it's within walking distance to the company. The Benson is a Portland landmark and still retains historic touches of its past, which I believe both of you will enjoy. I'll drop you off shortly and then swing by later at 7:00 p.m. for dinner. My secretary reserved a small banquet room at Ruth's Chris steakhouse."

"Will we be meeting anyone else for dinner?" Seyed asked.

"Not on this trip. It's strictly business, and I'm quite intrigued and anxious to look at your offer," Felix said, as he motioned for them to head up the hill to the car.

"Look at all these rows of beautiful roses. Is this a garden for research?" Al-Hadi asked as he lit up a cigarette.

"Yes, the gardens are used for the study, education, and conservation of rare and exotic plants. See that dome over there?" Felix pointed to a gray object situated in the center of the gardens. "That structure features hundreds of varieties of tropical foliage from Africa, Asia, and South America."

"I see why some of the plants are enclosed. Your climate is much too cold for sub tropical and tropical species," Seyed said as he opened the driver side rear door for Al-Hadi.

"Yeah, we're just above the forty-five parallel in the Northern Hemisphere, and Portland gets its share of snow and ice in the winters here. Its usually not much, but enough to screw up traffic," Jeffery added.

"Our problem with weather is heat and sand storms," Seyed lamented. "The stuff can be a nightmare for automobiles, air conditioning, and in fact, with all non-sealed machinery."

"We rarely have that problem except when one of the Cascade peaks decides to erupt," Felix said as he slid into the driver's seat.

"Yeah, I heard about Mt Saint Helens erupting in May of 1980 when I was studying for my electrical engineering degree at the University of Southern California. I was amazed at the pictures; thousands of acres of timber were blown down as if they were matchsticks. You were extremely fortunate for not losing more people," Al-Hadi said.

"We were somewhat prepared. The geologists had warned everyone to stay off the mountain a month before the eruption. But of course, some never listened," Felix answered as he wheeled the big Escalade out of the Botanical Gardens parking lot.

As Felix drove to the Benson Hotel, Seyed fell to silence and thought about how to approach Felix and Jeffery with their scheme. The meeting was to occur tomorrow and Seyed didn't relish the fact that he and Al-Hadi would be maneuvering through a mind field in order to avoid a firestorm with the gunrunners. He and Al-Hadi had to be on their best behavior and avoid any conflict if possible. He was particularly concerned with Felix's demeanor and knew that the big American could erupt with the slightest provocation.

FIFTY-THREE

OGDEN, UTAH 2010

S teve Kronoski waited until everyone was comfortable before he began the meeting. They had all just left the morning meeting with the assistant director, Jim Coffey, and they were still trying to wrap their minds around what they had heard.

Gene spoke first, "You're right, this is absolutely incredible! Now I know why Ted and I had been at a loss trying to find offshore accounts connected with Jamosa Enterprises." Gene turned to Frank and asked, "What are your ideas on this?"

Frank stood with difficulty and ran a hand through his thinning salt and pepper hair. He went to the whiteboard and listed a few bullet points and a rough flowchart to aid him in his explanation. As he pointed to the top item he said, "First, we need to get the names of the deceased mujahideen freedom fighters during the Soviet-Afghan war from DHS. Then we need to provide this list of names to Dr. James so his team can compare the deceased names to all corporate officials listed for corporations and companies in the Middle East. I'd start with Afghanistan since this is where the conflict occurred, and it's probably the most under-developed country in the Middle East. I would surmise that their government isn't very sophisticated or advanced and can easily fall victim to unscrupulous people like Mr. Jamosa."

"Mr. Mulligan, don't we have to search public records for death certificates?" Ted Hamilton asked.

"Yes, we do. Please call me Frank."

"Yes, sir."

"We'll search for death certificates, but you have to realize that people vanish in third world countries all the time and without a trace of formal documentation of their disappearance or death. And that's why it's critical for DHS to provide us with a list of deceased freedom fighters. Even when we get this list we still won't be able to link Jamosa Enterprises to these people or corporations. Our Muslim friend will have to do that, and I sure hope he is kept safe."

Frank was about to point to another bullet item on the whiteboard when Sheila Jacobson, a newer member of the team, asked, "In your estimation how do you think they're running these phantom corporations?"

"Like the assistant director said this morning, we believe that they have developed sophisticated software and hardware to mimic their corporations as real companies."

Sheila pressed on, "But how do they actually do this? I mean, if we were to look at their day-to-day operations it must be mind boggling."

"You're right. The technology behind this is phenomenal, and I for one would like to meet the person behind all of this. This is one smart individual."

"Frank, you said earlier even when we get the list of deceased corporate officials and the names of the corporations we still couldn't link Jamosa Enterprises without the help of our Muslim friend. Couldn't we trace backwards from the corporation's paper flow for evidence?"

"That's a good question, Sheila. And if you bare with me I will go over the remaining items that I have listed." Frank absent-mindedly massaged the discomfort in his right hip before he began. "There are five basic ways of sending mail including official corporate documents to the affected country's government and regulatory agencies. You can use e-mail, snail mail, fax, personal courier or a private mailing service such as FedEx. The last three can be pretty much ruled out. They're too cumbersome, and in the case of a courier or private mailing service you're adding an extra element in the form of a live person or company, and that person or mailing company can be traced. In my estimation I would use either e-mail or a country's postal service. In the case of physical mail, one can mail from anywhere in the world by simply dropping the documents in a mail receptacle without human intervention. Though the package origination and receiving points are documented, and this creates a trail. In my opinion, I believe using e-mail would be the safest bet if it were properly precipitated. I took the liberty to consult an old friend of mine last night to discuss the matter. He indicated under normal circumstances that e-mail addresses could be traced back to the physical location where the e-mail was initiated. However, technology being what it is, he also stated one can set up a botnet running physical and virtual servers where the virtual servers can prey on other physical servers on the Internet, in order to collect the physical server's address via scripted software and then e-mail documents from that address." Frank now looked at everyone to measure their reactions and said, "Does everyone understand?"

"Kind of," Sheila said with a glazed look in her eyes. "How does the process work?"

"I'll explain again at another time." Frank turned and pointed to the next item on the list. The terrorists also use a very sophisticated telecommunications service that allows them to send and receive voicemail without actually being there. This also holds true for three-dimensional holographic representation of human like avatars. Taken together this enables them to run companies with deceased corporate officials. We don't know all the individual pieces yet that make up this puzzle, but this is basically how they operate. And like the assistant director said, it does have an elegance to it. The big question I have is why don't they use fictitious names instead of deceased soldiers? It doesn't make sense. Are there any questions?"

Frank looked around the room and could tell everyone was thinking the same thing. How could this be?

Finally, Steve stepped in and asked, "Dr. James, is there anything you would like to say?"

"No, we're all set. Our team needs to search Afghanistan's public corporate records and build a database based on corporate company names and their corporate officials. Once we get the list from DHS we can then match the deceased names against our database."

"Okay, everyone, let's get to work and solve this mystery."

Steve motioned to Frank, "Can you hang back a minute or two?"

"Sure, what's on your mind, Steve?"

FIFTY-FOUR

PORTLAND, OREGON 2010

At 10:00 a.m. sharp the next morning, Al-Hadi and Seyed arrived at Jamosa Enterprises and Al-Hadi used the temporary security card given to him by Felix for use of the express elevator. In moments they were on the forty-third floor, moving toward the offices of Jamosa Enterprises. They went through the double doors and stood at the reception desk. Soon, a person arrived from one of the interior offices and introduced herself, "Gentlemen, I'm Ms. Hill, Mr. Jamosa's executive secretary."

"Ms. Hill, this is Dr. Seyed Mostakavi, and I am Mr. Al-Hadi Zafar, and we're here to see Felix Jamosa," Al-Hadi said with a smile.

"It's nice to meet you both," Molly said. "Can I offer you any refreshments?"

"How about some Cascadian bottled water," Seyed said. "I hear the Northwest has some of the best water in the world."

"I don't know about that," Molly said. "But it is really good. Please have a seat, and I'll bring some." Molly motioned for the two to take a seat on one of the dark brown leather couches across from her desk.

Felix, hearing the conversation, came out of his office and told Molly he would take care of it. After Felix collected Jeffery from one of the interior offices, all four stepped through the office's outer mahogany framed double glass doors and walked to the express elevator next to the regular elevators. Felix slid the dual smart card into the electronic card reader below the biometric fingerprint screen and pressed his right hand to the biometric glass plate and the elevator's door opened. After arriving on the forty-fourth floor, Al-Hadi asked, "Why all the secrecy, Felix?"

"I've taken great pains to design this building in such a way that to the casual observer there are forty-three floors. Even the express elevator doesn't show a forty-fourth floor. Exterior wise, the forty-fourth floor is camouflaged with two-inch thick titanium tungsten louvers with Kevlar and Ceramic technology. They're heat and armor-piercing resistant, and to this day I hate to think how much money I've invested in them. I've also swapped the building's original architectural drawings with plans showing only forty-three floors."

"Why bother?" Seyed asked.

"As you know, in addition to my textile business, I have an arms business. If the government comes looking they will have a hard time finding me. Who would ever look for me here?"

"I don't know," Seyed mused.

Al-Hadi looked at the two massive steel doors with ten-foot setbacks on each side of the elevator and asked, "Felix, what are these doors?"

"Well, let me show you." Felix swiped his security card across a tiny square embedded in the reinforced concrete wall, and the steel door slid downward into the concrete slab. Felix extended his right hand and said, "Gentlemen, welcome to my redoubt."

"Ah, a virtual fortress. I see the rumors are true." Al-Hadi exclaimed.

"Yes, they are," Felix said. "Gentlemen, this is my castle."

"Seyed mentioned that you had built an armed fortress, but I had no idea—" Al-Hadi's words trailed off as he looked around.

"Straight ahead you'll see Browning 50 caliber cannons on there own movable, rotating stanchions. Over there," Felix pointed, "are M61 Vulcan 20 mm Gatling guns, on movable turrets, firing nearly 6,000 rounds per minute. Further down are mounted RPG units with depleted uranium and magnesium rounds. Still further are mounted FGM-148 Javelin surface-to-surface and surface-to-air laser guided missiles with soft launch systems, which enables me to launch them within the confines of this space and not worry about blow back. These babies will stop a fully armored Cobra or Apache helo or an M1A3 Abrams tank in its tracks." Felix walked over to the other door and swiped his card, and the steel door disappeared into the floor. "In here are boxes of Kalashnikov AK-47s and Heckler-Koch HK G36 assault rifles with thousands of rounds of DU/magnesium and standard ammo. I also have gun turrets, arms, and ammo stashed all around the forty-fourth floor perimeter and reinforced steel doors are placed every two hundred and fifty feet for blast zones. The doors, louvers, and most of the mounted ordnance are controlled remotely, and the doors can be opened or closed section by section."

"What are those grooves or channels in the floor?" Al-Hadi asked, and before he received an answer he turned to Seyed and said, "Why didn't you tell me more about this place?"

"Felix doesn't exactly want this to be common knowledge," Seyed explained.

"I'm your friend; not just anyone!" Al-Hadi exclaimed. "You can trust me you know."

Before Seyed could answer Al- Hadi continued. "I've heard of Charlie Wilson's private war, but I think you've taken it to a new level. It looks like you have enough firepower to take out Portland if you really wanted to," Al-Hadi said in amazement.

Felix ignored Al-Hadi's last remark, looked at Seyed and said, "Since we're all here you might as well tell him the story behind this."

So much for being gracious, Seyed thought.

FIFTY-FIVE

ISLAMABAD, PAKISTAN 2010

The April sun was approaching the crest of the Margalla Hills when Jake and Slade landed in Islamabad on an urgent message from Paul Paulson. During the flight Jake had been thinking about Zoey and the fact that he very seldom saw her anymore. They had known each other for over a year, and the few times that they were together it was though the magic had never left them, although she seemed a little reserved as of late. He and Slade were so busy with the Jamosa investigation and the threat of a cyber-attack against the United States' financial institutions that there was very little time to do anything else. He would make it up to her.

Maria and Mohammed had been guests of the American Embassy for the last five weeks, ever since there had been an assassination attempt on their lives. The DHS agents had already checked into a hotel near the ambassador's residence and had just arrived at the first security checkpoint in their rental car. Ordinarily, when on embassy business, embassy officials would have escorted them to the residence. But they were going to stay a few days and also check to see how Mohammed's mother and sister were doing. While waiting at the gate for verification, Jake could see razor wire bristling in the late afternoon sun, sitting atop ten-foot high concrete barriers. He knew they were at the outer security perimeter just from looking at the ground. It was littered with cans, wrappers, and cigarette butts surrounding a cardboard like wood structure posing as a security shack. The Pakistani police and paramilitary had the responsibility for securing the outer checkpoints. The U.S. military had far too much pride and discipline to manage an area uncombed as this.

After going through a maze of similar concrete structures and checkpoints, each one tidier than the last, they finally reached the main gate. They saluted and identified themselves to a Marine in crisp, clean fatigues and complimented the soldier on his military protocol and politeness. After the guard checked their identifications and names on the visitor's log, he waved them through. As they drove inside the embassy compound, they could see a modern, u-shaped, two-story concrete building that appeared to have Kevlar embedded bulletproof glass for windows. The building was constructed in 1980 after the old American Embassy was burnt to the ground. In 1979, Pakistani students enraged by a radio report claiming the United States had bombed the Masjid al-Haram; Islam's holy site at Mecca, they had rioted and destroyed the old facility. There actually had been a terrorist attack, but the United States wasn't involved. After parking in a designated spot, two U.S. marines escorted them to a large, well-appointed reception area and asked them to wait while the receptionist contacted their embassy official. Before taking their seats, Jake and Slade saluted the two Marines and thanked them for their courtesy before they left. An embassy employee came over and asked them if they would like any refreshments while they waited. They declined, and she walked away. Jake turned to Slade and said, "Boy, wasn't she hot!"

"Don't you ever give up, buddy?" Slade asked.

Jake replied with his famous crooked smile, "Well, I'm thinking about adding another muscle car to my stable and—"

Slade cut in and said, "Adding another concubine to your harem."

"Good morning, gentlemen," Paul said, as he walked up to the two agents. "Did I miss something interesting?"

"No, not exactly," Jake quickly added. In a rare moment of self-consciousness he looked at Slade as if to say, "you take the lead."

"Paul, you sounded pretty excited on the phone when you called us earlier yesterday."

Paul looked at the two agents. "Yes, it appears Mohammed has more information for you."

"I hope it's about the U.S. targets the terrorists are planning to hit," Jake said quietly as the agents stood and shook Paul's hand.

"He didn't say, but he sure wants to talk to you fellas."

"Where is he?" Jake asked.

"Follow me. He's tucked away in a small conference room on the second floor."

After the two DHS agents shook hands with Mohammed and took their seats opposite to him in the small conference room, Paul asked if they wanted anything else besides espresso and water.

"How about some of those wonderful Pakistani pastries?" Slade asked.

"I'll have Maria bring some from the kitchen," Paul offered as he left.

Slade poured himself some dark Turkish espresso from the carafe while Jake helped himself to some ice water.

"Well, Mo, how's the embassy been treating you?" Jake asked.

"Too good, I'm afraid. I've put on a few pounds in the last month. But I am worried about my mother and sister. Even though I've been in contact with them by telephone, I'm still concerned." Mohammed said with an anxious look on his face.

"They're fine. We have a team of agents and Pakistani authorities watching them around the clock," Jake indicated and continued. "As a matter of fact, Slade and I will be visiting your mother and sister tomorrow to make sure they're all right and to see if they need anything."

"Can I come along?"

"Mo, it wouldn't be wise at this point," Jake said. "For all we know there might be people waiting for you to leave the embassy. No, I think you should stay here, for the time being, where security is tight."

"Have you found out who was trying to kill us?"

"Not yet, but we're working on it, Mo. And that's another reason why you need to stay put," Jake added.

Just then there was a quiet knock, and Slade went to the door and answered, "Come in."

Maria stepped through the door with a silver-serving tray loaded with pastries, another carafe of espresso, and three fresh glasses of ice water. As Slade held the door open, Jake stood, walked over, and took the tray while saying hello to her. He placed the tray on the table while Maria took a seat. After they had enjoyed some pastries, fresh espresso, and small talk, Maria excused herself.

After she left, Jake turned back to Mo and asked, "What's going on?"

"You remember the last time we spoke?"

"How could I forget, we had such a lively party going on," Jake quipped with a chuckle.

"The night I was on the patio at Seyed's house I now remember exactly what Felix and Seyed had been talking about. Like I said before, Felix was having trouble with a couple of holograms, and Seyed asked him specifically if it was the avatars representing Dimitri Gelashvili and Noe Lomidze. After he found out it was those two he really got upset. He told Felix not to use those because they were new and had some software glitches."

"Do you know which corporations were tied to the names?" Jake asked.

"No."

"Do you know where the companies are?" Slade added.

"No, just those two names," Mohammed replied.

"Did he say anything else? Did he mention anything about which U.S. financial institutions they were targeting?" Jake asked.

"No, they were only speaking about the phantom corporations and avatars."

"Okay, at least now we have a starting point, Mo, and thanks for your help." Jake said.

"When will Maria and I be released from protective custody?"

"As I said before it may take a while. We still need to tie up some loose ends and then you should be good to go." Jake said.

"I do have an important question though, and that's why I wanted you to come in person." He hesitated.

"Fire away," Jake said.

"I was also wondering if the United States could put my family and I on refugee status and send us to the United States so we could apply for asylum in your country."

"That's an excellent question, Mo, and I don't see why not. Do you have any relatives living in the states that could sponsor you?" Jake inquired.

"I have an uncle and aunt living in Bellingham, Washington."

"Excellent. We'll bring it to Paul's attention and see if we can get the process started," Jake said.

Slade picked up the house phone on the table and dialed Paul's extension. "I think we're ready to go, buddy."

"Be right up."

All three stood and Mohammed thanked them for being so kind. Jake stepped up and shook Mohammed's hand and said, "No, it's Slade and I and our country that should be thankful. You have provided us with some crucial information, and we won't forget that."

As Paul and Maria re-entered the room, the two DHS agents said their good-byes. On their way out Jake mentioned to Paul to check to see if it was possible for Mohammed, his mother and sister to gain refugee status and asylum in the United States.

"I'll look into it," Paul said. "Is there anything else you guys need?"

"Please make sure they continue to be well protected. I wouldn't want anything to happen to them." Jake said.

Paul looked at his friend in a respectful manner and said, "Don't worry as long as I'm here they'll be well taken care of."

"Thanks, Paul. I knew I could count on you." Jake said in a sincere voice.

At the front door, they all saluted each other, and Paul watched as two Marines escorted the two agents to their car. After driving through the embassy checkpoints and heading back to their hotel, Slade turned to Jake and said, "I sure hope our government grants Mohammed's wishes."

"I do too, buddy. But we have bigger fish to fry right now."

"I hear you, pal. We need to call our boss and apprise him of the situation," Slade said.

They drove in silence the rest of the way back to the hotel. Jake realized, even though they had a handle on the sham corporations, a much bigger and more terrifying problem was still in front of them.

FIFTY-SIX

PORTLAND, OREGON 2010

Seyed looked at his friend, and Al-Hadi nodded for him to begin the story.

"Remember four years ago when Abrahim Solasti had to leave on personal business?"

"Yes, go on." Al-Hadi motioned.

"Well it wasn't personal. I had Abrahim and a hand picked team of software and hardware engineers fly over here on Felix's request. Abrahim and his team worked with Felix and Jeffery to come up with a system to automate their armament so it could be controlled remotely. They designed the hardware and software with help from the team to make all this possible," Seyed said, as he motioned at all the equipment in front of them.

"I assume that you had Abrahim working for you in Iran on your nuclear reactor project?" Al-Hadi replied.

"No, he was over here," Seyed corrected. "And what they came up with was nothing short of brilliance. As far as I know, you're looking at the first fully automated AI, remote controlled armament system in the world."

"There are armed drones that operate remotely," Al-Hadi offered.

"I'm talking about an armed fortress, sir."

"Okay, please go on. How's this place work?" Al-Hadi asked.

"You're not going to believe what you are about to hear." Seyed said.

"Let me do the deciding," Al-Hadi said.

"There's a control room, a bunker if you will, with monitors below the building's sub basement. The bunker is hard wired to the forty-fourth floor. The system can also be operated remotely up to ten miles with hand-held devices using underground radio technology. These UGR devices operate on very low frequency signals in the three-to-thirty kilohertz range and use digital audio compression technology to send wireless voice and data messages."

"Why the overkill? Can't you use regular Radio Frequency technology?" Al-Hadi puzzled.

"No, because of all the concrete and steel in the urban areas," Seyed replied.

"Oh, I see. You need to transmit through buildings." Al-Hadi said, as the light turned on.

"That's correct."

"But you said that you can transmit up to ten miles?" Al-Hadi said with a confused look on his face. "How can you do that?"

"Yes. As you know we've been developing nano technology. This has allowed us to transmit digital packets of information on a molecular scale, which has allowed us to greatly increase the transmission range. And we have also found that the range and jamming capabilities are inversely proportional to the size of the digital packets. The smaller the packet, the better the range and it is more difficult to interrupt the signal."

"Unbelievable!" Al-Hadi exclaimed.

Seyed continued. "The mounted weapons not only rotate, but also can run laterally on their embedded steel tracks in the concrete floors. The channel system allows the weapons to move and lock into place every twenty-five feet. When they run out of ammo, they move to their respective collection points, reload, and continue firing."

"Amazing. Felix, what are you trying to do, go out in a blaze of glory?" Al-Hadi asked.

"Look, the government is trying to quash my arms business, and I will not tolerate it! Jeffery and I have worked too long and hard to go down without a fight. Besides, it's a great tool to promote the gun business." Felix swiped both embedded squares, and the steel doors rose and closed with a soft hiss. He walked down a short hall opposite the elevator and slid his security card into the concrete wall adjacent to an eight-foot reinforced steel door. After it opened, he invited his guests inside.

"Now, this is impressive," Al-Hadi said. "This is nicer then your place, Seyed."

"Sure looks to be," Seyed mused as he looked around. The massive great room had twenty-five foot ceilings, reinforced Kevlar skylights and a massive native stone, floor-to-ceiling gas fireplace.

"How large is this place?" Seyed asked.

"About ten thousand square feet," Felix answered as he swept his hand around and continued. "In addition to the great room, it has four large bedrooms with six tumbled stone bathrooms, state-of-the-art movie theater, two offices, exercise room, game room, conference room, dining room, library, a large professional kitchen and weapons storage. The mechanicals are on the backside of the complex, which controls heating, ventilation, air conditioning, sound, lighting and security."

"You're right. You do have a castle up here. Like I said, Seyed's house is very nice, but this is incredible. And to think it is all hidden and protected!" Al-Hadi exclaimed.

"Yes, it is. Now would you like some refreshments before we get down to business?" Felix asked.

"Still waiting for some Cascadian water," Seyed said.

"How about you, Al-Hadi?"

"Anything stronger? Perhaps a whiskey sour?"

"Sure."

"Jeff?"

"I'll have some Cascadian water too."

"Jeffery, why don't you take our guests into the conference room while I attend to the refreshments," Felix directed.

Felix went to the bar in the corner of the great room to fix the refreshments including a martini. He needed one. He was thinking on how he was going to turn the tables on Al-Hadi and Seyed. He was mad that they had alluded to his bungling on the Russian/Georgia conflict, and he sure as hell didn't like to be threatened or blackmailed. If he were forced to tell Jeffery about his screw up, his brother-in-law wouldn't be too happy to hear about it. In fact, Jeffery would probably be outraged; he knew it would take time to heal the rift. He hoped that it wouldn't get back to the family. "Damn Arabs and their deceitful ways!" he swore. Well he had some knowledge on their crap too. And if needed he would divulge it during the meeting and sit back and see if he could get any mileage from it. He would have to see how it plays out. He just hoped that Jeff would back him up if needed.

FIFTY-SEVEN

ISLAMABAD, PAKISTAN 2010

Returning to his hotel room, Jake picked up his satphone and was about to call the deputy secretary when he heard Slade say, "Hold it. It's 0300 hours Eastern Time. Do you really want to call at this hour?"

"I guess not. It can wait a couple hours. In the meantime I guess I'll continue to work on those dreaded government reports." Jake said.

"Yeah, I suppose I'll do the same. I'll see you at dinner, buddy."

At 0600 hours Eastern Time Jake called the deputy secretary. "Good morning, sir."

"How are you, Jake?" the deputy secretary replied.

"I'm fine, sir." Jake was surprised that his boss didn't launch in to the business at hand – he usually does."

"Is your encryption on?" the deputy secretary asked.

"Always, sir."

"Go ahead, what do we have?"

"Slade and I spoke with Mohammed at the embassy earlier today, and he graced us with some fortuitous news. As it turned out, he remembered a couple of the deceased corporate officials' names that could possibly tie Felix and Jamosa Enterprises to his sham corporations."

"Who are they?"

"Dimitri Gelashveli and Noe Lomidze."

"Wait a minute, Jake," the deputy secretary said. "Aren't these Georgian surnames?"

"You're right. Why didn't I think of this? Christ, we're on to something now." Jake agreed.

"Yeah, we have been beating ourselves up in the wrong place. It makes sense now since Felix stuck his nose into the Russian/Georgia conflict some time ago. Did Mohammed know the company's name?" Peterson asked.

"No, sir, he only mentioned the two surnames."

"Did he say anything about which financial institutions the terrorist were targeting and the method they were using? Remotely or on site?" the deputy secretary pressed.

"I asked him, and he didn't know."

"Okay, Jake, good job," Peterson said. "We'll start working on this and also forward the information to the affected agencies. We'll get these men."

Jake and his boss then discussed the forensics on the two dead assassins that had attacked the safe house in Islamabad and found nothing unusual outside of the fact that they were low-level al-Qaeda operatives hired by an obscure shadow group. Peterson persisted, "there's a connection here somewhere—I can smell it."

"I know, sir. Should Slade and I pursue this?"

The deputy director thought for a moment. "Jake, I want you guys to nose around while you're still in Islamabad and be sure to pay particular attention to Mohammed's mother and sister. If needed we can always move them to the embassy."

"I think they're fine, sir. We'll be checking on them and their security tomorrow. If we find a wind of doubt we won't hesitate to move them." Jake said.

"Any piece of information will help. You never know what angle it will provide, and it can possibly lead to more information." Peterson surmised.

"That's true," Jake agreed. He then asked if it was possible for Mohammed and his family to be given asylum in the states because of the extreme danger they were in.

"Jake, that's all fine and well, but as you know we don't handle refugee or asylum business through the agency."

"I know, sir. But if it helps to give them a recommendation, can we at least do so?" Jake inquired.

"I suppose," the deputy secretary answered, and then continued. "I want you and Slade back here next week. You'll be receiving your orders tomorrow. In the meantime, check things out and make sure our friends are safe. Understood?"

"Understood, sir."

"Good. I believe it's about dinnertime for you and Slade, so have a good Pakistani meal on me," the deputy secretary said, breaking the sat connection.

Jake knew when he and Slade got back to headquarters there would be a high-level meeting to discuss what they already knew and what still needed to be done. He was still concerned about who ordered the hit on Mohammed and Maria. If he found who was responsible he would make it personal. He was grateful for the information that Mohammed gave them and knew that it would be sent to the IRS division in Ogden, Utah and the FBI. He also knew that the tax auditors were looking for a key that would break open the Jamosa investigation, and he was more than happy to help them. But he was worried about the bigger problem. They still didn't know what targets were going to be hit. And just as important, when were they going to strike, and would it be from a remote location or on site?

Just then his satphone chimed, and he answered on the second ring, "Jake here."

"Hi, babe!" Zoey chirped.

"Well I'll be darned, if it isn't Zip. How are you, my sweets?" Jake asked.

"Fine, especially after our little tryst at Chesapeake Bay. I just wanted to call and thank you for the lovely weekend. You were such a gentleman."

"I hope I was more than that!" Jake exclaimed.

"You could never know."

I'm finally off the hook, he thought. "What do I owe the honor of your call?" Jake asked. "I know you better than you think."

Zoey sighed. "Hon, as you know I'm the operation manager for Fidelity Investments in Boston, Massachusetts. The other day, Doug Little, one of our senior investment advisers came to me with an interesting story. It seems one of his clients called him on an error he discovered on his last statement. The error was minor, and the client claimed Fidelity's accounting statement for the period of January through March of 2010 shorted his fund by $1.33. He indicated to Doug that he double-checked and still came up $1.33 short. This in itself would not pose any significant problem, but since then I have looked into some other accounts and have discovered the same thing. The funds are always shorted, never over, and they are all inactive accounts. I wouldn't have even mentioned this to you, but I have been on edge ever since our country has put the threat advisory system on red."

"What do you mean by inactive accounts?" Jake asked.

"They're usually small accounts held by our clients used for expenses and other purposes, and they usually have very little activity." Zoey replied.

"How long has this been going on?"

"Not too long, as far as I know. I've looked back on some of our smaller funds and accounts for the last year and discovered the anomalies only started to appear during our last accounting cycle. Do you have any ideas, sweetheart?" Zoey asked.

"No, not with more data. If I understood you, your statement cycles for most of your accounts run every three months. Is this correct?"

"Yes, it is," Zoey offered.

"Normally, I wouldn't stick my nose into your business. But with everything going on, it may be prudent. Going forward I want you to investigate and capture all anomalies on all of Fidelity's accounts for your branches in the Boston area for the next few weeks. Zoey, can you do that or am I asking too much?"

"Jake, without any formal or legal warrants, you're way out of line. But like you said with everything happening there may be a connection. I think I need to afford both of us wide latitude in this situation."

"I know this is asking a lot from you, Zip. And I also know that it could put your job into jeopardy, especially since this is being done unofficially. But if anything happens I will step up to the plate for you."

"That's all I wanted to know." Zoey said.

"I'm sorry, sweets, but I have to go. Is there anything else?"

"No, I just wanted to call and say hi and to thank you for the lovely weekend."

"I'll talk to you soon," and the line went dead.

Zoey took another sip of her coffee at work while creating another to-do list on her desk computer. She was worried about Jake. He seemed a little distant the last few weeks. Even though they had a great weekend together at the Bay, she wasn't sure if it was because of his workload or was he fading away from her life.

If the errors continued much longer on the accounts she would have to alert senior management, and she hoped it wouldn't take them long to notify the proper authorities. Everyone was worried and on edge these days. Who wouldn't be with the threat advisory system on red?

FIFTY-EIGHT

PORTLAND, OREGON 2010

Everyone was comfortably seated around the large cherry conference table, Felix standing at one end. He looked at everyone and asked, "Is there anything else anyone would like?"

Al-Hadi motioned at Felix with his lighter, "Do you mind if I smoke?"

"No, that's quite all right," Felix said, as he walked over to the credenza to retrieve an ashtray. "I just may have a victory cigar later myself." Everyone chuckled, trying to break the tension in the room. He passed the ashtray to Al-Hadi and went back to his spot, took a pull on his martini and peered over at Al-Hadi and Seyed. He took the conciliatory approach. "Look fellas, we've known each other for a long time and have had a good business relationship. Haven't Jeffery and I been square with you guys? In fact, Seyed, if you recall, I gave you your first arms shipment 'gratis' back in 1988?"

"Yes I do, but—"

"Damn it, let me finish, Seyed," Felix bellowed and pounded the table with his right fist. "Now you and Al-Hadi threaten me with this Russian/Georgia crap!"

"Now wait a minute. What's this stuff about the Russian/Georgia conflict?" Jeffery asked.

Al-Hadi and Seyed looked at each other in surprise as Felix answered his brother-in-law. "Look, Jeff, I had a little side deal going with Georgia awhile back. It's no big deal."

"No big deal!" Jeffery exclaimed. "Jesus, Felix, thanks for telling me."

"Jeff, it just happened. I received a phone call from a friend in the business, and he did most of the arrangements. I just supplied the weapons," Felix lied.

"Christ, do you know what kind of trouble this could bring us?" Jeffery warned.

"Yes, I know. Let's table this for now, okay? We have business to attend to."

"Well, I'm not forgetting this, Felix. We'll address this later."

"Okay!"

Al-Hadi stood and lit a cigarette, "Look, gentlemen, we're not here to cause trouble between you. We're here to work with you to achieve some common goals. Felix, we've only mentioned your mistake to get your attention."

"Funny way to do it, wouldn't you agree? Besides, if you wanted something why didn't you just come out and ask?" Felix huffed.

"Okay, you have a point," Seyed said, as he tapped his fingers on the table and then continued. "We need your help on something and in turn perhaps we can help you. But before I start, let me tell you something that precipitated this. This has been on my mind for a long time. So please bear with me," Seyed took a long pull from his bottled water and began.

"I have lived in your country for over twelve years while doing most of my academic studies. Even though I'm not a citizen, I have taken the time to look at your country's history and to study your constitution. Though it seems a little antiquated because of the time period it was written, it drives home the tenets of life, liberty, and the pursuit of happiness. Further, it professes that all men are born with God-given inalienable rights, not rights bestowed upon by the government."

"Where is this heading?" Felix asked as he ran his hand through his gray, thinning hair.

"Let me continue, Felix. You'll see soon enough," Seyed said. "I have to confess that even though I'm not a citizen I envy your country. Like you, I've traveled most of the world and nowhere can I find the level of freedom that your country has. You can travel anywhere without restrictions or checkpoints, speak your mind and practice your faith without fear of retribution. If you work hard, you can succeed and obtain anything you like. Sure, your country, like other nations, has experienced adversity throughout her history. There was the labor and social movement in the latter part of the nineteenth century that involved the formation of communist and democratic parties and organizations, the Ku Klux Klan in the latter part of the nineteenth and early to mid-twentieth century, and of course the growth of communism in the early to mid-twentieth century. Some of your institutions were battered and bruised because of these movements. But in the end your republic stood like a beacon of light to the world, dividing and conquering the fog of treachery, lies, and deceit, steadfast in following her principals of the constitution. Do you know why your country has persevered?" Seyed asked.

"Yes, I believe it is because of our people," Jeffery opinioned. "But what are you doing, giving us a civic lesson?"

"Oh, it's much more than that," Seyed intoned. "This time it's different. You cannot rely on the will of your people anymore. Some have given up traditions, values, and ideas that your forefathers fought so courageously for. Others have grown lazy, apathetic, and unknowledgeable on the principals of how your country operates under the constitution written by your founding fathers. I'm sure you know in order for a republic to succeed that it must rely upon the will, knowledge, and vigorous defense of its citizenry. You now have over three hundred million people divided by philosophical and political factions. Polarization of your country has to stop, otherwise your society will implode from within. Your political and free enterprise systems are out of control, dictated from the influence of money by your corporations and lobbyists. Prison incarceration and recidivism is rampant. Your technology has outstripped common sense. Your educational system is in tatters, under-performing and financially strapped. At least forty percent of your population is obese and overweight. Whole segments of your population cannot function properly. In my opinion, it appears that your society's elite has already decided that the tracks of history have been laid, the spikes of inaptitude have been driven, and the functioning part of your society is now inappreciable. Your democracy is changing to a plutocracy, or perhaps worse." Seyed paused and looked around the table. Everyone was quiet and fixated on his rhetoric. He took another pull of his bottled water and continued.

"Democracy. What a wonderful concept. In its simplest form, it's 'the free and equal right of every person to participate in a system of government, often practiced by electing representatives of the people by the people.' As John Adams said, 'Democracy... while it lasts is more bloody than either aristocracy or monarchy. Remember, democracy never lasts long. It soon wastes, exhausts, and murders itself. There is never a democracy that did not commit suicide.'"

"Why is that so?" Seyed asked.

"I guess it's what you just said," Jeffery offered.

Seyed stood and looked at the group. "There's no guessing about it. Quite frankly, I'm disgusted in which path the United States is taking. This path is fraught with peril. The United States doesn't enforce its laws or regulations anymore. Congress has many issues facing them, including the economy, immigration, and voting rights. Your administration and Congress are out of touch and out of control. Your nation believes that it can meddle in other countries' politics, even to the extent of nation building. Let me ask you this. How can a country, such as yours, expect to change cultures based on tribal tradition for millenniums to democratic societies in a decade? You think money and the military will do it? I think not. You know what happened with Afghanistan and the Soviet Union in the late eighties, and now your country is making the same mistake. And you wonder why the rift is growing between the east and west. I'm afraid if this continues history will repeat itself, but with far grater consequence and bloodshed. The Roman Empire lasted over five hundred years before it self-destructed. How long do you think the United States is going to last? At its present rate of decline, it will not even be close."

Felix stood and pounded his fist on the table and shouted, "Enough! I know the country is in trouble, any half-brain can see that. Now why are you here? What's so urgent?"

FIFTY-NINE

OGDEN, UTAH 2010

"Frank, thanks for coming by," Steve Kronoski said. "My what a gorgeous view of the mountains you have from your windows!" Frank exclaimed. It was another hot day in the middle of summer with all the sprinklers going in the downtown district. "Sorry it has taken me awhile to have a chat with you, but as you know we have been slammed with the Jamosa investigation."

"How well I know. Everyone's been up to their eyebrows, and I'm afraid there won't be any vacations taken this summer," Steve said.

"I know the heat's really on, both outside and inside. Now what's on your mind?" Frank asked.

"I've been wanting to get together with you for some time. I've been told that you have one heck of a background, spanning decades in the banking and financial industry. Frank, I'd like to have your thoughts on how did the banks get into such a mess, and how are they connected to the Wall Street meltdown."

"Do you mind if I take a chair? My hip has been bothering me again." Steve gestured to the nearest chair.

Taking his seat, Frank took a few moments to think about what he was going to say. "Well, in a nutshell, Congress, Wall Street, and the banking industry failed, and the common element was greed. It began in the seventies, picked up steam in the eighties and nineties and continues today. Steve, let's break this down into pieces, it will be easier to understand." Frank took another moment before continuing. "The official unemployment rate has been in the nine percent range nationally for two years with no sizeable improvement in the foreseeable future, though the actual rate is much higher."

"Yeah, I knew the true rate was higher then most politicians let on. Frank, how does the government figure the official unemployment rate, and what is the actual rate and how is it determined?" Steve asked.

"Well, it's quite simple really. The Bureau of Labor Statistics (BLS) is the principal fact-finding agency for the government. The parameters the BLS uses only look at people that are currently receiving unemployment benefits. It doesn't account for people that have exhausted their funds. These people have dropped off the radar and are the hidden faces of our society. In fact, there have been so many people that have exhausted their claims and are still looking for jobs that the BLS is in the process of redefining what constitutes the long-term unemployed. The ranks of these people have swelled since the recession officially started in December 2007, now numbering over two million and growing. If these people were included in the BLS statistics the official unemployment rate would be much higher. On the flip side of the coin is job growth. Every month there are one-hundred and twenty-five thousand new faces entering the job market, which means the market needs to hire one-hundred and twenty-five thousand people per month just to remain even. In the past few years the job market has actually declined. In order to bring the unemployment rate down to acceptable levels, let's say five to six percent, the job market needs to hire about two hundred and fifty thousand new employees per month for at least the next two years or so. Fat chance in that!" Frank blustered. "Now, if you add the new people who are looking but cannot find employment plus the ones that have exhausted their unemployment benefits and the ones that are still claiming their benefits, the true unemployment rate is much higher. I'd say it's actually between eighteen and twenty percent. Of course, like you said, our politicians never want to discuss this. They only refer to the official rate."

"Wow, I didn't know it was that high!" Steve exclaimed.

"Yup, it sure is," Frank said. "Speaking of hiding the facts the government does the same for the Consumer Price Index (CPI)."

"What do you mean?"

"The government, when computing the CPI, doesn't include a host of items that contribute to inflation such as rental and property insurance, some benefit costs, property taxes and utility expenses. Most cities, county, and state governments are under intense pressure to raise all forms of taxation because the economy has fallen off the edge. The insurance companies are doing the same. As an example, according to one source that tracks property taxes and home values, property taxes have risen on average thirty-five percent nationwide over the last four years while at the same time home values have fallen twenty-nine percent. Well, I have news for them!" Frank emphasized. "If this keeps happening you will see a mass exodus of people leaving their homes, not that it hasn't already happened."

"Where will they all go?" Steve pressed.

"Unfortunately, some will live on the streets and be at the mercy of civil services and charities. Others will move in with family, relatives, and friends, and they will be forced to consolidate their finances just to survive. And the remainder will rent; that's if they still have good credit."

"What will happen to all the vacated properties?"

"If this continues, between bank foreclosures, which are still rising and forced migration of home owners to rent rather than own because of increasing costs to maintain home ownership, the banks will eventually own nearly half of the residences in the United States. This will put enormous pressure on the default rates of financial institutions and the Federal Deposit Insurance Corporation (FDIC) that takes over control of these failed entities. Eventually, most of these properties will have to be razed because of blight, squatters and liability."

Steve just shook his head and looked at the consultant in bewilderment.

"Wait a minute there's more on the CPI. The government now is pushing for a new pricing system called the Weighted Chain Consumer Price Index."

"What's that?" Steve pressed.

"As an example, let's say that a family has allocated a certain amount of their budget to buy beef each month. But because other commodities such as energy and transportation have risen steeply over the last year or so they decide to buy more pork and chicken in order to shift the additional savings to cover increased energy and transportation costs. The government will look at this as a reduction of core prices and thus reduce CPI (inflation). Problem is that some wage contracts in the private enterprise, mostly unions, and most government contracts including Medicare and social security are adjusted annually by the Cost of Living Allowance (COLA), which is typically tied to the CPI. In essence the consumer is robbing Peter to pay Paul, and the government sees this as a reduction even though the core prices haven't gone done—they've actually gone up because of increased energy and transportation costs. Some experts say it is more accurate than the current system. I'm not so sure."

"Why those sneaky bureaucrats!" Steve huffed.

"Let's face it. They're rigging the official CPI the same way they've rigged the official unemployment rate. My bet is that social security recipients will not get a cost of living increase for three years. Rumor has it that Congress is using those savings to pay for an electronic medical records processing system for themselves."

"This is getting out of hand, Frank. We need to vote those Congress people out of office. Maybe even impeach them," Steve exclaimed.

"Not a bad idea. Another thing, people need to realize they cannot continue to receive the same amount of services that they have grown to expect. And the state and federal governments need to realize they must scale back those services, and this needs to be spread across all segments of our society. Right now the state and local pension system for government employees has an unfunded liability of three trillion dollars and growing. If this keeps going, all fifty states will be broke in a couple of years!" Frank exclaimed. "Did you know that, in many cases, state public employees not only get generous pay and benefits when they retire, but they also get paid for their accrued unused sick leave and personal time when they leave. That in itself is understandable. After all, they have earned this pay according to their contracts. But what I find surprising is that retirees are allowed, in some cases, to include this in their final year of employment in order to boost the amount that they will receive for retirement. In essence, they're receiving their accrued sick pay and personal time off year-after-year in addition to their retirement until they pass away or pass it on to their spouse. Did you read what happened in Camden, New Jersey?"

"No, I didn't," Steve replied.

"Oh, you're going to love this," Frank said. "The city of Camden discovered that they were broke. Imagine that. After the city had done their due diligence and discovered that they were in dire straits they needed to renegotiate their contracts with the police union. Otherwise the city would have had to lay off half of its police force. After the negotiations had been completed with the city, the union brought it before its members for a vote. Now here is where it gets interesting. The members rejected the new contract three hundred to one. Can you believe that? Only one person voted for the contract in order to spare their brethren and undoubtedly family members and relatives the loss of their jobs? Come on, what were they thinking? The way I understand it, Camden is a very dangerous city. But with the loss of half of the city's police force—need I say more? With this kind of attitude, I guarantee the states will go broke. It comes down to either the federal and state employees' union contracts be renegotiated in light of our present circumstances and past promises or the taxpayers pick up the tab." Frank was rolling. "Now I understand why some cities are in the process of conducting 'fire sales'."

"What do you mean by that?"

"Some of the cities' budgets are so deep in the red they are now forced to sell some of their municipal treasures in order to help balance their budgets. In fact, some cities are contemplating allowing corporate logos to be scrawled on some of their real estate. Unlike the federal government the cities and states are required to balance their budgets according to their constitutions. Speaking of the government, did you know for most federal and state employees their salaries have increased so much in the last ten years that they now average thirty-eight percent more per year than their counterparts in private enterprise? That doesn't include their bloated benefits. We have already contributed to the banks, large corporations such as General Motors, large insurance companies such as American International Group (AIG). Now, are we expected to do the same for the states and local governments? Do you see the irony in all of this?"

"I sure do; I just didn't know it was this bad," Steve said, as his face paled. "Even though I'm a federal employee I can certainly see where this is all heading. If this continues, the working middle class will be bifurcated. Employees in the private sector will be paying taxes with their hard-earned dollars supporting the bloated salaries and benefits for public employees and this will lead to a two-caste system, and possibly class warfare. If I'm not mistaken these are some of the errors that Greece had made."

"That's correct, Steve, and it's only getting worse. In less than six years the country's debt has more than doubled from seven trillion dollars to fifteen trillion dollars. Another way to look at this is six years ago every man, woman, and child was about twenty-two thousand and five hundred dollars in government debt. Today, they are fifty thousand dollars in debt and climbing. In fact the accumulation of debt in the past six years has now matched the entire debt of our country from its founding through

2004. It now takes better than forty percent of the country's gross domestic product (GDP) just to pay the interest on the debt. Further, at the end of 2011, provided Congress doesn't spend more than 1.5 trillion dollars projected by the Congressional Budget Office (CBO), the national debt will rise to seventy percent of GDP. If this continues at its present rate the United States will be where Greece is today by the end of 2012. And as the national debt grows the bond companies, who finance a good portion of this debt, will increase the interest rate at which they finance, and it will only exacerbate the problem. Worse case is that they might discontinue financing and where will that leave us? Can you spell 'default'?"

"You're telling me the entire bond market could collapse?" Steve asked, as concern swept across his face.

"Yup," Frank said, and went on. "In comparison, in 1980 the national debt was 909 billion dollars and 2.7 percent of the GDP. Based on year-end 2010 figures has your household debt gone up seventeen times? What about your income, has it gone up seventeen times since 1980?"

"Of course not. I would've been bankrupt if I followed those principles," Steve answered.

"Well, that's where the government is today. Insane, I tell you, just insane!" Frank exclaimed again.

"Jesus, you're scaring the heck out of me, Frank," Steve said, worry flashing across his narrow face.

"Well, do you want to be informed, scared and take action, or do you want to stay uninformed, take no action and some day wakeup to a dystopian society or no society at all."

"I see your point," Steve said.

"And speaking of debt, did you know the national debt ratio to GDP is at its highest point since the closing of World War II?" Frank asked.

Steve looked at Frank and answered, "I didn't know we had to go back nearly seventy years to match the current situation."

"At least back then we had a reason: we were climbing out of World War II. What are the reasons today, Steve?"

"Greed and laziness?"

"Bingo!" Frank said, as he peered up at Steve. "Back then Congress put the country on track in a year or so, but it's not going to happen this time. Sure, the conditions aren't the same and they never are—not exactly. But this time we've dug ourselves too deep of a hole and if we're lucky, and if we all work together with a single-minded purpose, it will probably take us a decade to dig out of this. Saul Sharken, the chairman of the Federal Reserve has fired up the government's printing presses again and injected six-hundred billion dollars into the bond market, calling it 'quantitative easing' in hopes that the banks would loosen up credit to the consumers and small businesses. I highly doubt it will work; the banks are just too greedy. But one thing for sure, inflation will hit with a vengeance. It's not a matter of if, but when!" Frank said with disgust in his voice.

"How high do you think inflation will go?"

Frank eased himself out of his chair and went to the white board and wrote a figure on it. Now it was Steve's turn to exclaim, "18.5 percent! Do you really think it could go that high?"

"I don't know, but it was that high during the recession of the early eighties, and we're in bigger trouble now," Frank said.

"Jesus that would be ruinous, especially with everything else going on."

"You said it, buddy. There's so much that the average citizen doesn't know. What about the rescission of the uptick rule in June of 2007 by the SEC chairman that had allowed professional traders and hedge fund managers to relentlessly short sell the markets day in and day out, which contributed to market exchanges experiencing new lows in 2008. Relatively few profited from this, but it ultimately ruined the long-term investors' nest eggs. Then there's the 'flash crash' in May where the Dow Jones plummeted nine-hundred and ninety-eight points in a few minutes. Again, this had allowed a few to profit by using sophisticated computer trading software in order to get out in front of the trading trends in milliseconds. Another debacle was when the Ahmad Administration and Congress passed the Consumer Protection Act (CPA) last month. It was supposed to enhance consumer protection from the fraudulent practices of the banking industry. Problem was they didn't fund the bill. What good are regulations if they aren't funded and enforced?" Frank asked. "Now the banks want it rolled back. And here's my favorite, the Healthcare Reform Bill. Janet Tselios and her minions pushed through the voluminous legislation, saying the health care law will be her crowning achievement and we have to pass the bill to find out what's in it. *Can you believe it?*" Frank bellowed.

"So you're saying no one read the bill before it was voted on?" Steve pressed.

"No, that's not what I said. Actually, very few Senators and their staffs took or had the time to read the bill before it was rammed through on the senate and house floor."

"What's in it?"

"That's a topic for another time, Steve. But suffice to say I will mention a couple of things about the bill. First of all, the act is flat-out unconstitutional."

"What do you mean by that?" Steve asked.

"Congress cannot force individuals to buy a product or service under the articles of the constitution. The new health care is a product and a service. For instance, if you like Buicks, but the government requires you to buy Chevrolets, what would you think?" Frank questioned.

"That's crap!" Steve exclaimed indignantly.

"Precisely," Frank said. "Now I'm not saying that all the products and services that will be offered in the bill are not well intentioned for society, but it was in the way it was delivered. Conversely, I do believe that there is far more in the bill that will create more harm than good, and there's one particular section in the bill that caught my eye."

"What's that?"

"The national healthcare tax. Some people refer to it as a national real estate tax, but it is actually a tax for Ahmad's healthcare plan. It applies to high-income earners (threshold for married couples is $250,000 adjusted gross income and all others are at $200,000 AGI). It also applies to real estate sales on your home. For a married couple it's $500,000 profit after your home improvement costs. I believe for all others it's $250,000 profit. Also, if you are a high-income earner over the income threshold and the sale of your house is over the sale profit threshold the government taxes the lower amount. The tax rate is 3.8 percent and it is effective January 1, 2013. And for some states that have real estate excise taxes, plus the standard real estate commissions for selling homes, you could be seeing close to fifteen percent taken from the sale of your house. With home values declining in the last four years to ten year lows or more and escalating home maintenance costs, you could be seeing even more home owners walking away from their properties in the future."

"You sure about that," Steve asked.

"Dead sure," Frank fired back. "Just to show you how poorly the health care bill had been drafted, all the king's men and all the king's horses tried and tried, but no matter how hard they availed when the bill was completed, they forgot to include a severability clause."

"They didn't!"

"Yup, and any beginning law student knows when you draft a contract with multiple items you always put in a severability clause. That way you keep the remaining items in force in case the other items are ruled illegal or null and void. That's how inept our Congress has become."

"I know we really need to pay attention and vote these deadbeats out," Steve said. "But another thing that worries me is what's going to happen to social security? It's been on the news so much lately."

"Ah, the third rail of American politics. You would have to mention that," Frank said. "Congress should have addressed this problem long ago, and the longer our representatives wait, the more difficult it will become. It's simply a matter of diminishing returns. In other words, the amount of money everyone will receive from the fund will progressively decrease as the factors/problems increase. It's a scalable and time-sensitive issue. If Congress had fixed social security a decade or two ago, they would have only needed to raise the full retirement age by a year or two and/or increase payroll taxes by one or two percent. But now since more time has passed more drastic measures need to be taken, especially since the fund has been showing a deficit since March. Of course, the fund's timeline on deficits and insolvency has been moved up, and the situation has been exacerbated because of our poor economy and the fact that baby boomers are now drawing from the fund. Congress is telling us that the situation is becoming so dire that recipients may have to take up to a twenty-five percent cut in their benefits and this undoubtedly is on top of rising the retirement age and eventually increasing the payroll tax for the younger generation. My question is: Will there be a grandfather clause or will all of us share in the pain?" Frank asked. "Now the Ahmad Administration, in all of its infinite wisdom, has decided to give most of the employed a holiday from payroll taxes by temporarily reducing the social security tax by two percent. It looks to me that they're heading in the opposite direction and making matters worse!" Frank exclaimed.

"Frank, you're scaring me again," Steve said.

Frank waved off this last remark and continued. "Who's to say our benefits won't be cut further, perhaps to fifty percent or more. Now there has been a surge in disability benefits for social security. What are the unemployed suppose to do? How are they going to live? How are they going to survive? Since the social security deficit and insolvency dates have been moved up a twenty-five percent reduction may be just a pipe dream."

"Well, I hope not," Steve said in a wishful tone.

"I'm sorry to have to tell you this," Frank said. "Congress doesn't have a vested interest in the system because they voted themselves out of the social security system in the 1950s and have created their own pension plan, and they only have to serve one term to get their full pension. In addition, there are a host of other problems such as incarcerated felons receiving social security and unscrupulous individuals drawing benefits from the deceased. And this holds true for other types of pensions as well."

"Other types of pensions?" Steve questioned.

"Sure. Look at your federal, state, and private pensions. Don't you think there is some level of fraud going on?"

"Sure, there always has been," Steve, answered.

"But now the level of criminal activity has spiked in recent years because our legislation and regulations aren't being enforced."

"I can certainly see that, Frank."

"And then there is our education system," Frank intoned.

"I know our kids are in trouble, but—"

Frank cut him off. He was steamed! "There are no buts about it, our educational system now ranks seventeenth in the world. Decades ago, we went to a tenure and seniority based system, and that has to change. Human nature being what it is, some individuals think this is an entitlement because of job security and have become uncaring and lazy in fulfilling their roles as educators, or they're not a good fit for the profession. After all, they have the unions to protect them. We need to move to a merit-based program where teachers are rewarded for outstanding work. Quantifiable performance should be measured by a metrics system on an annual basis, and when layoffs or hiring do occur, teachers' performance should be taken into consideration. Seniority should only play a deciding factor when the performance of two or more teachers is equal when competing for employment opportunities or eliminating positions."

"My God, where does the damage end?" Steve asked in amazement.

PATH TO PERIL   247

"It doesn't. There is simply too much influence from money. Congressional bills that should have not been written and passed, others not enforced, and most importantly the populace aren't keeping their eye on Congress and voting accordingly. As far as the connection between the banks and Wall Street, that's easy. Think about what I just said."

Steve looked at the consultant in amazement while Frank walked from the white board and eased himself into his chair. "I can hardly believe all of what you just said," Steve said with astonishment.

"Well you better believe it, buddy, because the tsunami is coming. Steve, did you know that I've been writing about this?" Frank asked.

"No, I didn't realize you were a writer."

"I didn't either until about twenty years ago. I was too busy raising a family, sending my children through college, working full time in my profession and going to school myself in order to advance my career. So I promised myself as soon as I retired I would transfer my life experience skills and begin the journey. I didn't realize that there would be so much to write about."

"How so?" Steve asked.

"Well like I told my friend, Clarence, the day I left Steel National Bank people need to step to the plate and help steer our country back on course. I just hope and pray that it isn't too late and that there are enough of us that will have the guts to make it their priority to do so. Otherwise, we will soon be waking up to a new world, and people will be dragged kicking and screaming to a hardscrabble life. Now let's explore some solutions."

SIXTY

ALEXANDRIA, VIRGINIA 2010

After a romantic dinner of roast duck complete with candlelight, mood music, and red wine, Jake and Zoey moved to the great room of his house with their after-dinner drinks. Very seldom did Zoey, or for that matter, Jake, imbibe. But she knew that Jake, being the considerate gentleman that he was, sometimes took extraordinary measures to make her comfortable and feel at home. And tonight that was exactly what she needed.

After sitting on the couch, Jake, turned and asked, "How did you get the nickname of Zip? I've been asking you for weeks, but you keep putting me off. Don't you think it's time to come clean, Zip?"

"Okay, hon. But it is rather embarrassing," Zoey said. "Besides, I like keeping you in a good mystery—keeps you off balance. A lady can't give away all her secrets you know."

"Come on, Zip! It's time to fess up and quit being coy with me," Jake flashed his famous crooked smile.

"Don't give me that grin of yours—doesn't work like it use to."

"Oh, come on you're so cruel. Don't keep me in suspense any longer," Jake chided.

She moved to the bank of tall windows at the far end of the great room. The day had brought an evening's chill. As Zoey peered through the windows she could see October's crescent moonrise over the Potomac. She was attired in an elegant black silk dress that showed off her beautiful curves, and her long, sable brown hair was more striking then ever with streaks of silver running through it. She was a stunning woman by any standard. "Okay, Jake, the simple truth. As you know I can keep a secret, and I'm not one to spill the beans or spread rumors. That's it. Not very entertaining but that's it."

Jake smiled at her from the couch and said, "You devil you, you're not going to tell me, are you?"

Zoey sighed. "When I was seventeen my parents took Sam, my older brother and I, to Whistler, B.C., for a summer break. While there, Sam and I visited one of their zip line parks. After looking around we decided to try their most difficult run. The zip line was suspended high above a breathtaking whitewater river that divided Whistler and Blackcomb Mountains. I was a Goth back then wearing heavy, garish makeup and sporting short, black, spiky hair."

"You're Gothic!" Jake said in amazement.

"Well, I was. But obviously I'm not now."

"Wait a minute, I kind of like that look. Can you dress Gothic for me sometime? Perhaps for the next Halloween party," Jake kidded.

"Are you serious? Now can I get back to my story?" Zoey said, in exasperation.

"Please do. It's getting more interesting by the minute, but I'd like to keep this Gothic business simmering on the back burner."

"Are you crazy, Jake? Anyway, here I was speeding down this steel line going for all I was worth, twisting in the wind when suddenly my zipper and clasp broke on the front of my pants."

"I tried in vain to secure my pants, but it was to no avail. Sam was already waiting for me at the terminus, having completed his run. I was terrified at the thought of being humiliated at the hands of my brother, and having other people see my condition. You have to understand that Sam and I were very competitive back then and whenever one of us had a chance to dish the other we certainly delighted in the effort. To make matters worse, by the time I ended my trek, my Goth makeup, eyeliner and eye shadow were streaming down my face in copious amounts mingling with my tears. I was a mess. I was horrified, Jake. To this day my brother still reminds me of that trip."

Suppressing a laugh, Jake said, "You've certainly have earned the moniker, I must say."

"Jake, its no big deal now but it was back then."

"Okay, babe, I see your point." Jake stood and walked over and held her in his arms.

"You have to admit that was funny, especially because of the competition between you and your brother." They looked at each other and busted out laughing trying to ease the tension, but her mind was troubled on other matters that had happened the last few days at work. She was thinking on how to tell him when he leaned over and whispered sweet nothings in her ear. As she turned to meet his gaze and looked up to those wondrous blue eyes, he took her in a tight embrace, and they kissed passionately for a long time.

"Whoa sailor, you better slow down, or you'll have a wild cat on your hands."

Jake flashed his crooked smile and answered, "That's okay with me, sweetheart." He swooped down for another helping, but she gently pushed him away.

"Not now, honey, I just have too much on my mind."

"What's troubling you, my sweets?" They moved to the couch, and Zoey took a sip of the Frei Brothers Private Reserve Pinot Noir. The vintage had a wonderful mellow bouquet with a smooth aftertaste. She admired Jake's thoughtfulness and the little things that he did for her since they had met over a year ago. Jake hit the remote to the gas fireplace and said, "You've been agitated ever since I picked you up at Reagan International."

Zoey looked at Jake in a thoughtful manner before she began. "I've talked to you about this six months ago."

"You mean the anomalies on some of Fidelity's funds?" Jake asked.

"Yes. I didn't want to bother you unnecessarily until I was sure. The errors stopped shortly after I spoke with you last time, and I'm not sure why. But I kept checking some of the inactive accounts periodically just to make sure."

"Did you contact senior management about the shortages?" Jake pressed.

"Yes, I did, but since they stopped Fidelity hasn't pursued it. However I did work with IT security after alerting upper management, and they didn't discover anything amiss."

"So what's the problem, Zoey?"

"The shortages have started again. Doug Little and I have verified it. And they are getting larger, and there are more of them."

"Are the shortages still occurring on the inactive accounts?" Jake asked.

Zoey took another sip of her Pinot Noir and said, "Yes, almost to the one."

"Have you notified senior management?"

"Of course and the CFO, Bob Sensari, said he would follow up on it. I gave him all the data that Doug and I had compiled. Jake, like I said, this is happening on other inactive accounts too, and they're never overages just shortages," Zoey said with alarm creeping into her voice.

"What's IT security have to say about this?" Jake said as he worked out the possible scenarios in his mind.

"The chief of security, Steve Carlson, said that they have checked everything; the cipher keys, portal gateways, server pathways and all IP security protocols including VPNs, and it all appears to be normal."

"Do you have any ideas, Zoey?" Jake asked with a raised eyebrow.

"I have one. All these funds have something in common."

"And?"

"Like I said, they're mostly inactive funds."

"Anything else?"

"Well Fidelity is currently scrutinizing these funds for more anomalies and without any definitive answers yet, I think someone has found a way to get around our firewalls and hack into these funds. Also, they picked these particular funds because they knew they were inactive."

"How would they know that?" Jake puzzled.

"I don't know," Zoey said, shaking her head.

"But why the inactive funds?"

"I think whoever is doing this thought the errors wouldn't be noticed for quite some time because of the funds' inactivity," Zoey ventured.

"Oh shoot!" Jake exclaimed.

"What wrong?" she asked, placing her wine glass on the coffee table.

He turned to her and peered into her beautiful blue eyes. "This is important, Zoey."

"What?"

"Do you know if any other Fidelity brokerage houses have reported the same type of errors?" Without stopping, he added, "Have other investment firms reported any suspicious activities that you're aware of?" Jake questioned.

"Why do you ask?"

"They're testing," He said with a concerned look on his face. "Now answer my questions."

"No. The Boston location where I work is the only incident I know of."

"You're sure?"

"Yes, Jake. What's going on?"

"I can't tell you right now. It may be everything or it may be nothing. Zoey, can you hang around here for a while; I may need you later for additional questions? In the meantime, I need to make a phone call. Oh, and if you like, there's more Pinot in the kitchen." Before she could answer, Jake was bounding up the stairs to collect his satphone and call his boss, David Peterson.

SIXTY-ONE

OGDEN, UTAH 2010

F rank Mulligan looked at Steve and continued. "You know as well as I the engine that drives a republic is its people. People hold the key to the nation's direction through the ballot box. However, in today's society some families think they're too busy to find the time to vote; too busy raising their families in this complicated world. Others simply do not care to vote, or are too confused and still others at the very least are complacent. How do we motivate people to find the time, get involved and vote responsibly? Perhaps we need to briefly look at our history of vote getting and its financial impact. Throughout the nation's history securing votes has taken many forms. Today, connected and non-connected political action committees (PACs) are used to funnel money to candidates and ballot measures. Just this year a landmark case, Citizens United v. Federal Election, changed the rules regarding corporate campaign expenditures. Even though direct contributions are still prohibited, some people are disenfranchised by the landmark decision because it allows groups trying to influence votes for candidates and ballot measures not to reveal their donors. In this age of non-stop media it has become vitally important for the voters to be able to vet transparency of information in order to determine where the money is coming from. Also to allow corporations, especially foreign-operated to have the right to finance candidates on behalf of their shareholders and employees doesn't sit well with some. This also is true for labor unions, health organizations and others. Steve, what do you think of the landmark decision?"

"I'm not sure. My guess is if unions and corporations provide a mechanism for their members, employees, and shareholders to choose which candidates to vote on their behalf, I believe it would be okay. But that raises issues. What about the flow of money and where is it coming from? Which candidates is the money going to? Is it divided equitably according to the way the members, shareholders, and employees contribute? How can you have that when voting is a privacy issue? It's a sticky situation fraught with pitfalls to say the least."

"That's my contention too," Frank agreed.

"And there's the issue of corporations headquartered here but operating in other countries. What overseas influence do they have?" Steve asked.

"Good point," Frank said as he leaned over in his chair to stretch his arthritic back. "Congress needs to scrutinize these corporations in order to find out if their philosophies and business principles lie in the best interests of the United States. If not, at least find ways to make them equitable in their alignment with U.S. economic policies. Another point of contention is Congress needs to clean up and streamline the regulatory agencies and rewrite regulations so that they are aligned with twenty-first century technology. I'm sure there are more than enough regulations in place; we just need to do housecleaning. Did you know that legislation was passed during the Carter Administration that required federal agencies to review federal regulations every ten years to ensure they were applicable?"

"No, I didn't."

"Steve, it's all about applicability and enforcement. Congress receives far too many bills in new regulations each day. No wonder the government is growing so large."

"I knew Congress was overloaded. Is it that bad?" Steve asked.

"It sure is. Our government needs to be reined in or we are going to end up like Greece. Over there, two out of three people work for the government drawing fat paychecks and retiring early with big pensions. And their government employees are only productive six to eight hours per week. The remaining third of their population is supposed to support this—I think not! Without loan guarantees from the Central European Union, Greece would have gone bankrupt, and they still might. You have to remember that most governments create bureaucracy to push paper in the form of regulations and taxation, not productive jobs. In a productive environment private enterprise not government drives the economy."

"I hear you, Frank."

"Another concern is lobbyist. Our representatives, with our best intentions at heart, sometimes become corrupt with lobbyists' influence and too much time in office. It escalates when Congress doesn't read house bills that are authored by their own and vote on them without knowing the consequences. This can allow legislation to be driven by self interest groups and bend the political will of the people for their own selfish causes. It's one thing when representatives advance their own standing through bipartisanship, sound business principles and hard work, and present well-written and meaningful legislation for Congress to read and vote accordingly. It's another when they write and pass bills that promote self-interests of a few against the majority. This leads to absolute power. Society should draw the line and take umbrage against such behavior. Simply stated: big money has taken over. Not only is it driven by greed, but also in the mechanics that deliver the results."

"What do you propose?" Steve asked.

SIXTY-TWO

PORTLAND, OREGON 2010

S eyed looked at Al-Hadi as if to say, "You take the lead."
    Al-Hadi fiddled with his pen thinking on how to broach the subject. He didn't want an uprising here, he just wanted a clear, concise, adult conversation with the gunrunners. "Felix, we know that you made a mistake by getting involved with the Russian/Georgia conflict."

"Now wait a minute. What gives you the right to meddle in our affairs?" Felix asked indignantly.

"Come on, it's practically common knowledge in the arms business. Besides, Seyed and I aren't here to cause you problems. We are here to help you with the IRS and the Russian/Georgia problem," Al-Hadi offered as he continued playing with his pen.

Felix stood and pounded the table and demanded, "How in tarnation did you know about the IRS investigation?"

"You just confirmed our suspicions."

"Are you trying to blackmail me," Felix bellowed.

"Now hold on," Al-Hadi said in a calm voice. "Wouldn't you think it's a logical step for the Ahmad Administration to take, in light of your blunder?"

Felix knew he was trapped and had no choice but to answer, "I suppose so." But he was really pissed now about the two terrorists interfering in his affairs, and he wasn't about to let the two of them get away with this."

"Al-Hadi, I want you to hear this. Since we're airing dirty laundry I might as well tell you a dirty little secret about Seyed." Al-Hadi looked at Seyed with puzzlement in his dark brown eyes.

"Al-Hadi, you know about the attempt on your cousin's life." Felix offered.

"Yes, what about it?"

With that, Seyed, jumped up and screamed, "You can't."

"Turnabout is fair play. I warned both of you not to swim where the waters are deep. I guess you didn't take it to heart."

Al-Hadi looked at Seyed. "What's this about? Is there something I need to know?"

Felix peered at Seyed. "Do you want to tell him or should I?"

Al-Hadi was now looking back and forth between Felix and Seyed. "What's going on here?"

Seyed glowered at Felix. "You're bluffing!"

"Try me," Felix roared.

Seyed sat, composed himself, and turning to his friend he placed a hand on his shoulder. "There's no easy way so I'll tell you straight up and please, please let me tell you why." Seyed said, in a calm steady voice.

"It was you behind the assassination attempt?" Al-Hadi shouted, as the full weight of realization descended upon him. "But why? Why would you do such a thing?"

Seyed, with tears in his eyes said, "I did it for Allah, for you, and for everything we had at stake. Mohammed was going to the U.S. authorities and tell them our plan."

"How did he find out?" Al-Hadi pressed.

"He overheard us talking about it," Seyed said.

"How do you know?"

"One of our team members, Abdullah Farahm, came to me a while back and indicated that his brother who is a friend of your cousin's said he heard some disturbing news coming from Mohammed and thought he should alert me. I didn't believe it so I checked some other sources to be sure. There's no doubt in my mind that your cousin was blowing the whistle on us."

"Why didn't you come to me first, Seyed?" Al-Hadi asked. "I could've talked some sense into him."

By now Jeffery was all-ears wondering what was going to happen next while Felix was still grinning, hiding a snub nose .38

in his lap—just in case. They were both thinking what plans were they referring to.

"It was too late," Seyed said.

"What do you mean by that?"

"He was already talking to American Embassy officials in Islamabad when the hit took place."

"You attacked the American Embassy?" Al-Hadi exclaimed incredulously.

"No, no. They were in some kind of safe house in Islamabad."

"You should have said something. This business with you flying Abrahim and a team over here to help Felix and Jeffery and now this!" Al-Hadi exclaimed. "Can't I trust you anymore?" Al-Hadi waved off Seyed and continued. "I know my cousin was a pain in the butt, and there were times when I suspected that he was leaning to the west, but in my wildest dreams I never thought he would go this far."

"Well, he did, and I had to do something. Comrade, from your point, it doesn't matter if he is alive or dead because he is in the clutches of the Americans, and undoubtedly you will never hear or speak to him again. He's facing a fate worse than death. Allah is the only one that can protect him now—praise be to Allah."

Jeffery frowned at Felix. His brother-in-law was still grinning, staring intently at the two Middle Eastern terrorists. He couldn't be reached.

Al-Hadi bowed his head and said quietly, "We'll talk about this later." He looked at Felix. "Now can I continue?" Felix nodded.

"Wait just a minute." Jeffery said. "What plan or plans are you referring to?"

Seyed looked at Al-Hadi and then measured his gaze at the two gunrunners. "Well for one, we're planning on helping you with the IRS, and we're worried about the grave situation in the Middle East."

"Whoa, you're moving too fast for us." Jeffery said.

"Well, if you let me continue, I can explain all of this to you." Al-Hadi said.

Jeffery and Felix nodded their heads toward the two terrorists.

"Even though I'm not a Saudi citizen, I do have high-level clearance. Seyed and I have worked with Saudi's oil minister for years and have helped the Saudi government strengthen its position in OPEC. With the oil minister's backing, King Abdallah bin Abd al-Aziz Al Saud has agreed to open diplomatic channels with the U.S. States Department in defense of you," Al-Hadi said.

"Why would he do that?" Felix asked, with a suspicious look on his face.

"Well, for one, the king is aware of the delicate position Saudi Arabia is in with its neighbors and decided to secretly work with the oil minister in order to have us broker a huge shipment of arms to the country. His highness is getting nervous over Iran's ambition to become a nuclear power in the region."

"You're saying that through all of your years of hard work, building trust and loyalty with the Saudi government, that you are now in a position to raise the specter of suspicion between the governments and pit one against the other?" Felix mused.

"You could say that," Al-Hadi lied.

"Hold on, I believe we're talking about 'The Twelfth of Never.'

"What do you mean by 'The Twelfth of Never'?" Al-Hadi asked.

"I mean this is something that will never happen. You do not have the position nor will you ever have the influence to pit two countries against one another. Besides, why would a country with this kind of clout and diplomatic reach go through us?" Felix asked. "They're not a rogue country."

"The oil minister only indicated that the king wants to keep it ultra quiet, because of the delicate balance of power in the Middle East," Al-Hadi said. "Undoubtedly, this will be the mother of all sales for your arms company. With some of the profit, it will help Seyed advance his dreams for a nuclear Iran. Felix, the bottom line is we both win. You get Ahmad's Administration off your back and still make a tidy profit, while we pull Iran in to the nuclear age. Seyed has been working hard on the technology for a long time, and with a little help from the Russians, Iran can realize its dream."

"How much money are we talking?" Felix asked.

"Half a billion dollars."

Felix let out a low whistle, then added, "You have to be kidding. I can't pull together that amount of weapons, especially in a short timeframe. Has the Saudi government done their due diligence; compiled their weapons, parts, and ammo lists? Have they completed logistics to transport the weapons?"

"Yes, most of the administration and planning has been done." Al-Hadi lied again. He knew that Felix was greedy, and he had him in his clutches now.

"What about training? What if I can't supply some of the arms request?" Felix pressed.

"Slow down, we can handle most of the training ourselves, and I'm sure you can find the weapons. Our timeframe will be generous."

"What type of weapons are we talking about? I'll probably need advance notice to acquire some of the arms." Felix said.

"You'll be receiving the lists within a month. Once you know how much time you need or if you have difficulty acquiring some of the arms, please forward the information to Seyed." Al-Hadi instructed.

Felix looked at Jeffery but could see that his brother-in-law was silent. "Okay, let's negotiate on the split."

Al-Hadi and Seyed could see the gleam in Felix's eyes and the numbers crunching in his mind. They had him, and they knew it.

In the end it was decided that they would bilk the Saudi government out of an extra two hundred million dollars. The split on the profit would be fifty-five/forty-five in Felix's favor since he was doing most of the work and supplying the weapons. Felix took a fresh Montecristo out of his suit inside pocket, fired it, and took a long pull. "Gentlemen, I really didn't know what to expect out of this meeting that you were so adamant on having. But it appears that we have a win-win situation. I don't know your personal relationships with the Saudi government, nor do I care. And I'm not sure how you are going to pull this off. But I do know I will need some advanced assurances before I deliver a single piece of hardware. Since this will be such a large order it will need to be done in stages. I will require the cost of the weapons and logistic charges for my end, plus a twenty percent surcharge before delivering each shipment. Of course, the surcharge will be taken into account when I complete all shipments and we divvy up the profits." Felix took another pull from the cigar. "You know this isn't going to be easy, and it will take time. I will also need concrete evidence from you, while the transactions are ongoing, that the government is closing the IRS investigation. Fair enough?"

"I know we are in agreement on the money arrangement." Al-Hadi took another sip of his whiskey sour. "However, your second demand is going to be more difficult. I suspect the investigation will take some time to wind down, perhaps longer than your shipment window. Maybe we can work out a compromise. Felix, how long do you think it will take to deliver the weapons?"

"Don't know until I receive your list," Felix said. "But I do know that it will take a lot of hard work. I'll tell you what I'll do. I'll deliver half of the weapons while the investigation is winding down. Once I have legal proof the charges have been dismissed, the rest of the arms will be delivered. Is that reasonable?"

"I believe so, but I will need to check with some of our government officials and get back to you," Al-Hadi lied.

"Fair enough," Felix said. "Now, is your flight scheduled to leave tomorrow?"

"Yes, at one p.m. your time," Seyed answered.

"Good, we'll have breakfast together in the morning, and then I will have you chauffeured to PDX since I have a busy afternoon.

But tonight, gentlemen, let's relax and allow Jeffery and I the privilege of showing you and Seyed what entertainment Portland has to offer."

"You're most gracious," Al-Hadi said as he and Seyed smiled and bowed their heads toward Felix.

"Jeff, do you have anything to add?" Felix asked, as he looked toward his brother-in-law.

"No, I think you've covered it all." Jeffery was still seething inside with the discovery of his brother-in-law's side business with the Republic of Georgia. How dare he go behind his back! When he entered the business he told Felix that one of the conditions were that he would be made aware of all transactions. And now this! *What else is he hiding?* Jeffery thought. Now, he was wondering about the IRS investigation and was Felix really telling him the truth. *Christ!* They could all end up in prison. *And the business about Al-Hadi's cousin?* He asked himself. It had to be a ruse. His brother-in-law sitting there, grinning and letting the prospect of earning huge sums of money getting in the way of common sense. No, he had to get out. He just didn't know when or how.

"Okay, gentlemen," Felix said. "You're on your own until Jeff and I collect you at the Benson, 7:00 p.m. tonight."

The meeting was adjourned. Jeffery escorted Al-Hadi and Seyed to the building's lobby and collected their temporary badges and Al-Hadi's time-sensitive security card for the express elevator and bade them good-bye.

In the meantime, Felix headed back to his office to inventory his weapons. He thought that his brother-in-law was quiet, for the most part, after finding out about his snafu. He normally would have been asking questions himself. He knew that he would pay. He simply didn't care, and if he had to, he would run the entire operation himself. He wasn't going to let anyone tell him what to do anymore, lest they stand in the line of fire.

SIXTY-THREE

OGDEN, UTAH 2010

Frank tugged at his tie and unbuttoned his collar on his starched white shirt; the building's air conditioning couldn't keep up with the August heat. After removing his tie, collecting his thoughts he continued. "We must change the mechanics on how Congress operates. This herein will help invalidate avarice, corruption, and graft in the system. Sure, money will always play a role highlighting the candidates and the platforms they run on. But we cannot continue to sidestep the will of the people."

"Here's what I think we should do. We should have term limits for Congress. I would think two six-year or possibly three six-year terms for U.S. senators, and change the U.S. House of Representatives term in office from two-year terms to four-year terms and limit their stay to three or four consecutive four-year terms. It's important that we continue to stagger the Senate and House of Representatives terms so we do not have an entire new class of Congress representing the people at any given time. It's also important that we give serious thought to balance Congress' time to serve their constituency against the time needed for re-election efforts. After all, how can Congress represent us fairly when half of their time is spent for re-election? Because of this I think we need to change Congress from full time to part time similar to the states, or at the very least have them split their time between the Capitol and their home districts. If I recall correctly before the advent of air conditioning, decades ago, Congress recessed in the summers due to the oppressive heat and humidity in Washington, D.C., and went home to work their farms and businesses. This enabled them to meet and socialize with their friends, neighbors, and business associates and to learn more about the concerns and problems of their districts and states. Another benefit had been that they could stump for reelection while being home. How can that happen today when they work full time at the Capitol, trapped and targeted by Washington's influence? I really think working part time or splitting their time would lessen the influence of Washington. Overall by enacting term limits, plus reducing their time in Washington, would minimize their efforts for re-election purposes, while at the same time maximize our representatives' service to the people and lower lobbyists' influence in Washington. Also, we should restrict seniority rules. One's standing should be determined by productivity, innovation, and bipartisanship, not how long they have been in office. Steve, this is a key one. Unlike states that debate their house bills on the Senate and House floors before they are voted the U.S. Congress only requires a roll-call, an up and down vote on whether they will formally debate a bill on the floor before a vote is called. This needs to be changed, especially for major bills. They need to be formally debated to ensure that Congress fully understands the bill's content before voting. This would also help to reduce bias and ignorance."

"So you're proposing that the U.S. Constitution be amended to include these changes?"

"Yes, I am, Steve. I firmly believe if these changes are made, it will make a noticeable difference on how Congress operates and will provide a better framework on how the people are represented," Frank intoned.

Steve nodded his head and thought for a long moment before replying. "You know, Frank, I think you may have a point here. It's not only that we need to vote for the right candidates, but we also need to change on how the system operates."

"I'm glad you agree," Frank said as he fiddled with his glasses. "But there is more. We should also encourage the elimination of interchanging positions with outside influential groups and lobbyists after the senators and House of Representatives leave

Congress. This would also lessen the influence that lobbyists have on them. Moreover, we need every state to have an open candidate system. This would help reduce the strangle hold of the two-party system. Further, we need to use the line-item veto more often to reduce pork. And finally every Congressperson needs to know the U.S. Constitution and how it should be properly applied within its framework."

"I'm with you on that," Steve said. "I'm sick and tired of seeing all the extras added to legislation in order to get bills passed. It has to stop. And more important, I'm appalled at Congress and the courts passing laws and regulations with little regard to the constitution. Now, how do we light a fire under the voters, and how do we get them to vote responsibly?"

SIXTY-FOUR

ALEXANDRIA, VIRGINIA 2010

"Sir, sorry to call you so late, but I may have some crucial information on the terrorists' plans."

"Jake, is your encryption on," David Peterson replied.

"Yes, sir, it is."

"Funny, I was about to call you on some important information I just received from Jim Coffey at the IRS." Peterson went on as usual without any preamble and said, "With the information we received from Mohammed, and the help of one of their accountants, Ted Hamilton, and a consultant, Frank Mulligan, we were able to find a clear connection that leads Felix Jamosa to Noe Lomidze and Dimitri Gelashvili."

"Great, what is it?" Jake asked.

"They found a mining and building materials company in Georgia's capital city of Tbilisi that had the names listed as executive officers even though they had both perished during the Russian/Georgia conflict." Peterson divulged.

"What's the company's name, and why would Felix be using deceased names for his company?"

"It's Constar Mining, Inc. Felix and his brother-in-law, Jeffery Star, think if they load their companies with deceased officials they can hide behind them in case there are any inquiries or government intrusion."

"But—"

"Let me finish, Mr. Cannon," Peterson huffed.

Jake knew when to back off. The deputy secretary never called him by his formal name unless he was annoyed or pressured about something. The fiery little man had his ways, and Jake respected that.

"The other side of this is how they run these companies, and Dr. Ferris led the way on this and has confirmed what Mr. Jabbar had told you. We now believe they are using very advanced and sophisticated AI software and communications gear that allow the deceased to be perceived as living and operating these companies."

"Sir, I understand about the possibility of phantom companies trading on the world's exchanges, but I can't quite wrap my mind around all the day-to-day activities that allow them to do this and the fact that they are using the deceased. They must be dealing with some enormously complex technology." Jake said, with confusion pulling at the edges of his mind.

The deputy secretary wasn't about to let Jake spiral him down, conjecturing about how the systems were developed and implemented. That was left to the big kilowatt guys. Peterson was more interested in the big picture and the strategies they use in order to stop terrorists' attacks.

"Jake, the consensus is if you interact with these people on a business basis through most forms of communication including e-mail, voicemail, courier, and conference calls, you would no doubt think you were dealing with real people."

"I guess so," Jake surmised. "How could you possibly know or even think these people were dead?"

"Precisely. If you perceive someone to be living, then they are living," the deputy secretary added.

"But what about video conferencing and face-to-face meetings?" Jake pressed.

"If my sources are correct, they have perfected the use of three dimensional human-like avatars for video conferencing."

"Yeah, that's what Mohammed alluded to, sir."

"And as far as meeting with these officials; there is really no need. As long as their companies conform to each country's regulations and laws, pay the appropriate fees and taxes on time; I don't see a need for it. Do you?" Peterson asked.

"I suppose not. But why use the dead? Wouldn't it be easier to use fictitious names?"

"Excellent question, Jake. Everyone connected with this mystery has asked the same thing, and no one has come up with an answer. We really won't know until we arrest Mr. Jamosa and Mr. Starr. I'm just as curious as you are."

"What's the next step?" Jake asked, shaking his head.

"The assigned agencies will continue their coordinated efforts and forward all their findings to us since we're the clearing house. Once we get incontrovertible evidence, we'll forward the information on to the Justice Department and aid them in any way we can to help build a case against them. Now, what's on your mind?" Peterson asked.

"Sir, I just received some information from Zoey Chamberlain I believe that needs to be looked into immediately." Jake went on to tell the deputy secretary what he had heard from Zoey.

"So you're telling me that the errors started to occur in some of Fidelity's funds six months ago and then abruptly stopped. But now they have started again?" Peterson asked.

"That's correct, sir."

"And the anomalies are occurring in inactive accounts?"

"Affirmative, sir. The funds' balances that she has checked are always showing shortages, never overages. Also the number of funds that are showing these peculiarities are increasing."

"Has the company done their due diligence in order to uncover these errors?" the deputy secretary asked.

"They're in the process, sir."

"What about other branches, any errors occurring there?"

"So far she hasn't received any confirmation."

"Perhaps it's a localized problem." Peterson offered.

"No, I don't think so, sir. For one, I think there's a good possibility that this will spread to other branches and possibly other brokerage houses. Zoey also told me that their security people haven't found any breaches in their firewalls. This leads me to believe that it's an inside operation. Sir, I think the terrorists have placed their people in some of the brokerage houses and are in the process of testing their capabilities. Mohammed did tell us that they were going to cyber-attack our financial institutions, he just didn't know which ones."

"Christ! You may be on to something, Jake," the deputy secretary exclaimed with concern sweeping across his face. "This could be a big piece of the puzzle we were looking for. It doesn't appear the cyber-attacks will be done remotely. But to be sure, I'll contact the proper authorities and have Fidelity send us a list of all of their employees at the branches they suspect illegal activities are occurring. Once we receive this list we'll have our team search for any terrorist connections or persons of Middle Eastern descent. We'll then narrow it to employees that have been there less than three years. If we find something then it's a localized cyber-attack, though the instructions to initiate the assault may come from elsewhere."

"Good thinking, sir."

"Anything else, Jake?" the deputy secretary asked.

"No, that's about it."

"Now back to the phantom corporations," Peterson said. "Once we assemble the evidence on Jamosa's sham company in Tbilisi, I'll use National Security Letters and have the Justice Department issue sneak and peak warrants. These warrants will be for their headquarters, Jamosa Enterprises, in Portland, Oregon and in Tbilisi. Hopefully, if the Justice Department gets off their collective backsides and promptly issues the warrants, I think we can go in on Friday night at their headquarters in Portland. I'll have the local fire department lock down their offices on some trumped up safety code violation. Wouldn't want any employees around. This should give us enough time before their offices open Monday morning to go through their documents, computers, and communications. We'll also do the same with their sham company in Tbilisi. Though I doubt if we'll find any employees working there, only the dead." They both chuckled, then the deputy secretary continued. "We wouldn't want our friends to know that we've been snooping. Now would we?"

"No, sir."

"From now on those two characters are going to be shadowed around the clock. We'll wire tap their business and house phones and bug their business and homes."

"Good idea, sir."

"Oh, one other thing. Is Zoey still with you?" Peterson asked.

"Yes, she is."

"Jake, I know this goes without saying, but can she be trusted?"

"Sir, I've known her for over a year, and I have never seen or heard anything out of the ordinary. You do know I met her on the cruise that you unceremoniously bounced me off of."

"Official business, Jake. When I need you and Slade you'd better come a running," Peterson chided.

"Couldn't resist the jab, sir."

The deputy secretary waved it off. "This is what I would like you to do. If possible, keep Zoey with you for at least the next couple of hours in case I need her input on any unresolved questions. And I'm sure this will not be a problem for you," the deputy secretary kidded. "I need to make a few phone calls now, and then I'll get back to you. Understood?"

"Affirmative, sir," Jake said smartly. "I already asked her to stick around and be available."

"I'm sure you did." In the next moment the line went dead, leaving Jake to his own thoughts. Before going downstairs, he walked out to the master bedroom's deck. In the still of the darkness, he could sense the pull of the Potomac and feel the chill of dread rolling toward him like the fog off the river. Things were progressing now, but he feared they were still missing something. He knew that he and Slade would be receiving their orders by sun up, but he didn't know what they were and where they were heading.

SIXTY-FIVE

FLIGHT TO RIYADH, SAUDI ARABIA 2010

"I sure hate these long flights, Seyed," Al-Hadi said while perusing the menu.

"Why don't you take a nap, sir," Seyed suggested as he was adjusting his seat belt.

"I think I will, but first we need to discuss the strategy on the IRS issue with Felix," Al Hadi said, and then continued, "I think Felix has removed himself from any friends he might have had on the hill with this Russia/Georgia thing. What do you think?"

"I think so. I looked into his dealings like you wanted, and he really blundered on supplying arms to the Republic of Georgia. Did you see how his eyes lit up when you indicated that we would take the Saudi government for an extra two hundred million and split it? Who does he think we are—fools?" Seyed exclaimed. "Why would we give him any of the money? I think greed is his weak point, and it's going to undo him."

"Yeah, he also bought the story on you trying to assassinate my cousin. Sure there was an attempt made, but it wasn't done by you. It was I that arranged the attempt. I just wished we could have found out sooner about that little melee-mouthed idiot. Seyed, it's interesting that he didn't bother to ask the right questions."

"What's that?"

"What were our plans and why we didn't ask how he found out about this."

"Well you were pretty convincing by quickly launching into the weapons ruse. I would have thought that Jeffery would have questioned us more, but he was busy thinking about his brother-in-law's blunder."

"I think we played it well. And as far as Felix, his rapacious nature is clouding his judgment." Al-Hadi looked at his friend and continued. "In fact it's more than that, Seyed. He's been doing this for so long that it's in his blood—an adrenaline rush for him. He can't quit."

"That's probably true, sir. I think he's at a point where he doesn't care who he screws. He has now lost the trust of important friendships and without it, it greatly hinders his ability to curry favors and determine any factual information."

"That's precisely how we are going to dupe him with the IRS investigation," Al-Hadi added.

"How's that?" Seyed mused.

"Actually it's quite simple, especially since Felix has undoubtedly lost his connections in Washington D.C. I have some ties with the king's senior administrative staff, and they can get me the names of the senior officials at the IRS and the Justice department. Together with their names on official-looking letterhead documents we can mail information to Felix's business address, periodically, indicating the progress of the investigation."

"What about the postal stamp origination on the envelopes?"

"Don't worry about that. We have some Muslim friends in the United States that will take care of that little problem."

"What if he decides to turn these documents over to his company's attorney, respond himself or he receives conflicting reports from the IRS?" Seyed questioned.

"That's the chance we have to take. I think the only fly in the ointment we have to worry about is if the IRS sends him documents that conflict with ours. Otherwise, I highly doubt that he will take the time and trouble to do so. It would open the door for more unanswered questions. No, if he thinks the investigation is winding down toward a favorable outcome, why would he? Besides, he thinks he's right in the middle of another arms deal with a country that the United States wouldn't think kindly of. Seyed, I don't care for the man anymore; he's losing his sense of propriety, and he's certainly not above reproach. I know we can at least get three or four large shipments of arms, with very little up-front money, before he discovers the ruse. By then it won't matter."

"You have a point."

"Seyed, I'm going to get some rest. We have a long flight ahead of us to Riyadh, and I need to catch up. After last night now I know why they call Portland weird."

"Okay. I'm going to check the movie selection to see if there is anything decent to watch."

Al-Hadi loosened his necktie and reclined the big leather seat. Before nodding off his thoughts drifted to the new quantum computing technology they had been working on for the better part of five years. *This had better work*, he thought. They needed the extra money to bring the science to fruition. They had invested vast sums of money, research, and hard work to ensure the application would work and could be applied properly. The science was a marriage between Nanotechnology and quantum mechanics, and like most technologies it was general purpose in nature and could have dual outcomes. There would be many benefits and risks derived from it both on a civilian and military basis. Once again, Seyed had stepped in and assembled a team of highly gifted scientists and engineers. The work had been highly compartmentalized to ensure that no one knew the scope of the project. They had bet the farm on it, and by the grace of Allah, it had better succeed.

SIXTY-SIX

OGDEN, UTAH 2010

" How do we get the voters to the polls and vote intelligently? Those are good questions, Steve. Well the basic idea is to change the process in the way we vote the same way we change the mechanics on how Congress operates and represents its people."

"Oh, I see where you are going with this. If we clarify and simplify the voting process, it will make it easier and less time consuming for our society to vote and hopefully vote more responsibly."

"Now you're getting the idea." Frank took a moment, stood, and began pacing even though his right hip was bothering him, thinking about what he would say next. "Let's break this down in pieces. It will be easier to manage. First, we need to revamp the voter registration system throughout the nation. Second, we need to disseminate and acquire accurate voting information in a consistent manner. Third, we need to understand the role that the media plays in all of this and to make them more accountable. Finally, computerized voting machines need to be standardized. This should make our republic stronger and enable us to strengthen our resolve to become a better country not to mention reducing the threat of terrorism.

"Right now they're at least two million people on the voter rolls that can't vote because they are dead. That's a part of more than 24 million inaccurate and outdated US voter records—more than one in eight. The states, if they haven't already done so, need to clean up voter registrations. They need to eliminate fraud by checking for non-citizens, felons and the deceased, and ensure that eligible voters only vote once. All fifty states and the

District of Columbia now offer voters options such as voting with absentee ballot, same day registration and voting, mail in ballots and permanent absentee ballots in addition to polling booths and electronic voting machines. I know we live in a free and mobile society, but certain things need to be set at a certain level of efficiency and done consistently and this is one of them."

Steve nodded and said, "I totally agree, Frank."

"Next, if not already available, we need to create websites with simple search engines that will reveal candidates' and incumbents' backgrounds, and the incumbents' voting record on congressional bills. We also need to develop websites, if not already in use, with a straightforward synopsis on legislation and house bills that list the benefits and drawbacks on each bill similar to the pros and cons for ballot measures listed in voting pamphlets. Now merge these databases so the voters can see both the representatives' voting record and the summaries of each bill they will vote on. Since our society is so mobile, we need to replicate and standardize this method throughout the nation on the federal, state, county and city levels."

Steve interrupted, "I believe most if not all the states already provide this information to voters."

"You're probably correct, but the method and information is not consistent from state to state. Moreover, we need to authenticate the websites as the only unbiased legal source," Frank explained.

"Oh, I see. It's like the credit agencies that administer credit scores. There is only one true source for calculating your credit score from the three credit bureaus."

"Exactly, Steve. Now where was I? Oh yes, it's incumbent that the media and other sources undertake a watchdog role to educate the public on how state and federal government enact legislation into law, and how money influences elections. Our constituency needs to study and debate this, in order to make improvements in the system."

"Aren't you asking an awful lot from the media?" Steve asked.

"Yes, I am. But the media needs to help educate the public on the mechanics of Congress. In other words, how does our republic work?"

"Fat chance of that happening," Steve mused.

"You're probably right, but we must try. We should also encourage the media to direct the public to the proper websites to acquire critical and accurate information in a timely manner, especially at least thirty days before each primary and general election. This information should include the candidates' and incumbents' backgrounds and the incumbents' voting record, and summaries of bills and legislation that will be voted. We must also prevent time lag as to when the voting public can see their representatives' voting record. I believe there is a thirty day blackout period before the primaries and general elections."

"There is? I didn't know that," Steve uttered in amazement.

"I believe so, and this is not to say that much of the information isn't already out there, such as the Congressional Records, but it needs to be presented in a form that can be quickly attained and easily recognized. It is vital that people be allowed to gather as much knowledgeable information as possible in the period leading up to elections. After all, how are they to vote intelligently without the latest, up-to-date and accurate data?

"Finally, we need to standardize the voting machines throughout the country to simplify and eliminate confusion on the voting process. In other words, keep everything the same across the entire nation including voter registration, dissemination, and acquisition of information and voting machines. If you move from Alaska to Hawaii, you register in the same manner, acquire information the same way, and you vote using the same machines."

"Point taken, Frank. Going through all this with you I can see what is happening. Technology and ideas are leaping ahead of common sense. All the tools are there, but we're not utilizing them properly. We are being bombarded by information from everywhere on a twenty-four-hour basis. What's true and what's not? Who knows? Everyone needs to be skeptical regardless of the source. Even though some of our populace is finally waking and trying to wade through all of this in order to find the right candidates, I see where it's becoming more difficult to separate the wheat from the chaff. In fact, there is even more confusion out there because these tools are being mismanaged and are yielding false information in some cases. Once authentication is in place and the right tools are being utilized consistently; it will make voting much easier, accurate, and will lead to a more informed voting public. This will enable voters to spend less time uncovering facts in order to make better choices, and this should bring more voters to the polls."

"Precisely. The Ahmad Administration and the previous five or six administrations knowingly or unknowingly crafted pieces of legislation that got us to where we are today. Through greed, arrogance, and laziness, they have set the table for us to join Europe. They're orchestrating the disappearance of the middle rung on the economic ladder. Generations of hard-working middle class families are about to disappear unless our society wakes up and takes tough action through the voting process."

"Frank, I don't think some of our society knows what's at stake here."

"I know, Steve. But now the work must begin. We need to put this out to the populace in the form of a write in campaign to our senators and representatives and perhaps a grass roots movement may develop from this. Like I said to my friend, Clarence, when we left the TARP meeting at U.S. Steel Bank of New York, there is a direct relationship on how a country's government operates and terrorism. Unfortunately we have more serious business to attend to," Frank said solemnly.

Steve nodded at Frank, "How well I know."

SIXTY-SEVEN

DHS NEBRASKA COMPLEX
WASHINGTON D.C. 2010

It was three weeks before Thanksgiving, and David Peterson was in melancholy mood. The weather had already turned cold, and he had a million things to do. Never mind that the nation's threat advisory system had already been elevated to red, his wife, Phyllis, had a full to-do list for him to finish before the holiday weekend. As Jake and Slade took their chairs before the Department of Homeland Security meeting began, David turned to them and said sarcastically, "Nice to see you're on time, gentlemen."

Jake and Slade nodded at the deputy secretary. They knew not to say anything to the deputy director at this moment. The man was under tremendous pressure to solve the incalculable dangers that lay before them. They were all under intense pressure. The country had never operated under a threat advisory of red and everyone was in a pensive mood to say the least.

Peterson looked at everyone with his deep brown eyes and collected his thoughts. "We have received data from the sneak and peak warrants, and we have found some interesting things. First, Jamosa Enterprises in Portland appears to be legitimate with no ties to Felix's arms trade. Second, we did uncover a smoking gun in the form of a diary. It appears that Jeffery Starr has been keeping a list of all the arms' activities since the mid eighties. It also points to a certain arms dealer, Simon Duke, being killed by Seyed Mostakavi at Felix's request in Afghanistan during the Soviet-Afghan war."

"Sir, how was Dr. Mostakavi involved in the conflict?" Dr. Ferris asked.

"He was brokering arms between the mujahideen and Felix, doing logistics and training the holy warriors."

"Quite the character," Dr. Tonya Franks commented.

"Indeed. He and his Pakistani friend, Al-Hadi Zafar, have known Felix and Jeffery for nearly twenty-five years and have had numerous arms transactions with them throughout this time."

"Third, and now this gets real interesting," Peterson said. "We did not find a single employee at their company in Tbilisi, not even a security guard. In fact we found nothing in the three-story building outside of some cubicles."

"What the heck is going on?" Tom Morrison, the agency's database director, asked.

Jake looked across the table at Tom. "We may have caught him in the process of setting up a major corporation in the Republic of Georgia, and he hadn't completed it yet."

"Why would he do that?" Tom pressed.

"You mean set up a complete operation that includes cubicles, offices, phones, computers and files?"

"Yes," Tom persisted.

"If there were any government suspicions or inquiries, within a short time Felix could move in employees, and it would appear the company was a going concern."

"Why would there be any questions? He's starting a company in their country. I'm sure the government would welcome the additional taxes from their corporation."

"That's true, Tom. But would they welcome the additional revenue from a company that is selling illegal arms and is operated by their deceased soldiers. Besides, Felix certainly doesn't want this to be known since he undoubtedly has other companies operating in this manner."

"You don't know that," Tom said.

"What else would it be?" Jake fired back.

The deputy secretary intervened. "Everyone, settle down! I know we are all under pressure, but I don't want us going down the road of conjecture so let's stick to the facts." Peterson glared at Jake, poured himself another cup of swill, and continued. "It's been confirmed there are phantom corporations! The diary lists fifteen such corporations and affiliated companies spread throughout the globe, and they are associated with over three hundred names. And I bet every name is a deceased person."

Slade let out a low whistle and exclaimed, "Unbelievable!"

Jake looked at Tom, and Tom just shrugged.

"Oh, it gets better than that. These fifteen corporations and some of their related companies trade on the world stock exchanges." Everyone just stared at the deputy secretary in stunned disbelief.

Dr. Clyde Ferris was the first to recover. "I was afraid of this, sir. If these are in fact virtual companies, they could vanish without a trace, without anyone ever knowing what happened. Bernie Maddoff would pale in comparison to this."

"That's what I'm concerned about, Dr. Ferris. Are there more phantom companies trading out there?" the deputy secretary mused.

Everyone now was looking at each other and shaking their heads. Finally, Jake stood, looked at the deputy secretary and asked, "Do we know where their seat of operation is? Is it in one place or multiple locations?"

"That's the questions we need to know; it wasn't in the diary. As I speak, our secretary, Mary Knappa, is conferencing with the Justice Department, the U.S. secretary of state, Tony Stein, and the attorney general, Teresa Struzan. We are going to issue arrest warrants for Felix Jamosa and Jeffery Starr. They will also contact the Saudi government and apprising them of the situation and asking permission to send a strike team to extract Mr. Zafar and Dr. Mostakavi. After the extraction the pair will be sent to Guantanamo Bay. Jake, Slade, when your orders come through you will be sent to Riyadh, Saudi Arabia and lead a small assault team. Saudi Special Forces will assist you. Understood?"

They both answered, "Affirmative, sir."

"How soon will you expect this, sir?" Slade asked.

"Soon," the deputy secretary answered.

"Not to interrupt you, sir, but what about the financial institutions?" Jake asked.

"I was getting to that," the deputy secretary huffed. "The proper authorities have alerted all the major banks and brokerage houses of the situation, and they are in the investigation phase of checking their employee databases, and we should hear back shortly. There's been enormous pressure put on these people to find out what is going on. Once we receive the information we'll start profiling and get to the bottom of this. Now, is there anything else?"

Everyone fell silent. "Let's get crackin'," the deputy secretary barked.

SIXTY-EIGHT

RIYADH, SAUDI ARABIA 2010

"Jake Cannon and Slade Swanson, this is Jerry Johnson and Ron Tate." Captain Jim Cramer was introducing his men to the Homeland Security agents.

Jake and Slade stepped forward and shook their hands. "Nice safe house you have here," Jake said as he looked around.

"Compliments from the Saudi's and the U.S. government," Ron said. "I see you and Slade are men of 'de oppresso liber' (to liberate the oppressed)."

"Yeah, we both toured with Delta Force a few years ago. Anything changed since we served?" Slade asked.

"Same o, same o," Jerry piped.

The Army's Delta Force squadrons were arranged similar to the British 22 Special Air Service Regiment (SAS). Squadrons were comprised of seventy-five to eighty-five operators and followed the SAS sabre squadron alignment. Each squadron could be broken down to four operators, including Intel, recon/sniper, and two direct action/assault troops. The group necessitated a broad array of skills. This mission had three operators. Captain Cramer was the recon/sniper expert while Sergeants Tate and Johnson were the direct assault troops.

"Jake, how was the flight to Riyadh?" Jim inquired.

"Too long, and the food was lousy. We had some turbulence coming in."

"Yeah, the weather can be unsettled here, especially in the fall and into the winter," Jim said.

"Coffee was good though. Now is everyone ready to get down to business?" Jake asked with a serious look reflecting from his blue eyes. He looked around, and everyone nodded in silence.

"You've all been briefed, correct?" he asked while sitting on the couch behind him.

Jim looked at Ron and Jerry and then at Jake, and answered, "All set from our end. We've studied the Intel and sat surveillance for Seyed's house, or rather his compound, and pics of Al-Hadi's limo. My God, that's a rolling bunker, and from the specs it's one hell ride! According to the route they take, I thinks it's prudent that we take them at the compound; less collateral damage."

"Yeah, Jim," Jake agreed, and went on. "The Pullman concerns me too, it's literally bristling with both offensive weapons and defensive counter measures. We will have to take them when the limo parks under the portico. That's when they'll be the most vulnerable. If they get inside the house, it'll make our job more difficult. Tomorrow, after Seyed leaves for work, Slade, you and I will go to the compound and check out the new security cards and remotes we received from Seyed's security company and look for any weapons he may have stashed."

"Yeah, Intel tells us that all the electronic locks are programmed off of one security card, and this will minimize the number of cards we need," Jim volunteered.

"Wouldn't matter, Jim, since I already instructed the security company to reprogram Seyed's house to have only one code," Jake said.

"Got a point there, but what about laser activated and motion security systems?" Jim asked.

"We checked for those when we were at Seyed's security company and we found no evidence of those type of systems being used outside of the standard motion/breakage detectors used for alarm systems. However, we have the tools to check for extraneous electronic devices including harmonics," Jake said.

"Good." The captain replied.

"Ron and Jerry, I want you two to hang at the safe house and work Intel until we get back. Comprende?" Jake asked.

"Gotcha, boss," they both answered.

"Also, as far as we know, Seyed will not be entertaining any guests this weekend and should be alone," Jake said as he looked down at the dossier in front of him, then continued. "If everything goes according to plan, Al-Hadi and Seyed should be safely ensconced in the United States by Sunday."

"Amen to that," Slade chimed in.

"What about his cars in the detached four-car garage?" Jim asked.

"You mean his Shelby Cobra and his Bentley Mulsanne?" Slade quipped. "Jake has his eye on the Shelby, and I'll take the Bentley."

Jim and his team gave the two government agents sideway glances. "You have to be kidding," Jerry said.

"No, we're not. Jake will disable the Shelby's ignition while I take care of the B. Wait a minute! You guys thought we were going to confiscate the cars for our personal use? Now that would be some trick, but we'll leave that up to the Saudis and the U.S. government," Slade said as Jake leaned back on the couch and began to roar. Jake and Slade looked at the bemused faces of their team, and soon everyone in the room broke out in laughter.

Jake took a moment to catch his breath, looked at Jim and his team and said, "Gotcha!" He composed himself, looked at everyone again, and in a slow and deliberate manner said, "Remember we want these two alive, especially Seyed. According to Intel, Al-Hadi's chauffer, Sied Hasson, shouldn't be a problem. He has no military background or specialized training, just a civilian driver. Seyed is the one we need to worry about. Even though he is now in his fifties, he stays in great shape and has considerable military training from the Soviet-Afghan war and is a weapons and explosives specialist, not to mention being a marksmen."

"Jake, is there anything this guy can't do?" Jim asked.

"Apparently not. You read his dossier. The guy is considered one of the most brilliant people in the world and undoubtedly has a treasure trove of information that could be useful to the United States, and that's why it is so critical we take him alive."

"What about extradition?" Ron asked as he ran a hand through his brown hair.

"No problem, the Saudi government has given the green light for us to bring them to the United States. It appears they really want Seyed Mostakavi out of the Middle East and under lock and key. King Abdallah bin Abd al-Aziz Al Saud, the Saudi government, and a few other countries aren't looking kindly toward Iran becoming another nuclear power in the region," Slade offered.

"Yeah, I can certainly see that," Jim commented.

Slade nodded at Jim and began to pace. "What really pissed off the Saudis was Al-Hadi's and Seyed's little soirée with Jamosa and Starr a while back. It was found that the pair were planning on swindling the Sheik and the Saudi government out of hundreds of millions on a proposed arms deal with the gunrunners."

"You don't say," Ron added.

Slade looked at Ron while waving his right index finger in the air to make a point. "I still don't understand why the king would deal with a couple of low brows like Al-Hadi and Seyed. I guess the Sheik was relying on too much trust from some of his family in regards to their credibility. You would have thought a country with their status would have gone through proper government channels, especially on an arms deal of this magnitude. In fact, they usually buy direct through American corporations and bypass the Pentagon. Word has it the king was so paranoid of Iran becoming a nuclear power that he was caught in a moment of fear and made the wrong decision. With Seyed tucked away, Iran will have a far more difficult time bringing their nuclear reactors online," Slade concluded.

"Not to cut this short, fellows, but what do we have for grub?" Jake asked. "My stomach's growling."

"The house is stocked pretty good, we have some good all fashion corn-fed beef, lots of veggies, potatoes and even desert," Jerry said.

"Now we're talking. Who's cooking?" Jake asked.

After dinner the team retired back into the gathering room to go over Intel, logistics, and any last-minute changes and alternate scenarios. The surgical strike team was nearly ready to go. They still needed to check and prep their weapons, armament, and supplies before they turned in. The assault was scheduled tomorrow, Friday evening.

SIXTY-NINE

RIYADH, SAUDI ARABIA 2010

Jake, Slade, and Captain Jim Cramer watched from their Chevy Suburban SUV as the big Pullman left Seyed's compound at 0900 hours the next morning. "God, that's an awesome looking machine," Slade said in his gravelly voice.

"Now you see why I want them out of the car before we take them," Jake commented.

"You don't have to tell me!" Jim exclaimed. "That's one heck of a rolling bunker."

After the limo was out of site they drove their black SUV, which was hidden a block away, up to the front entrance and Jake punched the remote. They watched as the pillared xenon-lit security gates opened. A week ago the Saudi government had notified Seyed's security company that an agent of the United States Department of Homeland Security, Jake Cannon, would be contacting them. The security company had been instructed to change the codes for Seyed's compound and issue new remotes and security cards for Jake's team. He had called the security company yesterday after he and Slade had arrived in Riyadh. They had swung by before going to the safe house to collect the new security cards and remotes and to study Seyed's security feeds. It was decided since Riyadh's November's weather pattern would remain unsettled for the next few days and there had been no activity at the house for the last few days, they would use yesterday's feed. Jake had instructed the technicians to patch yesterday's disk into the loop at 0900 hours, Friday morning. This was a critical piece for the extraction's success because they knew that Seyed was tech savvy and would undoubtedly be checking his security on his smartphone from time to time. He found that

Seyed's security was closed-looped and hard wired. This way it couldn't be breached by cutting alarm wires from the outside without interrupting the service, plus it afforded good protection from any nearby electronic interference. It had all the bells and whistles including hidden cameras, sirens, strobe lights and auto-call to the authorities and his smartphone. However, it could be breached by the right set of diagnostic tools and software by setting the protocols to 'false-closed'. Jake was surprised that the system wasn't military grade. Perhaps this was only the primary defense and Seyed had other, nastier surprises awaiting them.

"Jim, bring the car up to the portico and have it pointed street side," Jake instructed. "Slade and I are going to walk up the long drive and get a feel for the place."

They moved toward the house on the well-lit, wide-paved stone drive, inlaid with brick borders and diamond-shaped centerpieces. Flanking the drive on both sides were wide flowerbeds that were planted with well trimmed but now dormant white and purple Rose of Sharon from Lebanon and Chinese rose brought in from the Bahrain Islands and India. Behind the flowerbed on their left was a high stonewall, which lit up in the spring with bougainvillea from Italy and India. To their right of the drive was a large, manicured green lawn surrounded by high, reinforced stonewalls. Other flowerbeds, which outlined the inside of the walls, were filled with more bougainvillea and also lined with staggered rows of white and yellow poisonous single oleanders, and three types of lantanas—aculeate, camara, and alba.

"God!" Slade exclaimed, "What a beautiful place. I can hardly believe we are in Riyadh, Saudi Arabia. When I think of this place I have always thought of sand and wind—not this."

"Yeah, the Saudi's have taken great pride in their horticulture in the past few decades and have transformed many areas of their major cities into bejeweled gardens. I see that Dr. Mostakavi is a prime example of their thinking."

"How many acres does he have?" Slade asked.

"According to Intel, I believe it's ten. But don't you see something odd about this place?"

"Yeah, where are the trees?"

"I think that's because of security reasons. And look, just as the satellite photos indicate, there are security cameras everywhere." Jake and Slade could see cameras sitting atop stonewalls, spaced at 100-foot intervals.

They continued up the drive, moving past a long, lazy curve until the house came into full view. The mansion looked tall for two stories, because of its 10-foot ceilings on both floors. There was a massive eight-foot tall steel door for its front entrance. Jake turned and looked north, and he could see that the house held a commanding view that included the suburbs, mosques, and downtown Riyadh. In the far distance, beyond the city, he could see the sands of time with its shifting shapes, sometimes soaring 1,500 feet into the sky. The 7,200 square-foot house was done in sandstone with a reddish-brown tiled roof and large, bronze mullion windows. The house windows and the glass doors entering into to the east side of the house under the Porte-cochere were all heavily embedded with Kevlar and could withstand small weapons fire. The windows were all one-way view looking out. The bronze mullions, underlined with steel, were quite thick and layered in diamond patterns that provided additional protection for the windows. As they approached the captain, standing beside the SUV under the portico, they could also see a small patio west of the front entry surrounded by three-foot sandstone walls.

"Can you get a load of this place," Jim remarked.

"Yeah, it's sure nice," Slade answered. I can't wait to see the interior."

Jake interrupted, "Is everyone's radio on?" Slade and Jim both nodded. "Okay, Jim, I want you to inspect the front of the house and the four-car garage adjacent to the portico, but keep a sharp eye out. Use your canned smoke to check for laser activity and if you see anything unusual, you know what to do."

"Affirmative, sir," Jim said smartly.

Before Jake stepped up to the double glass security doors he sprayed smoke from one of the canisters he was carrying to check for any exterior laser systems. In fact, their plan indicated to check all exterior entrances for lasers and other security devices.

"Slade, check the house's perimeter entrances and report back here. In the meantime, I'll give the portico's entrance a thorough once over."

"You got it, buddy."

As Slade moved to the front entry, Jake peered at the portico's entry area for any security devices. The only thing he saw was a pair of brass plate outdoor lamps flanking the doors and external stereo speakers next to the lights—same pictures as the sat photos. They already had checked the surrounding neighborhood streets for hidden cameras, acoustical and other security devices and hadn't found any. Even though Seyed's compound was fifteen miles south of Riyadh, Jake wasn't taking any chances of getting surprised by newer technology. One of the reasons why Riyadh was safer than most of the other Middle East cities is because the Saudi government had installed ShotSpotter from SST throughout some of their major cities including Riyadh. The technology allowed law enforcement and other agencies to instantaneously determine the location and signature of gunfire and explosives wherever the video and acoustical-based systems were employed. For location it relied on GPS triangulation similar to finding cell phones. It enabled rapid response to these situations without relying on reports from citizens. Since this was a classified operation, Jake didn't want any local authorities showing up in case of gunfire or explosions during the actual extraction process.

After Slade returned and gave the green light, Jake slid the new security card into the slot right of the doors and watched as the big steel-grilled glass doors opened. Once inside the lighting on the north and east side of the house went on. Before going further, Jake sprayed canned smoke in front of them as they slowly walked through the portico's reception area and turned left onto a wide hall, which opened to a large well-appointed chef's kitchen on the right. They took a few more steps and then stopped. Jake took the smart card and slipped it into the wall slot and while he waited for the reader to open the double glass doors to Seyed's office he instructed Slade to search the kitchen for weapons, documents and any security devices.

Jake wished that he had his hands on the new sensing hardware that the Army was testing. The new hand-held systems were based on Doppler radar, materials science and nano technology. What he knew was when these devices where pointed at solid objects they gave the reader a three dimensional representation of the structure. It not only showed the structure itself and everything inside, but also defined the chemical composition of the materials and in some cases the brand name of the objects. This certainly would have reduced their time in searching the structures within the compound and drastically minimize any surprises.

Jake could see that the office was done in heavy birds-eye maple including crown millwork with crown wrapped faux maple beams. Opposite the double doors was a large celestial-style window with black custom shades that looked north. In one corner stood a state-of-the-art Sophia electric fireplace also in maple with a black marble insert. Jake whistled to himself thinking about how much money must have been spent building this place. He checked the room out quickly and found nothing out of the ordinary and met Slade out in the hall.

"You ought to get a load of the kitchen," Slade said as he ran a hand through his short, coal black hair. "He must have every gadget known to man."

"Did you see anything out of place, any documents?" Jake asked.

"Negative, just pure opulence."

Jake looked at the house's schematics and pointed down the hallway, "I'll check this side of the house while you search the front.

Radio me if you find something of interest." Jake moved down the hall and went through the glass doors into the master bedroom. Just then his radio vibrated. He unclipped the transceiver from his belt on his assault vest and hit the open COM button so Slade could hear. The Miniature Secure Handheld Radio (MSHR) was the world's smallest secure digital radio. It used flash memory embedded US Type 1 encryption for data and voice modes and was water immersible to one meter.

"Find anything yet?" Jim asked.

"Negative. You? Over."

"Just a couple of gorgeous cars. I mean these babies are beautiful. Over."

"Of course they are." Jake smiled. "Did you disable the ignition systems yet? Over."

"Sure have, and it was a piece of cake. Over."

"Man, you're fast!" Jake exclaimed. "Even for an old gear head. Over." Jake knew the captain's background, and he had been regaled more than once from some of Jim's friends about his prowess among car enthusiasts that included boosting any automobile he wanted in his younger days. "Okay, I want you to explore the cottage east of the garage and get back to me. Copy?"

"Copy that, sir, and out."

Jake peeked under the king bed and found nothing of interest and then looked around the room before going outside to check for weapons on the patio. Once again the courtyard was a study of over indulgence with its oversized hot tub, flat screen, Bose system and an outdoor kitchen flanked by ten-foot retaining walls. He searched around but found nothing unusual. He finally walked back inside and went through the master bedroom into an adjoining room and spotted a prayer rug next to a large window, facing east, and a bank of monitors on the adjacent wall. *Must be his prayer room,* Jake thought. Couldn't tell on the architectural plans—just a room between the master bedroom and master bedroom's closet. He checked the monitors and found everything normal. He moved into the closet and thought if he were going to find anything, he would find it here. He paid particular attention to the carpeting, looking for an outline of a trap door that would lead to the house's foundation. *Excellent spot for hiding weapons and documents*, he thought. Finding nothing, he then slid underneath the racks of clothing and examined the baseboards and walls encompassing the room. He almost missed it. He moved closer with his pen light to examine two tiny indentations, spaced three feet apart on one of the wall's painted wood moldings. He gingerly ran his fingers along the seams and wondered what these could be and all of a sudden, it hit him. *These are for door sills*, he thought. He pushed back the clothes and looked up and could see two small parallel grooves running upwards. He crawled from beneath the clothes, stood and thought, *where's the trigger?* He walked around the room searching and then began pushing and pulling back the lower and upper clothing racks in order to examine the walls behind them. When he pulled back the last upper rack of clothes he heard a faint sound. He stood back and watched in surprise as a portion of the wall dropped vertically into the houses' foundation to expose a short wide hallway with stairs leading to the second floor. He grabbed his radio, "Slade, come in. Over."

"Yeah, what's up? Over."

"Get over here. You won't believe what I just found. Over."

"Where are you, buddy? Over."

"In the master bedroom closet. Out." While waiting, Jake moved the rack of clothes in the other direction, and the wall moved upwards and clicked shut. *How ingenious*, he thought.

He heard Slade's deep voice behind him, "What's going on?"

"Look at this." Jake pulled the rack of clothes toward him, and again with a faint sound the wall descended to the house's foundation.

"Oh my God!" Slade exclaimed. "How shifty is that?"

"Would you like to enter my chamber of horrors?" Jake asked.

"Did you check for trip wires and other devices of mayhem?"

"Sure did. Even threw a half a dozen of Seyed's high end shoes in there and heard nary a sound outside of the clunking of leather," Jake said, as he flashed his crooked smile at his partner. They entered the short, wide hallway with their powerful penlights and could see stairs leading up to the second floor with a beautiful and obviously expensive split tapestry at the top of the stairway. They looked around and found a light switch on the wall next to the master closet opening and snapped it on. To the left of them was a large gun cabinet stocked with weapons and on the other side of the wide hall was a large ammo cabinet. Next to the ammo cabinet hung assault vests, flak jackets, and ammo belts filled with ammunition.

"Jackpot!" Slade exclaimed. "Look at all the guns in here. He has enough ordnance to hold off a small army." Slade sucked in his breath and said, "Do I see what I think I'm seeing?"

"Sure do. There are a half dozen Freedom Firearms in the gun case, and they look like they're in excellent shape. I have to admit the man has good taste in handguns." Jake took the radio and instructed the captain to collect the totes in the SUV and meet them in the room off the master closet. After they had confiscated the weapons, ammo, and other gear, Jake had Jim load the duffel bags into the SUV. Next, he instructed the captain to check all outside entrances to ensure the new security cards worked properly. While Jim was outside, Jake and Slade climbed the stairway and discovered by moving the right hand portion of the tapestry away from the wall the upstairs security door descended into the space in front of them. As they stepped onto the second floor landing, they noticed that both security doors closed behind them. They walked across the hall to the den. The room had a cherry credenza to their left and an oversized leather couch with a beautifully detailed glass top coffee table on their right. "Slade, you notice anything peculiar about this room?"

Slade examined the room and finally said. "You're right, there is something different here, but I can't put my finger on it."

"When I checked out his downstairs office appointed in maple including heavy ornate crown molding and ceiling beams, it was fit for a king. Look at the crown molding. Why would you cut expensive millwork at a ninety-degree angle? Plus, do you see any ceiling beams?"

"No, I don't," Slade said with a thoughtful look on his face. "This room looks out of sorts to the rest of the house."

"My thoughts exactly." The two agents carefully examined the room. Finally Jake turned to his friend and said, "I believe one of these walls either ascends or descends."

"Why do you say that?" Slade asked.

"Because crown molding is usually cut at a forty-five-degree angle to give the corners depth and a finished look. You can't have movement with a wall without its molding interfering with its adjacent side if it isn't cut at a straight angle. I should know since I have had intimate experience cutting crown molding with my miter saw when I was remodeling my house."

"You have a point," Slade said. The agents continued to search for anomalies in the room until Slade motioned for Jake to move to the back wall. "There, do you see the corners?" Slade pointed.

"Sure do."

"Do they look normal to you?"

"I think so." Jake walked over to one of the corners and peered at it while running his fingers along the crevice. "It's a millimeter too wide, and there's no paint contact. I have to say, Slade, you have good eyes." The two continued to carefully examine the room until Slade motioned Jake over to the credenza. Slade reached behind it and felt a slot outlined by a metal plate in the wall. He retrieved his security card from his assault vest and slipped it through the slot, and they watched in amazement as the back wall ascended upwards to expose a beautiful cherry back bar replete with lights, a large mirror, barware and expensive liquors.

"Maybe we should have a drink," Slade quipped.

Jake waved off his remark and said, "The more I discover about this house the more uneasy I'm becoming. I just hope we find all this place has to offer."

"I'm with you, partner. Looking around at this building it reminds me of a museum with its marble, massive eight-foot doors and expensive artwork. The guy has really gone over the top," Slade expressed.

"That's what I'm afraid of," Jake added. The two agents rifled through the cabinets and drawers of the back bar, and the cherry credenza and came up empty once again. "So far we haven't found any information that would help us in the investigation. Let's move on, Slade."

The Intel ops thoroughly checked the remaining rooms on the second floor and still couldn't find any documentation that would expose the terrorists' plans. They searched the three bedrooms, game room with its exotic Brunswick snooker table, the two bathrooms done in striated marble and the theater room. The only thing they found was that they were both amazed at the money thrown at the place. The theater complex alone was worth more than three year's of Jake's salary. He collected his radio from his assault vest, "Captain, do the security cards work for all outside locations? Over."

"Affirmative, sir. Over."

"Any hidden exterior features to the house, garage, and the guest cottage? Did you look for concealed entrances, doorways, and stairways? Over." "Affirmative, sir. I did a thorough interior search of the garage and carriage house and found nothing out of the ordinary. Also checked the perimeters of each building and found nothing unusual. Over."

"What about documents? Over."

"Nothing, sir. Everything looks clean. Over."

"Okay, post up at the portico and keep a sharp eye out. Over."

"Roger that, sir, and out."

Jake and Slade descended the front stairway to the gathering room and moved to the prayer room, checking the monitors. Everything appeared, as it should.

Jake looked at Slade and said, "Everything left the way it was?"

"It's cool."

"Okay, let's head out, we've been here long enough."

On the way back to the safe house Jake was thinking about what triggered the hidden doors to the gunroom. He had carefully inspected the clothes racks and the steel rods that encircled the master bedroom's closet and didn't figure it out until he moved the right hand side tapestry out from the wall and saw that it wasn't a standard rod that held the tapestry in place. It was a large hollow steel rod that most likely contained wiring going into the wall that connected to a transformer somewhere in the house that controlled the opening via a gear, sprocket or pulley system. *Pretty nifty*, he thought.

SEVENTY

RIYADH, SAUDI ARABIA 2010

Two black SUV's were parked a half a block away on a side street from the wide avenue that led to Seyed's house. The occupants in both automobiles were alert, waiting for the big limo to appear carrying Al-Hadi and Seyed from the bi-weekly energy meeting. It was 1815 hours on Friday evening. Soon the big black Pullman, followed closely by a blue SUV, turned off the boulevard into an exclusive neighborhood and went through a pair of large sandstone pillars and continued driving east up the hill toward Seyed's house. "Where did that other car come from?" Slade asked, as he turned to Jake behind the wheel of the lead SUV.

"Christ, I don't know. Intel indicated they always drove alone from the ministers meeting," Jake said with a concerned look on his face.

"Well they didn't this time."

"Slade, open the COM to Jim's car."

"Will do," He unclipped his transceiver from the belt on his assault vest and hit the open COM button so everyone could hear.

"Okay, everyone listen up. It appears that our friends have protection following them," Jake said.

"How many?" Jim fired back.

"Don't know, windows are tinted, but this is what we'll do," Jake replied. "Slade, contact the Saudi Special Forces commander for this detail. They have a couple of cars up the street from Seyed's house, and they need to cut off the blue SUV when Al-Hadi's limo turns into Seyed's driveway. We need to isolate them there."

While Slade was contacting the commander, Jake continued with his plans. "There's an alleyway perpendicular to Seyed's driveway, and we need to take the street behind us that runs parallel to his street and get ahead of them and lay in wait. Once they show the Saudis will cut off and secure their protection and will follow the limo into the compound. Thank God the property has a long, winding drive leading to the house, and this will give them just enough time to think that they can make it into the house. Otherwise, if they stay in the limo they will have the advantage. It's mobile, bulletproof, bristling with weapons and a frickin' pillbox. The timing is going to be critical. We'll lag back a few meters and off to the side; don't want to make it too easy for their counter measures. Once the limo pulls up to the portico and Seyed exits the car, we'll charge them. I'll take the chauffer and Seyed on the left. Slade, you have Al-Hadi on the right. Understood?"

"Yes, sir," Slade acknowledged.

"Jim, after the Saudis secure the blue SUV, I want your team to follow us in and lay back about fifteen meters to cover our backs in case anything happens. You follow?" Jake said, while barking orders.

"Affirmative. Weapons are at ready, and we're good to go when you are," Jim answered smartly.

"Okay, they're out of sight, let's go!" Jake barked again. The two SUV's made a U-turn at the top of the wide avenue and headed back down the street and made a sharp right and raced up the road parallel to the wide avenue. On the way Jake issued additional instructions to his team. They were only in place a few seconds when they saw the big Pullman heading their way.

"Where are the Saudis?" Jake asked.

"Boss, I see both of them coming up fast," Slade countered. In a blink of an eye, the lead gray Saudi SUV came around Al-Hadi's limo and wedged between the limo and the blue SUV while the second Saudi SUV forced the security car to the curb. Six Saudi commandos immediately jumped out with guns drawn. The first three took cover behind the second SUV that had pinned the security car to the curb while the other three hung back behind the lead SUV. The lead commando barked orders in Arabic to the occupants of the blue SUV to step out of their car with hands clasped behind their heads. At the same time, the big Pullman made a sharp right turn and crashed through the front metal gates and began accelerating up the drive. The two Black SUVs in the alleyway waited a moment before proceeding across the avenue to determine if the Saudi commandos had everything under control. Both of the security car's occupants were now kneeling in the street with hands clasped over their heads, surrounded by the commandos. The lead commando turned and waved the SUVs through the damaged gates.

So far so good, Jake thought. Now they needed to perfectly time when to approach the big limo as it pulled under the portico. One slip and this could turn into a firefight. Jake checked his rearview mirror and saw that Jim's SUV was following at about fifteen meters. As the big Pullman was about to pull under the portico, Jake gunned his SUV, and it shot forward, rapidly closing the distance between the two cars. As the three leapt out of the limo, the two agents exited their SUV with their .454 Casull revolvers drawn. In an instant Seyed bolted to the rear of the house, hopped over the coach gate, and disappeared around the corner. Slade ordered Al-Hadi to kneel and place his hands over his head while Jake attended to the chauffer and radioed Jim to bring his car forward. After the chauffer and Al-Hadi were secured, Jake handed them to Ron and Jerry and barked, "Jerry, stow them in your car and keep an eye out for any activity on this side of the house. Ron, reconnoiter the south side of the house and stay put for further orders. Jim, Slade, let's head to the back of the house and see were Seyed is. He's probably headed to the guest cottage around the corner, fifty meters away."

As the three moved to the back of the house, Jim quipped, "Christ, that man is fast!" Jake immediately used Delta's hand signal for quiet as they approached the northeast corner of the house.

Seyed barreled around the corner of the house and ran to the guest cottage, went behind it and slid the large potting table away from the house. He reached down, collected a key and unfastened a small padlock to a trap door, climbing down to a small basement door and went inside. The basement was as dark as a tomb with no outside windows and stocked with food and other supplies. He reached up and switched on a single dingy overhead lamp, moved to the far corner and crawled underneath a table and opened a small pistol vault and removed a pair of Heckler and Koch Mark 23 M auto .45 caliber pistols. The military version came with extended pistol grips to accommodate twenty round magazines instead of the standard ten for the civilian version. The handguns were extremely accurate, durable and really packed a wallop. He loaded ten magazines into his pant's pockets, reached back into the safe and removed a flak jacket. He left the safe door open and moved along the wall until he was centered under the stairwell. He used the same key to unlock a small door that led to a dimly lit passageway to the main house. He had excavated and built the tunnel six years ago without anyone's knowledge, except for three highly skilled craftsmen. After the three completed the work, they had the misfortune of meeting their untimely deaths. While walking through the tunnel, Seyed removed his suit jacket and put on his flak vest, stashed his ammo clips in the vest's pockets and holstered the pistols. He hoped his other weapon's stash was still in the main house.

As Jake peered around the corner of the house, Slade was on the radio a couple of meters back asking for an update on Jerry's situation. "No activity at the front of the house. Over."

"Okay, stay put and let us know. Copy? "

"Copy, FIFE. Out."

"FOW-ER, how say you? Over."

"Alls quite on the south side, FOW-ER, out," Ron, said.

They were on the International Civil Aviation Organization (ICAO) code for clarity in radio transmissions. The British and American armed forces adopted the ICAO alphabet in 1956. Jake was designated WUN that represented one by the code. Slade was TOO, Jim was TREE, Ron was FOW-ER and Jerry was FIFE.

"Jake, what do you see?" Jim whispered.

"Nothing, I think he went into the cottage. Will flank and use the side door approach. Jim, you take the west end. I'll stay on the east side, and Slade, you take point. Understood?"

"Affirmative," both men answered.

At the end of the passage, Seyed climbed a ladder that led to a trap door under his bed in the master bedroom. He crawled through the door and headed to the prayer room. He needed to see the monitors to determine what he was up against. He remembered seeing four SUVs, two across from his house in the alleyway and two that sealed off their security detail. *How many men?* he thought. He wondered if Felix had something to do with it. Even though he and Al-Hadi thought the meeting went reasonably well at Felix's redoubt a few months ago and official looking Justice Department and IRS documents had been sent to reel Felix in, he still couldn't help to think that something was amiss. *Wait a minute*, he thought. The two SUV's that cut off their protection were gray, the color of Saudi Special Forces. Why were they here? He wasn't exactly sure what was going on. It was so sudden. Was it one of his transgressions in the past? Was it his arms brokering, or perhaps helping his country, Iran, to become a nuclear power? He just wasn't sure, but he knew he needed to get out of here and fast. He needed to find somewhere safe, somewhere to buy him time to think. Seyed hurried into the prayer room adjacent to the bedroom and peered at the monitors. Everything seemed to be fine. He stood there looking at the screens awhile longer until he thought he saw something out of place at the front gates. He panned one of the cameras to get a closer view. "Crap, the gates are intact. *They're using a feedback loop*," he thought. *But how could they, surely he would have been notified by the security company if someone had tried to breach the compound.* Then it hit him. He had to get to his weapons stash.

***

Jake was heading to the east side of the cottage as Slade looked up from his position and saw a shadow in the prayer room. He issued a down signal to Jake. Frozen in his tracks, Jake hit the ground and saw Slade motion behind him at the window. Jake could barely discern a silhouette through the bronze tinted glass hunched in the prayer room as if looking at something. While keeping his eye on the figure, he slowly moved across the ground until he was able to stand at the far side of the master bedroom's patio with his back against the house.

Slade whispered, "Did he see you?"

"No, I don't think so, or I would have been toast. Christ, he's inside the house?" Jake said quietly as he looked at Slade.

"Couldn't tell who it was, but there's definitely someone there."

"Oh, it's him," Jake said in a hushed tone. They carefully moved further away as Jake hit the COM on his radio. "Ron, search the south and west facings of the house for forced entry and affirm, over. Jerry, you do the same out front. Jim, search around back of the cottage for any activity. Over."

"FOW-ER, copy, sir," Ron said.

"FIFE, copy, sir," Jerry intoned.

"TREE, copy, sir," Jim added.

Jake looked at Slade. "We'll find out what's going on."

Almost immediately Jake's radio vibrated, and he hit the COM button again. "Sir, found an opened trap door midway at the back of the cottage. Waiting instructions. Over."

"Jim, wait till Slade and I arrive. Over."

"TREE, copy, sir."

"Ron, Jerry, continue searching. Over."

"FOW-ER, copy, sir."

"FIFE, copy, sir."

"What do we have, Jim?" Jake asked as he and Slade approached him behind the cottage.

"We have a ladder going down to a basement."

Jake instructed Jim to stay put, and then he and Slade went down the ladder and went through a small door. "What do you make of it?" Slade asked as they made their way across the basement.

Jake ignored Slade's question as he spotted a table in the far corner and walked to it. He squatted down and saw that he was looking at a Lagerfeld's pistol vault tucked into the corner under the table. *"What do we have here?"* Jake thought as he pointed his penlight into the opened safe, reached in and retrieved .45 caliber ammo boxes and a couple of full magazines. While on his haunches, Jake turned his head toward Slade and said, "If I didn't know any better, I'd say these clips and ammo belong to an HK .45 caliber pistol. Search around and see if there are any other surprises."

While Slade checked the rest of the basement, Jake continued to search the safe. His radio pulsated again, and Ron and Jerry reported that they didn't find any signs of forced entry on the house's perimeter. Jake told them to standby.

What's going on? he thought. He didn't have long to wait.

"Just found a tunnel heading in the direction of the main house," Slade said.

"So that's how he did it."

"I believe so."

Jake switched channels on his radio and told the Saudi lead commando that they had found a tunnel between the cottage and the main house and to send four of his men into the compound and cover the drive and the house's perimeter. "I want one of your men stationed at the northeast corner of the main house, one at the southwest corner, the third midway along the drive and the fourth between the guest cottage and the four-car detached garage. Block the drive's exit with your SUV. Over." Jake barked.

"SIX, copy, sir."

Jake switched back to COM and told his team the instructions that he had given to the lead Saudi commando. "Jerry, when the commandos arrive, I want you to take up a new position behind the cottage and cover the trap door. Over."

"FIFE, copy, sir."

"Jim, we need you down here for cover as soon as Jerry arrives. Over."

"TREE, copy, sir."

"Ron, standby for new instructions. Over."

"FOW-ER, wilco, sir."

While they waited for Jim, they laid out their strategy.

"Slade, he's carrying at least two HK pistols."

"How do you know?"

"Because of the tour of his house this morning. Dr. Mostakavi has very expensive taste right down to his Lagerfeld's pistol vault under the table here. Fortunately for us, the safe is so luxurious and heat-resistant the interior is heavily padded with fireproofing material that leaves excellent imprints of objects stored inside, including his two HK's that were lying side-by-side on the floor of the pistol vault."

"So?" Slade said hesitantly.

"From the imprints on the safe's floor and the magazines, I'd say that HK makes two or three models that fit these marks. I already know their military issue because of the twenty-cartridge magazines he left behind. Let's see what we have." Jake unclipped his compu pad from his assault vest and punched in Homeland Security's small weapons database. "My guess is he's packing the same HK Mark 23 M auto .45 caliber pistols we're using for backup, and they're unpleasant to say the least." Jake looked down at his screen. "Ah, I was right. Now we know what he's using, but we still need to know where he's heading in the house and what he's doing? Any ideas, my boy?"

"Well if I was him I'd want to know yesterday what I'm up against, who are my adversaries, their capabilities, how many and where they are. And the first place I would check would be the monitors in the prayer room off the master bedroom. That's where I saw his shadow, Jake."

"Exactly. I'm sure he has seen our SUV's and knows this is a surgical strike. He'll probably head for his stash that was stored in the hidden hallway between his master bedroom closet and the second floor hallway."

"He'll be in for one heck of a surprise when he enters his gun room and finds that his weapons and supplies are gone," Slade added.

"Well, what are we waiting for?" Jake mused while tugging at his type III armor flack jacket.

The team was using the famed Delta Force black flak jackets for protection. The jackets were custom fitted for each person's torso with polyethylene plates for vital organs including the spine. The protection could withstand multiple high-powered rounds from rifles as well as small shrapnel and handguns up to and including .45 caliber rounds.

Seyed rushed into the master bedroom closet and pulled back one of the upper pant racks. He stood back and watched as a portion of the wall dropped vertically down into the houses' foundation to expose a short, wide hallway with stairs leading to the second floor. He walked inside, switched on the light and checked his large gun cabinet—it was empty. He frantically looked around the small room—nothing. Where were his Freedom Firearms, given to him by Felix, and where were his weapons from his days as a soldier in the Soviet-Afghan conflict? They took everything right down to his ammo, knives, and an old assault vest. Hatred filled his deep brown eyes. "Death to the infidels," he said to himself. He leaned up against the gun cabinet for a moment to collect his thoughts. He unclipped his satphone from his belt and while staring down at it, he thought about calling Al-Hadi. *That's foolish*, he thought. He knew that he and the chauffer were captured along with the two security agents. *How many were there?* he thought again. He spotted four SUV's. He could be looking upwards to at least twenty people. He could've used the extra weapons. He now knew it was time. He placed a call to Abrahim Solasti, his chief technologist. On the second ring, Abrahim answered. "Seyed, what's up?"

"Abrahim, listen carefully, I'm under assault at my house and praise be to Allah!" Seyed said emphatically and broke the sat connection. He knew his old friend would carry through. He had to get to the cars in the garage if he wanted any chance of escaping.

⬤

Jake unclipped his radio from his assault vest, switched to COM and began issuing orders while they made a beeline to the second floor hallway. "Jerry, are you at the trap door? Over."

"Just arriving, sir. Over."

"Jim, get your butt down here and provide back up. Over."

"TREE, copy, sir."

"Ron, use your e-card and go in through the front and post up in the hallway outside of the master bedroom. Seyed may still be in the master or the prayer room so heads up. Over."

"FOW-ER, copy, sir."

By now Jake and Slade were moving through the passageway when Jake suddenly stopped, peered down and picked up an article of clothing. "Lordy, this is his suit coat, and that only means one thing."

Before Jake could continue, Slade cut in and said, "Flak jacket, and he probably has an assault vest."

"Let's hope he's not as prepared as us," Jake said with a concerned look in his eyes.

Jake hit the COM again. "Listen up kids, our friend is now wearing a Flak jacket and probably an assault vest, and packing the same heat as we are. Copy?"

All three acknowledged.

Jake switched channels and notified the Saudi commandos of the new developments.

"Slade, get a move on. Hopefully we can trap him in his gun room."

"Hey, don't tell me to get a move on. You're the one that stopped, bubba. If you moved any slower you won't be able to keep up with your girl friends."

"Well at least I have some."

Jake and Slade's radios pulsated and Jake picked up.

"Guy's I'm in position. FOW-ER, over."

"Ron, stay there for further instructions. Copy?" Jake said.

"FOW-ER, copy, sir."

Jake hand-signaled Slade for quiet and whispered, "We're at the end of the tunnel," and directed his light upwards. "What do we have here? Looks like the underside of a trap door."

"Bet the master bedroom is on the other side," Slade interjected.

"Oh shoot, did I miss that?" Jake thought as he carefully slid the door aside, crawled through the opening and scooted underneath

the king bed with his gun drawn. He crawled out and took a crouch position and looked around. Everything was quiet. "Buddy, come on up, I'll cover you." Jake whispered. After Slade joined him, Jake looked around again and said, "You're right, and there's the prayer room with the bank of monitors." He hit the COM button and quietly said, "Jim, the tunnel leads to a trap door underneath our friend's king bed in the master bedroom. Copy?"

"TREE, copy, sir."

"How quaint," Slade said.

"Well what did you expect? King Arthur and the roundtable complete with trap doors, secret rooms, and passageways."

"Well, we have part of it," Slade quipped.

"These guys want to drive us back a thousand years. Okay, let's head for the backstairs off the kitchen," Jake directed.

"After you, my lady Marion," Slade said as a wide grin spread across his face.

Jake ignored the last remark and countered, "Move smartly, my friend, we need to catch this guy pronto."

On the way out of the master bedroom, they stopped briefly for Jake to give further instructions to Ron and then hurried to the back stairway. After they arrived at the spot where the wall leads to the gun room, Jake dug into one of the vests pockets and pulled out a listening device and put it to the wall and listened, "He's in there. He's talking to Abrahim." Jake stepped back and hit the COM button to his radio and whispered, "You in position, Ron? Over."

"Affirmative, sir. Over."

"What's the position of the entry door to the gun room? Over."

"The entry is open. Over."

Jake looked at Slade and said, "Darn, its open on Ron's side."

"Still should be okay, it's a pretty small enclosure."

Jake hit the COM again. "Ron, we're about ready to neutralize Seyed. Step aside and away from the opening. Copy?"

"FOW-ER, copy, sir."

"Slade, open the door," Jake whispered as he stepped up to the wall and collected a flash bang grenade from his assault vest. Slade inserted his e-card into the slot, and as the wall slid down, Jake released the trigger and flung the grenade into the small enclosure and stepped away from the opening.

———◇———

Seyed was clipping his satphone to his belt and looked up just in time to see a birdcage like object tumbling toward him. He instinctively stepped forward and threw out his left leg with lightening reflexes and booted the birdcage past him and into the walk-in closet and dove behind the wall, closed his eyes and covered his ears.

It was too late for Ron standing on the other side of the wall. He took the full brunt of the detonation. With his eyes blinded and ears ringing, he staggered to the floor totally disoriented. In an instant Seyed was by him, running through the master bedroom and out into the hallway to the portico's door. With a heave Seyed pushed open the heavy security door and bounded down the slate steps in full stride. The Saudi commando posted between the four-car detached garage, and the cottage was caught looking the other way, and before he could react Seyed was already going around the far side of the garage. Jerry saw him and hollered down to the commando, but he couldn't get a clean shot because the soldier was in the way. The other commando on the northeast corner of the house was out of position and didn't even see Seyed. In a flash, Jerry was on the COM telling Jake and Slade what had happened.

———◇———

"Christ, way to go," Jake barked.
"What's your location?" Jerry asked. "Over."

"We're in the gun room. Ron sustained some flash burns, and Slade's holding back to take care of him. I'm on my way out, and I want you to take point and have the Saudis surround the garage's perimeter. Copy?"

"FIFE, copy, sir and out." Jerry said.

Seyed fired a couple of rounds from the HK into the garage's side door and then kicked it in. He bounded inside, jumped in the Shelby Cobra and hit the ignition—nothing. *Man, they got to the cars too! These guys are good*, he thought. He shot out of the Cobra and picked up a crowbar from the workbench and began tearing out big chunks of sheet rock from the garage's rear false wall. Within seconds he had the Suzuki Hayabusa GSX1300R Electric out of the wall, his helmet on and cranking her up. This was one of the fastest production bikes in the world and could reach 100 mph in three seconds and had a 250-mile electric range. He had bought the bike six months ago and added an extra twenty-amp breaker in the house's main floor electric panel. He installed it under the two breakers labeled kitchen and gave it the same name. He trenched and ran the conduit and wiring out to the rear wall of the garage and attached the leads to the auto charger for the bike in the false wall. He pointed the high performance-racing bike toward the splintered doorway, revved it once, shot through the doorway, and turned left and rocketed down the drive.

As Jake cleared the portico steps he could see one of the commandos and Jerry with weapons drawn, firing at the disappearing figure. *I've got one chance*, he thought. Jake quickly drew his .454 Casull from his holster, took a wide stance and planted his feet firmly on the plush, green lawn. With both hands on the revolver's grip, arms extended, he carefully aimed and fired. The big gun roared and 150 meters away the bike's rear tire exploded in a pyre of dust, metal, and rubber. The rider pitched to the left and landed on his back in a wide swath of freshly turned flower beds as the bike continued down the drive, kicking up sparks and chunks of concrete before coming to rest in front of the commando's SUV blocking the drive's entrance. Jake holstered his handgun and quickly got on the COM and began barking out orders. "Jim, you take point. Jerry you have some medical training, correct? Over."

"Affirmative, sir. Over."

"Good, you'll come with me with one of the commandos, and will work our way down to the accident site and check out Dr. Mostakavi. Copy?"

"FIFE, copy, sir."

Jake changed channels to Slade's frequency. "How's Ron doing? Over."

"A little woozy, but okay. The flash burns on his legs don't look too bad. Over."

"Okay, stay with him and bring him out for some fresh air when he's ready. I'll have one of the commandos bring up a first-aid kit. Out." Jake instructed one of the commandos to fetch a kit. He looked at Jerry and the Saudi commando and said, "Fellas keep your guns drawn, we'll approach him slowly from three sides. I can't impress upon you just how dangerous this person is."

They both acknowledged Jake's instructions. Seyed was lying face down on the plush lawn about forty meters from the flowerbeds where he initially landed. He had rolled and skidded across the lawn and now lay motionless as the three men approached. Jake was the first to reach him and checked his pulse from his carotid artery. *It's weak*, he thought. He yelled up the drive for Jim to bring a blanket and first-aid kit. Seyed was bleeding from his right thigh, and he could tell by the angle of his left arm that it was badly broken. Jake got on the satphone and called Colonel Sam McGowan at a small airfield east of Riyadh. The United States had permission from the Saudi government to set up temporary operations for a small Delta Force detachment for the express purpose of extracting Al-Hadi and Seyed. There were two MH-6s stationed there with a Medivac team. The helos were a favorite of the Special Forces, and even though they were small, they were fast and carried a nasty sting. "Colonel, this is Jake Cannon, sir."

"Jake, is everything under control?" McGowan asked.

"Yes, sir, but we need Medivac at our location. Dr. Mostakavi appears to be seriously hurt, and one of our team has flash burns on his legs."

"I'll send both choppers. ETA in fifteen minutes, Jake," The colonel responded.

"Affirmative, sir." Jake broke the connection and focused his attention on the motionless figure in front of him. *I wonder what you've been up to*, Jake thought. He took a small-serrated knife from his assault vest, knelt down and cut Seyed's right pant leg away from his thigh and examined the wound. It was a clean cut, about seven inches long, but partially filled with dirt and bleeding profusely. *Must've snag his leg on one of the roses when he landed in the flowerbeds*, he thought. As Jim approached them with the first-aid kit and blanket Jake turned to Jerry and asked, "Can you stem the bleeding?"

"I think so," he answered as he knelt down, opened the first-aid kit and began to work on Seyed's leg.

They now could hear the two MH-6s, off in the distance, closing in on the compound. While Jerry was attending to Dr. Mostakavi, Jake walked down to the damaged gates and gave instructions to the lead commando. Three minutes later while the two helos were landing in the middle of the yard the second Saudi SUV with two commandos inside whisked the chauffer away. Jake walked up the hill to confer with Captain Cramer. "I want you to stay behind and help supervise and coordinate the search of Seyed's house. You can never be too careful."

"I hear you, sir. I'll report back my findings," Jim answered.

"Good. I want you to know that you and your team did damn well. There were no casualties and one minor injury to our men outside of what happened to Seyed. Damn fool, what was he thinking?"

"Don't really care, sir, and thanks for the complement," Jim said as the two men faced each other and saluted.

It took only fifteen minutes for the team to bid their farewells to the remaining Saudi commandos, Medivac to attend to Dr. Mostakavi and Ron Tate. After everyone and their equipment were loaded on board the two MH-6s lifted off. Back at the air field a CV-22 Osprey was waiting to receive the team and their captives. The Osprey with its vertical left off was perfect for this type of operation since the airfield's runway was far too short to accommodate standard jet aircraft. One hour later they were headed to NATO's Air Base in Incirlik, Turkey. Waiting there was a modified MC-130H Talon II to take them to Germany and then to the Naval Base at Guantanamo Bay, Cuba.

SEVENTY-ONE

RIYADH, SAUDI ARABIA 2010

Abrahim Solasti stared at his satphone. He wondered what had happened to Seyed. He had said something about being under assault and then Solasti heard the words, "Praise be to Allah." *How fitting*, he thought. It was November 16th, a Muslim holy day, Eid al-Adha, the "Festival of Sacrifice." *Perfect timing to offer the United States as a sacrifice to Allah*, he again thought. He hit the auto-dialer program button on his satphone. The button would set off a chain of events that would eventually send the world into a depression, or worse. The calls were automatically made to the five operatives working in the United States. Three of the team were senior investment managers for Fidelity Investments in Boston, Massachusetts; T. Rowe Price, in Seattle Washington, and Vanguard in New York City, New York. The others were bank officers for Bank of America in New York City and JP Morgan Chase, in Washington D.C. It was 7:00 p.m. in Riyadh when he made the calls. That made it 9:00 a.m. on the West Coast and 12:00 p.m. on the East Coast. By closing of business, today, chaos would reign supreme, and by the following Monday despair and hopelessness would set in as the world reeled from financial calamity. "It took years and a team of experts to construct the software (worms) that ultimately would wrought destruction upon the United States and the world," Abrahim mused.

At the onset of the project the team had planned to cyber-attack the banks and brokerage houses' firewalls' vulnerabilities on two fronts. Seyed decided rather than using the direct approach and have the team waste valuable resources in writing sophisticated software to break the companies' encryption and digital authentication ciphers for their firewalls, or look for zero-day elements that could be used to exploit their back door, he instructed his team to find the companies' manufactures of digital certificates and hack their list of keys. And if that was too cumbersome they could always obtain a list of high-ranking IT employees and hack into their home computers and possibly collect the information they were seeking. They knew that the possibility existed that some of the employees worked from home and would transfer information to and from their companies. The employees would unwittingly piggyback the viruses into their company's networks and thus circumvent the company's firewall ciphers. The worms would then lay and wait until they were instructed by the operatives to test the vulnerability of each financial institution. "Allah would find a way, Insah' Allah—God willing," Seyed had said.

The tests had begun months ago and were staggered, going from one company to the next. They had searched a wide array of financial applications for each company but always looking for seldom used accounts and once found, extracting small amounts of money from the funds. They had constantly monitored the big media in the United States, including social medias to see if there were any stories on any unusual activity on the five-targeted companies. As expected, there hadn't been any. Once again the United States had been asleep at the controls.

Once the tests had been completed, the plan would be to cyber-attack the financial institutions and banks simultaneously, from within, by activating a series of worms for each company. The viruses had already been implemented beyond each company's firewalls, complements of their employees working from home. They would piggyback through the company's servers by hacking into the lower-level ciphers and attack each company's financial system programs. Once the self-replicating virus had passed the companies' servers, it would change all of the cipher keys to lock out management from preventing further damage. The worms would propagate and grow at ever-increasing speeds, jumping from server to server, going through the companies' networks' of bridges, switches, and routers undetected. It would grow and adapt to not only the companies' security measures, but also learn and adapt to the financial programs before infesting itself on one finance system after another until every file and funds' proceeds were transferred to secret accounts spread across the Middle East. Afterward, the changed firewalls' and servers' cipher keys would be replaced with the originals; software trails and the viruses' code would vanish. There would be no trace of the worms' presence. It would be as though nothing had happened, except there would be no money left. Seyed had said, "That there was always the risk that the main power supply could be interrupted in order to mitigate the damages, but who would know until it was too late."

Abrahim wondered why he hadn't received any confirmation from the operatives yet. They were supposed to notify him within the hour via encrypted code on his satphone after they had unleashed the deadly worms. It had been three hours and still nothing. He had been monitoring the news media in the United States as they had, when testing, but there wasn't anything. *What's going on?* he thought. He knew he shouldn't call any of the team for fear of the authorities uncovering his location. But then again, it didn't matter. The initial calls had been made. He thought, *even if the operatives were caught and the operation thwarted, he still had one more deadly surprise for the United States. Allah would prevail.*

It had been four hours now since Abrahim Solasti initiated the cyber-attack, and he still hadn't heard from the operatives. There was nothing on the news, Internet, or the feelers he had put out. Well, he couldn't wait any longer. *It's time to start the second phase of the plan*, he thought. This he could do remotely. Early on, it was decided to target the cyber-attacks around the winter holidays, preferably Christmas or New Years. The team believed this would maximize confusion and damage since the infidels would be distracted by their celebrations. And as it turned out the timing of Seyed's phone call, though undoubtedly tragic from his end, couldn't have been more timely. He was still upset and confused to why Seyed didn't attack the U.S. banking and financial industry from Riyadh. For sure the technology was there, but he just waved it off saying he was too busy with his motherland. *If hindsight was worth anything, he should have done it himself,* Abrahim reasoned.

He had remembered when Seyed came to the team five years ago and unveiled a new project. He was very excited, and he was all business when it came to advancing new technology. Seyed had announced that he was assembling a team of very bright individuals with varied backgrounds from the physical sciences, computer science, quantum mechanics and computing and nanotechnology. He had said the best way to attack the United States was through advanced technology. Since his team already had permission from the Saudi government and King Saud University regents for time on their super computers doing molecular modeling and geological exploration for more oil deposits, he didn't see any reason why he couldn't add quantum physics and nanotechnology to the list. Besides, he had told us, molecular modeling was part of quantum physics.

Seyed had said that nanotechnology would open up new frontiers in all the sciences and affect our everyday lives in ways we wouldn't have thought possible. Nano machines held promise for a myriad of commercial and military applications. For instance, he said, these tiny nano engines working on nano, pico and even femto magnitudes could hold such small information packets that the entire contents of the Library of Congress could be stored in an area no larger than a sugar cube. He further expounded that medical science would be able to create devices with designer cells based on one's DNA that could travel through the human body, targeting and killing clusters of cancerous cells before they could spread.

He went on to say that he had researched both DNA and quantum computing and found that even though DNA computers held promise for faster processing speeds to solve a wide array of problems, he had chosen quantum computing because it was particularly adept at solving very large mathematical factoring problems and algorithms that were used in cryptography. And cipher keys were at the heart of digital certification. He had stated that most cipher keys are based on very large prime numbers, and in number theory, prime factorization is the disassembling of composite numbers into lesser non-trivial divisors, which when multiplied together equal the original number. He had ventured if they could build a quantum machine capable of 500 sextillion floating-point operations per second (500 zettaflops), then security on the Internet would be rendered useless. But first, he said, we needed to construct tiny nano and quantum machines that would enable us to produce ever-faster quantum computers.

He had compared quantum and digital computing by showing a ball and a coin lying on a table. We all knew that digital computing had two discreet states of zero or one just like the two sides of a coin. You flip the coin, and you have the other state. When you link these states (bits) together called bytes in the form of binary code, these structures give instructions for digital computer processors. However, he had showed us by rolling the ball across the table you have quaternary states called qubits of zero or one, zero and one, or a superposition of both. In other words, he had said, a qubit in its pure state can be represented as a linear combination of zero and one. He had also stated that you could look at that combination as being in two states simultaneously, or in the case of a light switch it shows various degrees of being on and off at the same time as in a dimmer switch. Each one of those states or chain of states can be interpreted as sets of instructions that go to the quantum computer's processors. He further stated by opening the doors to processing at the molecular level and harnessing the power of the atom's natural energy using ions, photons, and electrons without the tedium of constructing parallel processors in the classical sense, you could increase processing speeds exponentially. Besides, he had said, we are approaching the boundary in the digital world using Moore's law. He went on to state that Gordon E. Moore, co-founder of Intel, in his 1965 paper had noted that the number of integrated circuits had doubled every year since the invention of these circuits in 1958, and they would continue to double for at least another ten years. Needless to say it was well beyond the ten years that Moore had envisioned, and in fact, integrated circuits would continue to double every year or two until around 2020 when they would approach the size of atoms. At that point the era of integrated circuits etched on silicone wafers would end.

He then continued his discussion on quantum mechanics and elucidated on the issues of measurement and entanglement in quantum physics. He had stated that the team first must find a way to accurately measure the qubit states of one or more sub atomic particles without collapsing to the value that is measured. In other words, if one measures the state (spin, motion, and harmonics) of an atom, one or more neighboring atoms will take on the characteristics of the atom being measured. Such systems are then said to be in an entangled state if it cannot be written as a tensor product of its constituent subsystems. The team had eventually solved this problem by using a new type of photonic crystal laser to individually measure the spin, motion, and harmonics of each sub atomic particle and groups of sub atomic particles without artificially altering the decay of its orbit, motion, and harmonics and without changing its neighboring atoms or sub atomic particles' characteristics.

While part of the team was overcoming the barriers of super position, entanglement, distance, measurement and how to build quantum machines that would aid them in constructing faster quantum computers, the other team members were addressing issues of developing environments to control the interactions between sub atomic particles, and how to build nano machines that would enable them to send nano packets of electromagnetic energy to digital computers' information systems. The team had known that any form of energy could be transformed into another form and in all such energy processes, including total input, output and the exchange mechanism was equal to the total amount of energy in a closed system. Seyed had said in the case of quantum mechanics when using electromagnetic energy, the electromagnetic wave of these energy states were called quanta of light or photons, and that the electromagnetic radiation field could control these sub atomic particles by regulating the voltage in the field. Another method was to lower the environment's temperature close to zero degrees Kelvin (absolute zero) in order to control the atoms' interactions. In other words, he had said, these particles needed to be aligned in recognizable patterns such as strings to facilitate their measurements. So in the end he had decided to use atomic units of photons controlled within an electromagnetic field. He had postulated that he could generate enough electromagnetic energy through high-powered capacitors to create a strong enough field to control the sub atomic photons while at the same time boost the electromagnetic energy to the nano packets. Someone had asked him why he didn't convert and transfer some of the kinetic energy from the photons and use this to energize the nano packets. "No, no!" he screamed. "You don't want to interfere with the energy characteristics of the photons in any way. Besides, he said, he didn't know if this would be feasible, and it would certainly drive up the difficulty factor exponentially for measurements. He had said, based on their empirical evidence, their super capacitors generated more than enough electromagnetic radiation to properly energize the nano packets.

For testing, we had set up our own botnet with firewalls that had very sophisticated gateway cipher keys based on Shor's quantum algorithm for integer factorization. The new quantum computer running at nearly 400 zettaflops took less than five minutes to crack the prime factors of a very large semiprime. In retrospect, he had said, today's fastest digital super computers with its clusters of slave computers, or endless rows of parallel and quad processors would have taken a lifetime to do this. We had the breakthrough. This meant the widely held public-key cryptography schemes used on Internet sites were now useless. Further tests concluded that we were able to send nano packets of electromagnetic pulses of energy (EMP) and obliterate all information stored on digital computers' hard drives.

SEVENTY-TWO

RIYADH, SAUDI ARABIA 2010

Fifteen minutes after the CV-22 Osprey lifted off from the airfield at Riyadh, Saudi Arabia, Jake moved to the back of the plane and contacted his boss. "Did everything go smoothly?" the deputy secretary asked without any preamble.

"Ah, we had a couple of glitches, sir," Jake replied. "Ron Tate received some flash burns on his legs from a flash bang grenade, and I take full responsibility for that."

"What happened, Jake?" the deputy secretary asked with concern in his voice.

"I threw a stun grenade into a room where Seyed was hiding, and he kicked it into another room where Ron was, and he didn't have a chance to protect himself before it detonated."

"Jake, you can't blame yourself for the actions of others," Peterson said in a conciliatory tone.

"I know, sir, but it doesn't sit well."

The deputy secretary avoided Jake's last comment and asked, "Will he be okay?"

"Yeah, he'll be fine."

"Great. Now, what about Slade and the rest of the team?"

"Everyone's cool, sir."

"Good. Now what's the other snafu?"

"Seyed sustained some serious injuries, sir."

"Will he live?"

"Oh sure, he'll do just fine, and Al-Hadi's good too. As you instructed, we left the chauffer with the Saudi Special Forces for detainment and questioning. It'll be determined what level of involvement he has in all of this. We also left the security detail that was following Al-Hadi's limo."

"Security detail?" the deputy secretary asked in surprise. "I thought they traveled alone?"

"I thought so too until we saw a blue SUV following the big Pullman. Good thing the Saudi's were gracious enough to provide back up with their Special Forces, or we would have had our hands full."

"How did they do?"

"They were great, sir. They took care of the two occupants in the security car while our team extracted the subjects."

"Good to know. Now where are you?" the deputy secretary asked.

"We left Riyadh fifteen minutes ago and are on are way to Incirlik, Turkey. From there, as you know, it's on to Germany and then Gitmo."

"Okay. Now just to let you know, the Justice Department has issued arrest warrants for Felix Jamosa and Jeffery Starr. The warrants include capital crimes of treason and murder, and this should keep these two locked up for at least three lifetimes if not the death penalty. Problem is, I don't trust Felix. I don't think the FBI and the Portland police can waltz into Jamosa Enterprises and arrest them without some kind of incident. I'm still pissed at that federal judge, ah, what's his name? Oh yeah, James Law. Can you believe that?" the deputy secretary snorted. "The SOB had only issued sneak and peak warrants for their forty-third floor offices. Our attorneys had argued that all common areas of the building should be searched, especially since Felix is a king pin in the arms business. The piss ant said no!" The deputy secretary bellowed and paused before he continued, "and even though we received some good information from the search including Mr. Starr's diary, I still believe there are things about that building we're unaware of."

"I'm with you on that, sir. Should we remain on standby?" Jake asked.

"You bet your sweet bibby. I have a feeling their building is bristling with weapons."

"Jesus, you do?" Jake stated with alarm in his voice.

"Well, wouldn't you? They have been numero uno in the gun running business for years, and they probably have forgotten all the weapons they have laying around."

"You have a point, sir."

"We have another problem, Jake."

"What's that, sir?"

"You know Jamosa Enterprises is headquartered in Portland, Oregon?"

"So?"

"If you may recall the mayor and the city council had voted that they would not cooperate or be a part of the FBI's Joint Terrorism Task Force (JTTF). It had to do with the Brandon Mayfield arrest and detention over the Madrid train bombings in 2004. Though I suspect it runs deeper than that. And to this day, Portland is the only major city that remains outside and hostile toward JTTF. And to top it off, the FBI and us not only have to contend with the Jamosa Enterprise investigation and looming arrests, but also with the bomb plot at Portland's Pioneer Courthouse Square. Between the Jamosa and Mohammed Osman Mohamud investigations, the FBI and us have our work cut out in the Portland area."

"I'm wondering if Portland is becoming a hotbed for terrorists?" Jake questioned.

"I don't know. But I'm kicking this up to Admiral Eric Fulton, head of United States Special Operations Command (USSOC) and requesting a detachment of Delta Force operators. I have a real bad feeling about these gun runners, Jake."

"You've driven your point home, sir, we'll be ready," Jake said with even more alarm in his voice.

"Stay tuned. You and Slade will be receiving orders by the time you arrive at Gitmo. Understood?"

"Affirmative, sir," Jake replied, and then the line went dead. He stood there in the aft section of the Osprey for a long moment stunned, thinking about the conversation he just had with his boss. *He never recalled his boss being so concerned,* Jake thought. "God, I hope David isn't right or we could have one tense situation in Portland."

SEVENTY-THREE

RIYADH, SAUDI ARABIA 2010

Using the Saudi government in clandestine ways, Seyed's team had been able to uncover the locations of the four targets they were going to cyber-attack, using their quantum strategy. The information Seyed had received from the Saudis was highly classified and not given over to the Internet or any other source for that matter. *This had been the key to their success,* Abrahim thought. For months the team had tried to gain this information via conventional means, but to no avail. In the end Seyed and Al-Hadi had come through for them. The team knew it would be a long shot to try and break the targets' firewall ciphers with digital computer viruses, or search for companies that provided them. Instead, as they had done before with the financial institutions, they had received a list of the employees that work at the underground bunker sites and targeted their home computers with digital computer worms and waited to receive the information they were seeking. The sites had been placed underground decades ago in order to be impervious from electro magnetic pulses (EMPs) that were generated from fission or fusion devices such as atomic or thermonuclear bombs. Unlike the banks and brokerage houses, the targets' bunkers were a modified (distributed) open-air system similar to Iran's nuclear facility that was attacked by the Stuxnet virus. This meant the sites shared a botnet with each other and were completely self-contained from the outside world. The targets were autonomous to the Internet or any other source, and they could only transfer data amongst themselves. The plan had been to get the IP addresses of each site's firewall portals that ringed the gateways to their internal server networks. The assumption was made that if some of the employees worked from home and downloaded information along with the digital worms to their flash or thumb drives and then unknowingly uploaded the worms at work, this would circumvent the site's firewalls encryption keys. Once inside the target's network, the virus could then extract the portals' IP addresses.

Abrahim knew there had been two primary reasons to advance nanotechnology and quantum computing for their targets. First of all, it had been imperative to cyber-attack all four facilities simultaneously or as close as possible. Otherwise, it could afford the infidels time to lessen the damage by shutting down the remaining unaffected sites. Second, and as Seyed had suspected, the firewall cipher keys were changed on a weekly basis. It would have been impossible to decipher the keys, using digital technology, before they were changed again. Plus, it would have undoubtedly tipped off security that something was amiss. No, for the cyber-attack to be successful they needed to rely on stealth, speed and timing, and quantum computing was the ticket in. They could crack all the cipher keys at all four sites in a matter of minutes.

Abrahim had also known there was another reason not to solely rely on digital computer technology. Even if the team could break in and get pass the firewalls' and gateways' encryption keys, it would have taken much longer to instruct the operating systems at all four sites to erase the archived disk arrays. Besides, this would only logically delete the data. They needed to obliterate the information on the disk arrays in order to prevent any chance of recovering the data.

Just then his front door crashed in! "Praise be to Allah!" Abrahim said to no one in particular as he hunched over his laptop and typed in the passwords and executed the code (Allah) that would bring destruction to the infidels on Christmas Eve. "It's too late," he yelled, and laughed so uncontrollably that he had difficulty punching in the code to his smartphone. The last thing Abrahim Solasti and the special ops team heard was silence.

SEVENTY-FOUR

PORTLAND, OREGON 2010

David Peterson was on his satphone talking to Jake Cannon in Portland, Oregon, tying up loose ends on Felix Jamosa and Jeffery Starr's impending arrest when his secretary interrupted saying there was an urgent call from the base commander in Incirlik, Turkey. "Jake, I'll call you in a few, have to take another call." After receiving the horrific news from the base commander, the deputy secretary pick up his satphone and punched in Jake's number. "I have some bad news, Jake."

"What's that, sir?" Jake puzzled as he wondered what happened now.

"I just received word from Colonel James Strong, the base commander at Incirlik, Turkey. They lost everyone in an explosion at Abrahim Solasti's house in Riyadh, Saudi Arabia."

"Oh my God, everyone?" Jake asked as he stood and began to pace. "Your telling me all five of NATO's special ops and Saudi's Special Forces used as backup have all perished."

"Everyone, Jake. The only thing left was a huge crater where Abrahim's house used to stand. In fact the explosion was so intense that it wiped out half his block. He must have detonated 500 lbs of C-4."

"Could be Pentaerythritol tetranitrate (PETN) or Semtex, sir. Seems like the choice of explosives for the terrorists nowadays."

"You're probably right, Jake. I'm dating myself. I'm sure we will find out during the investigation from the forensic evidence. I can't tell you how horrible I feel about the men and their families. They won't even be able to bury their loved ones. When will it ever end?"

"Don't know, sir."

"Good thing you had Captain Jim Cramer hang back and help supervise the search at Seyed's house. At least we got some information from Cramer's team. As we speak, Saudi authorities are rounding up the rest of Seyed's team members."

"That's good, sir. Our team didn't have much time to search for documents. Our primary concern was weapons."

"I know, Jake. The main thing is you got Al-Hadi and Seyed out of there alive."

"Thank you, sir. I'm sure we're not going to find much evidence about their plans at Abrahim's property. I would have liked to take a peek at his computer's hard drive, but I'm sure it's been blown to smithereens. I can't help to think we are still missing something, sir."

"I know the feeling. Perhaps Mr. Jamosa and Mr. Starr's arrest will shed more light on their plans," the deputy secretary said.

"Let's hope so, sir."

"Now, have we covered everything on the Jamosa operation? If we keep to the schedule we'll be doing the extraction in about ten days."

"Affirmative sir, I think we're ready."

"Good, and let me know what you find out at the meeting with Portland's city council next week. Christ, they have to stick their noses into everything."

"I will, sir." As Jake was about to say good-bye, the line went dead. *Funny how the deputy secretary is with his conversations,* Jake thought. Very seldom a preamble and hardly ever a good-bye, he was very clipped and military-style. One thing for sure, the old warhorse was a leader and all business when it counted. *Couldn't ask for a better boss,* he thought. Before calling Slade, he sat back on his bed and thought about his conversation with the deputy secretary. He could tell David had the same uneasy feeling that he had. Slade could feel it too. Was it about the Jamosa and Starr's arrest or something more ominous?

SEVENTY-FIVE

WASHINGTON D.C. 2010

The weather is frightful driving in this morning, David Peterson
thought. It seemed as though the Washington D.C. area
was getting snow every other week for the last few weeks, and
with Christmas around the corner, the traffic congestion had
become especially cumbersome. The deputy secretary lived in an
old but well-kept stately manor in Chevy Chase, Maryland with
his wife, Phyllis. She was a carbon copy of her husband, except
for her red hair. She wore it in a sixties pixie cut that framed her
youthful looking face that made her cuter than a bug's ear. She
was petite with abundant energy, a wicked sense of humor and,
if needed, she could trash talk with the best of them. To put it
bluntly, she was like her husband in the sense that one would be
foolish to get on her wrong side. Phyllis was fiercely loyal to her
husband and their two daughters, Jenna and Jo, and she provided
a first cabin upbringing, which included prep schools in their
formative years and later private colleges for their post secondary
education. Both girls had graduate degrees and were married
to fine young men. Each had their own successful professional
working career. But there were no grandchildren yet.

Peterson usually took the most direct route to work that
followed Connecticut Ave., NW to Reno Road and thirty-fourth
Ave., NW. Then he hooked up to the Rock Creek and Potomac
Parkway NW, going across the Potomac using the Theodore
Roosevelt Memorial Bridge to get into the city. Sometimes he
took alternate routes when the traffic warranted it, especially
during the holiday season. As of late there weren't enough
alternate routes; everything was jammed. The Bluetooth phone
on his government-issued Lincoln Town car was chiming. He

hit the phone icon on the steering wheel and Dan Johnson's high-pitched voice came floating through the dash. He was the assistant director of the FBI and a good friend of the Peterson family. "Oh my God, we had a window of less than twenty-four hours before the virus struck the brokerage houses and banks!" Dan exclaimed. "We just squeaked by on this one, buddy, and if I were the president I would award Zoey Chamberlain and Jake Cannon the presidential Medal of Freedom."

David knew that the medal was one of the highest awards that could be presented to a civilian and was equivalent to the Medal of Honor for the military. "I know they saved our bacon."

"It's more than that, Dave. They saved the world's bacon, and I can't imagine what would have happened if these guys had succeeded in their plans."

"It would have been chaos for sure," Peterson said. "Have you obtained any more information from the five suspects?"

"Yes, we have received the name of the second in command, Abrahim Solasti, a Sudan national, and the names of some of their other team members. They're being questioned, and I believe we have verified the location of the initial call; it came from Riyadh, Saudi Arabia. We haven't been able to trace the ownership of the satphone yet, but two of the suspects indicated that Abrahim and Seyed were the only ones responsible for making the call. Seyed is sitting in Gitmo so that only leaves Abrahim."

"I concur, Dan. But we will not get any information from Mr. Solasti. We've already confirmed that it was his house involved in the explosion, and we're waiting on forensics to confirm his death."

"I know, and it's such a shame. Mr. Solasti could've provided a wealth of information to us."

"Well, we can't dwell on what might have been." Peterson said.

"Did you know that it took us over sixteen hours to get any meaningful information from the terrorists," Dan Johnson offered.

"I know!" Peterson exclaimed.

"Those damn attorneys and Ahmad's Administration policies caused us valuable time. God, I hope they don't close Gitmo; we need military tribunals for these types of people. You know if this circus would have gone on for a few more hours we would have been sunk."

"Don't remind me. It's another shoe bomber incident, but with far greater consequences," Peterson added.

"Another thing, all five of the operatives were Saudi nationals."

"Dan, I suspected as much. We are now working with the Saudi government to round up any other terrorists suspected working with Seyed Mostakavi and Abrahim Solasti in Riyadh. We have sent in special ops from NATO's Air Base in Incirlik, Turkey to assist the Saudi's in any way they can. Once they're corralled we're sending them to Gitmo."

"You sure that's a wise decision, especially for your career?" Dan asked. "You know how the Ahmad Administration feels about Gitmo."

"I don't give a hoot!" Peterson bellowed. "Don't they know the repercussions if the terrorists would have succeeded, for Christ's sake."

"Doesn't matter, Dave. You know as well as I it's all about politics. If it doesn't fit their views, they simply don't care."

"I'll tell you something, Dan. If we keep going down this path, one of these days something big like this is going to get through. Then politics won't matter one iota."

"I hear you, buddy," Dan said. "Now what's your take on unraveling this plot?"

"Well, as you know, we're putting some pretty bright people on this including white hat's and possibly black hatters too. Their plan must have taken years to hatch, test and initiate, and I'm sure it will take us some time to understand all the pieces, if we ever do. You know in some ways it reminds me of the Stuxnet worms that had attacked Iran's centrifuges, which enriches uranium for their nuclear reactors. Too bad Seyed won't be around to help them."

"What a pity," Dan said sarcastically. "I have one question, though."

"Shoot."

"Why didn't they do this remotely?"

"Good question." Peterson took a moment to rub his chin with his left hand in a thoughtful manner before speaking. "Like I said, I believe their plan has been in the making for years. It's possible that they began the project before all trans oceanic fiber optic cables were deployed in the oceans. Back then you didn't have high-speed communications running from continent to continent. The only way to succeed was by placing operatives in the countries you wanted to attack."

"Come on Dave, it has to be more than that," Dan Johnson replied.

"Well you guys are the profiling experts, I'd like to hear your side of it."

"Hey, you guys aren't so bad yourselves. Tom Morrison and especially Thaddeus Knowles are uncanny how they lead their teams over at your agency. I can tell you Thaddeus is well respected by the FBI's behavior science division. Our lead profiler, Sam White, really likes the man."

"Thanks Dan, I'll pass it on to Thad. Now what's your take?"

"Dave, as you are aware, your agency as well as ours has done extensive profiling on Seyed. He is one of the most brilliant people on the planet, but he is narcissistic, arrogant, aloof and really not interested in anything, except Iran. His pet project is helping his country to achieve nuclear status, and this is where he has channeled most of his energy since the Soviet-Afghan war. He's great at assembling teams and getting projects going in the right direction. But once they're running he refocuses his energy back on Iran. And in the last couple of years he's been overloaded trying to solve the Stuxnet virus situation that has plagued Iran's nuclear facility. I'm sure Mr. Solasti has brought this to his attention more than once to go remote, but Seyed probably just waved it off. You have to understand that most of his post secondary education has been done in our country, and he has been fully immersed in our culture. We believe he has developed a jaded view of our ways to the point where he thinks we are lazy and incompetent. And September 11, 2001 only reinforced his views. I'd hate to think of where we would be now if he had showed as much interest taking down our financial institutions as he had in bringing Iran into the nuclear age."

"I see your point, Dan. Since you're on the phone, I would like to discuss my concerns about Felix Jamosa and Jeffery Starr."

"What's going on? The arrest warrants have been issued by the Justice Department, and as I understand we are arresting them this evening. So, what's the problem?"

"I have an uneasy feeling about those two." David Peterson went on and told Dan what he had discussed with Jake earlier.

"You're putting a Delta Force detachment in place for this?" Dan said, alarm reflecting in his voice.

"Yes, just a precaution. Jake and Slade will lead the black ops from their end. They're only there to observe, and they will not intervene unless things get hot. And if they do, the Portland police and your team will assist as needed. Dan, I know your agents are exceptional at doing their jobs, but I don't want to see this getting out of hand. Besides, you have to agree that Portland isn't the friendliest place for the FBI to work in."

"Yeah, I realize that, and I still don't understand why Portland didn't sign on to JTTF like all the other major cities. Anyway, I'm sure the Portland police and my agents can handle this, but I will assign extra agents just to be sure."

"There probably won't be any trouble, Dan, but thank you for your cooperation. You won't even know our guys are there unless they're needed. The authorities in Portland will be alerted that special ops will arrive later today. Just wanted to give you a heads up, buddy. Have to go, talk to you soon."

Dan Johnson sat back in his chair and stared at the ceiling, thinking, *God, I hope this doesn't turn into a media frenzy. Portland is wacky enough without having the press and television revving them up.* They had been fortunate to keep a lid on the Jamosa inquiry because of the seriousness of the investigation and charges brought forth. Dr. Mostakavi and Mr. Zafar are in custody now, and the president is scheduled to give a press conference tomorrow evening after Felix and Jeffery are arrested. *Wonder how President Ahmad is going to sugarcoat this one*, he thought. He believed that the administration still didn't get it, still had their heads in the sand and still in denial. *Christ, we were within hours of looking at a whole new world.* Dan thought.

SEVENTY-SIX

PORTLAND, OREGON 2010

There was a stagnant, persistent low parked off the Oregon coast for the first nine days of December driving powerful, cold, east winds funneling down the Columbia Gorge and fanning out over the Portland area. The low pressure system was far enough off the coast to spare Portland of any precipitation, but it was cloudy and getting colder each day by pulling air in from Canada. The weather was about to change and so was Portland.

"Can you believe the weather out there?" Jeremy Leighton exclaimed. Jeremy was the senior FBI official assigned to the Portland field office.

"Yeah, it reminds me of Chicago, but not quite as cold," Slade volunteered as everyone took their seats in Jeremy's office.

"Speaking of cold, can you believe what came out of the meeting at city hall? I've been Special Agent in Charge (SAC) for the last ten years here, and I still don't understand why Portland is so anti-FBI task force. I mean enough of the Brandon Mayfield business. For crying out loud nobody is infallible, but yet the city council kept going on about it as if it happened yesterday. And their police chief, he's as gullible and naïve as the city council," Jeremy said.

"I know," Jake offered. "They were more concerned with parliamentary decorum and how official and important they looked than the topic at hand. I've never seen such self-aggrandizing pomposity in my entire life."

"Jake, if this thing gets out of hand like your boss thinks, they'll have far more to worry about then their egos," Harrison Stoner said, as he ran a hand through his coarse red hair.

Jeremy looked at the black ops squadron leader and said, "Let's just keep this in perspective. Captain, we're going in later this evening and evacuate the tower's occupants, and we will be cordoning off a large area around the building at the insistence of Jake's boss. At dawn we'll have a dozen agents on the street backed up by the Portland police and SWAT."

"You think that's going to matter," Harrison shot back. "You can't even keep track of your two suspects."

"No, I don't think so." Jeremy said. "We have had Felix and Jeffery's residences and their company under surveillance ever since the Justice Department handed down warrants for their arrest. The last time they entered their business was late this afternoon after they had a bite to eat at the Jackson Tower delicatessen across the street. Plus, the last triangulation on their smartphones came from the Fox Tower only an hour ago. No, they're in there."

"Anyone could be using their cell phones, Jeremy," the captain argued.

"That's true, but with close surveillance it's unlikely."

The captain waved him off.

"I thought we were supposed to grab them at their homes or when they were entering or leaving their business. Now we might have to contend with a forty-three-story structure—not a pretty picture," Slade huffed.

"We just received the warrants at 6:00 p.m. tonight, and we certainly couldn't arrest them until we had the papers in our possession," Jeremy glowered, defending himself.

"Okay, let's calm down, everyone," Jake said in a commanding tone. "We need to get down to business."

It was now Friday evening 2200 hours local time when the meeting ended. At 2300 hours Jake, Slade, and Captain Stoner met with the black ops team at a safe house in Northwest Portland. They went over last-minute details, prepped their weapons, inventoried their supplies and disappeared into the emptiness of the night. The skies had cleared and winter's full moon would be rising from the east at 0200 hours, and Jake wanted everybody in place by then for operation "Day Break."

SEVENTY-SEVEN

PORTLAND, OREGON 2010

At 0100 hours the black ops detachment met in the underground parking facility, directly below Director's Park. The area was just west of Jamosa Enterprises across from the lighted fountains in the 800 block on southwest Park Avenue. A 300-foot radius had already been cordoned off around the building, and all the tenants in the surrounding buildings and businesses had been evacuated. The team had reconnoitered the tower's perimeter, and it had been decided that the most advantageous position for the detachment would be to place three members each at the corners of the building, and Jake and Slade would take point outside the lobby of the Jackson Tower building across the street. They would have a good view of Jamosa's Enterprises east entrance, looking west across Southwest Broadway. Portland's SWAT would cover the parking exits at the north and west sides of the building and also the building's loading docks and bays. Additional members of SWAT and FBI agents were strategically placed throughout the building, and by 0200 hours everyone was in place. The arrests were to occur at dawn. Now came the tedious task of quietly removing the condominiums' occupants. The Portland police, FBI, and Jake's team had already acquired and reviewed the building's schematics that showed the floor plan, security, and mechanicals. The security at the entrances had proven to be more difficult to bypass than initially thought. Jake wondered why Felix had taken the trouble to install such a sophisticated system. *I'm sure his tenants appreciated it*, he thought. *But why all the trouble, what was he hiding?* After Jake and Slade watched the Portland police escort the last of the tenants from the building, Slade turned to Jake and said, "Two hours to go, buddy."

"So far so good," Jake replied as he adjusted his assault vest and peered out at the night from the Jackson Tower lobby.

The moon would be setting at 0700 hours, and the weather had been clear, but fog was now shrouding the streets from the nearby Willamette River. There was an icy chill in the air as rimes of frost began coating the streets and sidewalks. Jake stepped out to the street and looked up and surveyed the buildings around them, but all he could see was vague outlines of shadows trying to slice through the ghostly mist. As he looked down southwest Broadway, he could see that downtown Portland's gas style street lamps were bathed in dull orange halos trying to cast their glow from one to another.

"Christ, the fog's getting thick," Jake said.

"Icy too!" Slade added from behind him. "I just hope this goes down clean."

"We'll know pretty soon, partner." Jake said, as he collected his radio from his assault vest. "Captain, everything calm? Over."

"Affirmative, sir. But visibility sucks. Over."

"Don't sweat the small stuff, captain, and keep a sharp eye out, this thing is going down in a couple of hours. Over."

"Well do, hoss. Out."

Jake stepped back into the shadows of the Jackson building lobby and checked his magazine on the M249 light machine gun he was carrying. It was lightweight and a good all-purpose weapon and especially adapt for close quarter battle (CQB). A twenty- or thirty-round magazine or linked ammunition could be used depending on the circumstances and it used NATO approved 5.56x.45 mm ammo. Each team member had an accessory system called Special Operations Peculiar Modification (SOPMOD). The system allowed Special Forces operators to configure their weapons to individual preferences and mission requirements. The team was also packing HK Mark 23 M auto .45 caliber pistols and customized M203 grenade launchers. As always, Jake and Slade had their stock-in-trade Freedom Arms Model

83, .454 Casull revolvers with them. Jake had an uneasy feeling that they were underarmed. *Damn city council and their meddling ways*, he thought. He should have taken direct command from the beginning instead of acting in a reserve role. In the end the FBI was harangued into negotiating with the city council and Portland police on what type of weapons were allowed on the streets of Portland. The council was worried about collateral damage. *Big mistake*, he thought.

Jake had been monitoring the radio traffic between the captain and his team ever since they were in position. He was also monitoring SWAT and the FBI but providing no instructions or interaction. His team was only here to observe. Five senior FBI agents were set to enter the building at 0700 hours at daybreak and would take one of the elevators to the forty-second floor. There, members of the SWAT team would join them, and all would make their way to the forty-third floor via the building's interior stairwell. At that point, SWAT would provide cover for the agents as they made their way to Jamosa Enterprise's offices. Once the agents were inside, SWAT would continue to cover the hallway, elevators, and the stairwell, and if needed, assist the agents. There was nothing to do now except to wait and observe.

⚬⟫⟫◦⟪⟪⚬

"Felix, how is the arms shipment list coming?" Jeffery asked as he leaned his lanky frame over his brother-in-law's desk.

"Just about there. Only need to make a couple of adjustments."

"Well, hurry up. It's getting late, and I want to run the numbers before dawn. We've been at this all night, and I would like to get some shuteye. Think I'll go down to the vending machines to see if there's something interesting to munch on, hope you're finished when I get back."

Deep in thought, Felix rubbed his gray stubble with his right hand as he nonchalantly answered, "Sure."

Jeffery went through the office's outer double doors and headed down the hall to the bank of elevators. As he approached he could see that three of the regular elevators were moving down while one was moving up. He checked his watch and saw that it was almost 5:00 a.m. *What's going on?* he thought. *It's the weekend and the middle of the night, and the elevators are this busy?* Then it hit him. *Christ, they're getting ready to arrest us.* He turned and hurried back to the offices and rushed into Felix's quarters. "We're in trouble!"

"What do you mean?" Felix asked as he stared at his brother-in-law from behind his desk.

"There's all kinds of activity on the elevators, and it's the middle of the night."

Without saying anything, Felix put his espresso down, stood, and walked over to the bank of monitors on one of his office walls and scrutinized them. "Everything appears to be normal at all of the buildings entrances," he said as he motioned to the screens. He stood there a moment longer thinking. "Bet they're using the new west underground parking structure. Cameras haven't been installed yet."

"Wouldn't matter," Jeffery mused. "They're probably using a feedback loop for the security disks. I wonder if we can make a run for our cars?"

Felix went to his desktop computer and pulled up all exit and entrance cameras' logs from midnight to 5:00 a.m.; no activity, except for the security patrols. "Wait a minute," he said. "Was it raining when we came in late this afternoon from the delicatessen?"

"Why no, it wasn't." Jeffery replied. He peered at the screens and said, "I see what you're saying." They both rushed over to the glass wall of windows facing east and peered out. Even though it was difficult to see, especially at night, they couldn't see any tell tale signs of rain droplets on the windows.

Felix walked back to his computer and panned the cameras in sub level one parking and saw that his wife's Escalade and

Jeffery's black 740 Beamer were still there. Jeffery looked at the screen from behind him, "The cars are there, let's go."

"Are you crazy, Jeff? You said it yourself. They're using feed back loops, and even if the cars were there I'm sure they have been disabled." Felix switched to the hall monitor logs earlier in the evening and saw the usual activity of people coming and going from their condominiums. He turned to Jeff and said, "They have it covered pretty well, except for the rain. Jeff, it's a good thing you went out when you did, otherwise we may have not caught this."

"Yeah, but what are we going to do now?"

"Well, you know what this means, don't you?" Felix said with a strange light in his eyes. "We've been preparing for this for a long time."

"I know, I know. But I don't like it, and I never have," Jeffery said, while shaking his head.

"What do you propose for us to do? Give up!" Felix bellowed.

"I don't know. I was hoping this day would never arrive."

"Well it has!" Felix shot back.

Jeffery walked back to the wall of windows, turned, and stared at his brother-in-law. "I don't know if I can go through with this. Look at all the innocent lives that could be lost."

"Look, we don't know what's going on for sure, buddy. Let's head down to the bunker and check out the monitors for the hidden cameras. I'm sure they're still on a live feed," Felix said in a conciliatory tone.

"Yeah, let's go see."

As they walked into Felix's private bathroom, he was already formulating a plan. Even though he loved his brother-in-law and had to admit that they had been through a lot, he would kill him if necessary. No one, including Jeffery, would stop him from going down without a fight.

Felix stepped into the oversized jade green marble shower and inserted his smart card into a small slot at the top of the back wall, and watched as the wall descended into the space between the elevator and shower. The elevator opened and Felix and Jeffery stepped in. Thirty seconds later they were at the bunker below the basement's fourth sub level. As they walked into the bunker, the auto lights brightened, and Felix walked over to the bank of monitors on the far wall and checked for any activity. There wasn't any, but that didn't mean there wasn't traffic earlier in the evening. Jeff sat at the computer console and brought up each hidden camera's activity logs for the last five hours, and sure enough there had been all kinds of activity between midnight and 5:00 a.m. They could see the cameras' frames filled with Portland police officers going into the building and escorting tenants out.

"My, my, haven't we been busy for the last few hours," Felix quipped. "Jeff, pan the forty-fourth floor. I want to make sure the fortress is in order." After panning the redoubt and the building's perimeter, they could find nothing out of the ordinary at this hour. Felix lit a Montecristo and said, "Now we wait."

<hr />

Jake and Slade watched as the five senior FBI agents entered the east entrance and took one of the elevators up to the forty-second floor.

"Shouldn't be long now, buddy," Slade volunteered.

"Quiet," Jake commanded as he brought his night vision ITT PVS 16 monocular up to his eyes once again to scan the east side of the building. Even though the glasses afforded a wider field of view than other models, he still felt as though he was looking through a tunnel. The vision was sharp and clear but still suffered from tunnel affliction. "Now we observe and listen." It was 0700 hours and dawn was fast approaching the Pacific Northwest. The mist had turned to an ice fog a couple of hours ago, and the streets were now covered with a thick coating of rime.

He reached down and collected his radio and punched in the captain. "Heads up, Harrison, the agents have just entered the building from the east side. Over."

"Affirmative, sir. Over."

"Everything quiet? Over."

"Too quiet, sir. I don't like this. Over."

"I'm with you captain. Have your men on standby until I see them cuffed and coming out of the building with the FBI. Copy?"

"I copy that, sir. Out."

Slade walked out to the street and panned his field glasses up and down Southwest Broadway. Even though visibility was poor, he could still see SWAT huddled in different areas in Pioneer Courthouse Square adjacent and north of the Jackson Tower building, and Portland police were now lined up and down the street next to the buildings and across to Nordstrom. "Christ, there are too many people exposed out here," Slade said.

Jake switched channels on his radio, "Commander Stevens, pull back, pull back, do you copy?"

It was too late. Fire erupted from the top of the Fox Tower as the big fifty-caliber cannons strafed and pounded the surrounding area. The ground shook as chunks of asphalt and concrete from the streets and sidewalks hurled in chalky black dust as glass and mortar from the adjacent buildings shattered and clattered to the ground. North of the Fox Tower and across southwest Yamhill Street, Nordstrom's brown brick façade collapsed in a blizzard of smoke and dust as the big guns pounded away. Metal chunks turned to shrapnel as they flew off the rails of Portland's Metropolitan Area Express (MAX) light rail system at the intersection of southwest Yamhill and Broadway. It was Portland's answer to urban transportation and had over 100 miles of tracks and 150 stations and was world renowned as a model to follow. The Jackson building's façade of glazed terracotta and glass came crashing down, mixing with the black asphalt dust from the street below. The building's venerable old clock tower exploded in a pyre of metal, glass, and plastic. The Jackson Tower was an historic office building and had been home to the Oregon Journal back in its day. Pioneer Courthouse Square was stitched in craters, smoke, and reddish dust from its brick foundation as the fifty-caliber cannons reached out for its prey. Jake and Slade watched in horror as Portland's finest were cut to ribbons in their tracks, men and women scurrying, slipping and sliding everywhere. There was nowhere to hide and no way their flak jackets could withstand the withering fire from the heavy guns. The smell of cordite hung heavy in the air. Jake's satphone vibrated as he and Slade were retreating deeper into the Jackson Tower building for more protection.

"Jake, are you there? Over." Captain Stoner shouted.

"Go ahead, captain. Over."

"We're taking fire from all sides of the building, sir. What the bloody hell is going on? Over."

"We're in a war. Have your men pull back and take more cover. Over."

"I have. But we've already lost three of our men, sir. Our grenade launchers seem to have no effect. Can't really tell, though. We need heavier weapons, sir."

"Don't I know, captain. Standby. Copy?"

"Wilco and out, sir."

Jake knew they were outgunned. If only they had hand-held FIM-9 Stinger missiles or at least M136 AT4 anti-tank weapons, they might stand a chance. Jake and Slade could now hear the high-pitch whine of M61 Vulcan 20 mm Gatling guns laying down their deadly fire. They inched their way along one of the delicatessen's interior walls to get a better view. They both looked up and could see the top of the tower shrouded in fog and smoke with flashes of light piercing through the gloom. Dawn had made its presence with a bang.

"Damn, it looks like the fourth of July up there," Slade said. "They must have an army!"

"I don't know, but they sure have some heavy weapons." Jake got on the radio again and transmitted on civilian band to SWAT. "Commander Stevens, has your team pulled back? Over."

"Affirmative. But we sustained heavy losses. Over."

"You need to evacuate your SWAT team from the Fox Tower and move them to the west exit of the underground parking garage and wait for further instructions. Over."

"Why do we need to do that? Over." The commander pressed.

"Don't argue with me, commander, just do it. Copy?"

"Affirmative, sir. Over."

"As of now, I'm taking direct command of operations. Understood, Commander Stevens. Over."

"Affirm—"

Jake's incoming transmission died. "Commander, do you copy?" Jake waited for a reply. "Commander Stevens, are you there? Do you copy? Over."

"Oh crap, I think we lost the commander, Slade."

"We need air support, Jake." Slade shouted over the chatter of the guns. "We need to take out this building."

"Way ahead of you, buddy. Get me the coordinates of the building while I contact the base commander at the National Guard Airbase in Portland."

After contacting Colonel Robert Struthers, giving him the coordinates and putting them on standby, Jake's satphone vibrated, and he immediately picked up.

"Christ, Jake, can you believe this!" Jeremy Leighton, SAC, exclaimed.

"Actually, I can. My boss was leery of the operation, and his hands were tied except for getting a detachment of black ops," Jake said.

"We need military!"

"Jeremy, we're working on it." Jake went on to explain that they had contacted the base commander at the Guard Airbase. "Were your men able to get to their offices?" Jake asked.

"Yes, and they found zip, no one's home. They must be with their men at the top of the building."

"Did you find a way up there?"

"SWAT and us checked everywhere on the floor including the elevators. There's nothing. Where's the access?" Jeremy asked.

"I think there's more here than we know. Are your men out?"

"Yah, SWAT and my agents are about to make their way out through the underground parking facility west of the tower."

"Tell them to wait until I get more of my team to the west entrance of the parking structure for cover fire. Understood?"

"That's affirmative, Jake. I've been monitoring the civil radio transmissions, and I see you gave Commander Stevens an earful."

"He deserved it, sorry to say, but I think he's been hit. He was cut off in his last transmission to me, and I haven't been able to raise him. After your men are clear of the parking garage, I want them to fall back and wait for further instructions. Understood?"

"Affirmative, Jake. Out."

Jake's satphone vibrated again. "What in tarnation is going on? It's all over the news. The media is claiming there's a war going on in Portland," the deputy secretary said.

"You could say that, sir." Just as Jake was about to continue his conversation, he could hear explosions in the background rocking the waterfront.

"Jake, are you there?"

"Yes, sir."

"Did I hear a couple of explosions?"

"Affirmative, sir. They sound like they're coming from the vicinity of the Willamette River. They have heavy weapons that are pounding us from atop of their building. Slade just said that we are now receiving mortar fire. The Portland police and SWAT have sustained heavy casualties, and I've just put the Guards Air Base in Portland on standby."

"Jesus, Jake!" The deputy secretary exclaimed.

"Sir, all available police, fire and medical personnel have been rushed to downtown Portland and most of the inner southwest side is being evacuated. Slade just spoke with the governor, and he is mobilizing the Guard, and the city will be under martial law once they arrive, sir."

"God, I was afraid of this, Jake."

"I know. You did all you could, but it fell on deaf ears. Has the president been notified?"

"Just notified, and he will be kept informed of the unfolding events."

"Have to go, sir."

"Keep me posted, Jake."

"You know I will," and Jake broke the connection.

Slade turned to his partner and said, "Communications is getting spotty, and I'm having trouble getting through to the chain of command. Last I heard the Portland police and the FBI were in a command center on the east side of the city." Slade looked at the devastation around him. All the buildings within eyesight looked like they had been attacked by a giant buzz saw. Nearly all the glass on the lower stories of most of the buildings were blown out, and all were gouged and pockmarked and some showing their steel skeletons from the attack. Smoke and fires were everywhere. And yet the onslaught continued. Distant explosions across the river now rocked them.

"My God, they must have air-to-surface missiles!" Jake shouted over the roar.

"What are they doing?" Slade asked as he looked at Jake in horror.

"I'll tell you what they're doing. They're going absolutely mad!" Jake got on the radio and was finally able to reach the command center. "To whom am I speaking with? Over."

"SWAT commander, Jacobson, sir. Over."

"This is Special Intel Ops, Jake Cannon. Over."

"Yes, we know who you are, sir. The word's been put out."

"Good. Now where are you? Over."

"We're in a bunker at the central command center on the northwest side of Mt. Tabor. Jesus, we're seeing explosions from the lower east and northeast areas of the city from our monitors."

"You have to at least evacuate Portland's lower east and northeast neighborhoods. Do you copy?" Jake said.

"Affirmative. We're doing all we can, but it will take time. We're now also dealing with rioting and looting in parts of the city, and our resources are beyond the breaking point. We lost so many of our people downtown, sir."

"Hang in there, commander. The governor has called up the Guard, and they will be here soon to assist you, and they will lock down the city. As soon as southwest Portland is cleared, we're sending in the Air National Guard to take out the tower. Over."

"Thanks for the help, Jake."

"Your welcome, commander. Got to go. Out."

"I've never seen anything like this, except for the twin towers. Where are we heading, Jake?" Slade asked.

"We're just catching up with the rest of the world." The one thing that defined Jake was his inscrutability, his attention to detail. He was a stern tactician with an uncommon single-mindedness, and his objective now was to end this as quickly as possible with the least amount of casualties. "As soon as we get word that the downtown evac is complete, I'll contact the base commander again, and he'll scramble three F-15C's armed to the teeth and will put an end to this madness."

<hr />

Felix was hunched over the control desk in the bunker, peering intently at the four monitors in front of him. The system was designed to split Portland and Vancouver metro areas into quadrants of the compass and have the ability to zoom from street level to satellite surface coverage of Oregon and

Washington. The only flaw in the system was that they didn't have the capacity to view the topography on a real-time basis. At present, the technological expertise hadn't presented itself for them to commandeer and control one or more of DOD's keyhole satellites for their own use without their knowledge. And the red tape and cost to put one into space under the guise of their legitimate company wouldn't be cost effective, especially for such a narrow endeavor. They had to rely on commercial enterprise, such as Goggle Earth to get their topographical information, and the last set of satellite and surface views was posted six months ago. Even so, the action superimposed on those images was in real time. While Felix was operating the guns on the console, he locked in the coordinates on all twelve of the laser guided FGM-148 Javelin missiles and released their deadly payloads to Portland's east side. In a blink of an eye, Clackamas Town Center erupted in fire and smoke as three of the missiles found their mark. The main section of the Oregon Museum of Science (OMSI) disintegrated in a ball of fire from two more missiles. On the next screen he could see the twin glass spires and roof of the Oregon Convention Center engulfed in fire and smoke. Large chunks of concrete and steel were blasted from the Rose Garden, home of the Portland Trailblazers. On another screen, further north, he could see sections of the Lloyd Center broiling in flames and secondary explosions from the last three missiles. The mall was the largest shopping center in the Northwest when it was built in 1960.

"My God, what are you doing?" Jeffery exclaimed. "You're turning Portland into an inferno," he howled in horror as he stared in disbelief at his brother-in-law sitting behind the console.

"I'm doing to Portland what the ATF and IRS is doing to us," Felix hissed with that strange look in his dark blue eyes.

"You can't be serious!" Jeffery bellowed. "What about all the people you're killing, especially the civilians and children?"

"What about them, they're just collateral damage the same way the IRS and the government treats us," Felix roared.

"For God's sake at least put the system on auto to spare the children and civilians!" Jeffery shouted.

He was referring to the advanced AI systems for the guns that he and Abrahim Solasti's team had developed. It took nearly a year to write and test the programs. The artillery software, in milliseconds, could determine if it had a valid target to fire on. It calculated the height, weight, and body mass of its objects, and if the parameters fell within the range of normal children, the weapons wouldn't fire. If it were outside those parameters, the software would then determine if the targets were wearing flak jackets, carrying weapons or ammo belts. If so, the system would trigger the guns. Early on, Felix argued why adopt the parameters for children. If the targets were carrying weapons then initiate the guns. Jeffery pointed out that they were not in the Middle East and insisted on protecting the children. In the end Jeffery won out and now he knew why. His brother-in-law would simply switch the system to manual and kill indiscriminately.

"Felix, please stop the carnage, we can't go on doing this!" Jeffery pleaded.

Felix stared at his brother-in-law, wild eyed and with an utterly deranged voice, dropped to a whisper, said, "I don't know about you, but like I said, I'm heading to perdition."

Jeffery now knew that his brother-in-law was completely around the bend. As he stood behind Felix looking at the destruction on the screens, he quietly pulled out his Glock 17 and pointed it at the back of Felix's head. He was still seething about his brother-in-law's bonehead move supplying weapons to the Republic of Georgia. He had urged him not to sell arms to Saudi Arabia because it was a ruse and the United States wouldn't approve. He knew it was a trap. But Felix wouldn't listen; it was more money. He wavered while thinking how could he possibly kill him. He was married to his brother-in-law's sister, Carly, and Felix was married to his adopted sister, Clarissa, and then there was his niece, Sam. For years, he and Carly tried in vain to have children, but in the end it was found that his wife couldn't conceive. They were in the middle of adopting a young boy from Malaysia, but how could a son live in the shadow of unspeakable horror of the father? In a moment it all flashed in front of him, he raised the gun and pulled the trigger. Boom! Felix flinched, covering his ears, sounds of gunfire reverberating in the bunker.

"Jesus!" Felix screamed. Keeping his ears covered, he swiveled his chair and stood. Before him lay the crumpled body of his brother-in-law, blood streaming from a massive head wound. *What have I done?* he thought. He knew Jeffery was dead, and there was nothing he could do. He sat back in his chair, turned to the counsel and began rotating the controls again and watched as the big guns continued their reign of destruction on Portland. Somewhere in the background he could hear the sounds of shrieking and laughter as he played his video game.

Jake retrieved the radio from his assault vest, switched to civilian band and contacted commander Jacobson. "Commander, how long before the evac is completed in downtown Portland? Over."

"About fifteen minutes, sir. Over."

"Well hurry it up. I'll be in communication with the Air Guard's base commander shortly. Over."

"I will, sir. Has the National Guard arrived yet? Over."

"Any minute, commander. Over."

"Well, I hope so. Mall 205, Eastport Plaza, and Clackamas Town Center are being overrun with looters, and there are reports of random looting and fires in other parts of the city. Washington Square and Bridgeport Village are being looted on Portland's west side. Our resources are overwhelmed, and we haven't been able to receive assistance from our satellite cities; Hillsboro, Beaverton and Gresham, because of their own problems. Sir, civil unrest and violence are spreading rapidly. Over."

"What about your volunteers and auxiliary? Over."

"We've called up everyone we can. How many Guards, sir? Over."

"Five thousand on the first sweep split between the east and west sides of Portland and another five thousand two hours later. Joint Base Lewis-McChord (JBLM) in Olympia, Washington, has been put on standby in case we need them. Over."

"Hope it doesn't come to that, sir. Over."

"My sentiments too, commander. Out."

Jake was worried that this could be the spark to spread civil unrest to other major cities in the country fueled by the medias' frenzy. The masses were already unhappy with the Ahmad Administration. Jake contacted the base commander at the National Guard Air Base. "Colonel, commence operation Day Break. Do you copy?"

"Affirmative, Jake. Over."

"Commander, if possible, only take out the top of the building. We have enough damage and carnage as it is. Copy."

"Jake, I'll pass the word on. Out."

He knew it would be over in fifteen minutes. Three F-15Cs were being deployed from the Guard Air Base. The fighters were armed with 20 mm M61 Vulcan 6-barrel Gatling cannons and each carried either six air-to-air AIM-120-AMRAM missiles or six air-to-air AIM-9 Sidewinders. The tower's big guns, missiles, and mortars would be silenced. Jake deposited the radio back into his vest, turned to Slade, and said, "It's time to make haste."

"You don't need to prod me, pal. I don't want to be anywhere near this place when the air jockeys show up."

Jake collected his radio and contacted Captain Stoner. "Harrison, did everyone get out okay from the underground garage? Over."

"All accounted, sir. Over."

"Good, let's pull out and meet back at the safe house. Three F-15C's have just been scrambled from the Air Base. Copy?"

"Roger that, sir."

"We'll be meeting Colonel Ferguson from the National Guard there at 0900 hours. Out."

On the first pass the three military jets came in fast and low with their cannons blazing. They were flying spread formation to cover three of the four sides of the building's perimeter and to minimize any damage from enemy fire. As the fighters banked to the northeast after the first run Lieutenant Sullivan got on the Com to the squadron leader, "Foxfire, this is Delta-One. Over."

"Come in Delta-One. Over."

"Major, they must have some kind of hardened fortress up there. Didn't see much damage from our guns, sir. Over."

"It won't be hardened for long, Lieutenant. Out." The jets continued to bank and climb northeast to line up for their second run. As the F-15Cs came in they released half of their deadly payload, and the missiles found their mark. In a tremendous explosion it appeared that the upper third of the building momentarily lifted before collapsing in a cloud of smoke, fire, and dust. Huge chunks of super heated metal, concrete, and glass rained to the ground below, and secondary explosions rocked the tower and buildings around it. As the fighters headed back to the base, Lieutenant Chang opened the Com.

"Foxfire, this is Gamma-One. Over."

"Come in Gamma-One. Over."

"My God, what was that, sir? I know we pack quite a punch, but half the building must have come down. Over."

"Lieutenant, it appears they had a lot of ordnance up there, and that's what probably caused the additional explosions. Over."

"The commander isn't going to like this, sir. Over."

"We call it like we see it, Lieutenant. Out."

Major Conn was a hard-core military veteran who had flown his share of sorties in the Gulf wars and sometimes encountered some strange situations. *But this,* he thought, *was surreal.* As he left the target, he could see large fires dotting the landscape through the fog on both sides of the Willamette River. Who would've ever thought that once again our homeland was under assault and Portland would come under siege? He knew Colonel Struthers was a stern taskmaster and there would be butt chewin' for sure. *But, for Christ sakes, how much explosives can one pack into a building?* he asked himself. He would find out.

Felix was at the small fridge getting bottled water when the building shook all around him. He stepped over Jeffery's body and went back to the monitors. "Christ, they're blank," he said to no one in particular. The building shook again, and this time it rumbled, and the lights went out. He fumbled around at the console until he found his flashlight, snapped it on and scanned the room. The bunker seemed to be intact, but he didn't hear the faint hum of the mechanicals. *No heat, ventilation, or air conditioning,* he thought. He moved to the back wall and checked the crossover switch for the auxiliary power. The switch was in the off position; he flipped it on. Still nothing. He stepped to the elevator door and saw that it was out of level and damaged. Just for giggles he pressed the up button—nothing. *Christ, the elevator shaft must have collapsed,* he thought. And then he realized the horrible mistake he made. "God, I'm a nitwit. I should have switched the system to auto when I left the console."

Another piece of software that the team had written was patterned after Raytheon's AN/APG-63 X-Doppler radar system. It would have been ironic if he had known that the radar that had been developed to lock and target aircraft was basically a mini version and quite similar to the F-15Cs radar targeting his building. But how would he have known; he had been away from the console. Felix knew that he was doomed: five-inch thick steel and three-foot thick reinforced concrete walls surrounded him 120 feet below the surface with nothing except a few bottles of Cascadian water.

SEVENTY-EIGHT

DHS NEBRASKA COMPLEX
WASHINGTON D.C. 2010

David Peterson went to the seventh floor conference room at the Department of Homeland Security's headquarters well ahead of the rest of the team. He noticed that the coffee carafes had already been placed on the big oak table. He walked over to the small condiment table and poured some half and half in his cup, collected a stir, and then sat in his chair. He poured himself a cup of swill from the nearest carafe and began to collect his thoughts for the meeting. There was so much going on that Christmas didn't feel like the holidays anymore. Since 9/11 there had been no less then thirty-five attempts of terror attacks on the United States. In the last two years alone the FBI and DHS had uncovered fifty homegrown terrorists. Before then, everyone thought of terrorists coming from elsewhere, but not anymore. In the last year or so there had been the Maryland incident with mailings of incendiary envelopes, the Detroit shoe bomber, the Times Square bomber with a van filled with explosives, the Pioneer Courthouse Square bombing attempt in Portland, Oregon, and Yemen based terrorist trying to mail printer cartridges filled with explosives to the United States. And now they had to deal with the aftermath of the cyber-attacks on the United State's financial institutions and the horrible events that had happened in Portland a few days ago, not to mention phantom corporations trading on the world's stock exchanges. In every case the terrorists were either citizens or foreign nationals living here except for the Middle Eastern terrorists from Yemen and the terrorists that orchestrated the assault on the banks and brokerage houses. In fact it had become so busy the government now was in the process of possibly revamping the five-tier National Threat Advisory system to a new two-tier system. People began trickling in to the conference room taking their seats. They all knew not to bother their boss yet. They could tell he was still digesting notes that were in front of him. After everyone was seated, David looked up, and the meeting began.

"I can't say enough on how serious the events have become in the past few weeks. We are dealing with the consequences of terrorists' actions on our banking institutions and the infliction of horror in Portland, Oregon." The deputy secretary leaned over the table for emphasis, and with his deep brown eyes blazing and a stern look on his face continued. "So far there are over twenty-two hundred deaths and countless numbers wounded in Portland, and we're still counting. The city has lost over fifteen percent of their police officers and firemen. There are billions of dollars of damage to the city's infrastructure and will undoubtedly take a generation to repair. Emotional damage, no doubt, will take much longer to heal. In addition to the direct assault, there were numerous riots and fires that broke out in various parts of the city that contributed to the death toll. More troublesome, there were riots and mayhem that broke out in other west coast cities and then fanned out across the country because of this. The death toll is still rising in some of those cities. Fortunately, the National Guard and in some cases the military were called out quickly to stop this madness. Quite frankly, I'm ashamed of our nation. Apparently it has gotten to the point where large segments of our society seem to think that they can practice civil disobedience and outright violence because they are unhappy with the current state of the nation. Well, join the club, I'm unhappy too, but that's not the way to change."

"Sir, you know as well as I that you did all you could to ensure that we were prepared for the gun runners' arrests, but it fell on deaf ears," Tom Morrison, Homeland's database director and chief profiler, said.

"Tom, you're missing the point. It shouldn't have come to this if our country was on the right track." The deputy secretary took another sip of coffee and looked around and could see that everyone was in agreement. "As far as the gunrunners it's too early for verification as to their whereabouts, but we now believe that they had a very sophisticated computerized armed fortress sitting atop of their building, and it was remotely controlled. Again, I cannot emphasize this enough; this would have not happened if our country was operating under the principles of our constitution. And if it wasn't for certain people in our government such as Jeff Faye, the senator from New York who stepped forward to place undue pressure on the Ahmad Administration to interrogate the five operatives in the proper manner, we wouldn't be sitting here today."

"How is the Solasti investigation progressing, sir?" Jake asked.

"As you know nobody survived. NATO lost all five of their special ops, and the Saudi government lost six of their special forces. Initial reports indicate that Pentaerythritol tetranitrate (PETN) was used, and the explosion originated from the basement area of his house. The detonation was so intense that it destroyed an area of one hundred square meters around the house and left a huge crater over twenty feet deep. Because of the extraordinary circumstances, the Saudi government was kind enough to grant permission for us to send teams of forensic scientists to Abrahim's house, or rather where the house used to be. We're still in the process of gathering information on site, and once we're finished we will pack up the house and its contents, or what's left of it, and fly the remains to the FBI's central forensic lab in Quantico, Virginia, for further analysis. It's going to be a difficult process since Mr. Solasti blew everything to smithereens."

"I assume the investigation for the cyber-attack on the financial institutions will take some time for computer forensics. I mean the way they pulled this off?" Dr. Tonia Franks, Homeland Security's computer guru, asked.

"Well doctor, you're the expert in the field. What do you think?" Peterson said.

"Well, sir, it's too early to make any definite calls on the software, except to say that they covered their tracks well. It will take time to determine the method of coding and how they attacked the financial systems' programs. The big question I have at this point is why they didn't do it remotely. I'm sure they had the expertise to do this. It just doesn't add up. In all probability if they would had used this method, and God help me for saying this, I believe they would've succeeded."

"Perhaps Dr. Mostakavi can help us with this," Peterson mused.

"I hope so, sir. It would help our end of the investigation," Dr. Franks opinioned.

"Okay, lets move on. Our secretary, Mary Knappa, will fly to the White House tomorrow. She will be meeting with the president, vice president, and cabinet members to help formulate new strategies to ensure this doesn't happen again. The scuttlebutt is that the government might scrap the existing National Threat Advisory system for a simpler two-tier system since we are having so much activity. I don't know if this will make us any safer, but we can sure try. We have a lot of issues and problems facing us, and central to this is our right to privacy."

"Sir, how's the new system going to ensure this?" Slade asked.

"For one, we don't know if we are going to a new system. Two, if and when we do, I'm not sure how it would reduce risks and yet not erode our privacy. The government is still in the planning phase," the deputy secretary responded.

"Well, I always thought the present system was a bit much. We either have a creditable threat or we don't."

"Now that will be up to government, won't it Slade." The deputy secretary huffed.

"Yes, sir!"

Peterson paused and looked at everyone before going on. "We just uncovered another possible plot where terrorists could be planning on poisoning our food and water supply using Ricin and Sodium Cyanide or other toxic chemical substances. Their targets are open-air water reservoir systems, hotel and restaurant buffets and salad bars for large events. DHS has already briefed the hotel and restaurant industry and put out alerts to the major water facilities throughout the country. Where does it stop?" the deputy secretary said. "They're altering the very essence in the way we live, and I hate to say this, but if they continue they will make us all paranoid."

"What they say they can do and what they actually can is not always the case, sir," Slade intervened.

"Don't you think I know that?" Peterson questioned. "You're missing the point too, Slade."

"Meaning?"

"They have enough technology to continually keep us on edge and cause internal strife in our society. Lord knows, our population is already under considerable stress from multiculturalism and splintered ideologies. Political discourse has grown coarse over the last few years and is becoming more vitriol and inspiring some to violence. Nowadays everyone is watching. They see our weaknesses and shortcomings and use it against us. And some of the more radical factions such as Jihad are trying to accelerate this and destroy us from within."

"I see your point, sir," Slade said.

"Dr. Knowles, I want your team to stay on top of the forensic information as it comes in. The FBI will be sharing the datum with your team, and you're going to be very busy between Riyadh and the Portland sites."

"I'll be all over it, sir," Thaddeus Knowles responded. "In fact we are getting feeds from Mr. Solasti's site as we speak."

"Any significant finds yet?" Peterson asked.

"Nothing earth-shattering, but you'll be the first to know, sir."

"Okay, thanks, Dr. Knowles."

The deputy secretary wasn't worried about Thad. He'd been with the agency for five years and was a crack forensic scientist when it came to uncovering this type of evidence. His team was composed of architects, mathematicians, medical, weapons, physical and organic chemists, physicists and even archeological forensic experts among others on his team.

"Jake, Slade, I want you back in Portland by tomorrow evening. We need your eyes and ears on the investigation and recovery efforts. I don't want to miss anything, and we need to find Mr. Jamosa and Mr. Starr. I've checked with Dan Johnson over at the FBI, and they're in the dark as well as us as to what happened to those two. I want them found. Understood?"

"Affirmative, sir," they both answered.

The deputy secretary stood and walked around the table to where Dr. Ferris was sitting. He put out his hand and said, "Clyde, I want to thank you for your insight on the phantom companies. You're the one that put us on the trail."

Clyde Ferris was a little guy like his boss but not near as physically fit as David Peterson. At first he tried to slump in his chair. He hesitantly put his right hand up to partially shield his face to in order to deflect his boss's gaze. "Why thank you, sir," Clyde whispered.

The deputy secretary shook his limp hand and said, "I mean that, Clyde. You know how to think outside the box, and that trait is highly valued here."

"I don't know what to say, sir," Clyde said as he adjusted his thick, horned-rimmed glasses.

"You don't need to say anything. I just want you to continue doing the outstanding work you're known for."

"Oh, I will, sir. You can count on it," Clyde said with a slight blush on his face.

Everyone in the room knew that Dr. Ferris was an introvert and mainly stayed with his small team of neural net engineers.

But they also knew that the man was constantly thinking and burned big kilowatts.

"Good." David Peterson said, while standing behind Clyde's chair. "Is there any other business?" he asked. Everyone was quiet. "Okay, you know what to do." As the team stood to leave, the deputy secretary turned his attention to Jake and Slade. "Can you two hang back for a bit, I need to discuss something with you." The two agents looked at their boss and said, "Sure, no problem."

SEVENTY-NINE

DHS NEBRASKA COMPLEX— WASHINGTON D.C. 2010

"Hey, guys, thanks for sticking around," the deputy secretary said. "I've never seen so much media coverage in my entire life. It's been everywhere, and most of it is blaming us for bungling the operation in Portland. Christ, what's wrong with those idiots?" Peterson bellowed. "I knew this was going to happen. Why would I think otherwise? The big question I have is where is Felix and Jeffery?"

Jake and Slade looked at each other, and Jake took the lead. "Sir, there are a number of possibilities at this point, though I think they're somewhere in the rubble of what's left of the building."

"What gives you that idea?"

"Sir, after the National Guard arrived, martial law was called immediately and a dragnet was cast over the city two hours later for the gunrunners," Slade volunteered.

Jake rubbed his cleft chin and added, "I wish it would have been sooner, sir. With pandemonium everywhere they could've escaped, but again I don't think so. I don't see how they could have escaped the building's rubble in that short of time. Fires were everywhere and ammo was still igniting from the intense heat. Plus, after the second wave of the Guards came in, we were able to lock down all public transportation, including taxi and limo service. All interstates and state routes that led in or out of the city were also closed. We kept the lid on everything for seventy-two hours, except travel for essential personnel and still nothing. As you know their communications have been monitored for some time, and their last outgoing transmission via smartphone was to their wives on December 10th at 2330 hours triangulated from the 800 block of SW Park Avenue, which is their building, sir. There haven't been any incoming or outgoing calls since, and I think they're buried somewhere in the building. It may take time, sir, but we'll find out."

"What about the looting and riots? Exactly how serious were they?" Peterson asked. "From what I have seen on the news and feeds from official authorities, it was pretty bad."

"It was, sir. The media wasn't overly exaggerating this time. It was as though every lunatic in the city was waiting for an excuse, and they found it. Quite frankly, I'm surprised at the speed and voracity of the violence. The first places to be hit were the shopping malls. First came the looting then the fires and finally the killings. My God, shopkeepers and employees alike were literally gunned down until all businesses were closed. Even the Guard sustained heavy losses in some of the shopping malls. Cars and trucks were overturned, burning everywhere as well as some of the private residences. Some sections of the city are still without power and water. Civil authorities were overwhelmed, ill equipped and not prepared for such a violent assault. Did you know the gunrunners had pods of additional weapons and ordnance stored along the waterfront? Those were the explosions you heard in the background when you were speaking with us, sir."

"I thought you said it was mortar fire, Jake." Peterson said.

"Mortar fire was what set off the explosions."

"That makes sense. I see JBLM wasn't called up."

"That's affirmative, sir. We really didn't want to get the military involved unless it was absolutely necessary. Civilians and the military mix like oil and water under these types of circumstances. But it was close," Jake ventured.

The deputy secretary paused and looked closely at his top two Intel ops. "How are you boys holding up? I know you both are running close to empty."

"We're fine, sir." Slade answered.

"Yeah, we need to get down to the bottom of this." Jake added.

"I know you just flew in from Portland yesterday, but I want you two back in the mix by tomorrow evening. Your team is still there, correct?"

"Of course, sir. You know that Captain Harrison Stoner lost three of his men in the assault, and two others were injured." Jake sighed bitterly with sorrow reflecting from his blue eyes.

"Yes, I know, and their families have been notified. It's such a terrible shame and especially on our soil. Jake, how are Johnson and Craven doing?" Peterson asked.

"They're fine, sir, just flesh wounds."

"Good, I'm glad to hear that. Now let's get you guys back there and see what happened to those two. Portland needs all the help they can get, and you may be there for some time."

After Jake and Slade left the conference room and arrived in Jake's office, Slade turned to him and said, "You know it will probably take some time to recover their bodies, that's if they're there."

"Oh they're still there. I can feel it. They're probably trapped somewhere and can't get out. And like you said, it will be awhile."

Peterson sat in his chair thinking about Portland and the looting and violence that had followed and the fact that it had spread to other major cities in the country. After hearing Jake and Slade's account red flags were waving in his head. They had to be prepared and call out more military if needed. *God help us all if it came to that*, he thought.

EIGHTY

RIYADH, SAUDI ARABIA 2010

It was Christmas Eve in the West as the monsters sped along the 'light pipe' on the ocean's floor from Riyadh, Saudi Arabia to the United States and Canada like a vicious pack of wolves closing on their prey. In moments, they were at the doorstep of their quarry, working their insidious code into the gatekeepers' portals. The Canadian and three U.S. targets were now under full assault. The quantum machine unleashed its full power of 500 zettaflops and cracked the guardians' complex ciphers within minutes for each underground site. Mere digital computing machines could only hope to decipher cryptography at this level in one's lifetime. Once past the sites' ring of firewalls, the pack attacked the gateways' ciphers with ferocity. They carried their deadly payload of nano packets of Electro Magnetic Pulses (EMPs) through the servers' bridges, switches, and routers. Relentless in their assault from all possible network pathways the carnivores closed in on the IBM mainframes' input busses. Once in, they replicated their EMPs driven by high-powered capacitors and traveled to the big mainframes' operating systems with lightning speed. The operating systems' management programs and fences were no match for the wolves; nor should they be. The creatures were now past most of the guardians and nearly had free reign. They weren't interested in any of the mainframes' ancillary systems. Single purpose in mind; they were all focused on their prize, and the prize was the mainframes' disaster recovery repositories. Each site's archive system was composed of farms of disk arrays and each held at least a quadrillion bytes of sensitive information. With brute force the night runs smashed through the last of the gatekeepers and emitted highly concentrated electromagnetic pulses of radiation behind the cloaked vault walls. In an instant, endless rows of disk arrays containing countless bytes of information on multi-terabyte disk drives vanished. Even though the vaults were cloaked to protect multiple forms of electromagnetic wave inductions they were only cloaked from the outside. The systems had never been designed for these types of cyber-attacks, and technology at this level would not be available for at least another ten years in the United States.

EIGHTY-ONE

WASHINGTON D.C. 2010

"What, what did you just say?" Ron Duncan exclaimed. It was Christmas morning, 2:00 a.m. in Washington D.C., and the IRS director had just been awakened at home by a call from his chief of security, Tim Smith.

"We've just been attacked, sir."

"What?" the IRS director exclaimed again.

"All four of our underground bunkers were just attacked, and it appears that all of the individual and corporate income tax information has been erased. In fact all information has been destroyed," Tim explained.

"In Canada too. Jesus! What happened? What about backups?"

"Everything is gone, Mr. Director," the chief of security said.

"But how, how could this have happened?" the director asked. "I thought there was redundancy built into the system. We moved the information underground decades ago, and we have around-the-clock security. What's the casualty rate, Tim?" the director asked.

"As far as we know there isn't any, sir."

"Good. Now tell me how they got in." Ron Duncan was now out of bed and heading to his home office. Thoughts were flooding his mind. He was trying to comprehend the gravity of the situation and what had happened.

"Sir, I don't think you understand. There were no intruders and no physical breach at any of the sites. We were cyber-attacked, sir."

"You mean to tell me that all the information disappeared at all four sites without physical intervention?"

"That's correct. We are in lockdown mode, and the grounds of all four sites are being searched, and so far we haven't come up with anything. I have a bad feeling about this."

"What else have you found?" the director pressed.

"My team has been in contact with IT, and it's much too early to get any quantifiable evidence let alone a preliminary assessment of the situation, but they believe that some type of new or advanced technology had been used to get through our defenses and degauss and destroy the bunkers' archive systems."

The director cleared the last of the cobwebs from his mind and barked, "Christ all mighty! This is all we need on top of everything else, a nation of no income tax records. Tim, you know what to do. Follow the protocols and keep me informed."

"Yes, sir, I certainly will. But it's Christmas, and it will take some time to bring in more staff."

"Tim, I don't care what it takes, just do it."

The director broke the connection and eased himself into the leather chair in his office. *What were they going to do?* he thought. The country had enough trouble as it was. The near miss on the financial institutions, the recent events in Portland, Oregon, phantom corporations trading on the world's stock exchanges, and now this! He didn't like where all this was heading. It had all the earmarks of a major cyber-attack. "But from where and from whom? And how was it done?" he asked himself. He knew the United States was vulnerable to attacks from both domestic and international terrorists. This had been readily apparent in the last few weeks. All countries were. The Brits were having their own problems, too. "But our tax system? Who would have ever thought of that?" he asked himself again. Hopefully they would find out soon. But now he needed to make some phone calls.

EIGHTY-TWO

WASHINGTON D.C. 2010

Ron Duncan was so nervous and upset that he couldn't remember the password to his video conferencing software so he called the FBI director, William Thompson, and the secretary of Homeland Security, Mary Knappa, directly at home.

It was now was after 3:00 a.m. when Mary heard a ring tunneling into her dream. "This had better be good," she huffed. "The only time I like being interrupted at this hour is on my golfing vacations."

Ron proceeded to briefly tell them that the IRS had been cyber-attacked and indicated that he would videoconference them in a few minutes. After the short phone calls, the IRS director went down to the kitchen and started the coffeemaker. God, he wanted a cup of coffee; he couldn't wait. After the coffee was done, he poured himself a cup and went back upstairs to his office, found his password, and brought up the videoconference software on his desktop and punched in the numbers for Liam and Mary. "Can you see and hear me okay?" he asked.

"Yes, you're coming in fine," they both answered. Mary was the first to speak, "Now what's this about?"

"We have a major problem," Ron said as he peered at the split screen images.

"What's happening, Ron?" Liam asked.

"All of the disaster recovery systems for the individual and corporate income tax records have disappeared."

"What!" There was stunned silence.

Liam was the first to recover, "Ron, what do you mean they disappeared?"

"They have all vanished according to my chief of security. I just received the call from him an hour ago."

"You do have redundancy?" Mary asked.

"Yes, we have three underground bunker sites in different locations in the United States and one in Canada."

"You're telling us that all the information from the four sites have vanished?" Mary said incredulously.

"I'm afraid so," Ron answered.

"How could this have happened? Ron, how were the sites breached?" Liam asked.

"Don't exactly know yet, but I can tell you one thing for sure—there was no human intervention. Besides, if there were, it would probably be all over the media by now."

"Then what happened?" Mary asked.

"From the reports I've been receiving, it appears that some type of new or advanced technology was used to destroy all the data from the archives."

"Do you have any idea on what the technology is?" Mary asked.

"It's too early yet to know much of anything, except that the data is gone."

"What actions have you taken?" Liam pressed.

"I've already alerted the chain of command at our agency, and everyone is working feverishly on this."

"Christ!" Mary exclaimed. "This is going to have far-reaching consequences."

"Tell me about it," Ron said. "We're going to have to make a big decision quite soon. The new tax season is upon us, and we need to decide if we want to scrap the present system or go to a simpler process."

"What about your tax records at the regional offices around the country?" Liam asked.

"Well, without looking into it, I would venture we have millions of outstanding individual and corporate tax cases we are currently working on. And most of these cases are audits that go back anywhere from one to seven years. But the information we currently have is minuscule compared to our archives. What are we supposed to do? Continue investigating on some because we have all the information at hand while we drop investigations on others because of a lack of data?" Ron questioned as he tapped his desk with his fingers.

"The law is the law," Liam volunteered. "You can't be serious about not having your people continue prosecuting tax cheats?"

"I didn't say that, Liam. I think we need to continue investigating people and corporations who evade their taxes but at the same time explore ways to at least give individuals and companies options to come clean."

"We did that already," Liam said.

"What are our other options?" Mary asked.

"That's the big question," Ron ventured. "Perhaps we'll build tax records on the fly."

"Ron, that's not going to work. If what you have just said is true, the hole is too deep, the loss too wide, and the risks too high. We'll have to scrap the old process and come up with a new simpler tax system. Besides, if we go with what you have suggested, the present tax system could even become more convoluted and possibly come down like a house of cards," Liam advised.

"Don't you think it's high time to simplify the process?" Mary pushed. "Look, the tax code has been changed and amended so many times that even your own accountants are confused some of the time. That's why when some people take their tax forms to more than one tax preparer they sometimes get different results. The original federal tax code was thirty-eight pages when it was first established in 1913. Today it's over seventy-two thousand pages. Something has to give."

"What about the job loss that will occur as a result of this?" Ron argued.

Liam interrupted the dialogue between Mary and Ron. "The loss of employment will eventually correct itself. Don't you see by moving to a more straightforward income tax system that in a relatively short period of time it will dump more money into the economy and eventually create more jobs as a benefit? Ron, this is an opportunity of a lifetime, an opportunity for the government to show the people that it can do something constructive for a change."

"But, but—" Ron blurted.

Mary cut him off and said, "Liam's right. We need to move to a flat tax system or something similar. Even though your suggestions might have some merit, I'd hate to think of what would happen if we went down this path and it collapsed and blew up in our face. Can you imagine the outright confusion and chaos it would create? Sure, the crooks would love it. But do you think the majority of our citizens would stand for this, especially after all our country has gone through in the last decade or so?" Mary pointed in a persuasive manner.

Ron felt like he was getting ganged up on, and he wasn't about to let them get the better of him. "I still think my suggestions warrant heavy consideration, and if we implement the changes properly it will work."

"Come on, Mr. Duncan, cut me some slack," Liam glowered. "I wasn't born yesterday. It appears after all of our suggestions; you're still running with your ideas. Come clean, Ron. You just want to grow your agency."

"No, that isn't so!" Ron exclaimed.

The secretary of Homeland Security stared at Ron's image in front of her and chimed in, "Liam and I have known you for too long and know when we see a bluff."

"Okay, all right. Perhaps your suggestions have good merit." Ron Duncan was already forming strategy in his mind in order to push his agenda. "Who wants to call the president?"

EIGHTY-THREE

DHS NEBRASKA COMPLEX
WASHINGTON D.C. 2011

David Peterson, deputy secretary of Homeland Security, was standing at the bank of windows facing east on the seventh floor of DHS headquarters in Washington D.C. Spring had come early to the Capitol this year, and it was unusually warm this morning. The cherry trees around the district were in full bloom, and the humidity had already made its presence. He had been thinking about the series of meetings that were held in the last couple months between the president, his cabinet, and Washington insiders on how to resolve the income tax dilemma. He had been shocked to learn they would keep the present tax system and go with Ron Duncan's original ideas. He had remembered how his boss, Mary Knappa, beseeched the president and other high-ranking officials to scrap the old system and start anew. But the only thing the secretary got for her troubles had been an exercise in futility. Even though the Republicans had made strides in the mid-term elections the progressives still held control and were hell-bent on making the government grow larger. *Spend, spend, spend! That's all they could think of,* David thought. Just last week a press conference had been held by Ron Duncan, the director of the IRS, indicating there would be a tax holiday and all individuals' tax returns wouldn't be due until July 15th. Of course you could hear corporations scream bloody murder. What about them they asked. You would have thought that people would have been suspicious of the rollback. But to his surprise the opposite had occurred. It was like New Year's Eve all over again. Throngs of partygoers throughout the country had celebrated in the streets for days afterward. David had known that Mary and Ron were good friends and that their friendship went back at least two decades. *Well, you can trash that relationship,* David thought.

He and the Secretary had discussed the situation at length ever since the cyber-attacks on the IRS, and both were fully aware of the terrible consequences that lie ahead for the nation if things didn't go smoothly. He had remembered the secretary saying that she couldn't believe the thinking on the hill. She had warned them repeatedly that if they chose this path they would be entering a minefield for which there might not be a return. But for all of her oratory skills and suggestions, it had been to no avail. Once again the president and his cronies had prevailed. *God help us all,* David thought. His only hope was that the people of our great nation would vote intelligently in the 2012 general election and augment the 2010 freshman class.

His thoughts now turned to Al-Hadi Zafar and Seyed Mostakavi. He remembered sending Jake and Slade to Gitmo in order to aid in the interrogation of the terrorists. It was vital that they uncover as much information as possible to guard against future cyber-attacks. They were particularly interested in how the terrorists had developed quantum technology. The military interrogators spent weeks using all kinds of physiological and psychological methods including the Reid technique. They used suggestibility, deception, and pride-and-ego-down—attacking their personal worth and self esteem in order for the subject to redeem their pride. They deprived them of their sleep, rationed their food, and injected white noise into their environment. They threatened their families and relatives, but without their families in custody, it was nothing more than an empty promise. In the end Jake did get Al-Hadi to break, and he provided a lot of valuable information, such as their sources of income, money laundering activities, friendships, and arms contacts. Jake even received information from him on their level of involvement with the Saudi government. But Al-Hadi wasn't a scientist and could only provide general information on how they developed quantum computing.

Seyed was an entirely different matter. The man was a juggernaut; stonewalled everyone throughout the interrogation process, including Jake and Slade. Jake wanted Seyed extradited to France to visit the judge. Jean Niviere was retired now but still had the clout to round up family members of terrorists and have them extradited. He was legendary in certain circles and had been widely hailed as a key player in the global war on terror, and even though he had been accused numerous times of heavy-handed methods, the French government usually granted his wishes. *Once the terrorists and their families were in his clutches—well you got the picture*, David thought. He went as far as discussing the matter with his boss, Mary Knappa, secretary of Homeland Security. But the secretary told him that the Ahmad Administration would never stand for such tactics. *He couldn't believe that Mary's suggestions on revamping the IRS had not even been given the time of day, why would they listen to her now*, he thought. The only thing Seyed had told them was that our day was coming, and the world would be driven back to the seventh century. "Allah would prevail!" he said.

Members of his team were filing into the conference room, and he needed to shift gears and think about today's agenda. They needed to discuss the whereabouts of Felix Jamosa and Jeffery Starr and also the progress on the investigations of the financial institutions and the IRS cyber-attacks.

EIGHTY-FOUR

DHS NEBRASKA COMPLEX
WASHINGTON D.C. 2011

The deputy secretary continued to stand at the wall of windows, peering out until everyone was seated. Finally, he turned and acknowledged his team before taking his seat. "Okay, we have a lot of ground to cover today. First, I would like a progress report on the clean up in Portland, and the whereabouts of Felix Jamosa and Jeffery Starr." The deputy secretary motioned in Jake's direction and said, "You have the floor."

"Sir, the clean up is going as scheduled. Portland's southwest side is still busy with activity in clearing the rubble and will be for quite some time. Other areas of the city, especially the major shopping malls, are seeing the same work, and that also includes the Oregon Museum of Science, the Rose Garden and the Business Convention Center. The city has been hit hard both from a standpoint of personal loss and a loss of property."

"What's the timeframe on the clean up?" the deputy secretary asked.

Jake ran his fingers through his wavy blond hair and shifted his muscular frame before he continued. "It's going to take a few years before everything is shipshape again. The demolition of the remaining sections of the Fox Tower will be delayed until all the debris on the ground is cleared. The demo team doesn't want to bring down the remaining portions of the building for fear of overflow into the adjacent buildings. I still think Jamosa and Starr are somewhere on site, especially since architectural forensics found evidence of another elevator shaft leading from their forty-third floor offices to somewhere beneath the surface. The elevator shaft was not in the original architectural plans."

"Yes, we're finding that the building held many secrets, including the hidden cameras," the deputy secretary added. "Jake, is there any safe way into the building at the present time?"

"Well, we could enter through the underground parking structure at the west side of the building, but in my opinion the area is too unstable. Besides, I doubt if we would get too far before we encountered more rubble. No, I think it's going to be awhile before we find them, sir."

"Dr. Knowles, do you concur with Mr. Cannon?" Peterson asked. The deputy secretary wasn't above pitting teammates against each other, especially when it came to gleaning as much information as possible.

"Jake's correct, sir. Members of our team along with a group from FBI's forensics have been on site almost from the beginning, and the building is extremely unstable. Some of the adjacent buildings aren't much better. Though I would like to add that the hidden elevator shaft terminus was actually next to Mr. Jamosa's personal bathroom. Rather ingenious I thought."

"Yes, Thaddeus, we have learned quite a bit about the building including the hidden forty-fourth floor fortress that Jake mentioned earlier. Christ, they had enough ordnance up there to take on a medium size country, not to mention the additional weapons and ammo stashed in pods along the waterfront. What were they thinking," the deputy secretary mused. "Now what about the financial institutions? Dr. Franks, what have you found?" Peterson asked.

Tonia Franks, the department's computer guru, looked at her boss and collected her thoughts before beginning. "There's over a half million lines of code we're sifting through and thank God we are receiving help from two of the operatives. They didn't write the code, but they're showing us the procedures they would've used in order to release the worms, and that in itself has proved invaluable. Sir, the code itself is very sophisticated and incorporates elements of artificial intelligence that enabled the virus to learn the financial systems and security protocols of its targets as it traveled through the servers' networks. They didn't need to worry about breaking through each company's firewall's ciphers since the employees, unwittingly, had already done that. This had been accomplished by infecting some of the IT employees' home computers with the terrorists programs, and once these employees uploaded information to the company's servers, the game was over."

"Dr. Franks, why didn't the operatives download the viruses directly to the company's business systems while they were at work?" the deputy secretary pressed.

"Yes, I wondered about that too until I spoke with one of the operatives. Kashif Naru said it would have been easier and less time consuming if all five of them downloaded the viruses themselves. After all, once they had logged in, they were already beyond the companies' firewalls and wouldn't need to worry about cracking the gateways' ciphers. But he told me that Seyed didn't want them taking any unnecessary chances for fear of getting caught, and even though it was more effort, he decided to let the infidels do the damage to themselves. Just more embarrassment, Seyed had told them."

"Did Kashif or any of the other operatives know about the quantum computing plans?" Slade asked.

"No, I had asked him the exact same question. What I believe had happened was that Seyed wanted to use this method to test their digital viruses on the financial and banking employees browsers and home computers since they would be using very similar procedures when cyber-attacking the IRS. Beyond that, as we know, Dr. Mostakavi was very security conscious and used extreme methods to compartmentalize the quantum technology."

"That makes sense, Dr. Franks," the deputy secretary chimed in.

"We also found that the worms were self-replicating and self-learning as they spread throughout the financial programs, and if the transfer of assets would have been made to the five Middle Eastern sites, as Al-Hadi had told us, the code would have destroyed itself."

"So, doctor, you're telling me if we wouldn't have intervened when we did, the money would have been transferred, and the code would have vanished without a trace."

"I'm afraid so, sir."

The deputy secretary whistled and said, "My God, just as we had suspected."

"Yes, that's right, sir," Dr. Franks responded. "There's more, sir, but that's the fat of the matter."

"Now what about the IRS situation?"

She grew excited, and her delicate features animated as she exclaimed, "Oh my God! I can't believe the technology they used to cyber-attack the IRS. It's incredible, sir. They are so far ahead of us it's unbelievable." She launched into the field's background in order to help explain some of the concepts to the team. "Even though quantum physics had been discovered in the 1920s, initial experiments with pairs of photons to study non-locality in quantum mechanics didn't start until the 1970s. Then ideas began to circulate. In the 1980s it was discovered that quantum systems might possibly be used to carry out certain computations. The field really didn't take off until the mid 1990s when Peter Shor devised quantum algorithms that could factor large numbers very efficiently using quantum computers. Developing quantum machines for general all-purpose processing is still years away, and we're just beginning to scratch the surface. In essence they have found a way to accurately measure the qubit states of large numbers of sub atomic particles that enables them to process information to the sextillion magnitude in order to factor incredibly large numbers. I can't say if they have advanced their technology to a state of computing general all-purpose applications, but for the purpose of cracking cipher keys, they have done it. For all intents and purposes they have rendered digital ciphers used to protect gateways on the Internet and botnets useless. I hate to say it, but they stormed in and blew down our doors using this technology. And as far as using nanotechnology to build those quantum machines, well—"

"Dr. Franks, I know we were caught napping, but please stick to the question."

"Sorry, sir. Haven't been getting much sleep lately."

"I don't think any of us have been getting our rest. Besides, sleep's overrated. Don't you think?" Peterson asked.

"Yes, it is, sir, especially when it comes to defending our nation."

"Good, now continue."

Dr. Franks collected her thoughts again and went on. "They not only cyber-attacked us remotely, sir, but they were able to send nano packets of electromagnetic energy (EMP) through the shielded cabling to the IRS's mainframes and servers. They totally bypassed the bunkers' archive vaults' defenses for EMPs. Brilliant, just brilliant!" she exclaimed.

"Enough with the adulations," the deputy secretary huffed. "For Christ's sake, Dr. Franks, terrorists attacked the United States." He knew she was brilliant in her own right and understandably amazed at the technology used against the IRS, as they all were, but they needed to stay focused on the problem.

"Sorry, sir," Tonia said. "I'm just appalled that the United States is so far behind in some technologies."

"Another topic, another time," the deputy secretary quipped. "Now let's get on with it."

"Yes, sir. Do you know about the Stuxnet virus?"

"I believe all of us know about the virus. After all, we make it our business to keep informed about such situations."

"Sir, they entered the IRS bunkers the same way that the Stuxnet virus attacked the Iran nuclear facility. Like the Iran nuclear plant the IRS has an open-air system, except it is a modified open-air ring containing the four underground bunker sites. Essentially this is a distributed botnet, if you will, where all four sites can communicate with each other. They operate like the Internet, but they're not connected to it." She looked at everyone and asked; "Is this making sense?" Everyone nodded yes.

The deputy secretary interrupted and asked, "Where is this all going, Dr. Franks?"

"I'm almost finished, sir."

"Please continue."

"Basically, the terrorists used the same strategy as the Stuxnet virus. They infected the home computers of IRS employees living around and working at the sites with digital viruses. They knew that some of these employees had authority to download and upload information to and from their work sites, and they infected those employees' flash drives and thumb drives in order to gain entrance to the botnet. In this case, the terrorists were only interested in gaining the firewalls' IP addresses. They weren't concerned in implementing the digital viruses' programs behind the firewalls, as was the case for our financial institutions. Once they had the IP addresses to the firewall ports, they unleashed the date-sensitive quantum computing software, and were able to crack the firewalls' ciphers for all four sites in a matter of minutes. And unlike the cyber-attack on our financial institutions, they succeeded, and all traces of the quantum viruses and code have been totally destroyed."

"Do you have any idea on how their technology works?" the deputy secretary asked.

"Not really, sir. As I said, our quantum technology is in an early stage. If we could've stopped this before it occurred, we could've learned a great deal from it."

"Thank you, Dr. Franks." The deputy secretary took a sip of coffee and now directed his attention to Jake. "You're at bat. Have you found any information that would shed some light on this?" Peterson asked.

"Well, sir, for the last three months along with the Saudis we have scoured the locations where the terrorists had stayed, and we haven't uncovered anything significant. I thought for sure we would've discovered more at Seyed's compound besides the names of his team but no such luck. We have also checked Al-Hadi's condo in Riyadh and have found nothing there. The five operatives along with six others of their team haven't yielded anything beyond the initial inquiry. We're suspecting, at this point, any documents with crucial information, especially on quantum technology have either been secreted away or have been destroyed. Sorry we couldn't be of more help."

"Well, keep looking," Peterson directed.

"You can count on it, sir."

"Dr. Knowles, what has your team and FBI forensics discovered about the contents of Abrahim Solasti's house?"

"We've uncovered some information on charred documents that were in the explosion but not to the extent that they mean anything. But we are still working on that, sir."

"What about Solasti's hard drive?"

"A total loss, sir. We could only find charred fragments in the rubble, and there wasn't enough left to cobble anything together. However, we did find Solasti's explosive signature."

"What was it, Thad?" the deputy secretary asked.

"Jake was right. It was Pentaerythritol tetranitrate (PETN), sir. And I might add that he detonated a large amount of the substance. We found the compound's explosive residue on fragments that belonged to a fifty-five gallon steel drum. We believe the PETN was detonated via his smartphone."

"Anything else?"

"Not much. Everything within the perimeter of his house was pretty much vaporized, except for the items that I just mentioned."

"What about the NATO ops and Saudi Special Forces? Any evidence found on their bodies?"

"Sorry, sir, there gone, just gone—totally vaporized."

"Okay, I have a couple of items before we convene." The deputy secretary stood and leaned his short athletic frame toward his audience, and with his deep brown eyes in full concentration, continued. "With the help of Jeffery Starr's diary, we have been able to notify the authorities around the globe and shut down all of their phantom companies operating on the world's stock exchanges. I do hope we have them all," the deputy secretary commented warily. "Hopefully, in time, the legitimate stockholders will be duly compensated."

Jake interrupted the deputy secretary and said, "Sir, something has been bothering me for a long time."

"What's that, Jake?" Peterson asked with great restraint in his voice.

"Why didn't they use fictitious names instead of the deceased to operate their phantom companies?"

"Good question," the deputy secretary replied. "I think we'll never know the answer until we find them. And that's if we find them alive. Now where was I, oh yes, as some of you know we haven't been able to get any information from Dr. Mostakavi. He simply will not cooperate. As far as Mr. Zafar, he has at least given us some information on their sources and activities. But it appears we are at the end of our solicitations, and they are now waiting to be rewarded by Allah. The rest of their team imprisoned at Guantanamo Bay is following the same tack, except the two operatives that came forth and helped us on the financial institutions. The only good news on the horizon is that President Ahmad was forced to sign House bill H.R. 6523. It limits his ability to transfer detainees from Guantanamo Bay to civilian courts. The only reason why he signed the bill is because it releases money to keep the military funded." Still standing, the deputy secretary looked around the room and asked, "Is there anything else to discuss?" The team was quiet. "Okay, let's get to it."

As the team filed out of the conference room, David Peterson moved back to the bank of windows facing east and peered out. He was still worried about how the income tax dilemma would play out. He knew that the secretary's suggestions were now filed in the dead letter box and only hoped that Duncan's strategy would go according to plan. But somehow he knew it wouldn't. Only time would tell.

EPILOGUE

DHS NEBRASKA COMPLEX
WASHINGTON D.C. 2011

The deputy secretary hastily called the meeting to order. The tides were rising, and the agency had to get a handle on it. It was nearly as hot inside the conference room as the fall weather outside. The D.C. area had been experiencing unusually hot and humid weather even by their standards. And to make matters worse the building's air conditioning was clanking again. *Thank God everyone is in attendance*, David Peterson thought. He had a lot of gritty issues to disseminate, and he wasn't looking forward to it. "Okay, let's start with the Jamosa and Starr situation in Portland. Thad, you have the floor."

"Sir, the demo teams have finally cleared the rubble from the Fox Tower. Last week our team and FBI forensics had the opportunity to examine the building's bunker. We found Jamosa and Starr's decomposed remains inside. It appears from ballistics that Jeffery Starr had killed himself with a single bullet to the right temple from a Glock 17 handgun. His time of death based on the rate of decomposition and other factors was early December of last year. Jamosa's death came later and had been determined to be sometime in the middle of January. We found scarred indentations of his distant phalanx apexes that indicated he tried to claw his way out. This is also consistent with the condition of the sheetrock in the bunker. He practically stripped off all of the plasterboard on the bunker's interior steel walls. He literally had ground his fingertips to stubs. I still can't believe how he survived down there for six weeks with a few bottles of water. It must have been horrible—just horrible, sir."

"Enough of the theatrics, Dr. Knowles. Now, was there any evidence or documents found on the bodies or in the bunker that would shed more light on the investigation?" the deputy director asked.

"No, sir. As you know the only information we have found so far was Starr's diary and some documents at Jamosa's residence indicating some of the gunrunner's revenue streams and contacts. And, if I may, I think those documents only involved his side jobs. Nothing points to the reason why he became a terrorist. And I guess we'll never know why he used the dead for his phantom corporations instead of fictitious names."

"Not really, he took the enigma with him to the grave. Thanks, Thaddeus," the deputy director now looked at Jake. "Any new information on Mostakavi and Zafar or their team?"

"No, sir. I think all the information we had received early on is all the knowledge we'll get. We even tried to coerce information from Seyed by threatening him through his mother. We told him that his younger brother, Niv, and his elderly mother and family would be branded as terrorists. Niv would be thrown out of Iran's elite military service, Al-Quds, and he would be considered a traitor and lose his officer's pension or worse. He just laughed at us. He thinks his mother and brother will be glorified, not disgraced. They're all sitting at Gitmo waiting for their judgment day in order to be exulted by Allah. Seyed made an interesting comment though."

"Yes," Peterson prompted.

"He wrote it in Arabic, "God is coming"–"الله القادمة."

"Well we know that. Anything else."

"Yes, there is." Jake stood and faced the deputy secretary. "Sir, I still think Mostakavi needs to pay a visit to the judge. If we can extradite him I believe Seyed will eventually come clean with his plans and perhaps advance our knowledge in quantum mechanics. I don't trust the guy. Who knows what other plans may be in motion on his behest?"

"Jake, I share your concerns and for what its worth, Mary and I have tried more than once to convince the president, but he won't listen. Perhaps in time Dr. Mostakavi will give us more information. Besides, the secretary and I have to balance the delicate nature of the information and allowing the doctor out of our jurisdiction against what the French may find out. We have to consider the information he would give to the French government, especially knowledge on quantum physics. In the end it could haunt us. And with all the negative publicity surrounding the arrest of IMF chief, Dominique Strauss-Kahn who happens to be a French citizen, it would give the French government even more of an incentive to steal away information. The majority of the French people think it's nothing more than a trumped up plot now that the U.S. authorities have released him. No, we have to stay the course."

"I understand, sir."

"Good." The deputy secretary now turned his attention to Dr. Franks. "Have you found anything else on the cyber-attacks against our financial institutions?"

Tonia Franks turned to the deputy secretary, and Peterson could see that she was deep in thought before answering. "Mr. Deputy Secretary, now that we have had time to study their rogue code and method of implementation we have determined two things. First, their code was quite sophisticated, especially the sections that enabled them to commandeer the institutions' financial systems and security protocols. The code was written in such a way that once one part of a company's financial systems and security had been breached and learned, the code replicated that knowledge to other parts of the system where it made sense. It's called commonality duplication, and it's one of the central tenets of the cognitive science of artificial intelligence. Of course this greatly enhances the speed and destruction of the viruses.

But the real genius behind this is not in the replication or self-learning techniques but in the method it was delivered."

"What are you saying, Dr. Franks?" Peterson asked.

"Somehow they knew at what steps to insert the code that would maximize the most damage in the least amount of time. They knew exactly what, where and how to attack, and in the proper sequence for all their targets."

"Interesting," Peterson replied. "So they knew how to inflict the most damage in a very short period of time."

"Yes. Even if someone quickly switched off the main power supply to the mainframes and servers it undoubtedly would have been too late."

"What else did you acquire, Dr. Franks?" Peterson said.

"We learned this information from two of the operatives. In addition to releasing the viruses, they also had been instructed to learn as much as possible about each company's systems and vulnerabilities. Once this knowledge was gleaned, it was sent back to their team in Riyadh to incorporate it into their AI software. They were really on top of it, sir. But, I still don't understand why this wasn't done remotely. They certainly had the expertise."

"Well, Dr. Franks, we'll have to leave that up to the psychologist and psychiatrists to unravel that mystery. Like I said before, in time, Dr. Mostakavi may shed some light on this." The deputy director now turned his attention to the IRS. "What have you found out about the quantum aspects of the investigation?"

"Two words—Trojan Horse!" Tonia exclaimed.

"Meaning?"

"Sir, they used our own technology against us. Notwithstanding their knowledge of quantum computing, Dr. Mostakavi being a nuclear physicist knew that the government would have incorporated Electro Magnetic Pulse (EMP) defenses in order to shield the IRS bunkers against atomic or thermonuclear detonation. And that included the bunkers' conduits leading into each building."

"Where is this going, Dr. Franks?" Peterson asked.

"Bear with me, sir. I think you'll find this interesting."

"Okay, carry on."

"The IRS bunkers' exterior walls only had electro magnetic pulse protection from incoming threats. Once through the outside walls there were no additional defenses. In other words they loaded their quantum viruses with nano packets of EMPs, generated by super high capacitors, and used the conduits' shielding to get past the EMP defenses. Once inside it was checkmate."

"How ingenious, Dr. Franks," Peterson said.

"I thought so, sir."

"Now, have you found anything else that would help us to understand on how they built their quantum machines?"

"Not really, sir. As I said before our nano and quantum technology are still in the toddler stage. If we only could've retrieved a few pieces of the quantum viruses' code, this may have helped us on how they advanced the technology. But as you know everything vanished."

"Yes, how unfortunate."

"Is there anything else?"

"You'll be the first to know, sir." Tonia leaned back in her chair and shook her head as if to say incredible.

"Thank you, Dr. Franks," the deputy secretary said. Peterson looked around the room. "Is there any additional information I should know?" The team nodded a collective no.

"I'm surprised," Peterson said. "There is one important question that's been keeping me up at night. How in the heck did they get the locations to the IRS bunkers? This is top-secret classified information. If the terrorists weren't privy to this knowledge they wouldn't have been successful. Anyone?"

"Sir, I think either the terrorists paid a handsome sum to acquire the data from a government source, or someone in the Middle East knew of the locations," Jake ventured.

"Do you think!" the deputy director exclaimed. "One thing for sure. I won't stop until I find who was responsible and how it was obtained. Christ, isn't anything sacred anymore?"

"You know it would almost be worth the risk of sending Seyed to the judge for that single piece of information." Jake opinioned.

"Jake, I almost agree with you," Peterson said. "Oh, before I forget, how are Mohammed and his family doing?"

"They're doing fine, sir. They're living with their uncle in Bellingham, Washington, and Mo and his sister are already taking citizenship classes. I want to thank you for helping them. Mo keeps in touch with me via e-mail and can't thank me enough for what we have done for them."

"Yes, he turned out to be a fine gentleman and the United States owes its gratitude to him. Will have to work on that, Jake."

"Perhaps we can attend their graduation ceremony on becoming citizens."

"Good idea, Jake. Anything else?"

"Yes, it's shocking what Al-Hadi attempted to do to his cousin. Mo thought they were close and such good friends." Jake added.

"Well it just goes to show what the world is like nowadays." The deputy secretary now paused and looked at everyone with grave concern reflecting on his face. "Now, listen up. I've got some troubling news to share with you." Peterson bounced out of his chair and began to pace. "Some of the things I'm about to tell you will surprise or even disturb you. But you need to know, we all need to know in order to prepare for what's coming."

"What can be worse than what has already happened in the last few months," Tom Morrison interjected.

"Plenty," the deputy secretary said. "Most of it centers around the income tax debacle."

"I suspected as much," Slade interrupted.

"Everyone hold your comments until I am through—this is important." Peterson huffed. "As you are all aware, President Ahmad fired the IRS director, Ron Duncan, last week because of his bungling of the tax situation. Of course, Mr. Duncan, was just an escape goat because the administration supported his plan. Tax receipts are down by 25 percent even though the due date for individual income taxes had been extended to July 15th. Also, corporate taxes are down 20 percent. It appears that a segment of our population has decided not to pay them, not that it is a surprise to anyone. To further exacerbate the problem, the government doesn't have a leg to stand on since most of the IRS tax information has been destroyed. The government has no legal recourse."

"Sir, you and Mary did all you could to warn them of the consequences of following Ron Duncan's plan, but they wouldn't listen," Dr. Ferris said.

"I'll give you a pass on this one, Clyde, but don't interrupt me again. You understand?"

"Absolutely, sir."

"Team, this is the result of two failed generations. Congress and millions of people looking for an easy way out, shirking their responsibilities and always putting the onus on their fellow man. This is so serious on so many levels that I want to throw my hands up in the air and say screw it!" Peterson scowled. The team looked at their boss with stunned silence. "But I won't. That's not the way I operate. What's the government to do? Incarcerate everyone, or estimate taxes on individuals based on their 2010 Census profiles? Lord knows how accurate that would be? And what about corporate taxes and the deficit situation? This all could lead to defaulting on our national debt and losing the bond market in the process, not to mention the de facto gold standard of our currency. And now we need to worry about the markets. All three major indexes have been heading south for months ever since the country discovered it is without a viable tax system. The Dow is trading in the five-thousand range and the NASDAQ is barely keeping its head above one-thousand." David paused to let his remarks sink in. "Okay, let's find out how they found the IRS locations. Meeting adjourned!"

As everyone filed out of the conference room, he noticed there wasn't the usual chatter between his team. Perhaps he had been too tough on them, but he needed answers especially on the IRS locations. They were running out of time. "One of the quickest ways to anarchy," *he worried*, "was for a republic to quit paying its taxes." The administration and Congress had better get their act together or all would be lost. He knew that empires rose and fell and society's social order changed every few hundred years; it happened to Greece, Rome and more recently to the Ottoman empire. He wondered if the United States was next? He could now sense uneasiness, a stirring in the cities. There was talk of launching predator drones (UAVs) over our major metropolitan areas in order to monitor the growing unrest of its citizens. He knew that robotics' technology was growing rapidly, and more than forty-five nations were now involved in various Predator and Reaper projects. They were tools for the eyes of a government, and soon they would far exceed human piloted planes in speed, range, and weaponry not to mention intelligence gathering. He just hoped that the United States wasn't marching down the road to ruin, lockstep to civil war.

**Turn the page for an excerpt from H.D.
Duman's next exciting novel.**

ROAD TO RUIN

It was 2300 hours in Baghdad, Iraq and the November sun had set hours ago giving way to another chilly evening. Jake Cannon was sitting in a mess hall in one of the Army's green zones at Camp Victory having a late night snack. The camp was scheduled to close within the next few weeks. The Ahmad Administration decided to stay on schedule and had been pulling troops out for months. The United States invasion had started in March of 2003 under the previous administration to remove Saddam Hussain from power and eventually had met its objective with the execution of Saddam on December 30, 2006. However, NATO and the United States had lost many lives in the process and by some reckonings the total cost of the war was now over three trillion dollars—an enormous sum. Jake thought the U.S. had made a mistake staying in. Sure we needed to get Saddam, but after that we should have pulled out. There's no way for a nation to rebuild a country's infrastructure and change its government in a decade or so, especially with traditions going back millenniums. Now in advance of the final draw down the Sunnis, Shiites, Kurds and other factions were ready to continue their age-old battles. Who knew where this would lead; the money, sweat equity and lives that had been spent would go for naught.

Tonight's menu included a bit of creamy walnut cake, coffee and a conversation with a striking, young brunette with piercing emerald green eyes. Her name was Jacqueline Smith and she had been recently promoted to the rank of Major, and invited Jake over to the mess for a little celebration and some cake. How could he ever resist such an invitation, especially from a young good-looking lady like Jackie? He was still troubled by his break up with Zoey Chamberlain. Nonetheless he had a weakness for certain things, and this was high on his list.

She had that sensual look about her he so liked. It shouted, don't let the smoke get in your eyes, he thought. With her smoky, charcoal locks gracing her beautiful face, clear olive complexion, and piercing green eyes, not to mention her sultry voice, she would be a natural opposite Bogey instead of Bergman sitting in a dimly lit smoky bar in Casablanca overlooking the Moroccan shores of the Atlantic. Besides, his affection for women of the 40s and 50s ran deep; it matched his fondness for cars and music that stretched into the sixties and seventies.

Jake was in the middle of a conversation with the Army Ranger Intel officer, discussing breeding habits of female yellow jacket queens. He had been telling Jackie that when the government and private enterprise were developing organic insect bots for military use, it had been very difficult for the microbiologists to modify the isolated DNA strands of the fully developed female yellow jacket queens. They particularly had trouble reducing their inherent sexual activity. The military didn't want the bot queens distracted by colonies of real yellow jacket males when on assignment. Jackie had gazed into his blue eyes and said, "Are you trying to get into my pants by telling me a big fish story?"

"Naw, I wouldn't spoof you like that, would I?" Jake flashed his famous crooked smile again.

"I don't know, I've heard stories," Jackie kidded.

"Actually science hasn't progressed to that point yet. That's the next generation—DNA computing."

"What?" She puzzled.

"You do know that the military has created computerized life-like humming birds?"

"Sure, that's been on the news awhile back."

"Well, next week we'll be testing nano scale artificial insects with your group and I believe you'll find it quite interesting. There's so much to this technology that most people haven't realized the amazing breakthroughs that science has made."

"From the advance briefing, I knew we would be working with nano bots, but I had no idea …"

"Hold on to your bonnet, Jackie, because a whole new world is going to open to you." Before she could respond, Jake excused himself to get a second piece of walnut cake. While serving himself, he thought about how this technology would affect Iraq. He wasn't sure, only that the parting gift the military would leave behind would serve as the eyes and ears of the United States for future intelligence. Sure, most of the military equipment and almost all personnel would be leaving—not the insects.

While Jake was getting more cake her mind drifted back to when they had first met. It had been a week ago when Jake, Slade and their team from the Department of Homeland Security had arrived on base. They were here to train the Army Ranger's counter intelligence unit on the maintenance, and operation of the new nano bots. She went for the big athletic type with lots of muscle, though she would take more brains than brawn any day. She knew that Jake more than fit the criteria in both categories. In fact whenever she was in the same room with him, she found herself having a hard time concentrating and her furtive gaze kept wandering in his direction.

She remembered the first time that Jake and his team had been introduced to the Ranger's Intel unit shortly after their arrival. Once her green eyes fell on Jake everything else during the introductions became white noise. Even in loose civilian clothes she could tell that he was in excellent physical shape. He wasn't overly tall for a man, well maybe not for her, standing about six foot two with wavy ash blond hair and quite tan. But those eyes! Oh those sparkling blue eyes. Jake had seen her gaze fix on him during the introductions and he locked his eyes on her and gave her that signature crooked smile. She knew that he had seen her face blush. She asked him later what he was thinking when they had first met, and he had told her, "I need to know this lady better!"

After digging in to his second piece of cake, he continued telling Jackie about the nano bots when his Sat phone rang. He picked up on the second ring and answered, "Jake here," still grinning from Jackie's last remark.

"Jake, how are things progressing with the Army Ranger's Tactical Intelligence Unit on the new bots?" David Peterson asked, without preamble. David was the Deputy Secretary of the Department of Homeland Security (DHS) and Jake's boss.

The Department of Homeland Security had been created after the 9-11 attacks. The government had coalesced twenty-two agencies together to focus on the primary responsibility of protecting the

United States from terrorists' attacks domestically. Even though its mission was within the U.S. borders, it also monitored and received Intel from agencies worldwide. And if warranted, DHS could act internationally to protect its citizens back home from present and future threats. David Peterson had served two tours in the Gulf Wars and was a decorated full bird Colonel that ran the agency in a quasi-military fashion. He knew the importance of accurate Intel and was especially diligent in this area. He also knew the faster the agency could respond to problems the less collateral damage the United States would face, and he wasn't afraid to call in favors or use his clout with the military. His team was hand picked and almost all had come from branches of the Armed Forces and had exemplary military careers. He especially afforded wide latitude to his lead senior intelligence officers, Jake Cannon and Slade Swanson. They were both black ops and had come from Delta Force E-Detachment (Communications, Intelligence and Administrative Support). While on assignment and if they were working with the Armed Forces, Jake and Slade always followed strict military protocol and were accorded the same courtesies as if they were still in the service.

"Everything is going according to plan, sir, and we should begin training next week." He mouthed to Jackie that he would take the call outside and would be back afterward.

"Is your asymmetric encryption device on?" Peterson asked as he ran a hand through his course, gray hair. He always asks this question to his ops when discussing sensitive information.

"Affirmative, sir."

"Jake, you don't have next week. In fact, we need your team and the nanoids deployed to Mumbai, India as soon as possible. There has been another attack."

"You have to be kidding, sir. India is still cleaning up from the last one."

"Well, it appears this one is more concentrated and we believe that some of the targets include India's financial center." Peterson said. "Jake, I just got off the phone with our Secretary, Mary Knappa, discussing the situation. According to latest Intel, it appears that dozens of Islamic militants have come ashore via the Back Bay on

Zodiac inflatable boats earlier this evening. They are now fanning out across the city, and killing most everyone in their path. So far the attacks have been isolated to the Leopold café, popular with foreign tourist, the central train station, and a hospital. We have also learned the terrorists have retaken the Taj Mahal Palace on the Arabian Sea and the Trident-Oberoi hotel on the Back Bay."

"My God, the same hotels!" Jake exclaimed.

"Makes sense. The terrorists already know their weaknesses and India was caught napping."

"I guess so, sir."

"Reports out of Mumbai indicate that both hotels are once again being rocked by explosions and fires, and the terrorists are seeking expatriates and tourists for executions or ransom. This time there are more of them and they are all heavily armed with automatic weapons, rocket and grenade launchers. Some of them have taken control of one of India's primary television stations and they're demanding the return of all mujahideen, imprisoned in Pakistan. They have already specified ransoms for some of their captives. They indicated that if their demands were not met, they would torture and kill the hostages on live broadcast. This time, they say that they are better prepared and will use high tensile explosives to bring down both hotels and other important religious landmarks. General Christopher Cox, head of Army Intelligence for the Middle East, has already briefed President Ahmad and his staff. I need Slade and you to quickly assemble your team and the bots within the hour. Your team's operation is now officially called 'Intrepid', understood?"

"Understood, sir," Jake answered heavily with a sigh.

"I've already contacted camp Victory's base commander, Colonel Sy Jacobson, and briefed him on the situation. I want you and your team to go over to the Med Corp building and receive flight sickness inoculations."

"Flight sickness, sir?" Jake asked, as he wondered about the deputy secretary's last statement.

"Don't interrupt me," Peterson barked. "Just listen."

"Yes, sir," Jake said smartly.

As the deputy secretary continued, his deep brown eyes showed concern as his tone grew more serious. "After your team is prepped including your Land Warrior systems you will report to Sergeant Ross at 0130 hours local time, and he'll have two army transports waiting to move your team and equipment to Al Taji airfield, northwest of Baghdad. There you'll meet Air Force Colonel, Clancy Callahan, and his flight crew. Your team will board the new Air Force's FX-61 hyper scramjet that's coming from Ramon Airbase in Israel, and your team will fly to an undisclosed Indian airfield near Mumbai. You will arrive at the airfield at approximately 0300 hours and meet Indian Air Force Colonel, Raj Srider, and his security chief. They will direct your team to the nearest hanger where you'll change into your Land Warrior systems. From there you will be escorted by unmarked security to a safe location near the Trident-Oberi hotel. Your ETA in Mumbai is 0600 hours. Intrepid will receive additional information in transit. You will report to Sergeant Ross in ninety minutes. Do you understand?"

"Affirmative, sir!"

"Are there any questions?" the deputy secretary asked.

"Many, sir."

"Keep it brief, Jake."

"I didn't know the scramjets were already in operation, sir."

"The prototypes have been for six months, though it's not well known."

"I know it's a ways, but why are we taking the FX-61?" Jake asked.

"Because ever since Seyed and Al-Hadi tried to take down our banks and brokerage houses, Intel has been acutely aware of situations like this and now it looks like al-Qaeda and Lashkar-e-Taiba have jumped into the mix and this time they're going after Mumbai's financial center. It's the heartbeat of India and time is of the essence."

"Sir, we haven't field-tested the bots," Jake said. "We're only half way through our prep cycles."

"This will be your field test. The Prime Minister of India has indicated that the situation is escalating rapidly, and he is now considering calling in the Army and the Elite Indian Commandos. President Ahmad has told him to bring them in, but only as a show of force. He indicated to the Prime Minister to keep them negotiating until we get there. By the time your team arrives, I'll have the hotels and financial district's buildings' schematics along with the latest locations of where the terrorists are. The Defense Department's keyhole satellites are working on this now. Once we receive the information it will be programmed into the nanoids' network. I'll also have more information on weapons and explosives they are using. More importantly, we need to find out if any of the terrorists have direct ties with Pakistan. If so, this could create a sticky situation between the countries. Any more questions?" the deputy secretary huffed.

"Yes, just how fast is the FX-61?"

"Jake, you know that's classified. But I can tell you once you take off from Al Taji, it will take you less than 30 minutes to arrive at the airfield near Mumbai. And I might add, this is just a walk in the park for this baby. You do the math," Peterson said and then smiled to himself.

"I just did and it's at least mach 7—holy cow!" Jake exclaimed with a stunned look on his face.

"We'll be in contact," the deputy secretary broke the encrypted sat connection.

Jake stood outside the mess hall to compose himself before walking inside. He told Jackie that he just received a call from his boss and that he and his team would be called away for a few days, but to keep the home fires burning. He turned and was about to leave when she walked over and gave him a quick peck, and told him to be safe and out of harms way. He promised he would and then left to awake Slade Swanson and his team.

While walking to Slade's quarters, he thought about the FX-60 and FX-61 shuttle space plane program that was designed and co-developed by Northrop Grumman and Lockheed Martin. He knew the planes would replace the United States aging shuttle fleet. In comparison, the new birds made the Air Force's SR-71 Blackbirds developed by Lockheed's Skunk Works look slow. The new hypersonic scramjet shuttles (supersonic combustion ramjets) didn't require gantry type launches from Cape Canaveral. Instead, they could take off and land like ordinary jets. By definition, ramjet engines have no moving parts, instead operating on compression to slow freestream supersonic air to subsonic speeds by a converging chamber and a diffuser, thereby increasing temperature and pressure, and combusting the compressed air with fuel injectors and subsonic burners. A diverging nozzle that accelerates the exhaust to supersonic speeds, resulting in thrust, completes the process. He knew that current technology supported scramjet operation with a starting freestream Mach number as low as 4.0. The heated air was a natural by-product of the plane's forward speed. The resulting process took place in milliseconds and could push the space-plane to phenomenal speeds, theoretically over mach 24. And unlike conventional jet engines, there is no need for turbines to increase wind velocity for combustion.

What he had remembered about the basic design of the FX-61 was that it included two conventional, spear shaped jet engines sitting back on stubby delta wings of the space-plane. The airfoil shape of the plane provided as much lift as the wings. The airlift ratio between the two components had to be precise in order to allow for both subsonic and hypersonic flight. The inlet chamber with its diverging nozzle was part of the plane's belly aft of the cockpit. Additionally, there was a two-stage rocket engine centered at the back of the plane's fuselage. The break through came when a new hybrid hydrogen fuel mixture was discovered that ignited at a relatively low freestream mach number and burned efficiently with a low oxygen content ratio. This would allow scramjet engines to flashpoint at mach 4.0 and enable the space-plane to fly in extremely thin atmospheric conditions to altitudes approaching 180,000 feet. The premise was that the aircraft would accelerate to mach 4 using conventional jet engines. At that point, the scramjets would take over and push the shuttle to very high altitudes. The two-stage rocket booster would then ignite, fueled by compressed hydrogen, and lift the space-plane to a geosynchronous orbit 220 miles above the earth. This would enable the orbiter, if you will, to match the angular velocity of the earth and thus facilitate docking with the space station. Jake was just shocked that the Air Force already had the prototypes in production. He entered their quarters, flipped on the lights, and awoke Slade.

"What's this, you don't bring me coffee and Danish," Slade said in his gravelly voice and sat up and rubbed his dark brown eyes.

Jake tapped him on the head with his knuckles. "If you don't hurry up, you'll be getting a knuckle sandwich instead of pastries."

While Slade dressed, Jake quickly briefed him on the situation developing in Mumbai. He then instructed Slade to make ready for an away team, and indicated that a general briefing would be in fifteen minutes in situation room A. Afterward, Slade left the barracks and collected Dr. Clyde Ferris, Homeland's bot expert, Dr. Tonia Franks, Homeland's AI and computer guru, and their toxicologist, Dr. Hans Frances. Normally the three scientists wouldn't be on a mission like this. They were only here for testing the nanoids and instructing their military counterparts on the operation of the insects. But because of the gravity of the situation they were pressed into service. Slade knew that they were central to the operation and would have to keep a sharp eye out for them, especially after they arrived in Mumbai. Fifteen minutes later they all were huddled in the situation room. After getting hot coffee from a tray that Jake offered, he cleared his throat and with his team in front of him, began.

"Okay, everyone listen up. We have a critical situation brewing in front of us. Earlier this evening, a team of terrorists landed in Mumbai, India via the Back Bay and…" Jake went on to describe what he had learned from the deputy secretary.

He finished with, "I can't impress upon you enough how important it is to stop these guys cold in their tracks. If they take down Mumbai's financial district and or some of their prominent religious landmarks, and if the terrorists are tied to Pakistan, it will send shock waves around the world and possibly a precursor to nuclear war. And just as important, this could lead to a major disruption of the world's financial markets. From here on, our team will be designated 'Intrepid'." Jake paused, and then asked with a grim look, "Are there any questions?"